# Texas
# Puppy Love

**Helen R. Myers & Amy Woods**

Previously published as *The Dashing Doc Next Door*
and *Puppy Love for the Veterinarian*

**HARLEQUIN**® MUST LOVE DOGS

ISBN-13: 978-1-335-69085-2

Texas Puppy Love

Copyright © 2018 by Harlequin Books S.A.

First published as The Dashing Doc Next Door by Harlequin Books in 2014 and Puppy Love for the Veterinarian by Harlequin Books in 2016.

The publisher acknowledges the copyright holders of the individual works as follows:

The Dashing Doc Next Door
Copyright © 2014 by Helen R. Myers

Puppy Love for the Veterinarian
Copyright © 2016 by Amy Woods

PLEASE RECYCLE
THIS PRODUCT IS RECYCLABLE

Recycling programs for this product may not exist in your area.

HARLEQUIN®

Printed in U.S.A.

™ www.Harlequin.com

# CONTENTS

**Helen R. Myers** is a collector of two- and four-legged strays, and lives deep in the Piney Woods of East Texas. She cites cello music and bonsai gardening as favorite relaxation pastimes, and still edits in her sleep—an accident, learned while writing her first book. A bestselling author of diverse themes and focus, she is a three-time RITA® Award nominee, winning for *Navarrone* in 1993.

### Books by Helen R. Myers

#### Harlequin Special Edition

*It's News to Her*
*Almost a Hometown Bride*
*The Surprise of Her Life*
*A Holiday to Remember*
*The Dashing Doc Next Door*
*Groomed for Love*
*A Man to Count On*
*The Last Man She'd Marry*
*Daddy on Demand*
*Hope's Child*
*It Started with a House...*

Visit the Author Profile page at Harlequin.com for more titles.

# THE DASHING DOC NEXT DOOR

Helen R. Myers

With special thanks to Dolores Dugger,
Leslie King, Gail Reed, Carolyn Bolin, Paula Rogers
and Norma Wilkinson for sharing anecdotes,
as well as your beloved pets with me.

And to animal lovers everywhere,
especially those of you who give the abused
and abandoned new hope.

# Chapter 1

"Humphrey? Here, sweetie. Nice dog. Time to come in now."

Brooke Bellamy felt like a fool. How the heck did you convince a dog to return to its home when what it wanted wasn't back there?

Although it was almost midnight, and only the first Tuesday in June, it was plenty warm already. Most sane—and lucky—people were in their air-conditioned houses, probably in bed. Brooke, however, was spending her third night in Sweet Springs, Texas trying to make metaphorical lemonade out of lemons.

"Oh, *no,*" she moaned, upon coming to a new hole dug under the chain-link fence. She'd just spotted the evidence she most feared: her aunt Marsha's beloved basset hound had escaped again!

On Sunday morning, seventy-year-old Marsha Newman had fallen in the shower and fractured her right hip. As soon as Brooke had gotten the news, she had packed a suitcase and raced from her house in Turtle Creek in Dallas to her aunt in Central East Texas to offer what assistance that she could. Never would she have dreamed that her life could turn upside down in such short order; life-changing upheaval had occurred not once but twice in a month. Then again, she also hadn't expected it likely that the daughter of business tycoon Damon Bellamy would find herself unemployed!

"Humphrey!" she called in an urgent whisper. "Where are you? C'mon, boy. You'd better get back here before you get yourself run over," she added. Actually, at this hour there wasn't any traffic that she could see or hear, and this Cherokee County town, south of Tyler, only had a population of fewer than four thousand people; but the way her luck was going, she wasn't taking any chances.

How long had she left the not-so-little tubular test on her patience in the backyard in order to take a shower in peace? Not more than ten minutes. Yet for someone who tended to move at the pace of an armadillo, Humphrey must have recognized this as a prime opportunity and had kicked his short legs into gear. Now he was out, and who knew where? Wearing only her sleep shirt, she wasn't exactly dressed to go prowling through the neighborhood in search of the critter. But she would because, heaven forbid that, come morning, she had to return to the hospital to confess to Aunt Marsha that she'd lost her beloved companion of ten years.

Aiming her LED flashlight toward the double gate,

she hurried to open it and check the driveway in case she could see muddy prints to give her new clues as to Humphrey's whereabouts. Why she expected prints when it hadn't rained in days, and she hadn't yet had a chance to water, was testament to her fatigue and growing anxiety.

"Humphrey, sleepy time. Let's go in and have a cookie."

That coercion had worked Sunday night, the first time he'd snuck off, and a variation of it had been successful last night. Not this time, though. Humphrey was a fast learner, even if in dog years he was her aunt's age. Surely dogs didn't get dementia…or could they?

"Humphrey…sit! Stay!" In the past, Aunt Marsha had bragged that a horn blast from a passing freight train couldn't budge her obedient pet once those orders were given. "I guess it depends on who's doing the ordering," she muttered to herself. Then again, the dog would have to be within hearing distance to cooperate.

Increasingly worried, Brooke made her way around the outside of the fence to where the escapee had gained his freedom and focused her light on the grass hoping for some hint as to which way the dog had gone.

"At it again, I see."

Gasping, Brooke spun around. Wholly preoccupied, she hadn't heard that Doc had come outside and joined her. Dr. Gage Sullivan was the local veterinarian, who owned Sweet Springs Animal Clinic on the outskirts of town. He had come to her aid last night as well, and had been a great help. What a relief that he'd either seen or heard her out here. Correction, it would be if she'd thought to put on something over her nightie. Last night she'd only just returned from the hospital and had still been wearing her street clothes.

"Hey, Doc. My, you sure do stay up late for a guy who says he heads to the clinic at the crack of dawn." Despite the limited lighting provided by their porch fixtures, she had the strongest urge to fold her arms across her chest, which might have something to do with the way he was smiling down at her. Not that it was anything remotely lecherous; his expression was more like someone seeing a line of sevens appear on a casino slot machine.

"Lucky for you, I'm behind on paperwork." Gage directed his own flashlight at Humphrey's latest escape hole. "Looks like he worked fast. At this rate, he won't need a nail trim for a while. How long since you last saw him?"

"Ten minutes…. Well, fifteen now. I've been out here for at least five calling for him. I should never have given him his private time, but I was dying for a shower."

"You think Humph needs private time?"

Brooke grimaced her agreement that the phrasing sounded ridiculous to her, too. But she had her reasons for putting it that way. "He gives me a look if I don't turn away while he's, you know, doing his business."

Gage choked on a laugh. "He was just setting you up, rookie. That hound can play an innocent the way a pickpocket can work a mark."

With pessimism fast becoming a knee-jerk reaction, Brooke asked doubtfully, "And what do you know about pickpockets?" It seemed an unusual analogy to use.

With a philosophical shrug, Gage replied, "We had a black sheep in the family tree."

Brooke studied his appealing, all-American face capped by shaggy, medium-brown hair still wet from his own shower. "Seriously?"

"It was when my uncle was young. After a few run-ins with the law, he wisely tried magic instead, and had a pretty successful career."

Brooke didn't know whether to take him seriously or not. After only three brief conversations with Gage Sullivan, she'd come to the conclusion that he was very laid-back and just as amiable. Her aunt sang his praises every time she had a chance to bring him up in a conversation. But at the moment, there was no sign of the serious, disciplined person Marsha described. As a bemused expression played across his face, she thought of him as someone who liked to just throw ideas out into the cosmos to see what kind of reaction he would get from people. If he hadn't chosen the profession he had, he could have been a popular college instructor. At least the female students would have enjoyed fantasizing over him.

"Is that something you should be telling a near stranger?" she asked, hoping he got the hint. She wasn't in to gossip, and this was not the time to be practicing some stand-up comedy routine or whatever it was that he was doing.

"I figured it would be better to get the awkward stuff out of the way. Did you happen to look under that sweet BMW 650i of yours?"

It was sheer reflexes that had Brooke glancing toward the silver metallic convertible in the driveway before resuming her studious inspection of the man who was built like a sequoia compared to her own stretchto-get-there five foot two. "Uh—yeah. Get the awkward stuff out of the way because…?"

"I'm going to ask you out. When Marsha is feeling better and you're not so pressed for time."

That startling bit of news left Brooke without a clue as to how to answer him. She couldn't deny that he was an attractive man, solid and relaxed in his own skin, even though his white T-shirt and jeans were clinging to his body as though he hadn't taken time to towel off from that shower. In comparison, she had to be reflecting sheer self-consciousness, as she gave in to the need to cross her arms over her purple satin-and-lace sleep shirt.

"You…work fast, Doc."

"My parents would disagree with you, considering that I'm thirty-six and still single. But," he added with almost boyish pleasure, "I've had the advantage of seeing a few photos of you at Marsha's. Combined with her delightful gushing about what a thoughtful niece and smart woman you are has convinced me that I have to make an impression before everyone else realizes you're back in town."

"Oh, Aunt Marsha," Brooke groaned softly. "Really, Doc, I may be Texas born and bred, and spent a good portion of my childhood here, but no one died of a broken heart when Dad relocated us to Houston after my mother died. What's more, it's been too long between my visits back for anyone to get their hopes up." To get his attention off her, Brooke gestured toward the street. "About Humphrey… Do you think if you called him, he might respond? Aunt Marsha has told me plenty of times that he adores you."

"Until I take his temperature and a blood sample,"

Gage drawled. Nevertheless, he cupped his hands around his mouth and whistled sharply. Then he called, "Yo, Humph. Here, boy."

Yesterday, the basset hound had yelped from two houses away and come waddling up Gage's driveway, eager for familiar company and the promised treat from Brooke. When several seconds passed and only crickets and tree frogs broke the silence, Brooke sighed. "I'd better go change into street clothes and initiate a wider search."

"I'll get started on that while you do."

Guilt forced Brooke to protest. Her conscience wouldn't let her allow him to do that when she had been told repeatedly by Aunt Marsha what long hours he worked. "That's good of you, Doc, but—"

"Gage."

After a gently reproving look at his unabashed flirtation, Brooke continued. "All I was going to say is that I'm sensitive to the fact that you're probably already dead on your feet. You need to get what rest you can."

"Do you think that's going to happen knowing you're out here wandering about by yourself? A Saint Bernard could grab you by the scruff of the neck and carry you off like a pup. You're certainly no match for anything larger."

That gave her pause. There were still less than fifty thousand people in all of Cherokee County, and most of them lived around communities like Rusk, the county seat to their northeast. Had things changed around here so much? "My aunt says Sweet Springs is still the friendliest town, and that this remains the quietest of neighborhoods."

"Okay, but then what if you come upon Humphrey

having a face-off with a rabid skunk, or a mother raccoon protecting her young?"

Brooke's stomach lurched, and she pressed a hand against her abdomen. She so did not want to have to deal with either scenario. While Marsha was a second mother to her, especially after the death of her mother when Brooke had been barely twelve, she just didn't share her aunt's love for indoor pets. As far as the wilder creatures were concerned, she would be content to know they'd been exiled farther out in the country or to a zoo!

"Too much information," Gage said, upon noticing her distress. "Come, take my Windbreaker. I keep it by the back door. It'll save you the time it would take to change, and we can search together."

With long-legged strides, Gage backtracked across the yard until he could reach inside the door of the two-story, colonial-style dwelling; Brooke followed with less enthusiasm. Had he meant it about wanting to ask her out? She hoped not. He'd been nothing but kind and helpful since her arrival, and he really was a good-looking man. She would forever be grateful that he'd been outside on Sunday morning when he'd heard Aunt Marsha crying for help from inside her house. On the other hand, Brooke wasn't here to date, especially since her plan was to return to Dallas to get her career back on track as soon as possible.

"Thanks," she said, once he held the lightweight dark jacket up for her. Sliding into it, she tried to flip her still-damp blond hair from under the collar and found long sleeves thwarted her efforts. With a wry smile, she rolled them several times. "This reminds me of when I was a kid and up here for Halloween. I borrowed one of my uncle's sweaters for Halloween to create my Robin Hood costume."

"I would never have guessed. Not a princess? Not even Maid Marian?"

Brooke shook her head at his stereotyping. "You only think you have me figured out."

"Interesting. You do tend to look and act as though you came out of the womb wearing high heels and a business suit. Extremely well tailored, but sexy," Gage added, his blue-gray eyes sparkling with good humor in the glow of the overhead light.

Her tendency to fixate on looking professional had started later, after her father had taken over directing more and more aspects of her life. Until then, she'd enjoyed playing games, watching Saturday-matinee movies and indulging in a healthy fantasy life—all of which her mother and aunt had supported. It relieved Brooke to realize that Aunt Marsha hadn't gotten around to sharing that bit of information with him. Yet. It was challenging enough when Gage Sullivan looked at her with those kind but knowing eyes that seemed to see way beyond flesh and bone.

Averting her gaze, she dealt with his comment by changing the subject. "Where do you think we should start? Even though your jacket is lightweight, I'm already about to melt."

"Well…the hospital is that way," Gage said, nodding toward the west, the direction both their front doors faced.

Disconcerted, Brooke asked, "Do you think Humphrey would actually try to go *there?* I'd about convinced myself that he was simply running away from me. Can he actually pick up her scent from that distance?"

Gage shrugged. "It's not two miles, and something is compelling him to ignore his obedience training. Since I don't think you'd be cruel to a pet your aunt loved so much, it has to be pure heartache for his mistress that's compelling him to escape. Let's take a left out of the driveway and see if we can hear or spot something. Considering his age, and with legs as short as his, speed and endurance are on our side."

As she followed, Brooke glanced from her size-six designer flip-flops sparkling with rhinestones in the artificial light to his size twelve or better athletic shoes. "Speak for yourself."

Looking over his shoulder and following the direction of her gaze, Gage chuckled. "I'll try to remember to cut my strides in half. I'm sure he hasn't gotten too far, and he's bound to trigger someone else's family pet to bark sooner or later." As he reassured her, Gage directed the beam of his flashlight across the street to scan each yard for any sign of movement.

Following his lead, Brooke used her flashlight to check houses on their side. Although most dwellings were dark, suggesting their inhabitants were already in bed for the night, she uttered, "I feel terrible about abusing people's privacy. What do you want to bet some insomniac spots us and calls the police thinking we're prowlers?"

"Relax, I know everyone in the department," Gage assured her. "Plus, their drug dog is a patient of mine." After only a few more steps, he paused. "Aha! Hear that?"

Brooke was about to ask him how long he'd been in

Sweet Springs, when she, too, heard an excited sound ahead—part bark and part yodel-howl. "Oh, dear. I hope he's not standing under someone's bedroom window."

They hurried the rest of the way, crossing the street, into the next block, where they came upon Humphrey running around someone's koi pond. Illuminated in the center by accent lights was a fat, indignant-looking bullfrog.

"Whoa, Humph." As the winded but excited dog tried to circle the pond again, Gage scooped him up into his arms. "Some dog on a mission, you are. One chubby amphibian and your whole master plan to get to your lady flies out of your mind. And look how you upset Brooke." In the soft pinkish glow of the streetlights, his eyes twinkled with humor as he turned the dog to face her.

What with Gage being almost a foot taller, Brooke found herself practically eye to eye with the panting hound. She primly clasped her hands behind her back and said, "I'm just glad you're okay. But this is the last time I let you outside unchaperoned."

"Aw, don't be too hard on him. No damage was done," Gage told her.

As they started back, Brooke couldn't help but feel a need to defend herself. "I know I'm not my aunt, but am I really *that* bad? The more I think about it, the more I believe he pulled this to get back at me."

"For what?"

"He's not getting to go to the shop with me the way he does with Aunt Marsha."

"Whoa. That would do it."

"I did come home twice to let him outside. And I petted him extra this evening when I got home from the hospital. Oh—and he'd had the canned food that she says is his favorite, that she only gives him on special occasions."

"Ah, the truth emerges," Gage said, lowering his head to speak into the basset hound's ear. "A pat on the rump and canned meat byproducts, and she thinks she's got you under control."

With a choking sound, Brooke stopped in her tracks. "Then you *do* think I'm not being good enough to him?"

"I think he's lonely. Why can't he be at the shop with you?" Gage asked, sounding more curious than judgmental. "It's his second home. Customers would give him the extra attention he's used to getting."

Brooke understood that Humphrey was a replacement for *her* in many ways, now that she was an adult and unable to visit Aunt Marsha as often as she would like. She also grasped that animal care was Gage's calling, but that didn't mean he or anyone else had a right to put a guilt trip on her. She did that well enough without any help. "Not everyone and everything should or can revolve around Humphrey, Doctor."

"Gage."

Ignoring his mischievous reply, she continued, "You probably don't think there's much to running a florist—"

"I didn't say that."

His tone was quiet, even gentle, which made Brooke press her lips together as she accepted that she'd jumped to conclusions again. "What I mean is that it's taken every bit of my attention and ability to get arrangement orders filled, what with the store being busier than ever, now that one of the other two florists in town has retired and closed down her business. Don't get me wrong, Naomi has been good to come out of retirement to help in emergencies, and Kiki is managing the front just fine on her own, but—"

"I thought you worked at the shop when you visited?"

"When I was a child. I could put a single rosebud in a vase with a sprig of baby's breath or a fern. In time I learned a few more things, but I've forgotten most of that, and styles change. The point I'm trying to make is, first and foremost, I'm here for my aunt, not to entertain a dog. Then there's the matter of the doors opening every few minutes. I'd be a wreck if I'm constantly checking to make sure someone didn't inadvertently let Humphrey out into the street."

Gage nodded, then began walking again. "You should have called me and told me you were struggling. I would have told you to drop him off at the clinic. He'd fit right in with Roy and the boys."

It was that simple? "I'm afraid I don't know who they are." *Boys?* Her aunt hadn't said anything about children, and he'd just said he was single.

"Roy Quinn is my manager," Gage said, amusement entering his voice again. "Anywhere else, he'd be called a receptionist, but he tends to get all puffy and glares if he's called that—and he has the Neanderthal eyebrows to do it. Besides, he does too much other stuff for such a restrictive title. He could be a full-fledged technician, but he balks at fulfilling the necessary requirements to get certified."

"Stubborn. I see why you think Humphrey would fit in."

After a soft chuckle, Gage admitted, "There's no denying he can be. But behind all of that gruff exterior, he's mostly a teddy bear. He's sure been a welcome change from the young ladies who thought the receptionist job was step one to becoming Mrs. Sullivan."

"Awkward," Brooke said with a nod, able to finally speak from experience and sympathy. She'd witnessed enough behavior like that in her professional world, where some girls only went to college to find the wealthiest husband possible. "Then again, I don't know what options girls have out here where the pickings are undoubtedly slimmer. A big-hearted, patient doctor must seem like a fairy tale come true."

"You left out cute."

His charm was potent, and Brooke had to work at keeping her expression benign. "Definitely cute." But not willing to venture any farther down Flirtation Lane with him, she asked, "So is it Roy who has the sons? They help out at the clinic, too?"

"Say *what?*" After a brief, confused look, Gage uttered a low, "Ah! The boys I was referring to are his military veteran pals. Roy's single, too, and his one request in taking the job was for me to allow a table and chairs in the corner of the reception room. He has some VFW buddies who like to congregate daily. The male version of the female coffee klatch of old. They'd already been run out of the local donut shop, and the grocery's deli department, and they'd worn out their welcome in the bank's lobby."

"Are they all single, too?"

"Not quite. One has a wife in a nursing home, but her Alzheimer's is so advanced that he can't bear to spend more than a few minutes a day with her. Another is divorced—and that's not a bad thing, as far as he's concerned. The rest are widowers."

"Well, it's another testament to your generosity and goodwill that you're so accommodating," Brooke said.

"They're not in the way," Gage replied with a dismissive shrug. "Interestingly, after their military service, they were all farmers or businessmen in the area, so they pretty much know everyone who comes in and can supply me with a wealth of background information on clients and their livestock if I'm not familiar with someone."

Brooke could see both the pros and cons of their arrangement. "Were you, by chance, in the military, too?" she asked as they turned into her aunt's driveway. "I sense respect as much as affection when you speak about them."

"I spent eight years in the U.S. Army Reserves."

His almost apologetic reply won a quick glance from her. "What? That's noble, too."

Gage took several seconds to answer. "The guys ribbed me about it at first. It was the usual taunting about trying to avoid active duty, which I wasn't. I took that route to get through school and get my practice established. It was only after they learned what a trial it had been not to lose my business that they really rallied behind me. We're pretty much one big mutual-admiration society now."

Sensing that he'd been modest and had struggled greatly, Brooke felt humbled. "Here I've been feeling sorry for myself because I've lost my job, thanks to government regulations, and can't interview for a new one because I'm here helping Aunt Marsha, and all the while you've endured much heavier and *dangerous* burdens." With new respect and concern, she asked, "Is there a chance you'll have to go away again?"

"Nah, I finished up a couple years ago. As much as I gained from the experience, it was tough on my clients, as well as the friends who donated their time to keep the clinic running. I'm relieved, too. You know how hot it gets in Texas, but that's nothing compared to the Middle Eastern deserts. It's not an endurance test I ever want to go through again, especially at my age."

"Right, all that gray hair is practically glowing like neon in the moonlight," Brooke said, matching his easygoing tone. If he did have any gray hair, she had yet to notice it, even in daylight, amid the various shades of brown and gold.

"Hey, I have all of the scars and aches that come with this profession."

Brooke paused at the gate. "Still very young for having experienced as much as you have. Thank you for sharing that. Also for your time. It helps me better understand why Aunt Marsha speaks of you with such affection—and not just because you saved her countless hours of suffering after her fall."

"I'm partial to her, too." Gage stroked Humphrey soothingly as he waited for her to open the gate. "She's helped me every bit as much as I may have her. She keeps an eye on things when I'm not around. Did she tell you about how she called me one morning on my cell phone? I'd already left to get an early start at the clinic and she'd spotted a squirrel gnawing its way into my attic. By the time I could return home, the critter was inside and had almost chewed through wires in two spots. That could easily have resulted in a costly fire if left untended."

While cute enough in cartoons and on greeting cards, the creatures were rats with couture tails, to Brooke's thinking. "Doesn't that make you want to cut down all of the nut-bearing trees around here to force them to move?"

As Gage threw back his head, his laugh filled the humid night air. "Are you sure you were born in Texas? Nature may not be perfect, but we civilized folks aren't, either."

"At least we don't carry fleas and diseases."

"You mean you've never had the flu? Chicken pox? Measles?"

Brooke should have known better than to criticize creatures in front of such a devoted animal lover. "Okay, okay, I get your point." She began reaching for the basset hound, only to see Gage step out of her reach and nod toward the house.

"How about I set this old boy inside for you? I have a feeling that if you put him down after we close this gate, he'll just waddle straight for the hole and crawl under the fence again."

"Good thought." Brooke made a mental note to get the key to her aunt's storage shed first thing in the morning and get a shovel to close that latest exit spot.

Once she unlocked the back door, Gage set the placid hound on the hardwood floor. By the time he'd shut it behind Humphrey, Brooke had removed his jacket and handed it over to him.

"Thank you," she said sincerely, as she discreetly crossed her arms over her chest again. "You're as much a gentleman as you are a lifesaver."

"I meant what I said about bringing Humph to the clinic. His species may have been bred for work, but in the end he's quite the social animal. I can guarantee you that he'll be coddled and get plenty of exercise. By the time you finish at the shop daily, he'll be as grateful as you are to get home and crash on his doggy bed."

"Let me run the idea by Aunt Marsha," Brooke said, to buy herself a little more time. Gage's idea did sound like a gift to *her* sanity, but would Aunt Marsha approve? "Remember, it could be some weeks before she gets to come home. This isn't your usual broken hip. There was extra repair work to do. It might be several days before she's even ready to relocate to the rehab facility."

Gage shook his head in sympathy. "For such an active lady, that will exasperate her. When I first bought my place, she was about your size, which I still think is Tinker Bell tiny, and in the past year, I know she's lost a good ten pounds that she can't afford."

His visual perceptions served him as well as his instincts obviously did. "This is probably no surprise, but she does have osteoporosis issues."

"I worried it was something like that."

Sensitive to his increasingly searching gaze, Brooke reached for the doorknob, hoping he would take the hint. "Thank you again, and for so much, Doc. Gage," she amended at his gently reproachful look.

"You are more than welcome. It was good to spend a little while with my favorite neighbor's favorite niece instead of settling for a wave as we dash for our vehicles in the morning."

They *had* been leaving earlier than everyone else in the neighborhood. "Yes, it was. But it's *only* niece. I was the sole yield from my parents' short but loving marriage."

"Nicely put and poetic for a math head." At her grimace, he added, "Did you think that if your aunt has been bragging about you that she'd leave out how smart you are?"

"I guess not. It's a wonder that she hasn't set me up with an account on some online-dating site."

Gage shook his head. "She wouldn't do that. She's too protective of you. Do you miss not having any siblings?"

"Sometimes. But it was nice having all of the attention, too. You?"

"Two sisters and three brothers. Privacy was the challenge in our house, since I was number five out of six kids. Fortunately, I lack most ingredients required to be a type A personality."

"I can't imagine… I mean, having that many siblings." Along with being an only child, she'd spent the second half of her childhood with little time for fun or friendships, what with her father directing her extra-curricular activities as much as her school focus. Faced with the reality that he would have only one child, he had been a veritable Tiger Mom, as hands-on as though he'd been managing a lab project, determined to make her the best at what he directed her toward. Only since having her job liquidated when proprietary trading won the government's evil eye did it strike her that focusing so determinedly on networking might have served a purpose, but it had left her emotionally vacant compared to what family and friendship provided. Experience had also taught her sobering lessons on the difference between friends and acquaintances.

"Are you okay?"

Pulled back to the present, Brooke saw that Gage

was studying her with unusual intensity, despite the hint of a smile curving his inviting lips. That smile was a ruse, she realized. It was meant to hide how serious he'd suddenly become. Well, she didn't need all that magnetism directed at *her*.

"Fine," she assured him, flashing him an equally deceptive but brighter smile. "You just made me realize that I'd promised to report on Aunt Marsha's condition to my father, which is going to be a challenge since I'm not even sure what time zone he's in."

"He sounds like one of the original wheeler-dealers."

How much of *that* side of their lives had Aunt Marsha shared? "He's an unapologetic workaholic." It was on the tip of her tongue to add with no small self-deprecation, "And I'm afraid this acorn didn't fall far from the tree." It was only the cold chill that ran through her—a chill that belied the sultry night's warmth—that had her editing herself in the last second. Instead, she whispered in entreaty, "I really need to get inside."

Gage took a halfhearted step backward. "Don't hesitate to holler if you need my Sherlock services again."

With a wave, Brooke hurried inside and, upon closing the door, she quickly twisted the wand to shut the miniblinds. Only then did she exhale her relief. What on earth was she doing almost making such admissions to a near stranger? Had she been subjected to some version of dog psychiatry, hypnotism or what? She glanced over her shoulder, taking in Humphrey's resigned look.

"Please don't put me in this position again. I don't have the time, understand? Not for you *or* him. You're both sweethearts—I get it—but I'm not in the market for anything like that, so behave!"

* * *

By seven forty-five Wednesday morning, Gage was up front at Sweet Springs Animal Clinic enjoying a rare extra cup of coffee with the old-timers and Roy before the early-bird clients arrived to drop off a beloved pet for some procedure, or were overeager to pick one up after an overnight stay. However, the first person to pull in was Brooke Bellamy.

As the others began noticing her flashy, metallic-silver BMW convertible that shouted her previous professional success, a rush of pleasure swept through him. So, he thought, she'd not only approached Marsha about his suggestion, his sweetheart of a neighbor had given her blessing. He would have to send Marsha a bouquet in gratitude for assisting him in gaining more access to her lovely niece.

"Be still, my heart…" drawled sixty-six-year-old Jerry Platt, who sat closest to the window. Retired from the air force and divorced, he was considered the "kid" in the group and frequently taunted the others with tales of his romantic escapades—true or not. "Say, isn't that Marsha Newman's niece? Wow…. She grew up to be a pretty little thing."

"Looks a lot like her aunt," Stan Walsh replied. Stan was sixty-nine and an old navy man turned sheet-metal fabricator. He'd passed his business over to his son earlier in the year following the death of his wife. "Every bit the lady, too, from what I hear, so behave, Platt."

"Did she ever marry?" Pete Ogilvie asked, craning his head to watch as Brooke went around to the passenger door to let Humphrey out. The eighty-two-year-old ex-marine and widower was the oldest in the group and still looked the part of the rancher he'd been.

"What is she now? Twenty-nine? Thirty? Back in my day, a girl would be afraid to be called an old maid if she hadn't hooked a guy by then. Good for her, I say. You have to be pretty successful to afford wheels like that. What's to want in today's crop of guys anyway? Present company excluded, Doc," he quickly added.

"No offense taken," Gage replied, although he did plan to keep a close eye on that wily fox Jerry Platt.

Having waited patiently for his turn to speak, Warren Atwood said, "Back in your day, telephone operators sat in front of circuit boards, you old dinosaur." The intellectual seventy-year-old had gone on from the U.S. Army to being the D.A. of Cherokee County. His wife was at the community's nursing home in the advanced stages of Alzheimer's. It was only his closest friends who knew what a toll that was taking on him.

"All right, you guys," Roy Quinn said, as Gage put down his mug to go welcome Brooke. "Behave yourselves for a minute. She's not going to be as used to your nonsense as we are."

Gage barely heard him as he pushed through the two sets of doors. Reaching the fresh air, he saw Brooke look up and give him a ready-or-not shrug and smile. She looked as fresh as the posies she worked with in her three-quarter-sleeve teal silk top and matching slacks. The gold earrings and necklace added another layer of elegance. With her blond hair deftly swept up into an artful knot, he knew that, inside, jaws were slack with admiration. She did powerful things to him, too.

"Good to see you." The words felt slow and heavy to his ears, but then his tongue felt as if someone had poured concrete in his mouth.

"You, too," Brooke replied with visible relief. "I

was half afraid last night's offer was sheer politeness on your part. As it happened, I had to drop off some papers at the hospital this morning, and when I peeked in on my aunt she was wide-awake, and we had a quick chat." As Gage held the door for her, she led Humphrey inside the green steel building.

"So she gave her blessing?" It fascinated Gage that as her nerves grew more visible, his eased. He even touched the small of her back, unable to resist stealing some tiny physical contact for private savoring later.

*"Blessing?"* Stan asked from across the room, his hand to his ear. His years on an aircraft carrier and in a sheet metal shop had all but destroyed his hearing. "Did they get engaged? I thought she just got back in town?"

"Shut up, you fool," Pete replied, swatting at his arm with the editorial section of the *Tyler Morning News*. "What kind of eavesdropper are you?"

"My hearing-aid battery must be giving out."

Brooke sent the men a bemused glance, then said to Gage, "She did—and said to tell you that she'll make you her renowned apple crumble as soon as she gets back on her feet."

Gage uttered a throaty groan of pleasure, then crouched to pet the basset hound, who was wagging his tail cautiously, not sure if this was an official visit or what. "Relax, Humph. You're about to be spoiled rotten, just like when you're at the flower shop."

He unclipped the lead from the dog's collar, after which Humphrey shook his whole body, clearly relishing the freedom in this, of all places. Brooke, on the other hand, looked anything but reassured.

"You're certain it's going to be okay for him to run

free like that?" She looked unconvinced as she rolled up the blue nylon leash around her hand.

Gage rose, knowing they had precious few minutes left—and not even private ones—before the parking lot started to fill. He wanted to tell her that he liked her hair up. It showed off her slender neck so much that his fingers itched to caress the baby-fine hair there and her even finer skin. She was exceedingly fair for this time of year, but on her the look worked. However, the sum of all of her delicate parts didn't fool him: inside that petite body was a backbone of pure steel and a strong will to match it. The irony was *that* just made her all the more irresistible.

"We'll make sure he doesn't get into anything he shouldn't—nor goes outside without supervision." Gage then addressed the others. "Everybody, this is Brooke, my neighbor—although you probably already know that."

"We do," Jerry said, as the others waved and called greetings. "How's Marsha, darlin'?"

"Still in a lot of pain from the surgery. Thank you for asking. But she's determined not to depend long on that walker they're forcing her to use."

"She's a fighter. Give her our best."

"I will." Brooke turned back to Gage, worry creasing the smooth skin between her finely arching tawny eyebrows. "As I drove here, it hit me. We close at the same time, but occasionally I'll have to wait on Charles—our delivery man—to return the store's van. Or you may have to leave on a call. How do we work this?"

Acutely aware of all eyes on him, Gage shrugged to show as little concern as possible. "If you're running late, give me a call, and if I have to leave for an emergency, Roy can wait for you, can't you?" he asked him.

"Sure, boss." Roy expanded on his answer directly to Brooke. "We tend to hang around after hours with whomever stops by. Not to worry, Ms. Bellamy. From here on, Humph will be treated as family."

Although looking far more confident about the arrangement, Brooke remained poised and formal as she stepped to the counter and offered her hand. "That's very kind, since I feel as though I'm taking advantage. You're Roy? Please call me Brooke."

When Roy's brown eyes all but glazed over under the full effect of her warm smile, Gage took hold of Brooke's elbow. "I'll walk you out."

He ignored the feeling of daggers pricking at his back as they exited the building, but he didn't care. A familiar truck was coming down the service road and he knew it was heading here. Another hectic day was about to commence, and he wanted these last precious seconds with her to be his alone.

"I saw that you beat me to filling the hole Humphrey dug last night," Brooke said, pausing at the driver's door. "You're being too good to me."

"It didn't take more than a minute. I was concerned that you might forget and he would take advantage."

"Is that really black pepper you spread over the area?"

"It is. I often tell people to spread it over their pets' graves to repel varmints from trying to dig them up. It should work to thwart Humph from another escape, too." As the sunshine lit flecks of gold in her brown eyes, Gage felt something akin to hunger pangs grip his stomach. "At the risk of embarrassing you... You look particularly beautiful this morning."

After another of those cautious pauses that Gage was starting to recognize, Brooke's shimmering lips curved into a private smile. "A woman who can't accept a compliment is out of her mind. Thank you." She reached for the door handle. "I do have to hurry, though. Kiki has a dental appointment in an hour."

"Then I guess I'll see you later. What are you doing for dinner?" It was foolish to ask, since he could easily be dealing with emergency farm calls by then, but he couldn't resist.

"I'll grab some takeout and go keep Aunt Marsha company as she has her supper."

The look she gave him from under her long eyelashes added a warning not to pursue what he was intent on achieving. Nevertheless, he needed for her to know that he was determined, too. "What about a glass of wine afterward?"

"By then I'll be totally drained and my feet will be killing me. The only thing I'll want to do is kick off these shoes, have a soothing shower and collapse in bed."

Gage glanced down at the cork-and-leather platform sandals that added a good three inches or so to her height. "Very pretty, but why on earth don't you wear something—?"

"More sensible?" Brooke offered when he abruptly edited himself.

"I would have tried for 'less dangerous.'"

"Very diplomatic. But I've worn heels since I was in junior high. Couldn't wait for my first pair. When you're practically the runt in the entire school, you don't mind taking a few risks to fit in better."

Gage suspected that she would always stand out regardless, and guessed that any grief she took was more about jealousy than her petite size. "I guess in your male-dominated profession, you liked being taller because the guys tried to make you feel insecure even without the height disadvantage?" When she offered a one-shouldered shrug that suggested it was a moot point, he added, "Well, with or without the extra inches, I think you're—"

"I *really* have to go."

"Adorable." Gage grinned as she cast a self-conscious look at the pickup truck now turning into the parking lot as though the driver could read lips. "Sue me. I've seen you smile. You have dimples that should be seen—" and kissed frequently "—and when you're not stressing over your aunt, the shop or Humphrey, those brown eyes make me feel like a kid facing his first fudge-caramel sundae."

"Oh, Lord." Pressing her lips together to repress a smile, Brooke quickly climbed into her BMW. "Have a good day, Doc."

"*Gage.* Give me that at least. You know I'm going to go back inside to deal with all kinds of abuse from those guys." He nodded his head toward the windows where everyone was unabashedly watching.

She keyed the ignition, and, once the engine sprang to life, Brooke put the sports car into Reverse. Just after she shifted into Forward, she wiggled her fingers at him and drove away.

Waving to Carter Spears as Spears drove around to the back where he would be picking up the family pet—a potbellied pig—that had survived eating one of Carter's leather work gloves, Gage returned inside. After pausing at the surreal silence that greeted him, he suddenly faced five sets of wiggling fingers waving at him.

Knowing it would be worse if he said anything, he just nodded his acceptance of their ribbing. In his opinion, he'd made progress—minimal, but in the right direction. Brooke liked him. More than she wanted to. He could feed off that all day.

Pete Ogilvie started the Greek chorus of commentary. "So that's the way of things, eh? You'd better work fast because you've got your sights on a city girl, my friend. She's not going to hang around these parts a day longer than she has to."

"My back hurts just thinking about all the bending you'll have to do to kiss the little thing," Stan Walsh groused.

Jerry and Warren hooted and laughed, and Jerry said, "Listen to him. The guy on the most medications is having sympathy pains over your love life, Doc."

"My money is on you, son," Warren said, only to scowl at Jerry. "What are you trying to do, get us thrown out of here, too?"

"What do you think, Humph?" Gage asked, crouching to give the basset hound another affectionate rubbing. The dog was visibly curious as to what was going on. "You're one of the guys now. We have to support each other."

As though understanding, the dog rolled on to his back and offered his belly for scratching.

"That's exactly what I think." Chuckling, Gage obliged the dog. "Everybody has his—or her—soft spot. It'll be your job to help me find hers."

# Chapter 2

"Give him a few more days. He'll win you over."

Brooke did a double take when her aunt said those words. Yes, she had just been complaining about Humphrey trying to block her from leaving him when she'd dropped him off at the house a little while ago, but then her thoughts had inevitably veered to Gage. As luck would have it, he *had* been called out on an emergency this evening when she'd gone to pick up Humphrey from the clinic, and she'd been surprised at how disappointed she'd felt that he wasn't around.

"What? Oh." Embarrassed, Brooke self-consciously fussed with a strand of hair that had worked free during the day and now tickled her neck. "It's not that I don't think he's a good dog," she assured her aunt. "It's just that he's confused by what's going on, and, at his age, he probably doesn't like his routine being upset. Sometimes I suspect that he thinks I'm the cause of it all."

"Nonsense," Marsha replied with a genteel wave of her hand. "It is what it is—he's old. Wait until you're our age. You'll have your share of confused and cranky moments, too."

Brooke shook her head. "You're never cranky."

That won her a wry laugh from her aunt. "Bless you for that, but you're wrong. Just ask the nurses who were on duty today. As for Humphrey, I know this is a terrible inconvenience for you, sweetheart—"

"Don't even think that. I'm relieved to be able to be here for you. I just wish—" As she filled the water pitcher to refresh the low reservoir in one of the flower arrangements filling the room, Brooke tried to think of something that her aunt would like to hear. "—I wish I'd interacted more with Humphrey during my other visits, so I wouldn't feel like such a stranger to him, and an incompetent one at that."

"Silly, you could never be that, and it's not your fault that you have your own interests that don't include pets." Marsha glanced out the window, her expression slightly pensive. "It's just as well—your father would never have allowed you to have a dog or kitten in the house, and I wouldn't have been able to bear it if you'd ached for one." Forcing a bright smile, she changed the subject. "Listen to this. Today I managed to sit up and swing my legs over the side of the bed without help from the nurse. I wasn't sure I would make it—it hurt like blazes—and I was utterly exhausted afterward, but proud of myself."

"That's terrific!" However, Brooke couldn't help but worry, too. She thought her aunt looked quite drained—dear as ever, even with her short, permed, silver hair a bit mussed, and wearing her old-fashioned bed jacket over her hospital gown—but if trying too much too soon was the reason, how could that be a good idea? Grateful that they had the room to themselves, she spoke frankly. "Is that what your therapist wanted, Aunt Marsha?"

The older woman patted the bed opposite from the table that bore her food tray. "You spoke with the surgeon. This was an extremely invasive procedure, and my muscles and tendons are as sore as everything else. Stop fretting and come sit down. You're making me dizzy with all of your puttering and fussing. Have a bit to eat. I noticed that you didn't bring anything tonight, and there's way too much here for one person."

Although she had little appetite herself, Brooke did sit down. All that was on the dinner plate was a broiled chicken leg and thigh, a dab of sautéed spinach, a scoop of wild rice and a green salad. Even the bran muffin on the side was small, and the bowl of strawberry Jell-O wouldn't keep a toddler happy for more than a minute or two. Hardly the excess Marsha suggested.

Her aunt was still a pretty woman, despite the dark shadows that remained under her eyes. Her slender face showed few wrinkles for a woman who loved spending her free time away working in her yard. They shared the same large, doe-shaped brown eyes and petite build—as had Brooke's mother. Brooke often wondered if this was what her mother would be starting to look like if she'd lived. Unfortunately, Marsha had long been taking her health for granted, and her doctor had cited concern over her low blood pressure and anemia, as much as the osteoporosis.

"Don't worry about me. You're supposed to build up your blood as well as your strength," Brooke said, and set to work opening the silverware packet, then pulled off the foil lid on the juice cup. "Take a sip of this apple juice. I'll bet you haven't taken enough liquids today to help dissolve all of those vitamins and medications they're giving you."

"Please. The other half of my exercise is reaching for the call button to get a nurse in to empty my bag," her aunt muttered. "At any rate, I don't like juice, you know that. Too icky sweet. If I promise to drink some water, will you pour this down the sink?"

"Fair enough." Once Brooke returned, she said, "I was so eager to tell you about how good business was at the shop today that I forgot to tell you that I met the older gentlemen who spend the day at Gage's clinic. They all asked about you and sent their best."

"How sweet. They can be such a bunch of characters." Marsha halfheartedly broke off a bit of muffin and nibbled on it. "Isn't it kind of Gage to let them roost there? That's how I think of them—a motley group of roosters trying to still strut their stuff."

"Having come from a rather large family, I guess Gage misses having more people around," Brooke replied without thinking. Belatedly intercepting her aunt's look of amusement and unabashed satisfaction, she quickly regretted the comment.

"You two have been visiting more," Marsha said with a satisfied nod.

"Not really. There's been no time."

Looking unconvinced, her aunt pointed out, "You've been sharing details about *family*."

Brooke took great pains in cutting chicken off the

bone. "I felt I had to make polite conversation while walking through the neighborhood with him to find Humphrey. It would have been rude not to, what with him donating his time and showing so much interest in how we're doing."

"Yes, it would, and I'm proud of you," Marsha replied. "Because, although I adore you, you can be a bit—"

Brooke's breath all but locked in her throat. "A bit what?" Her aunt was never anything but complimentary and supportive. Was she about to get criticized?

"Insular."

"That's an awful thing to say."

"I'm not being judgmental. It's the place you've found yourself at this point in time. The sad thing will be if you stay like that."

Her aunt's opinion stung because Brooke wasn't stuck in any mode of behavior; she was *unemployed,* and that had happened because of decisions out of her control. She hated feeling like just another piece of flotsam as a result of "government regulation"—and her helplessness and the injustice of it made her all the less eager to talk about it. How did she explain this to her aunt when Marsha could barely balance a checkbook, let alone do quarterly reports for Newman's Florist and Gifts? She was that clueless about how the financial world operated; never mind what it meant to be a young, single woman holding her own in such a male-dominated cutthroat world. Why, if Brooke wasn't handling the accounting side of her aunt's business, Marsha wouldn't still be open today! What seemed "insular" to her was savvy and self-protective to Brooke.

"Anyway," Brooke said, forcing herself to put her

aunt's need for calm first, "Gage told me that he left Montana because he didn't like freezing for that much of the year."

Marsha looked a bit dazed for a moment and then caught up with their conversation. "That's what I remember, too. Having emergency calls in blizzards can't be any fun."

As her aunt reached for the muffin again, Brooke sighed, scooped a bit of rice and chicken up with the fork, and held it up to Marsha's mouth. "Try this."

"Oh, Brooke, I'm not totally incapacitated. You don't need to feed me."

"Well, you don't seem to want to do more than pluck at crumbs like a finch. Cooperate—and then I'll let you hold the fork." After her aunt obliged, Brooke set the fork on her side of the plate. "Now that I have your attention, there's something else we really should discuss."

"That doesn't sound fun at all."

Able to smile at her aunt's childlike tone, Brooke launched into news she was sure her relative would like. "It's about the store's windows. Kiki offered to spruce them up and put in some Fourth of July decorations." What Kiki had actually said was that it was embarrassing to still have the spring/Easter decorations up, and that even customers were asking when they were going to catch up with the calendar—and the rest of the shops on Main Street.

"It's still spring," Marsha protested. She suddenly looked smaller and weaker as she sank deeper into the pile of pillows behind her. "This whole acceleration of holidays is getting out of hand. You watch, in August, they'll have Halloween decorations on the same aisle as school supplies. Tell her to wait until after the fifteenth. By then I should be able to help her."

Incredulous, Brooke said gently, "Aunt Marsha… dear…you'll be lucky if you're moved to the rehab facility by then. Now, Kiki is more than capable of doing this. You taught her well, and she's had good schooling in marketing and design. At least let her draft an idea for you about what she'd like to do."

"That sounds expensive. For once I'm taking your advice, Ms. Financial Expert. There shouldn't be any spending on new things. There are plenty of decorations up in the loft."

Years ago, Newman's Florist and Gifts was the site of Sweet Springs Farm Supply, and the upstairs—still accessible by the back steps—was still a good second-story storage place for inventory, decorations and supplies. But after talking to Kiki and jointly taking a look up there, Brooke had agreed with the younger woman's perspective.

"Most of what's up there is showing its age and should be thrown out, Aunt Marsha," Brooke reported, combining both her and Kiki's conclusions. "Why not let us do a real renovation and scrap what isn't up to the store's standards?"

"But people always look forward to the displays I do."

"And next year, they'll enjoy it again. But in the meantime, there's another good reason to do some purging. If—Heaven forbid—there was a fire, there's enough clutter up there to burn down the whole block."

Marsha suddenly moaned. Seconds later, she pressed one hand to her hip, then the other to her chest.

"What is it?" Immediately concerned, Brooke was on her feet. "Is the pain worse?" She knew her aunt's chart as well as the nurses and remembered Aunt Marsha wasn't due another pain pill until ten o'clock. "I'll get a nurse."

"Just give me a minute." Marsha's voice was all tight, the words clipped, as though she was enduring a cramp or spasm of some kind.

Finally sighing with relief, her aunt shifted her gaze out at the pretty landscaping. Amid decades-old pines, there were beds of azalea and rosebushes providing blossoms three seasons of the year.

"Whew. It's moments like this that you realize you're getting old." She slid an apologetic glance at Brooke. "It's not that I've intentionally neglected taking care of things upstairs. There just never seems to be enough time to do the serious cleaning out that it deserves."

"Oh, Aunt Marsha, we know," Brooke declared. "Look, I'm here. There's no reason not to make good use of that. What's more, Kiki has a strong affection and devotion to you, too. We can do a little work upstairs every day, and before you know it, we'll have things refreshed and the inventory in good shape." "Kiki," as Kimberly Katherine Webb was known around town, had just graduated from the community college nearby and had worked at the shop since high school.

"She's been a good girl," Marsha admitted.

"She's twenty-one," Brooke reminded her patiently. "A young *woman,* and if the economy wasn't so challenging, she would probably already be gone trying to make better use of that business and marketing expertise. You have to let me give her more responsibility or she might yet take the gamble and fly off on her own. I promise you, Aunt Marsha, gifts like Kiki don't come every day."

As Marsha opened her mouth to reply, Brooke's phone buzzed. She rose to take it out of her pocket and saw the caller was Gage. He'd given her his cell phone number upon her arrival in town last Sunday.

"Is something wrong?" she asked, certain that he wouldn't have intruded on her time with her aunt if something hadn't happened.

"Humph is howling. It's not a complaining type of cry. This sounds serious. Could he have gotten into something that could hurt him?"

*That dog,* Brooke thought. "I can't see how. Hold on." To her aunt, Brooke said, "Humphrey seems to be in distress."

"Is he choking? Could there be smoke coming from the air conditioner? Did you leave the oven on?" Marsha asked with growing concern. "I don't remember when I last gave it a good cleaning. Oh, go, Brooke. I won't be able to live with myself if my little boy gets hurt."

Was her aunt tearing up? Disconcerted by the idea, as well as the thought that she might have done something she couldn't remember that was endangering Humph, Brooke said into the phone, "I'm on my way."

Minutes later Brooke pulled into the driveway at her aunt's house. Gage stood at the gate using the time to do some texting. What's more, he'd been home long enough to shower—his wet hair was a clear giveaway—and to change into a clean white T-shirt, khaki shorts and flip-flops. Although she couldn't ignore the little flutter inside from noticing how good he looked—wide shoulders, flat stomach and strong legs—she wondered why he wasn't at the door or windows peering into Aunt Marsha's house to see if the fire department or sheriff's office needed to be called, too.

"I'm so sorry for the noise," she said, as she got out of her BMW and used her remote to lock up. Almost immediately she heard Humphrey's wails coming from inside. That stopped her from asking the countless questions that had flooded her mind between the hospital and here. Humphrey was so loud it was a miracle the neighbors across the street hadn't yet complained. Then again, they were much older than Aunt Marsha and liked to watch TV in their sunroom in the back of their house. No doubt the volume was set high, too. "I didn't realize you would make it home this early," she added as Gage opened the back gate for her.

With a grimace, he said, "The owner had waited too long before calling me. The only humane thing to do was to put down the cow."

The jarring news sent Brooke stumbling over a concrete step stone. She would have fallen if he hadn't caught her by the waist and steadied her. She cast him an apologetic look over her shoulder. "And now I'm making you listen to this. I'm so sorry."

"No need. But I'll come with you if you don't mind, in case Humph needs medical attention."

Brooke had already sent up a quick prayer that wouldn't be the case. She didn't want to think about having to bring bad news to her aunt.

Her hands weren't quite steady as she unlocked and opened the door. Then she saw Humphrey sitting a few yards away. When he gave her a toothy grin and wagged his tail in welcome, she thought, *What on earth?*

After glancing around to see that nothing seemed amiss, she muttered, "Devious dog." Both she and Gage had been played for fools. "I should have known you were a born con artist."

As Humphrey hung his head and eyed her sheepishly, Gage tried but failed at subduing his laughter. That had the basset hound trotting to him and woofing as though in total agreement that what he'd pulled was great fun.

"Stop that!" Brooke protested as Gage stooped to rub the dog's extra rolls of skin. "You know this is all because of your bright idea about him being lonely and in need of companionship. Now you've made things worse with all of that dog-sitting psychology."

She set her purse and keys on the kitchen counter and returned, hands on hips, to confront the four-legged conniver. As Humphrey raised his paw toward her, she muttered, "Don't even pretend that you're experiencing separation anxiety from me. I left Aunt Marsha near tears. She thinks that you were somehow injured or in danger."

With one more reassuring pat for Humphrey, Gage rose. "What you need is a glass of wine. Do you mind?"

Before Brooke could respond, he headed for the refrigerator, which quickly had her narrowing her eyes with growing speculation. Sure enough, he brought out an open bottle and then took two glasses from the china hutch in the breakfast nook.

"Why didn't you tell me that you know your way around here?"

"I was waiting for the right moment. Would this

be the time to tell you that I know where the spare key is hidden?" Gage's look held no less appeal than Humph's had.

Meaning that he could have come inside and checked on Humphrey himself if there had really been an emergency. The stinker...and so was her aunt! Marsha had to have surmised quickly that there had been no crisis. She'd just wanted to escape finishing a conversation she didn't want to have and, too, eating a dinner she had no interest in.

"So much for thinking Humphrey's the only conniving one," she began.

"I had hoped that Marsha would have told you by now." As he poured the red wine, Gage did manage to look uncomfortable at finding himself in this position.

Able to appreciate he'd been caught in an unenviable position, Brooke wearily rubbed at her brow. "There's been too many other things going on."

Nodding, Gage said, "If it will reassure you, move the key until she's out of the hospital. The last thing I want is for you to have doubts about me."

He was as sensitive as he was a gentleman, and she'd been around him enough to gauge he was sincere. "What I should do is go back and make Aunt Marsha eat every bite of her dinner. I just know she feigned angst to force us to spend more time together, too."

"Don't be too hard on her." Gage handed her a glass, his smile coaxing. "She means well. She probably could see that you're burning the proverbial candle on all sides and could use an early night. Beautiful as ever," he assured her, as she self-consciously rubbed at nonexistent mascara under her eyes, "but in need of a break from being a perfectionist."

Was she that? Disciplined and devoted, maybe; however, accepting that to argue would only prove Gage right, Brooke gestured to the back porch. "Would you like to sit outside?"

"Don't you want to call your aunt just in case?"

"She showed you where the extra key was hidden," was all Brooke replied. It struck her that was how Gage had gained entrance on Sunday to help Marsha after her fall. In all that had been happening since Sunday, she'd overlooked that critical detail. "If we turn on the ceiling fan, it should be pleasant," she added, trying to suppress her annoyance with her relative. "And the breeze will help keep the mosquitoes away."

"Perfect." Gage whistled to Humphrey. "Come on, old man. You get a reprieve. Go roll in the grass and maybe a dragonfly or two will come by to entertain you."

Humphrey waddled outside and eased himself down the three stairs. Then, with a deep sigh of relief—or contentment—he plopped himself on to the grass and gazed at his domain with satisfaction.

Brooke and Gage settled on the glider and tasted their wine. The flavor was lush and fruity with a teasing peppery finish—exactly what the end of a hot summer day called for. Brooke couldn't remember when she'd last given herself an evening to just…unwind.

"I wish I could understand him half as well as you do," Brooke said, nodding toward the hound.

"I have an added edge—I see him more often than you do, and I've been around animals all my life."

"No, it's more than that. You have a gift. Aunt Marsha calls you a dog whisperer."

Gage uttered a dismissive sound. "There's no magic.

All the old guy—or any animal for that matter—wants is food, security and companionship."

"That sounds fairly universal for humans, as well. It's the quantity and timing that seems to cause the problems." Realizing that she could well be discussing her own life, she said abruptly, "So tell me, how was *your* day?"

"You've heard enough. It doesn't get better."

"How awful."

"Well, you're saving me from dwelling too much over it."

That pleased her. "You really have a tough job for someone who's so easygoing and good-natured," she said. "I guess I've never thought about all that goes into being a veterinarian."

"I wasn't fishing for sympathy…but I'll take the compliments." After Brooke's soft laugh, he grew philosophical. "There's a downside to every occupation. What would you be doing in Dallas on a gorgeous evening like this?"

"Not enjoying it, that's for sure. Before my department was shut down, I'd probably be taking a meeting or eating takeout while studying client portfolios." That sounded as dry to her as the actual work could be.

"If you have to work late, you should at least eat well."

"And I do. Did. I have to confess, I'm not much of a cook. Besides, it's always seemed a waste of time to go through so much trouble for just myself." That earned her a concerned frown from Gage, and she concluded that he thought her boring. With a twinge, she thought he hadn't been the only one.

"Marsha was concerned for you. She always felt you worked too hard."

"I liked being good at what I do."

"Same here. Only not if it starts to dictate almost every waking hour of my day."

Brooke couldn't help but be dubious. "Really? Aunt Marsha has talked about you, too, and when she wasn't calling you a dog whisperer, she was describing a twenty-first century Dr. Doolittle. Do you mean to tell me that there isn't a house full of cats and birds, fish, turtles and maybe a monkey over in that house of yours?"

He lived in a two-story colonial, but without the extra gingerbread-style ornamentation that adorned her aunt's Texas Victorian home. Painted a country blue with white trim, it was well tended, and the metal storage building in back looked large enough to keep a vehicle, as well as any yard equipment he might own.

"Want to come over and find out?" Gage teased, breaking into her thoughts.

Charisma emanated from those blue-gray eyes as his gaze locked with hers. Whenever he looked at her, she felt as though he was analyzing every atom of her being. When he openly challenged her, as he now did, she became all but mesmerized.

Tearing her gaze from his, she shook her head. "I'll never sympathize again for that unwanted female attention you complained about. You're a relentless flirt."

"With you." He glanced at her hands. "I don't see a ring, and your aunt said that there was no one serious in your life."

"Note to self," Brooke muttered. "Remember to take duct tape to the hospital tomorrow to repair loose lips."

Chuckling, Gage lifted his glass to inspect the wine's deep red coloring. "This is nothing like Marsha's boxed wine. I should have looked at the label more closely. There are hints of currant and undertones of something spicy."

"Glad you like it." Relieved to have something else to focus on, Brooke explained where it had come from. "It was a Christmas present from a client. He sent a case, and I brought two bottles with me."

"You have seriously generous clients. I tend to get homemade dog biscuits."

Bursting out laughing, Brooke sputtered, "You're not serious?"

"I wish. My clients tend to think I'm the animal world's version of the *Good Housekeeping's* seal of approval. They think if I like their concoctions, it's not only okay to feed the stuff to their four-legged children, they should consider going into commercial production."

"How funny. I'm glad you like the wine, though," she added, regaining her composure. "If I'd had to guess, I would have bet that you preferred beer."

Gage let his head drop back and groaned, "More aspersions on my character. Do I have to get a marine haircut and wear my clinic jacket 24/7 to get any respect?"

"No, no, you're absolutely right. In fact, you remind me of another client who came into my office several times dressed in worn jeans and dusty Western boots and an equally weathered hat. He cross-examined me relentlessly during his first two appointments. The third time he came, he gave me full control of his five-million-dollar portfolio."

Gage grunted. "If I had that kind of money, you can bet I'd be giving you the third degree, too."

"My point," Brooke said, hoping a few sips of wine on a half-empty stomach wasn't turning her into a complete ditz, "is that that I'm usually more sensitive and don't make such perception errors."

Gage stretched his legs before him, crossed them at the ankles and beamed at her. "Take your time. I'm happy to be your refresher course." When Brooke failed to play along, he relented. "Actually, it does take a while to really get to know a person. Rush things and you're apt to regret it."

"This from the guy who announced he was going to ask me out the second time I said more than ten words to you."

"'Announced' being key. I was planting the seed of an idea." When Brooke only sipped more wine, he amended, "So I let my eagerness at getting to spend some time with you get the better of me. Are you going to hold it against me?"

"I can't when you're being so good-natured about my teasing you."

"Is that what's going on? It sure feels like flirting to me."

*"Teasing."* Brooke knew she sounded about as prim as an old-time schoolmarm. But she could feel herself softening toward him with every minute they spent together, and she had to be careful that she didn't let things go further.

Hoping to change the subject, she drew in a deep breath, only to inhale the subtle fragrances emanating from the yard where the sinking sun was triggering long shadows and her aunt's pocket of four-o'clocks and moonflowers—both nocturnal bloomers—were beginning to open. "I loved summers here while growing up. I would sit for hours on this porch reading *Anne of Green Gables, Little Women, The Three Musketeers*.... When my mother got sick, she made me a list of what to be sure and read, knowing she wouldn't be around to guide me."

"Did you get through it?"

"No," Brooke admitted. "The following summer, my father decided it was time for me to read 'serious books'—biographies about successful businesspeople, world history, that sort of thing. He wanted me to recognize trends and warning signs of manufactured or sociopolitical conflict."

"Wow," Gage drawled, "you weren't just smart, you must have been a little Einstein."

Feeling undeserving of such praise, Brooke replied, "It was more about wanting to please my father. He's the brilliant one."

"Where does he live? You said he's out of the country? I can't help noticing that he hasn't come up to see your aunt yet."

It struck Brooke that he misunderstood which of her parents Aunt Marsha was biologically related to. "She's my mother's older sister. By fifteen years," she added, knowing that he would be confused, considering her own age. "Marsha never did warm to my father. And I have to admit that went both ways, so my father tends to keep his distance. But a lovely arrangement of flowers arrived from him the evening I arrived." Or from his secretary, Brooke thought with some cynicism. She also wouldn't tell Gage that as other gestures arrived from dear friends, Marsha had donated her father's arrangement to the nursing home in town. All she offered was, "My father runs his own investment business, which is based out of Houston, but he travels the world over."

Looking neither impressed nor intimidated, Gage said, "Obviously, you admire him. I hope he's equally proud of you?"

"Sometimes," Brooke demurred, ignoring personal hurt to reach for diplomacy. "He thinks I'm being foolish in how I've chosen to handle things here."

That sent Gage's eyebrows rising. "What would he have you do? Leave your aunt alone in the hospital and let her business flounder?"

"My aunt would never be totally alone," Brooke replied, her loyalties torn. "As you're aware, she knows virtually everyone in town, and then there's that broad network of friends in church. She'll never want for company. As for the shop… I could have asked Naomi to handle things—at least temporarily. She retired, but she's helping me with the more involved orders or a big event. Only, Naomi doesn't need or want to work full-time again. Despite being two years younger than Aunt Marsha, her own health isn't that great."

"The other younger woman there—Kiki, you called her this morning?"

"Yes. Kimberly Katherine is her real name, only her talents lie in the front of the store. She never trained to do arrangements, and my aunt isn't close to giving her full management authority—Kiki has only just graduated from the community college. In Aunt Marsha's viewpoint, she's still a child, so my coming seemed the least disruptive for everyone."

"Except for you," Gage said quietly.

"Please," Brooke entreated, "forget I complained about having to leave Dallas."

"Okay... If you'll tell me why there's no one back home miserable that you're here?"

It wasn't a matter she let herself dwell on too often. "Let's just say that I've been luckier in business than I have in love." Hearing that phrasing had her immediately covering her eyes with her free hand. "Considering that I'm unemployed, that's not saying much, is it?

"The problem is that the men who show interest in me either don't react well if I'm more successful than *they* are, or—if they don't mind, or find value in that—they still want me to be available at a moment's notice like some trophy wife. I'm *not* someone who can spend half a day in a spa and the rest shopping while waiting for a guy to text me that he's ready for my company."

Gage just sat there watching her, but Brooke could read his mind as though he'd spoken. "You're wondering how often that's happened," she said, with more than a little chagrin. "Enough times to be content to focus on my career at this stage of my life."

"What I think," Gage replied, slowly amending her opinion, "is that it sounds like someone hurt you pretty badly."

Having had a few months to think over the matter, Brooke didn't hesitate in her response. "No. He made me angry. His lack of respect disappointed me."

"Does *he* have a name?" At her arched look, Gage offered amiably, "Just in case he happens to show up acting like he owns the place and you need some backup."

"Parker. Parker Minot. But he won't do that. When I close doors, they stay shut."

Nodding slowly as he digested that, Gage said, "Strong woman. I'm relieved."

Glad to have that done with, Brooke thought it only fair to see how he acted when the tables were turned. "What about you?"

"Pretty much the same story."

"What, you couldn't handle half a day in a spa, either?"

Grinning, Gage rubbed the back of his neck. "I don't know—there are days when a good massage would be heaven. But no, I was referring to the unlucky part. On principle, I'm just a guy who likes to do the chasing, not be wearing a target on my back—or on my checkbook. If you ask my mother, though, she'll tell you that I'm more fickle than my sisters ever were." He struggled for and failed at a scowl of indignation. "I thought only women could be fickle."

"Ho-ho," Brooke replied. "Men are perfectly capable of being changeable and less than faithful." Curiosity got the best of her. "So even after resolving the office situation by hiring Roy, you're being chased, huh? Do the ladies bring their poodles and Pekinese into the clinic under false pretenses?"

"It's calmed down some, but it happens. I have more work than I can handle, and it's not fair for clients with animals in crisis to have to wait because of something clearly superficial. Then there's the perfume they douse themselves and their pooches with. I confess there are times we can't get them out of the building fast enough."

"The things some women will stoop to," Brooke lamented in mock protest of her sex.

As Gage leaned over to gently nudge her with his shoulder, Humphrey uttered a soft "woof." Mounting the stairs far more slowly than he'd descended, he waddled to Gage. With a baleful look, he put one paw on his almost bare foot.

"What's that all about?" Brooke asked. "Is he wanting me to get off his side of the glider?"

"Nah, this probably just reminded him of the good old days. My dog, Joey, used to come over with me to visit with him and Marsha, and even though Joey was a big chocolate Lab, he was really gentle with Humph. Joe made it to the ripe old age of sixteen, but he passed away right after Christmas."

"How sad…but what a wonderful friendship you must have shared—and Humphrey, too." Brooke leaned over to scratch the hound under his chin. Could it be that this was another reason for the poor dog to be having such strong separation anxiety from her aunt? "I guess, then, that he's asking when things are going to get better?"

"Pretty much. I know he's ready for me to bring him a new playmate, but I just haven't been ready yet. That's another reason it's good for him to come to the clinic. We have dogs being boarded all the time if the family is on vacation. There'll usually be someone for Humph to play with if he tires of human company."

Knowing she had yet to fully appreciate what people like her aunt and Gage felt toward their pets, Brooke shifted to face him. "Was Joey one of those dogs that went everywhere with you?"

"You bet. He knew when he could jump out of the truck and when to stay put. He liked everybody—well, almost everybody," he amended with a secret smile. "He instinctively gave wide berth to people with short fuses, even when they were behaving."

When he took a deeper swallow of wine, Brooke recognized that he was ready to change the subject. "You still haven't told me what made you settle in Sweet Springs?"

"An aversion to being cold."

"Where did you go to school?"

"Texas A&M. I finished my training here at the clinic."

"No kidding? I guess Aunt Marsha may have mentioned that, but I must've been just getting out of high school and was totally fixated on college at the time. How long have you lived next door?"

"Just over two years."

That explained why they hadn't met sooner. "I haven't been getting over here as much."

"And prior to that, there was college and grad school."

That again confirmed that her aunt had confided plenty in him. "Well, Dad expected a 4.0 average daughter."

Gage's expression turned pained. "I don't mean to offend, but your father sounds more like a field marshal or a paid personal trainer than a dad."

He was partly correct, and Brooke could only admit ruefully, "He's definitely one of a kind." Not liking this subject any better, she nodded to Gage's glass. "Are you ready for a refill? Now that the wine temperature has had a chance to warm to perfection, you should really like the bouquet."

"I shouldn't drink all of your present."

Knowing by the halfhearted protest that he wanted her to coax him, she reached for his glass. "Wine is always better when shared."

He outmaneuvered her and took her glass instead. "In that case, at least let me do the legwork. You enjoy the rest of this sunset."

As he disappeared into the house, Humphrey looked perplexedly from her to the door. "Oh, don't worry," she assured the pooch. "He'll be right back. You won't have to suffer my company for too long."

The soulful-eyed dog let his front paws slide, and he settled on his tummy, then rolled halfway over to press his back against her feet. After a second of surprise, Brooke leaned over again to stroke his sleek, short fur.

"Well, thank you, Mr. Charming. So if he likes me, you're going to give me the benefit of the doubt? How magnanimous of you."

Gage returned with the wine and a beefy treat from the pantry for Humphrey. The dog sprang up to a sitting position, grinning in pleasure. As soon as Gage gave him the snack, he lay down and started to chew enthusiastically.

"I thought treats after dinner were frowned upon?" she asked, accepting her glass.

"When I saw him scooting over to you, I thought he should get some reward." After resuming his seat, Gage touched his glass to hers. "Here's to things continuing to work out to everyone's satisfaction."

The openly inviting look in his eyes told Brooke that he was also talking about matters that had nothing to do with Humph behaving and bonding with her, or Aunt Marsha. But they soon fell into easy conversation again, and before Brooke knew it, their glasses were almost empty once more. They had covered several other topics—local politics, who was closing their business, who was opening one and finding a reliable lawn-care person. That last subject had Gage reacting right away.

"Don't worry about it—I've been doing Marsha's yard at the same time I've been doing mine. With my big zero-turn machine, it takes no time at all."

"You're sure? I already feel as though I'm taking advantage."

"Positive. If the guilt gets too bad, just invite me over for another glass of wine." When Gage noticed her slapping at mosquitoes for the third time, he reluctantly rose to his feet. "We'd better call it a night before the bats join the mosquitoes and try to carry you away."

"Was that a diplomatically phrased short joke?" She narrowed her eyes with playful speculation.

"Only stating the obvious—you're the one with the most tempting skin."

Cocooned in the amber glow of the porch light that had just come on automatically, Brooke felt more than relaxed; she felt part of a special moment that she honestly wished wasn't ending. What a surprise, considering her previous intent to keep him at arm's distance.

"Thank you…and for the visit. I can't remember when time passed so quickly or pleasantly," she admitted, rising herself.

"That's good to hear. That means if I suggest it again, you'll say yes."

Before she knew what was happening, Gage leaned

over and tenderly kissed her cheek. The caress sent such a unique warmth through her body that Brooke tried to quickly blame it on the wine.

"That would be nice, but you're the one who said you have more work than you can handle," she reminded him, before any additional romantic thoughts—and ghostly yearnings—tripped her up. "And I have to get back to my schedule of spending evenings with Aunt Marsha." Then doing the bookkeeping when she got home. That wasn't going to happen tonight. Right now all she felt capable of doing was to shower and slide into her comfy bed.

Giving her a patient look, Gage handed her his empty glass. "One thing I'm going to insist on is for me to take Humph on my way in tomorrow morning. There's no reason for you to make a special trip out to the clinic. Besides, he can't be wild about the view from your BMW's floorboard."

*"I know,"* she sighed, "but those claws—trimmed though they are—are not going to test my leather seats."

Nodding his understanding, Gage drawled, "Just say, 'Thank you for being sweet, Gage.'"

"I do appreciate your thoughtfulness," Brooke replied instead. "There are several things that I need to get to at the store, and the extra time will be welcome."

"My pleasure—now, isn't that worthy of a kiss on my cheek?"

Trying not to laugh at the rascal, Brooke said, "Dr. Sullivan, any trouble you have with unwanted female attention, *you* invite!"

However, when he gave her a crestfallen look, she

couldn't resist. Rising on tiptoe, she aimed for his cheek. However, Gage proved what a scoundrel he could be when in the last second, he turned his head, and her kiss landed directly on his warm, welcoming lips.

# Chapter 3

"Are you blushing?"

Jerked out of her daydreaming, Brooke glanced over to find that Kiki Webb had quietly entered through the back door of the shop. It was unlocked because their deliveryman, Charles Rollins, was outside checking under the hood of the florist's van, as he always did before heading off on his first run of the day—and today was Thursday, usually one of their busiest.

The heat in her cheeks told Brooke that Kiki was probably correct in her estimation, and that flustered her, too. "Is it warm in here to you, too?" she asked, hoping to fool Kiki. "Do me a favor and ask Charles to check the air conditioner before he leaves? Hopefully, only the filter needs cleaning."

"Ms. Brooke, the thing is blasting enough cold air to turn Mount Kilauea into an iceberg," Kiki replied, her expression a mix of amusement and concern. "You could shut off power to those storage coolers and the flowers wouldn't notice. So what's up that has you gazing off into another dimension? Oh! Excuse me— is it your guy in Dallas? Is he coming to visit for the weekend?"

Since she'd arrived at the store, Brooke had encouraged Kiki to work as she always did. But the young woman was shy and deferential, calling her "Ms. Brooke" at every turn. Hoping to find some happy middle ground, Brooke replied, "There is no guy and no visit happening, and considering what our schedule has been and is about to be, that's good news!"

The energetic blond cutie with the impish smile clasped her hands in excitement as she instantly made mental lemonade out of lemons. "That sounds promising. What's up?"

"I talked Aunt Marsha into letting you get after those window displays."

As expected, Kiki was enthused. She pumped the air with her fisted hands and filled the room with the music of jangling bracelets. Her colorful jewelry matched the rest of her artsy outfit—a gauzy pink blouse over an orange tank top, over a deep purple sports bra. Her jeans were enhanced with her own beadwork, and her purple flip-flops sparkled just as much as her metallic-orange toenail polish did.

"Oh, Ms. Brooke—"

"Please…just Brooke."

"*Thank* you! I was afraid to hope when you said you'd do your best to get me permission." With a new enthusiasm, the perky young woman shoved her bag— another of her own designs fabricated out of old blue jeans—under the workstation where Brooke kept hers and did pirouettes to the front of the store.

Catching a flirty fragrance, Brooke demanded, "Hold it! What's that scent you're wearing?"

Kiki shoved her hands under her shoulder-blade-length hair and flipped it to send more scent through the room. "You like? I've been working on this recipe for weeks."

Nodding as it played through her senses, Brooke replied, "Adore it. Put me down as a guaranteed customer. That's pure romance."

Kiki snapped her fingers. "I couldn't think of the right description, but it is, isn't it? I feel so girly wearing this."

"Defined notes without being heavy or too sweet."

"Unfortunately, Ralph Lauren already trademarked the name *Romance*."

"He would rethink his recipe if he got a whiff of yours."

Retracing her steps to the worktable, Kiki reached for Brooke. "This is the best news I've been given in months."

Although startled by the hug, Brooke found the impulse endearing. "You know what? When you get that and your perfume packaging finalized, we should put it in the store. I think it should be right on the front counter so you can do samples. I mean, if that was something you were interested in?"

"Are you kidding?" Kiki did another little dance of joy. "I can't wait to tell my folks."

The young woman had shared that, while her mother loved having her—the only girl born between two brothers—still living at home, her father was ready to see his offspring spread their wings and leave the nest. Brooke thought giving her creativity such a boost might help her reach that goal soon.

"I'm sure they'll be even prouder of you than they already are. Aunt Marsha realizes that you need to put more of your training and talent to work. I think her delay in doing that is partly due to her having lost almost all of her family—my mother, then their parents—so early in life. Then, when my Uncle Sam died, I think she developed a certain fear of change." She nodded to the front of the store. "After you get the window displays finished, we'll talk about some improvements we might tackle in the rest of the place."

Kiki looked like a kid on Christmas morning. She pressed her right hand to her heart. "I don't know what to say, Brooke. I won't let either of you down."

"I'm fully confident that you won't." Brooke glanced around the store. There was no denying that things were looking a bit dingy and uninspiring. No doubt Aunt Marsha's customers and friends loved her too much to have told her the truth. "It's about time the place gets an update—including a brighter paint job. You were right when you told me that Aunt Marsha has faithful clientele, but that she's not getting the younger crowd's attention."

"I'll be happy to go online and get some paint color samples for you to show her."

Setting the arrangement she'd just finished by the other four waiting for delivery, Brooke nodded, although she thought she might just want to keep this bit of information to herself to surprise her aunt with the new and improved store. "In the meantime, let me go up to the loft and take a look around while you watch things in here. Once I'm back, you can go up and start purging what's showing its age and bring down anything you think will work for the display. Then we can figure out what else we need."

"Sounds like a deal."

Outside, Charles Rollins was just slamming the hood on the delivery van. A gangly senior with silver hair and a neatly trimmed mustache, he wiped his hands on a paper towel and beamed at her. Handling deliveries was exactly the amount of work the retired math teacher wanted to keep himself active between afternoons gardening with Chloe, his wife of forty years.

"All set when you are, Brooke," he said.

"Everything is ready for you." She gestured back to the store. "You have four deliveries and the tickets are under each vase. But do me a favor and grab an extra cup of coffee and keep Kiki company while I'm up in the loft for a quick check. With both the front and back doors unlocked, I don't want her being in there alone."

"Understood. Be happy to," he said, only to look up the two levels of stairs. "You sure you don't need me to help up there? Are you planning to carry down something heavy or complicated?"

"More likely I'll be yelling, 'Look out below!' and tossing things into the Dumpster," she replied, indicating the big unit beneath the stairs. "We need to catch up with the rest of the community and prepare for the summer traffic by redoing the front windows, but from what I remember being up there, the pickings are slim."

Charles nodded, his look sympathetic. "Marsha has just been too busy to give the place the attention it deserves. After I make these deliveries, why don't I come back to help?"

Brooke had always liked Charles and appreciated his gentlemanly manner. He was a low-key throwback to another age. "If Chloe can spare you, I will definitely take you up on that offer, Charles. Thank you. That will allow Kiki to get to work in the windows all the sooner."

As she went up to do a quick inventory, Brooke's thoughts inevitably drifted back to last night and the kiss. In truth, that was what she'd been doing when Kiki had arrived. She was amazed that she'd gotten the good rest that she had, considering how her mind had been churning.

For such a brief incident, Gage had really left her thrown off balance. She'd had two serious relationships in her thirty years—the last being when she'd thought things might progress to marriage—until Parker had received a great job promotion/transfer that would relocate him to California. Before they'd had a chance to talk, he'd accepted, convinced that Brooke would give notice and come with him. Stunned, she had only voiced one question.

*Why?*

*Because you love me.*

She'd thought she did; however, she'd never said the words because he didn't. He'd said he'd *loved* a gift, *loved* some impressive function they'd attended that her father had invited her to, *loved* the parties she'd arranged for their friends…until it struck her that there were degrees of love, or maybe she'd confused contentment and caring for that deeper feeling?

Upon realizing that she didn't feel enough to walk away from everything she'd accomplished career-wise, she'd said goodbye to Parker. How ironic that only weeks later, her so-called career was snatched from her.

Now there was Gage, *the unexpected one,* as she was coming to think of him. She had no time for frivolousness, let alone romance, and yet he was making her feel all fuzzy and fluttery at just the thought of him, the way she hadn't felt since Bobby Stafford had kissed her outside of their high school gym back in the ninth grade. The problem was that she was thirty, not fourteen, something she'd felt compelled to warn Gage of last night.

"Cat got your tongue? You should see your face."

"You shouldn't have done that."

"Because there's no sense in starting something that has no future," he'd recited. "You've more or less already said that."

"I wish you'd take me seriously."

"I don't want to. I'd thought after two glasses of wine and an hour more of my irresistible presence, I'd have started to wear down that argument. How many thousands of relationships have started with seemingly no chance at a future? What about the soldiers heading for war who met a girl at a dance or airport? What about the soldiers who met girls overseas and instantly felt something special? Were war brides a bad idea because of inevitable challenges?"

He'd enjoyed picking apart her logic, while she'd countered by suggesting that he was way too romantic to have managed to stay single for this long, and she suspected he just liked the chase—as he'd admitted—and saw her as safe entertainment.

"Try me," he'd challenged, a gleam in his sexy blue-gray eyes.

She had demurred, of course, and sent him home. However, once in her room, Brooke had stopped before a full-length mirror and touched her lips. Letting her eyes drift shut, she'd relived the moment of his brief but sensual assault. What would it feel like to lay breast to thigh with him and feel those strong arms drawing her closer yet? To be kissed deeply as he entered her?

"Be honest," she said to her reflection, "you want to find out."

"Pardon?" Gage asked, looking up.

He had hoped to lock the front doors at the stroke of five and get the rest of his obligations here done so he could get Humphrey home. It probably wasn't likely that Brooke was of the same mind, but a man could hope. Instead, Liz Hooper had swept into the clinic with her obnoxious Chihuahua, Banderas, named after Liz's favorite Latino-heartthrob film star. This afternoon, "Bandy" had been stung in the face a few times when he'd stuck his curious nose down into an underground bee nest.

"I said, 'Come over and find out.'"

Gage blinked at Liz, although the image of Brooke after he'd kissed her good-night lingered before him.

"Earth to Gage—you wondered what kind of bee it was." As Liz explained herself, her wrist full of bracelets jingled when she gestured in the direction of town. "I certainly can't bring one to you without getting stung myself."

"It was just a— Never mind," Gage replied, mentally berating himself for the slip in concentration. Liz was a handful under normal circumstances. He didn't need to let his guard down and give her any ideas.

"There's some swelling," he said, gently feeling around the wounded dog's neck, "but there doesn't seem to be any signs of anaphylactic shock. I'll go ahead and give him some Benadryl to reduce his discomfort. Let's go with half of a child's dosage, considering his size." He did so, using an eye dropper to get the liquid into the Chihuahua's mouth. As the small animal licked and swallowed, he handed Liz the box. "Follow the schedule on the box. Unless something gets worse, you should be able to stop tomorrow."

Liz looked disappointed. "You're sure you don't need to keep him under observation for a few hours? I would rather wait than put him through the stress of another trip here, not to mention having to call you back."

Gage didn't believe the shapely brunette. She wasn't the most subtle woman on the planet and had made it clear since their first meeting that he would be welcome in her bed anytime. That was why he'd left both doors in the examination room open, so Roy could hear what was happening at all times. The last thing he needed—especially after last night with Brooke—was for Liz to start unfounded rumors about them being an item.

"I don't think that will be necessary," he told her. "Besides, you look like you're on your way somewhere."

Liz immediately ran her hand over her white figure-hugging dress. "Why, thank you for noticing, Gage. Aren't you the gentleman? But no, I'm just not one of those women who can allow herself to be seen in public looking anything less than her best."

Even if her dog was gasping for breath? Gage wondered.

"It would just seem disrespectful to Darryl's memory."

The late Darryl Hooper had been mayor of Sweet Springs for two terms before dying prematurely of a heart attack last year. The tongue-in-cheek gossip around town was that second wife, Liz, had, one way or another, worn out the poor guy.

"Well, I'm sure he believes you're doing him proud," Gage drawled, handing the dog back to her. "Just make sure to keep Bandy calm and out of the sun. If he continues to rub at his face, you might cool him off with a cold compress. That'll also help the swelling recede faster." Hopefully, that would also keep her off the phone, calling him to give him updates he wasn't asking for.

"All right, I'll do my best." Liz gave him a beseeching look that included a fluttering of her expensive false eyelashes. "Do I need to bring him in for a follow-up?"

The sound of Roy clearing his throat saved Gage from having to reply to that. Glancing over his shoulder, he saw Roy poke his head in the doorway.

"Sorry, Doc, but we have a dog that got into antifreeze."

Gage winced. "Damn. Will people ever learn?" Dogs found the taste of antifreeze appealing, and humans were warned relentlessly to keep such things in closed containers out of reach of animals, but he had to deal with at least a few cases a year of an animal that had imbibed some. In all but two cases, the liver damage was such that the animal had died.

He gave Liz an apologetic look. "Sorry. Time means

everything in this case. Ah—no follow-up is needed. Roy, please get Mrs. Hooper checked out."

Gage dashed out of the room, leaving Liz in Roy's care. Under normal circumstances, he wouldn't have charged for this service, minimal as it was. But he'd been more than generous to Liz in the past and suspected she was seeing that as encouragement. At this stage, she came here as often as high school kids showed up at the local Dairy Queen's drive-through window.

In the main examination/operating room, Gage was surprised to see there was no one waiting for him, which wasn't exactly a surprise, since he was belatedly realizing that he hadn't heard anyone enter the building. He then went to the other three examination rooms, but they, too, were empty. What the heck was going on? he wondered.

"Thank you, Mrs. Hooper! Hope Banderas feels better soon."

Roy never spoke in such a booming voice, unless he shouting a warning to Gage that he was about to get stepped on by a half ton of beef. That seemed a strong hint to Gage to wait for the sound of the front door buzzer indicating that Liz had left. Only then did he venture out front.

Coming to stand beside Roy, they watched Liz spin her metallic cashmere-colored Jaguar into a sharp U-turn and speed out of the lot. If Bandy wasn't safely in his carrier kennel, he was definitely worrying about more than bee stings.

"What did you say to her?" Gage asked.

"I asked her to swipe her credit card. She's been

here four times in seven weeks, Doc, and hasn't paid for any of the visits."

"I felt guilty charging her when I didn't do anything. Was it really four times? I thought it was two, maybe three. Well, thank you, Roy."

"You're *welcome*."

It didn't slip by Gage that Roy was issuing a message, something akin to "Let's end this before it becomes town news." That was fair. It was one of the many reasons he relied on him so much.

"I take it there's no dog with a ruined liver?"

"Nope. Sorry for the momentary distress, but I knew anything less might not be enough to get her out of here."

From the corner, Pete Ogilvie asked, "Do y'all think that tight dress is cutting off her circulation?"

"First, you need blood in your veins for that to happen," Jerry Platt told the oldest member of their group. The so-called "kid" of their group had been seen in the company of Liz several times, the latest only a few weeks ago. This was the first time since then that he'd made any comment about her.

The other two men laughed, and Humphrey raised his head where he'd been laying contented between the old-timers. He wagged his tail as though amused, too.

"Let's get the front door locked, and then we can neuter the two Delaney Labs."

"The— Right. Let's get it done." Gage wasn't about to tell Roy that he'd completely forgotten about the pups. That was a testament to how badly he wanted to get home and see Brooke again.

He'd tricked her into kissing him…and she hadn't gotten angry. After a moment's surprise and what had seemed a halfhearted protest, she'd looked at him differently—and in a good way. Before that changed, he wanted to kiss her again. Sadly, that wasn't going to happen as soon as he would like.

For the first time since he could remember, he wasn't grateful for being up to his neck in clients. Until now, he'd liked staying so busy that he had no time to think about what was missing in his life. But Brooke's arrival was changing that fast.

"Remind me to do more than just talk about adding to our staff," he told Roy.

The dark-haired man did a double take. "Be happy to, boss. You feeling okay?"

"Never better."

When Brooke pulled into the driveway that night, she shut off the BMW's engine but then just sat there in the dark, slumped against the seat, her eyes closed. What had begun as a successful and rewarding day had unraveled by the time she'd reached the hospital in the evening. Eager to share the day's progress with her aunt, she'd found the room vacated. To her astonishment, Marsha had been transferred back to ICU!

Almost too weary to move, she forced herself. Humphrey would have heard or seen her pull in and would start barking and wailing at any moment. Gage's pickup was in his driveway, and she didn't want to disturb him. To be honest, she also wasn't prepared to face him yet.

Exiting the car and locking up, she let herself inside the back gate and immediately saw more lights shining inside than she had left on. What on earth was going on?

As she started up the porch steps, the back door opened, and she came face-to-face with the man who had possessed more of her thoughts in the past twenty-four hours than was wise. Ignoring the jolt in her chest, she focused on something rational—the reason for him to be here. Kiss or no kiss, he wouldn't take such liberties to just come over without an invitation. That must mean only one thing.

"Don't tell me," she groaned. "He acted up again?" She looked beyond him to where Humph was sitting, watching them and wagging his tail. "What is wrong with you? I intentionally left it darker in the house so you'd nap."

Stepping back to let her enter, Gage explained, "I only got home a few minutes ago myself, and he must have seen my lights. That's when he started a ruckus worse than last night. Maybe it's only because you're later, too. I hope you don't mind me coming over, but he was getting tangled in the front drapes, then scratching at the door."

"No, of course not, but I hate that you're inconvenienced."

"I'm not. Don't give it a thought."

But his news sent Brooke's heart sinking as she set her purse on the counter. What else did they have to do to keep this animal behaving? Couldn't she have at least an hour of pure silence to adjust to what was happening? What if the curtains were torn or the paint peeled? She had no time to deal with repairs. Feeling the avalanche of bad news threaten to overwhelm her, she covered her face with her hands.

"Hey." Gage came up behind her and gently grasped her upper arms. "It's really okay. He stopped as soon as he heard me, so there's no real damage done. I checked. He helped." His brief chuckle at his own humor ended quickly when he realized she wasn't joining in. "Brooke?"

"I'm sorry, I can't *do* this!"

"Aw, come on." Gently turning her, Gage tilted his head to better see her face. "He's just a dog, hon. Not even a very big one. A bit spoiled, agreed, and somewhat set in his ways—"

"A bit?" she cried. "It's too much—and unfair. And added to everything else—"

The desperation, followed by a telltale hitch in her voice, had Gage frowning. "What's happened that has you this shaken? Talk to me."

She didn't want to. She wasn't ready to talk to anyone, particularly a man she didn't want thinking the worst of her; but it was apparent that he wasn't going anywhere, so she dropped her hands and said simply, "Aunt Marsha collapsed this afternoon."

Gage's expression mirrored what she thought hers had been when she had been told the news—shock and then dread. However, faster to recover, he drew her against his solid, broad chest. "Ah, jeez. I'm almost afraid to ask.... How is she?"

"Weak, but stable. They're keeping her in ICU for the night."

Kissing her on her forehead, Gage said, "You look ready to collapse yourself. Come, sit." He urged her to a chair in the breakfast nook, then tugged out the one beside it and sat down before her, his long legs boxing her in. Resting his elbows on his knees, he enfolded her hands in his. "Start from the beginning," he coaxed. "Did she reinjure her hip?"

"No, thank goodness. She was standing, but her therapist was with her at the time, and he managed to catch her. Only... Gage, it's her heart."

He bowed his head to her hands, resting his forehead against them before kissing them. "Sweetheart." Then, raising his head, he looked deeply into her eyes. "They're sure?"

"They'd done some tests before I got there—"

His expression reflected confusion. "When on earth did they call you?"

"They didn't."

*"What?"*

Brooke appreciated his guttural sound of indignation in her defense. Initially, she'd been offended, too; however, she'd soon learned enough to be more understanding. As concisely as possible, she told him about arriving just after dropping Humphrey at home and finding her aunt's room vacated. Naturally, she'd thought the worst.

"Dear God. What a scare you had."

"I think the shift change, along with their urgency to make sure she wasn't having a heart attack or stroke, created the inevitable glitch in contacting me." Brooke closed her eyes, trying to remember everything said and done. She was still dazed and felt terrible for her newly distressed aunt, who was now more exhausted than ever, after all she'd been put through to get data for the doctors to peruse. "They'll repeat a few tests tomorrow, but they're increasingly certain that it's a heart-valve problem."

"Damn," Gage murmured, stroking the soft skin on the backs of her hands with his thumbs. "How's she taking the news?"

"Oh, she's trying to put up a good front…until I finally kissed her good night so she could try to get some sleep. She dropped her guard then, and I could see her fear and need for reassurance, yet at the same time her concern for me and for what this would do to my schedule."

"Of course she would," Gage replied. "I understand a valve replacement is a more dangerous and invasive procedure than a pacemaker, and that's likely to lengthen her recuperation time."

"Exactly," Brooke said, only to add with determination, "but I can't let her go back into surgery feeling guilty for needing more of my time."

"Nevertheless, it's a tough blow for you." Gage gave her hands a gentle squeeze. "What can I do to help?"

The man was entirely too appealing for his own good. Wanting nothing more than to dump everything in his lap and curl there herself, she straightened her spine and said firmly, "You're already doing plenty." Then she added wryly, "Well, you could will me some of your patience with that one."

As she nodded toward Humphrey, Gage scoffed at her self-deprecation. "You're doing great with him. What you need is something to relax you so you can sleep. Mind if we open that other bottle of wine?"

Brooke gave him a droll smile. "I was planning to, so by all means."

While he got busy, she used the time to slip out of her heels and the butter-yellow jacket she'd worn over an ivory silk blouse and matching slacks. Hanging the expensive jacket over the back of the chair, she thought she really had to find time to check out the boutique across from her aunt's shop for some more casual clothes. Everything in her wardrobe made her look as though she was taking a Wall Street meeting. Granted, the jacket had been helpful in the cold hospital, but otherwise, it had felt pretentious and stuffy.

By the time she'd taken the clasp out of her hair and shaken it free, she was feeling the stranglehold of panic ease its grip on her throat, and she was breathing normally. "Thank you, you're a lifesaver," she told Gage as he brought the two glasses of wine to the table.

"Hey, if there's any way my handing you your own wine makes you feel indebted to me, who am I to argue?" he teased, his gaze warm, although still concerned.

"It's about more than that, and you know it." Brooke took a grateful sip. "I will make this up to you, if only to prove I'm more competent and less selfish than I've been sounding this week."

Resuming his seat, Gage looked completely perplexed. "What are you talking about? You've stepped up to the plate better than anyone could ask or would expect. You're simply drained and dealing with this new blow just as Marsha is, and in your case, you have the added responsibility to keep a stiff upper lip for her sake."

"You're generous to look at it that way." Encouraged by his logical thinking, she decided to share something she'd been pondering since learning her aunt's latest health challenge. "There's something I've decided to do that should help a little stress-wise. I have to get back to Dallas and let a real estate friend sell my place."

Gage didn't respond as fast as she had expected. He, too, looked caught between opposing emotions.

"Leaving my personal feelings out of this," he finally replied, "I have to ask—aren't you being a bit premature? You're still reeling, and, as a financial expert, you know it's never wise to make such a big and lasting decision so soon."

"I know," she replied, "but I also know that sometimes you don't have the luxury of putting things off, and this is one of those times. They'll undoubtedly do surgery at the most opportune moment when she's stabilized and they're certain about what they need to do. Thereafter, Aunt Marsha will need me more than ever. Better to get things rolling in the small window of opportunity that's available."

"There's always the possibility that the doctors will alter their prognosis after tomorrow's added testing."

Brooke gave him a mournful look as she shook her head. "They're not wrong. I've noticed her fatigue even before today, and made myself believe that she was naturally slowing down a bit." Her tone grew wry. "What are you doing? You and Aunt Marsha have both been conniving to get me back here, and now you're trying to talk me out of it?"

"It's the circumstances. It will break Marsha's heart to learn that you're giving up your pride and joy—don't tell me that your house is merely an investment. She talked about how much work you've put into it, and understood your need for independence." As she raised her eyebrows at that latest admission, he shrugged. "Yeah, she used me as a sounding board at times and asked me for advice now and again—one of those times being when you stopped renting and chose to buy your own home.

"I understand how family can weigh in on major decisions," he continued. "When I came down here for school and then stayed, my family wasn't overjoyed, either, regardless of my feelings about the weather. My father thought I should set up practice up in Montana, so I could handle his stock in between dealing with my other clients. There were some stiff-necked attitudes for a while."

"I'm sorry about that," Brooke replied. "But this is different. You have a larger family. My aunt has no one but me—and as I think I told you, I'm the daughter she never had. If I can walk away from her in this moment of dire need, what does that say of my feelings for her?"

"Nobody has the right to judge you, even her, and she wouldn't want you to give up your life for her, let alone your dreams, especially if she realized you were feeling trapped."

Brooke uttered a sound of sheer misery. "Please, forget I ever admitted my feet of clay. The real truth is that no matter whether I had a job or not, I would be here."

"That's the bottom line, isn't it?" Gage asked. "You had to work through some issues, but in the end your love and devotion for her came first."

With no small admiration, Brooke replied, "You should have been a psychiatrist. I just hope Aunt Marsha doesn't end up regretting me taking the liberties I have at the shop."

Gage swirled the remaining wine in his glass. "I passed the store on my way to the bank this evening and saw the window-display changes. I'd say you're doing great."

"That's all Kiki's doing," Brooke assured him. "She'll appreciate the positive feedback."

Taking another sip of his wine, Gage rose. "Well, if you're wanting better feedback, I need nourishment, and considering how long you've been at the hospital, you do, too. How are you about omelets? I know Marsha always has some eggs and cheese in the place."

Rising herself, Brooke protested. "I love them, but I wouldn't feed you anything I make…except to maybe open a can of chicken soup and toast some bread. I think I can almost pull off a facsimile of bruschetta."

"Which you could probably use to sustain yourself for two days," Gage drawled. "I need more. Allow me."

He set to work getting the essentials from the refrigerator, and within minutes the smell of frying bacon and onions was filling the kitchen. Brooke couldn't stand not helping somehow and washed her hands in order to set the table.

"After the long day you've put in yourself, I can't believe you have the energy for this," she told him as she worked. "Weren't you out on a call this evening?"

"Late surgeries," he said over his shoulder.

When he left things at that, Brooke decided to not question how that had gone; in all honesty, she didn't think she was ready to hear any more bad news. Instead, she noted as he grated the cheese and then whisked the eggs, "Aunt Marsha often made herself scrambled eggs, toast and jelly for dinner. You're doing all that so efficiently, I can see you two are probably like kindred spirits in the kitchen when you get together."

"Ah…no. I tend to make her sit down. I'm afraid of stepping on her small feet or poking her in the ribs with my elbows—and, by the way, I do see you're barefoot. If you don't want to see sweat turn this shirt into a floor mop, kindly remove those dainty things from my reach."

His good humor and protectiveness with her made his description about time spent with her aunt all the more heartwarming. In fact, she barely caught herself in time as she started to reach out to rub his back with appreciation and affection.

*What's this? Not even Parker incited the touchy-feely impulse in you, unless he initiated it first.*

"Do you think the bruschetta would be overkill or should I stick to making toast?" she asked, aware that she was sounding a bit breathless. She could easily stay out of his way by using the far side of the counter and the toaster oven, and she needed to do something to keep her imagination from getting out of control.

"Heck, no, get after it. Those tomatoes on the island look perfect. Besides, food tastes better if you had a hand in preparing it."

She was grateful for his casual manner, and took the remaining half of a loaf of French bread from the refrigerator. "I thought the saying was that food tasted better when cooked outside over an open fire?"

"If I thought you owned a pair of jeans, I might prove that to you at the first opportunity."

"I own jeans."

"The designer kind, of course."

He had her there. "There aren't many hoedowns in my neighborhood."

"Believe me, I fully appreciate the way you look. You're elegant and at the same time quietly grab-your-larynx sexy. Nothing in-your-face about it."

Something about his tone had Brooke wondering. "That sounds like you were describing someone in particular."

Gage made a guttural sound. "There's this client..."

"A lady."

"You're being overgenerous."

Already convinced that Gage strove to be a gentleman at any cost, Brooke was totally intrigued. "It's not just about too much perfume? She comes dressed for seduction? To the *clinic?* In front of your senior audience?"

"That about sums it up."

"Other men might call you a lucky man," she mused.

"None that know me. I told you—I like to do the chasing."

She remembered, in this case, though, it was fun to play devil's advocate. "On the other hand, for casual sex, do old-fashioned rules need to apply?"

With the spatula hovering over the sizzling pan, Gage intoned, "Liz isn't the kind of woman one should risk casual *anything* with. Particularly sex."

"Liz… I'm not sure I remember—"

"Hooper. Her husband—"

"Was once the mayor. Didn't he pass away?"

"Almost a year ago, yeah." With a soft snort, Gage added, "The guys at the clinic were enjoying a few laughs at Liz's expense as to why and how."

"Sweet Springs' own Greek chorus," Brooke mused. "No dull moments at your place. I may never have the courage to walk in there again."

"Then you'd be making a mistake," Gage said, suddenly and completely serious. "You're as respected and admired as you would be anywhere."

*He wants to kiss you.*

The realization hit Brooke the instant he turned so their gazes met and held. The fact that she wanted that—to experience the feeling of his lips on hers again, his taste, being held against that rock-solid body—left her almost weak-kneed, so much that she jumped when the toaster popped behind her.

Laughing in embarrassment, then sniffing at the telltale smell, she groaned. "Some help I am. I've burned the bread!"

Once they sat down to plates laden with steaming, aromatic food, Gage refilled their glasses. All the while he kept Brooke entertained with anecdotes from the clinic. In between, he slipped in a casual question or two—mostly harmless, nonsensical stuff—in order to relax her again. It eventually worked, but not totally. After that sexually charged moment, she'd withdrawn a bit into the comfort of her cool executive persona again.

*It's because she's still committed to eventually leaving.*

Not if he could help it. Gage felt terrible for Marsha's latest crisis, but he damned well wasn't going to let this opportunity for more time with Brooke go to waste.

"Better?" he asked after they'd spent a few minutes quietly and appreciatively feasting.

"Mmm…" Brooke closed her eyes as she finished chewing a bite of omelet. "It's sublime. Why do my omelets taste like I'm eating a page torn from a magazine, while this is so moist, yet the vegetables have a crunch?"

"You have to stay close. I think the general rule is to cook scrambled eggs slowly, but omelets go in a hotter pan, therefore it's done faster."

"I'll try to remember that. I guess the downside of growing up with a housekeeper is that I didn't spend much time in the kitchen learning." Brooke gave him a bemused look. "It seems my tab with you keeps rising."

"We're friends. There's no counting."

"I only meant—"

"I know." Gage decided he'd been too sensitive and said with a sly grin, "Wait until you taste my tortilla soup." The day would come, he thought with determination. "Whenever your aunt gets the sniffles, I make it for her."

"Taking the cures with Gage," Brooke quipped. "That sounds like it should be the title of a tiramisu-rich indie film to enjoy on a lazy Sunday afternoon."

His insides twisted with hunger and did it again when she glanced at him from under her long lashes. Those peeks were more shy than flirtatious; such a contrast to the character she strove for outside of this safe place. He found that beguiling, as tantalizing as the sleek body she framed in professional suits, silk though they were.

Feeling himself getting aroused, he shifted in his seat. "Ah…when were you planning to return to Dallas?"

"As soon as possible. I'll know more tomorrow after the doctors finish their tests, but I'm thinking that I should be able to get over there on Sunday and at least pack my clothes and talk to my friend Andi—Andrea Demarco, the agent I mentioned. We can do the detail work later, and fax forms back and forth to formally get the house listed."

"I'll come with you." Gage knew he would have to clear a few things off his own calendar and arrange for someone to cover for him, but he would IOU himself to his neck to manage that. "We'll use my truck.

Don't argue," he said, as he saw protest in her eyes. "You can't carry anything in that bracelet charm of a car you drive."

That had Brooke choking and needing a sip of wine to recover. "That's funny," she finally managed. "And you're right—practical it isn't. But…you're serious? There's no denying what a help you would be. On the other hand, you have such responsibilities here. You're on call 24/7."

"In emergencies, we arrange for another vet willing to cover for us. I can even free Monday if need be. If you could arrange something similar for the store, I think we could get you fairly squared away."

"Undoubtedly." Brooke stared at him as though he was someone a fairy godmother had conjured for her. "Gage, seriously? I'm no pack rat, so it shouldn't take that long. Maybe half of Monday at the worst. Only… you have such little time for yourself as it is."

Until now, he'd had as much as he needed. Now he was aiming for what he wanted. Ignoring her latest protest, he playfully held up his hands to frame her like a photographer, and said, "The truck's backseat will probably hold the entire contents of your clothes closet—even if you're more of a fashionista than you look."

"Ho-ho, mister," she said, pointing her fork at him. "May I remind you that I'm into quality, not quantity."

He knew that, without needing to see that closet. She wore the same diamond-and-gold knot earrings every day, and the same gold chain. She wore no rings or bracelets, only occasionally a gold watch.

"Any furniture that you can't live without until the sale?" he asked. "We'll have an empty truck bed. We'll just need to bring blankets and rope to keep things from getting scratched."

After only a slight hesitation, she shook her head. Her expression almost sad, she said, "I don't think so. Just personal belongings. The house will show better with furniture anyway. Besides, you've undoubtedly noticed what a collector Aunt Marsha is. It doesn't need one more thing added to it."

The admission had her quickly dropping her gaze to her plate. It was obvious that she regretted even that much criticism.

"Are you okay?" Gage asked gruffly.

"Not really. It's just that…this is actually going to happen. All of it, and it feels so déjà vu."

Understanding that she was being reminded of the upheaval she'd lived through when losing her mother, Gage muttered, "Hell, Brooke, please don't cry."

"Easy for you to say," she said, dabbing under her eyes with her napkin.

"Well, think about this—if you do, I'll feel obliged to carry you upstairs, and if that happens, angel, all deals are off."

# Chapter 4

"Whatever you want—it's yours."

It was Sunday, and Brooke had unlocked the door to her Turtle Creek home, welcoming in Gage. After his outburst on Thursday night, he'd half believed that she would cancel this trip—or make different arrangements. Then on Friday when her aunt's condition had worsened and the doctors were thinking that the valve procedure was impossible, he'd wondered if the trip would happen at all. However, later Saturday, Marsha had rallied, and here they were.

Brooke's house bordered University Park, near SMU, another of the most desired neighborhoods around the heart of Dallas. He'd passed through the area a few times while familiarizing himself with the region during holiday breaks, and it was still a prime real estate area. No surprise, then, that Brooke had claimed a piece of it for herself. In her world, the world her father had groomed her to live in, prestige meant a great deal.

"Now who's being provocative?" He wasn't referring to her welcome, rather her laughing gasp, then gentle demurring, after he'd seductively warned her on Thursday night.

"I was referring to whatever is in the kitchen or wine cooler," she explained. "Please help yourself." But the schoolmarm-like enunciating didn't work because she was failing at keeping a straight face. "Just get your mind out of the gutter, *Doctor*."

"That was nowhere close to where my mind was," he murmured.

As he followed Brooke into her cozy cottage, he thought it was welcomingly more romantic than what he'd expected from a fast-tracking young executive. The 1950s dark brick-and-mortar structure with pronounced V-roofing and diamond-shaped lead windows reminded Gage of the dollhouse his sisters had played with as kids, and he said as much to Brooke.

"I played with one, too," Brooke replied. "People sometimes call them gingerbread houses. Our housekeeper had been a German widow and her name for the style was *Hexenhaus*. Witch house," she translated, "like in the Hansel and Gretel story."

"No wonder I feel like a giant in here."

"Don't worry, it's not so small that you'll bang your head anywhere."

She was right, and despite what the outside suggested, the interior had been totally updated, including fixtures and appliances current to what today's homeowners desired. The decorating scheme was sophisticated, the colors soothing—a mixture of taupe, ice-blue and ivory, a theme carried throughout the house, except for the ivory and gold in the kitchen, designed to please a weekend chef. Gage was tempted to tease Brooke by asking if the owner's manual was still taped to the top rack in the oven, but one look at her biting her lower lip, and he decided not to push his luck. Instead, he noted that the furnishings were inviting but true to her claim that she didn't equate quantity with quality on any level.

"I can see you in here," he said, slowly nodding as he continued to look around.

"That's sweet, but after a week away, it already feels like someone else's home." Brooke set her leather shoulder bag on a brass and ivory-suede bar stool and waved her arms to encompass the room. "Well, I meant it—make yourself at home. That door across from the laundry room is a bathroom. There's another midway down the hall leading to the bedrooms, and another in the master suite. Andi should be here at any minute, so I'm going to check in with Aunt Marsha and let her know we've arrived."

"I'll start getting the boxes from the truck."

Gage understood Brooke was still basically winging things emotionally. No matter how Marsha's doctor tried to soft-pedal around issues, Gage knew the dear woman would need to take things more slowly from here on, and it was likely that her days of running Newman's Florist and Gifts were also at an end. Brooke hadn't said more about that and was remaining stoic, and Gage couldn't have been prouder of her. It was totally human to dread, or at least worry about, what was going on, and it was a true example of character that she did it with such grace.

On his second trip back to the truck to retrieve more boxes, a sleek white Mercedes SL550 pulled into the driveway, stopping him in his tracks. Although it was a cloudy day, the raven-haired driver lowered her Jackie Kennedy-style sunglasses to eye Gage over their black rims. So this was Andi, he thought. Brooke's college friend and the BFF who'd helped her purchase this house some three years ago. Also true to advertisement, Andrea Demarco emerged from the sporty coupe like a model filming a pricey commercial. Gage watched long, gleaming legs, then the rest of an attention-getting body, finely encased in a silk khaki dress, emerge. The four-inch heels were leopard print, as was her briefcase-style purse. The woman looked ready for a shopping safari…or to bid highest at a charity auction—particularly if the next item up was male. Another Liz Hooper? he wondered. He couldn't see someone like Brooke being anything more than polite with someone like that.

"You must be Andi," he said, stepping forward to extend his hand. He expected quick rejection, since he was wearing a T-shirt and jeans—in his case the shirt was Texas A&M maroon and white. But this was as good a time as any to find out if this modern-day Queen of Sheba would be a help or hindrance where Brooke was concerned.

"I must if you're Gage," she purred. "Goodness, Brooke told me that I had a treat in store, but she didn't tell me that her doctor friend was such a specimen."

"Just a veterinarian," he replied, accepting her slender limb that was adorned by an array of gold bangles and diamond rings.

"Woof."

He couldn't help but chuckle at her easy flirting, especially since her sultry gray eyes held a subtle acknowledgment that she knew where to draw the line if necessary. At least Andi's approach was far more relaxed than Liz Hooper's edgy, almost desperate style.

"Brooke will be relieved that you're here," he told the undeniably attractive real estate agent. "She could use your moral support. It's been a hard week for her."

"I've gathered as much. Having expected her to stay in this place for several more years, I know it would be no small thing to make her put it on the market." Andi eyed the house and the lush and whimsical landscaping. "On the other hand, I've been drawn to this property since I first showed it to her. Believe me, it looked nothing like it does now. I hate that her aunt's not well and that Brooke will have to stay put in Sweet Springs for some time, but I'm thrilled with the chance to get her the price she deserves."

"She'll appreciate that. Someday."

Andi turned to study him anew. "Not only handsome, but sensitive."

"I'm nice to kids and senior citizens, too."

Laughing, Andi said, "Lead me to our fair friend before I forget that I'm supposed to be here on business."

With a wry smile, Gage grabbed up the last bundle of boxes and opened the door for Andi. As soon as Brooke spotted them, she rushed to the taller woman and hugged her.

"It's *so* good to see you. Thank you for coming. I

know the property is small potatoes compared to what you're handling these days."

"Nonsense. Besides, a storage shed is worth a nice bundle in this neighborhood, and your precious abode is anything but." Then Andi leaned back to study her friend. "What a spell you've had. I've been worried for you—and Marsha, of course. How is she?"

"Scared. A hip is bad enough. A heart…" Brooke shook her head.

"I can't imagine. But having you there has to be a huge reassurance." Andi hugged her again. "So tell me—what stays and what goes?"

"I've drawn you up a list."

As she went to pluck it up from the kitchen counter, Andi gave Gage a look of pride. "I'm efficient. That one makes me look like a rank amateur. If all of my clients were this thoughtful and thorough, I could handle twice the clientele that I do, and there would be fewer misunderstandings." But when she looked at the list that Brooke handed over, her carefully tweezed eyebrows arched higher. "Good grief. Darling, mad friend, you have obviously been working too hard and lost all sense of reason. Practically everything is on this list."

Although Brooke's gaze held regret as she inspected the room, she still ended up shrugging. "I hate the idea of these beautiful pieces being locked away out of sight for who knows how long. At least this way they would be used and enjoyed…if you happen to find the buyer who will fall in love with them as I did."

Andi remained confused. "Why would you need to put anything in storage? You said your aunt's house is as large as some museums."

"Also as full as one," Brooke replied, drily. "And

then there are all of those stairs. After two trips up to the attic, which is my option, although probably crammed, too, the movers would likely abandon the rest of my things on the veranda and back porch and run for their lives."

Leaning against the counter, Gage raised his right hand. "Permission to interject? You know I'm going to help," he told Brooke. The look he gave her underscored that the matter wasn't up for discussion.

"You're doing plenty helping me this weekend," she insisted. "Not to mention everything you've done up until now. What if you injure your back? I have enough on my conscience as it is."

"It is a *very* nice back," Andi murmured from behind them. "And—oh, my—strong."

Casting Andi a wry look, Gage told Brooke, "This is clearly a good time to tell you that I have plenty of empty rooms at my place—and half are on the first floor. Anything not sensitive to dust or humidity—garden tools, lawn furniture—could go in the barn. The movers could back a truck halfway inside and let the hydraulic lift do the majority of the work."

Stepping forward to lean against the counter, Andi gave Brooke and Gage a narrow-eyed look, then drawled to her friend, "Don't let me leave without getting the number of your fairy godmother. If there's another man half as good as this one appears to be, I'll take that introduction as payment of your IOU."

All but blushing, Brooke uttered, "You're embarrassing him—and me."

"And me," Andi replied cryptically. Then with an ironic laugh, she set down her bag and took out her Android and notebook. "No damage. I'll get started on taking measurements and pictures. Call me when you two are ready for wine. I want to know if there's anything else worth seeing in East Texas."

Brooke waited until the door shut behind Andi. Only then did she say quietly to Gage, "She's a wonderful person, but she recently broke up with her live-in boyfriend. It's made her a bit more sardonic than usual. They'd been together for years, and she'd believed that they were together for life, wedding or no wedding. On her birthday, instead of a gift, he told her that he wasn't having any fun anymore and was ready to move out and move on."

"Sorry to hear that," Gage replied, as he tried to play catch-up. Something was clearly going on. "She's an attractive woman."

"She's stunning! She's like an exotic bird."

Brooke's almost hurt expression had him wanting to take her in his arms. For a sophisticated businesswoman herself, she was something of an innocent when it came to personal relationships. It seemed that when she finally embraced someone, she did so with a child's wholeheartedness and acceptance. Gage had yet to be convinced that Andi deserved such trust. After all, she was sure giving him strong hints that she would like to do more than get to know him better. On the other hand, he was beginning to think part of that was due to Brooke encouraging that.

"Cosmetics help," he said, watching her closely, "but the jury is still out on what she's like on the inside."

"Men like women with legs that go up to their armpits."

"Especially in Vegas," Gage drawled. "But I can't see how a physical asset would help in a struggling relationship. I do like her frankness, and she seems to have a good sense of humor."

"Since when do men care about a woman's sense of humor?"

"Always." Gage smiled grimly. "Particularly when they're in trouble—like now."

Brooke relaxed somewhat. "I want you to like my friend."

"I think I will. Only don't hold it against me if I can't help liking you more. Much more."

The moment was out of a movie scene set up where the woman was meant to go all soft and willing, and the guy, reassured, would move in for a sigh-winning, applause-worthy kiss. Instead, Brooke turned away and started fluffing up the pillows on the couch and then an armchair.

"You just know me longer, that's all," she told him. "Give her a chance."

Gage couldn't believe what he was hearing. After all of the tender and tempting moments they'd shared in the past week, he felt worse than let down. He felt… what? Betrayed? Used?

"I think a better use of my time would be to get these boxes put together." With that, Gage picked up the armful and went into the living room before he said something he would regret.

Some three hours later, the three of them sat in the breakfast nook finishing their lunch. Brooke had ordered Asian takeout from her favorite restaurant only blocks away. Having had enough of her sesame chicken, she sipped at her Chardonnay and watched Andi and Gage engaged in an animated conversation.

She was certain that it was her imagination, but both of them seemed determined to prove something—to *her*—and it was making Brooke increasingly uncomfortable.

"Why shouldn't I have a dog?" Andi wasn't just challenging Gage, she clicked her chopsticks together as though tempted to pluck something off him.

"Because he—or she—can't provide you with what you're really looking for." On the surface, he appeared all calm reason, only to stab his fork into a piece of broccoli with a bit too much relish. "Besides, you work too much. Ask Brooke about Humphrey. A dog needs attention, companionship and exercise. Unless you're willing to invest that kind of time, you're not going to get the pet you're expecting."

Andi didn't respond well to that. "For pity's sake, it's not like I'm talking about adopting a rescued greyhound from a racetrack that will be kenneled all day. I meant something small, a toy something that I can carry in my bag. They make black poodles in that size, don't they?" Andi turned to Brooke, looking for affirmation as much as confirmation.

"I hear the last place producing them refused to go union, so the employees walked off the job and the operation went bankrupt," Gage drawled. "Now you have to order them from Guam, and you can only get them in white."

That bit of outlandishness had Brooke reaching for the bottle of wine. As she poured a little more into her glass, she thought perhaps she should have warned Gage that Andi saw contention like another dimension of foreplay. He wasn't going to upset her; he was playing right into her hands.

As though reading her mind, Andi said to Gage, a glint in her eye, "You're getting annoyed with me."

"Not at all. Only you remind me of the woman who was eager to breed her young dachshund, and, considering its age, I asked if it had even gone into heat yet. She told me it had been curling up by the hot water heater since the first day she brought it home."

Just in case she was wrong in her estimation, Brooke eased the chopsticks out of Andi's grasp.

"Well, I think it would be adorable for me to enter clients' homes toting a little poodle version of me," Andi said to Brooke.

Not daring to look at Gage, she replied, "No doubt about it."

"What will the homeowners say when they discover only one of you is housebroken?" he drawled.

"Gage!" Brooke sent him a pleading look.

As though she'd heard nothing, Andi continued. "We could wear matching nail polish and bling."

"Dogs aren't fashion accessories." Gage enunciated each word.

Wondering how a pleasant hour could go so horribly wrong, Brooke snapped. "Enough, you two!" She said to Andi, "You'll long turn heads whether you adopt a pet or not. The point is that you've never been any more drawn to animals than I have. Is adoption really right for you?"

"What is?" Andi tossed back the last sip of her wine only to set the glass on the wooden table with a thud. "Okay, here's the thing. After several dates since breaking up with he whose name will not be spoken, each guy has been worse than the next. Remember *Must Love Dogs?* Diane Lane's website-generated applicants were *princes* compared to the characters that I've been paired with."

"I'm so sorry! Here, take my wine." Brooke slid over her glass. Although she could have lived the rest of her life without Gage hearing this, she replied, "You're way braver than I will ever be by doing that. I've seen the commercials, sure, but to actually go online? No way."

"Besides, think of what your father would say?" Gage asked, his expression benign.

Not only did Brooke glare at him, Andi joined her.

"Well, fear not," Andi soon added. "I've given up the whole business, but look where that leaves me. You're pulling up stakes. My Friday-night safety net!"

Brooke shook her head, not buying into her angst out of sheer necessity. "I'll be barely more than two hours away, not across state lines. By the way, during the week, don't we mostly text anyway?"

"But I live for our sleepovers." Andi reached over to squeeze Brooke's hand. "They're like a weekend at a spa, without strangers judging your body." She turned to Gage. "No doubt you've already grasped this, but this one is the best listener on the planet."

"Only because your stories are always far more entertaining than mine," Brooke quickly assured her, afraid of what Gage might say.

"Sadly, true." Andi's chuckle was short-lived when she added in all seriousness, "The fact is that you were fine-tuned by Daddy Dearest, who believed in the archaic notion that children should be seen, not heard, and you've yet to really escape that demoralizing indoctrination.'"

"Thanks," Brooke replied with a wry twist of her lips. "I love being called a robot."

"You know the financial world better than anyone I know. Probably as well as The Donald at your age—maybe even Warren Buffet. I just wish you'd be as confident about yourself."

As Brooke lowered her eyes, Gage offered to Andi, "As the minority voice on the subject of dating, might I suggest that your bad luck in love is relative to some people finding themselves unable to get pregnant?"

The raven-haired Realtor smiled into his eyes. "Probably because my motto is do it well or not at all." As mischief lit her sultry gray eyes, she all but pleaded, "Please tell me you at least have a twin?"

"Sorry. I do have three brothers and two sisters, though."

Her interest sharpening, she straightened in her seat. "Any of them single? The brothers, I mean."

"Two. But you'll never get them out of Montana."

Andi turned to Brooke, giving her a "You see? I have no luck" look. Pouring Brooke's wine into her glass, she rose. "I'll take this with me if you don't mind. It's time for me to return a few calls and otherwise get back to work, so you can get to yours."

As the back door closed behind her, Gage said to Brooke, "She's definitely a live wire. I would never have guessed that you two could be such good friends."

Simultaneously wondering if that could continue, and thinking she now knew what an abused tennis ball at Wimbledon felt like, Brooke could only reply, "You provoked her."

"Hit the rewind button, sweetheart. Only after she started it."

Since he was right, she could only defend her friend on merit. "Andi *is* more of an extrovert than I'll ever

be, but she has a big heart, and from the first, she protected me and my interests as I shopped for a house
that would be a home as much as an investment. She's
become my best friend."

"I want to agree—especially when she referred to
your father as Daddy Dearest."

"Your ears almost went to attention like Humphrey's
when she spoke of him." With no leftovers to see to,
Brooke stacked one container into the other and carried them to the trash. "Just don't misunderstand. My
father was never physically abusive."

"Okay, but what about emotionally?"

The question had her struggling for an answer. "Not
everyone is born the demonstrative type. That doesn't
make him a bad person."

Gage rose, too, and carried their plates and silverware to the sink. "And how often did you cry yourself
to sleep? Not because he was busy, or because you were
missing your mother?"

She knew what he was asking, and his challenge
made her feel as though she was having that awful na-
ked-in-public dream; however, she couldn't stay upset
with him. She knew he was trying to understand and be
supportive. But the need to keep some walls up seemed
wisest, even if it would hurt him. "I'll say it again, you
should open a side business as an analyst, Doc."

"I'd go broke, my problem being an interest in only
analyzing a certain individual."

Brooke added the empty wine bottle to the trash
and, too, a fantasy. "I'm not sure I'm worth that much
of your time."

"I disagree, but I wouldn't expect a modest person
like yourself to say anything else." He came to her and

took hold of her arms, forcing her to meet his somber scrutiny. "Let's just get one thing cleared up. Stop trying to hook me up with your friend."

"Groan and blush," she said, lowering her gaze. "I'm embarrassed enough without hearing how easily you saw through what I'd attempted."

"Failure was inevitable, since your heart disagrees with your head."

It felt so natural and right to be standing like this that Brooke didn't realize she was stroking his chest until he covered her hand with his and stayed it so she could feel the powerful rhythm of his heartbeat. That drew her gaze to meet his.

Brooke forgot about where they were and that Andi was only beyond a door or wall. She was transported to the other night when they'd sat together and all had seemed safe and right with the world. "This is such a mistake," she said, helplessly focusing on his mouth.

"Let me prove otherwise."

As he lowered his head, Brooke felt her body react as though someone tripped a switch. The mere brush of his lips—incredibly tender yet coaxing—made her feel both cherished and desired. When she yielded to invite more, he didn't disappoint, soon kissing her in a way that had her uttering a soft sound of yearning and wrapping her arms around his neck.

"This is the woman I've seen watching me," he said against her lips.

He initiated another kiss, lifting her off her feet as he drew her tightly against him to align their bodies. Brooke could feel her nipples harden to sharp points against his chest, and his growing arousal between her thighs. After concluding that she was a woman of limited passion and sensuality, it was as thrilling as it was startling to realize there was someone who could bring her this high this fast that she couldn't voice any cohesive thought.

"I wish we were alone, so I could *really* kiss you."

The shiver that rushed through her body was all about the assurance that there could be more, that his kisses could get any better. As much as she wanted that, Brooke made herself push against his shoulders until he set her back on his feet. "Andi," she said simply.

With a sigh, Gage allowed, "Yeah, I know. Sorry." He looked as thrown as she was.

"It's not like I don't want this, too." Seeing her lip gloss on his mouth, she quickly wiped it away with her thumb.

"It's about time." The smoldering look he gave her made Brooke feel as though she was a heartbeat away from being in his arms again. "For such a small slip of a woman, you have annoyingly strong willpower."

Not anymore she didn't. Not where he was concerned, and when he reached out to brush his thumb over her taut nipple, exposed due to her thin T-shirt and sheerer bra, she moaned and crossed her arms over herself. "Please. I have to go outside and talk to Andi."

"If she tries to talk you into anything kinky, try to remember that I'm a one-woman man."

Unable to suppress it, Brooke burst out laughing. "And *bad.*"

Minutes later, when Brooke got outside, Andi wasn't where she'd last seen her. That wasn't unwelcome news. Still feeling her lips tingling from Gage's kisses, she suspected they remained a bit red and swollen, as well. Buying herself another minute or two, she went to check the mailbox, even though she'd had her mail transferred to Sweet Springs. Finding it as empty as it should be, she headed to the back of the house.

"I was about to come ask you if all of this garden sculpture stays," Andi said, taking a photo of the man-size tiered concrete fountain tucked in the corner where the kitchen nook's bay window looked out over the backyard. "It's not on your list."

Brooke's felt a wave of relief knowing that if Andi had been any quicker in her work, she would have witnessed way more than was helpful.

"I'd only gotten around to inside things so far," Brooke replied. "But, yes, everything was bought to fit this landscape. It would be aesthetically wrong to remove it."

Andi nodded her approval. "You're going to make someone very happy, and my job easier yet. This will definitely be a move-in-ready property, both indoors and out."

"Well, even though I never expected this moment, you taught me what it takes to get a fast offer," Brooke reminded her. "And a quick sale will, hopefully, make this less painful."

As she focused on her notes, Andi asked, "Will you buy something in East Texas? You do have to think of some kind of reinvestment to avoid getting hit with taxes."

Oh, God, Brooke thought. She just hoped that Gage wasn't watching. "I don't know. I hadn't thought that far ahead. It's not like I need another house to maintain, and all signs are such that Aunt Marsha may never be able to resume residence in her own home. At least not without live-in help."

"Then there's Gage's house next door," Andi said, bringing matters closer to the real subject. "He said you haven't seen it yet? You'd better go have a look. You need to find out if it's a single-guy nightmare or a king's castle awaiting the right queen. Even at that, it will need some feminine touches."

Brooke gave up and blurted, "Andi, seriously, that's the least thing I—"

"Uh-uh!" Andi held up one perfectly manicured finger to silence her. "Don't even try to go there. We're friends, correct? I am well familiar with your ladylike ways and how you try to do no harm. I know *you*."

"I honestly did mean for you two to meet."

"I believe that. Just as I believe that while you didn't want to have feelings for someone, you'd planned— may still be planning—to say goodbye to soon, that's exactly what's happened." Andi shook her magnificent raven mane behind her shoulders. "And face it—he's half besotted with you. Don't think I don't wish otherwise. Believe me, I was ready to give him my business card in the hopes that he would find some time to race down the interstate and address *my* issues."

Knowing better than to insult her friend's intelligence with any more denials, Brooke reached for her. "I'm sick over this. I didn't go looking for it, and it's a complication that I don't need."

"Oh, shut it," Andi scoffed good-naturedly, as she hugged her back. "He's all man in that classical-cowboy sort of way. He knows who he is. How often do you run across someone so balanced? Don't blow this, which you could, since you've never been one to compartmentalize. You gave those bloodsucker employers of yours your undivided attention. Granted, that probably saved you from marrying a clueless jerk, but now you're giving your aunt and her business that same devoted focus. Let me tell you, Gage is no Parker, and he'll demand you change your ways. He wants his share of those soulful, melt-your-heart, brown-eyed gazes, and you'd better give them to him."

Andi checked her latest picture and then pocketed her phone. "I'm done. Time for me to head to the office to start on the paperwork. You'll probably be back in Sweet Springs before I get everything set. I'll fax everything you need to sign tomorrow." Suddenly stopping midway to her car, she announced, "We haven't even talked a price yet."

At that moment, Brooke was torn between laughter and tears. "You're the expert. I trust you."

"Are you sure?"

It was nearly seven-thirty in the evening when Brooke came into the study to tell Gage that they should call it a day. While his back was getting stiff from packing and stacking boxes of books and his stomach had begun to growl from hunger, he knew—finished or not—they had to head back to Sweet Springs tomorrow, and there were still things to do. At this point, that's all he wanted to focus on.

"Let me get these last two boxes done. Then how about I get your kitchen packed?" he asked. "I've checked it out, and it won't take me another hour. You have the emptiest set of cupboards that I've ever seen outside of a model home. I know you don't cook for yourself, but what? No dinner parties? Not even catered?"

"Not here." She shrugged. "Most of my clients are

men, and not all of them are married. Those who are don't always bring their wives to a dinner meeting. To avoid complications, it's best to hold dinners elsewhere. The same with private parties. I just didn't have the time to spend in the kitchen."

For once, Gage was pleased with the news. No wonder the fridge held mostly wine, beer and bottled water. On the other hand, he was also convinced that Brooke would spend more time in the kitchen if there was someone there that she wanted to be with. He'd already proved that to himself.

"You have to be exhausted from tackling your bedroom and bathroom. Why don't you make us something to drink and keep me company?" He requested a scotch and water for himself.

"Consider it done. I'll be the designated driver. If I drink now, I'll fall over on the couch and sleep until sunrise. While I'm gone, you decide where we should go to eat. There are some casual steak houses and breweries that serve great burgers and grilled food close by."

The idea of having to share her again didn't appeal to Gage at all. "It's Sunday night—everything is going to be so packed, we won't be able to hear ourselves think, let alone hold a conversation. We could go to that gourmet market we passed on the way here."

"I can't let you cook after all you've already done," Brooke said, her tone adamant. "What about pizza?"

"Sounds great."

"Then tell me how you like yours. I'll call as soon as I bring you that drink."

In fact, it was just under an hour later that Gage washed up, then got the door for the kid delivering their dinner. Brooke was still on the phone checking on her aunt one last time for the day. The sun was sinking fast, and as he carried the pizza box to the kitchen nook, he admired the way the light played off the live oak and juniper trees artfully framing the small but photogenic backyard. If this property was in East Texas, he could live contentedly here, he mused, as he set the box on the table.

About to refresh his drink, he pantomimed to Brooke, asking whether she wanted wine or whatever? Still listening to her aunt, she went to the cooler and got out a bottle of cabernet, which she handed him.

Winking at her, he opened the bottle and poured so it could get to its best temperature before attending to his glass. He didn't pretend not to be listening to Brooke's side of the conversation. It reassured him that there was no hint of the cool, formal financier in her tone; she was all warmth and concern.

"No, dear, I'm not coming tonight. We're still in Dallas. Yes, that's right, I did explain earlier today, but you were in between nurse and doctor visits. It's perfectly reasonable to have gotten confused. I'll see you tomorrow afternoon for sure, as soon as we unload." She deftly took two plates from a cabinet and handed them to Gage. "I know where to put things, Aunt Marsha, not to worry." Lifting a roll of paper towels off its pewter pedestal, she passed it to him, as well. "Humphrey is doing fine. Gage spoke with Roy earlier. Humph has a girlfriend, a yellow Labrador named Lily. No, Gage didn't get a new dog yet. Her people are out of town, and she's being kenneled at the clinic." Brooke looked toward Gage and grinned. "Well, I'm sure you're about to make his day. I'll tell him. Try to get some sleep, dear. I'll be there soon."

"Now you're ready for this wine," Gage said, as soon as she disconnected and set down the phone on the counter.

Thanking him, she settled in the seat next to his and indulged in a slow sip. Only then did she pass on her message. "Aunt Marsha says to consider yourself kissed for making sure Humphrey is being so well taken care of."

Pretending to be unconvinced, Gage replied, "I think she told *you* to give me a kiss for her. I caught that smile—it was a dead giveaway."

"You'll just have to ask her when we get back to Sweet Springs."

"I'm being cheated," he muttered, but he couldn't keep a straight face as he opened the pizza box. If there was any grace and justice in the universe, he would get kissed before the night was over. "Is she holding up okay? It sounded like she was having some memory or focus issues."

Sighing, Brooke nodded her agreement. "But there's good cause—since my last call, she learned that they're bumping up her surgery."

"Is that right? How soon?"

"It's now scheduled for Thursday."

On Friday, the doctor had said that they'd scheduled her for Tuesday in a week. "Wow," Gage said. "Did something happen to make them do that?"

"She couldn't remember their specific reasoning." The look she gave him signaled that it brought back the concern about her memory. "I suspect the doctor didn't like her numbers. It's the first thing I'll look into tomorrow."

The mask of the calm nurturer was gone. In its place

was the face of a niece wracked with doubt and dread as she picked up his plate and slid on two slices of the pie.

"It will be all right," he assured her, reaching over to stroke her cheek.

"What if she's too weak, or there's some other problem they haven't factored in?"

"You can't think that way." He accepted the plate. "The point is that she's in the best place possible if there is a problem. You certainly won't be of help to her if you make yourself sick."

Taking a sip of her wine, Brooke assured him, "Believe me, she won't see this side of me when I step into her room."

"Then I'm doubly grateful that you're being so open with me."

"Well, let's eat before this wine makes me a total goofball," she declared. "The pizza smells out of this world! Andi and I usually try for a modicum of restraint and order the thinnest crust and veggie kind."

That won her a pitying look from him. "Women. Then what's the point?"

He'd asked for a pepperoni, sausage and jalapeño, thick crust with extra cheese. Brooke had already warned him that she would be plucking all peppers off hers, which she proceeded to do.

"You don't know what's good for you," Gage scoffed, as he held his slice close for her to dispose of them.

"Some of the juice will still be on there. That's about my speed."

"I should have known when you ordered sesame chicken for lunch. I guess I should be glad you didn't ask for half of this to be Canadian bacon with pine-apple."

Gage ate with relish, but he enjoyed watching her more ladylike restraint and how she dabbed at her mouth with a paper towel after each bite, although there wasn't even a crumb lingering on her lips. "Have you ever so much as dropped something on your clothes since you were…maybe in training pants?" He seriously doubted it.

Brooke's brown eyes lit with self-deprecating humor. "I have terrible luck with Italian food. It's so bad that I've learned *never* to order it unless I'm eating here at home. It's the spinning-in-the-fork thing. I think I'm doing well, but my clothes end up looking like a TV drama's crime-scene splatter photo."

"That's impossible," Gage replied. "Anyone who handles chopsticks as well as you do? At lunch I was thinking you must have an Asian great granny in your family tree. I wish I'd have thought of Italian. I'd make a donation to your favorite charity to see sauce on your nose."

About to reply, Brooke paused when her cell phone buzzed. She immediately dabbed her mouth and rose. "Sorry. I wasn't expecting any calls since I spoke to Aunt Marsha. I should have turned it off. It's my pet peeve when people think they're so important they need you to see them taking inane calls during a meal." But her wry smile froze the moment she picked it up. "Oh, damn. It's…my father."

Gage didn't care for the way she pressed her hand to her abdomen as though she was about to lose the few bites of dinner she'd consumed. What kind of parent did that to a child he supposedly loved? Sure, things hadn't always gone smoothly between him and his father, but he'd known his old man would lose a leg before seeing one of his kids suffer.

Brooke took the call and turned her back to Gage. "Hi, Dad. Just back in the States?"

Damon Chandler Bellamy. Gage had heard his full name earlier in the day, sardonically spoken by Andi, and had seen a few pictures of him in the study. He was a good-looking guy, something like the European who was playing that superspy these days in the movies. Cold and calculating as he was lean and elegant. From the family photographs, Gage had taken some small satisfaction in guessing he was below average in height—somewhere between Napoleon and Tom Cruise. His blond hair told him that Brooke's hair color was natural, and that she'd inherited her gorgeous brown eyes from her mother. Damon Bellamy's eyes were the gray of steel buried in Arctic ice.

*"You're doing what?"*

The sharp exclamation yanked Gage back to reality, and he saw Brooke shakily moving the phone a few inches away from her ear. When she glanced over her shoulder at him and he saw her embarrassment, he had to reach for his drink. His only other option was to take the damned phone and yell back, "Exactly what is your problem, pal?"

"It can't be helped, Dad. I can't make any appointments yet when Aunt Marsha is dealing with so many problems. Didn't you get my message about her condition being graver?"

Hell, Gage thought. The guy must have treasury ink in his veins instead of blood to not even ask up front how his sister-in-law was doing.

"It's nothing she can control. I only just learned they're going to do the heart-valve-replacement procedure on Thursday. Moving it up must indicate they're worried."

As Gage heard her father issue a lengthy list of directives, he watched Brooke cross to the table to reach for her glass and take a fortifying sip of wine. Her hand exposed the subtlest trembling, and he had to fight the urge to go stand behind her and draw her against him to offer his moral support. But would she accept it?

At the end of what seemed a lengthy rant, Brooke said dully, "That's impossible, Father. She's afraid, and I won't leave her in that condition. The hospital staff are fine people, but they can't provide the reassurance that family can."

*You tell him, sweetheart.* Gage was heartened even for that modicum of formal rebellion. He'd been half worrying that he would hear "Yes, Daddy."

After another lengthy rant by her father, she recited, "I understand that the longer I'm out of circulation, the harder it will be to find a good position, but that can't be helped."

Whatever Damon Bellamy said next had Brooke gripping the back of her chair.

"That was uncalled for. I respect that the countryside doesn't hold any appeal for you, but I spent some of the happiest days of my childhood there with Aunt Marsha. I know I'm no longer a child, and I don't see myself as a martyr. Listen, I have to go. A neighbor is at the door. I'll get back with you after the surgery. Thank you for the call."

As soon as Brooke disconnected, she turned off the phone and pushed it as far away from herself as she could. When she returned to the table, she reached for her wine glass. "I'll probably regret this, but—" She took too long of a swallow to appreciate anything but the alcohol, and when she set down her glass, she glanced at him with no small chagrin. "I guess you could tell that didn't go well?"

"He tends to speak loudly when he's annoyed."

She exhaled shakily. "I underestimated how unhappy he would be with my decisions."

*Underestimated his ability to be an ass.*

Wanting badly to reach for her, Gage said, "I should have left the room to give you more privacy, but the truth is that I didn't want to. I have a low tolerance for anyone, particularly a parent, bullying."

Brooke winced at the word. "He's not really that, he's…just used to getting things done."

"Well, you're his daughter, not his protégée. Excuse me prying but…he seemed annoyed with your aunt, as well as you?"

"He feels that Aunt Marsha has lived her life and that she shouldn't burden me with her problems."

Gage could tell just by her expression that even repeating that was upsetting and distasteful to her. "Much better to get back to wheeling and dealing and chasing that all-important dollar, eh? Helping is part of what families do. Isn't a prime vow in a wedding ceremony 'For better or worse'?" It never ceased to astonish him when people were in a hurry to say those words, only to be among the first and fastest to indicate, "I didn't mean *this!*"

Brooke fingered the remnants of her first slice of pizza but didn't try for a bite. "My father was an only child, and his parents had very little and didn't achieve much more. It made him extremely ambitious. He could have stepped out of a Dickens novel."

"Was he on your mother's reading list?"

"Never let it be said there's anything wrong with your memory." Brooke shook her head, her expression sad. "Maybe those books helped my mother understand him, and it may have helped her reach his compassionate side, but once she was gone, he reverted back quickly." She shrugged, then tried for a resilient tone. "Don't worry. This isn't the first time I've been on the receiving end of his criticism, and I doubt it will be the last."

"Thinking of you developing a thicker skin is doing wonders for my state of mind, too."

Brooke abruptly shifted her gaze out the bay window where now the timer-set lights around the fountain shrubs twinkled. "Don't be too nice to me. I'm just tired and emotionally drained enough to make a fool of myself and burst into tears. Believe me, I can handle my father's censure far easier than your tenderness."

That made all the sense in the world to Gage, but it wouldn't help him sleep tonight. He was tied in knots for her. Finally, slowly shaking his head, he said, "You're asking for too much, sweetheart. My sisters taught me that classic romantic movies held a lot of advice if I ever was in relationship trouble, but I never saw one where the guy gorging on pizza made the girl throw herself at him."

Staring at him, Brooke eased her fingers over her mouth as new tears flooded her eyes. But this time they were tears of laughter. "Neither did I," she said as giggles burst from her lips. "But his error might be in that he didn't save her a piece for breakfast."

Taking his time to pretend to ponder that bit of wisdom, Gage ultimately shook his head in rejection. "That can't be right. Cold pizza for breakfast—who are you, a former trash-bin scavenger?"

Sniffing, Brooke reached for a slice. "I happen to like cold pizza."

As she took a bite and chewed, Gage ripped off a fresh sheet of paper towel and dabbed at the moisture under her eyes. "You finally found some jalapeño juice, I see."

After a grateful glance, Brooke played along and said huskily, "I still don't know how you stand the things."

Smiling into her eyes, he said softly, "They're worth the trouble." Taking another sustaining sip of his drink, Gage thought they should get the rest of tonight's awkwardness out of the way. "In case you were figuring out how to bring up the subject, I'm going to camp out on the couch in the study tonight."

Brooke wiped her hands and reached over to gently rub his forearm. "I'm sorry. I honestly intended for tonight to go differently. I was going to let you seduce me."

With a slow, full nod, he asked, "I knew it. Thick crust is the secret aphrodisiac, isn't it?" When she smiled, he took hold of her hand and lifted it to his lips for a kiss. "You're physically exhausted and mentally beaten up, and you're about to say goodbye to a big piece of your independence for a while."

"And you deserve better than leftovers," she said, rubbing his lower lip with her thumb.

"Lovely, I would crawl on all fours for your leftovers. But for our first time, I have this fantasy."

"That's nice," she whispered, transfixed. "I don't know that I've ever been part of anyone's fantasy before."

"Stick with me, kid."

"You make me want to."

# Chapter 5

"I can't believe you did that. What happens now?"

Brooke stroked her aunt's shoulder as Marsha waved and blew kisses to the scene outside where Gage stood holding Humphrey by the window. It was Wednesday evening, and Gage had just brought Humphrey to the hospital grounds to say hello before Marsha's surgery in the morning. The older woman had acted like a child, laughing and crying and clapping her hands at the sight of her beloved pet.

"*Now,* you settle down and get yourself a good rest," Brooke told her as she adjusted the bed to bring it down to a more comfortable sleeping position. "You need to be rested and in a good frame of mind so they can fix you up tomorrow."

"I'm so happy to see my old friend, my sweet boy." Although Gage had carried Humphrey to the truck,

Marsha continued to gaze toward the window as though her pet was still there. "Be sure to tell Gage that he's an angel for bringing him to see me."

Considering the way Humphrey had writhed and howled, the pleasure of this impromptu visit was an equal treat for her basset hound. "I will. This was his idea, you know. I was worried that the staff would frown on this."

"They couldn't possibly. Humphrey is such a well-behaved boy. He could have been much louder if he'd wanted to be."

Mostly due to experienced Gage, knowing how to rub the gleeful dog under his chin and to massage his ears, she thought, smiling. She wasn't about to inform her aunt that earlier at the clinic, her "well-behaved boy" had chewed one of old Warren Atwood's shoe-laces completely in two while lying under the front table as the old-timers were playing dominos. It had only been when nature had called that Warren—try-ing to stand—had felt resistance and heard a growl. As the rest of the old-timers had looked under the table, they'd realized Warren had become the dog's chew toy.

"Will you make sure they call you as soon as I'm out of surgery tomorrow?"

The pensive question yanked Brooke's attention back to her aunt. Not only did Brooke not like that Aunt Marsha was sounding so anxious, this was the third time she was having to reassure her.

"There'll be no need," she replied, crossing the room to lower the blinds and pull the curtains shut before returning to her aunt. "I told you, I'll be here waiting."

"Oh, that's way too long for you, and what if it's busy at the shop?"

It didn't matter if Brooke was eighteen or thirty, she was still a child in her aunt's eyes, ever in need of older and wiser direction. But in such a gentler way than her father. "I'll go in early to check the computer and phones," she replied patiently, "and take care of whatever is necessary. Naomi is going to fill in while I'm here. Later, when you're in recovery, I'll go back to the store, and return here after we close to see if you're awake yet and ready to be moved to a room again."

"I feel like I'm causing you all too much trouble."

Brooke sat on the edge of the bed and took her aunt's hand in both of hers. "Not in the least. I have to lay down the law to get any time with you at all. The phone rings if I'm at the house, the store… People want to help. You'd blush if you knew how concerned and kind everyone is being."

It was the truth. Every day someone came by for an update on Marsha, or to offer to sit with Brooke during the surgery, to help clean the house, or to cook once Marsha returned home. There were plenty more messages left daily on the answering machine at the house. She'd never experienced anything like that in the city. You were definitely surrounded by more people there; however, unless your house caught fire, or you called 911 for another emergency, people tended to leave each other alone. Of course, most of them were professionals and focused on careers, or had families involved in lots of activities, she thought wryly. She only knew one set of neighbors well enough to converse with beyond "Good morning" or "How are you?"

"I'm so blessed," Marsha said, squeezing Brooke's hands. "Pastor Wilson came by just before you arrived. He'll stop by tomorrow, too."

"See? You have the power hitters in your corner. What more could you ask for?" Leaning over, Brooke kissed her aunt good-night. "Now you really have to settle down and get some shut-eye, dear. I don't know that they'll want to give you anything to help you what with having to use anesthesia tomorrow."

"Then I'm going to be watching TV all night. You can't sleep in these places otherwise. There's something going on all the time, and if you do doze off, they come in to check your numbers again, or to take blood, or give you a pill." Marsha paused, her thoughts drifting elsewhere. "You said Gage and Humphrey are waiting for you outside, didn't you? Go! Get something to eat—I think you lost weight since I last saw you. You don't want to end up scrawny like me."

"You're as beautiful as ever, Aunt Marsha, you're just not feeling well enough to eat."

"It would be nice to crave a cheeseburger again. Give my boy a good snuggle for me, will you?"

Brooke kissed her again. "I will, dear. I love you."

When Brooke climbed into Gage's truck, Humphrey—sitting on the backseat— wagged his tail in welcome and woofed softly. She leaned back there and rubbed his neck and scratched his ears.

"Yes, you did good, you ham. To hear Aunt Marsha tell it, she thinks you're ready for a Hollywood agent."

As she turned forward and pulled on her seat belt, she said to Gage. "She thought you were pretty terrific, too."

Although he looked pleased, he scoffed, "I doubt she even noticed me. I saw who she was getting all excited over."

"I told her this was your idea." Brooke reached over to stroke his arm. "Thank you for that—and for us using your truck."

"My pleasure. How's she doing otherwise?"

"Trying to put on a good show, too. But she's so anxious, her mind is skipping all over the place. So if she gave me instructions on Humph, or the store, or feeding *you* once, she repeated herself three times over. I'm as ready for this to be behind her as she is. This behavior is so unlike her."

Gage stroked her hair, free and flowing straight down her back tonight. "Stress will do that to people, especially older people."

"I know. This side of my brain grasps that very well," she said pointing to her left temple. Then she pointed to her right side. "*This* part of me wants to catch the next flight to… I don't know where, and pretend none of this is happening."

"Never mind that flying business." Gage contorted to open his arms, careful to avoid bumping her or the windows. "Here's all the island fun you can handle."

As Humphrey barked, clearly thinking this was the start of a new game, Brooke laughed softly, grateful for Gage's willingness to be silly in order to lighten the moment. "That is tempting. Does this offer include lounge-chair drink service?"

He narrowed his eyes as though flipping through memory files. "Do you remember where we put your liquor inventory?"

"In the pantry. Thank you for reminding me that I need to relocate it somewhere else before Aunt Marsha gets home. She's no teetotaler, but if some of her friends come to visit or help, I wouldn't want to put her in the position to be embarrassed."

Gage nodded his agreement and added, "I seem to recall packing tequila. I can have you a margarita made before you can kick off your shoes and feed the pooch."

"Seriously, let's save that for the recovery celebration," Brooke replied. "I would like to have a clear head tomorrow. I'll join you if you have the Chivas, though."

Minutes later, Gage drove into her aunt's driveway and parked. He lifted the basset hound out of the back and set him on the driveway, where Humphrey trotted, tail wagging, leading the way to the back gate. Walking beside Gage, Brooke felt as though they were a married couple returning home for the day. Amazing for someone she'd known such a short time—and how sweet this taste of domesticity was.

As though sharing the same thoughts, Gage said, "If I don't have any late calls tomorrow, I'm going to mow both of our lawns."

Their yards were getting a bit overgrown compared to their neighbors', but for good reason. Since their return from Dallas on Monday, Gage had been nonstop busy as well, and their contact had been mostly hit-and-miss, or at best brief catch-up calls.

"Are you sure? I was going to look through Aunt Marsha's telephone book to see who she used before you began helping her so much."

"Never mind him. He's the other reason that I started doing Marsha's yard when I did mine. If things don't level off, we'll discuss options."

Once inside, they went in opposite directions to wash up and get comfortable. As Brooke removed her heels and hung her rosemary-green linen jacket by the stairs, she smiled, replaying Gage's comments. She'd never liked the way Parker had always thought he knew best and tried to direct their every decision, even though he was usually repeating someone else's advice—as Andi had pointed out. On the other hand, Gage said "we" not "I." They hadn't even been intimate yet; nevertheless, she felt as though they had been. She felt as though she could trust him with anything.

Well, she amended, not completely intimate, she mused as her thoughts went back to last night in those few minutes before Gage had received a call and been forced to rush off on an emergency. She'd been left weak-kneed and yearning for more of his talented touch.

The memory of those minutes, and his kisses, left her feverish, and she brushed her hands over her matching slacks and silk eggplant-colored top as she returned to the kitchen. Seeing Gage was making their drinks, she checked the answering machine on the kitchen bar. Two calls left no messages and were only identified as "local" on the screen, while the other two were people from the church asking about Aunt Martha.

"I'll hold off on answering those until after the surgery tomorrow," Brooke said, for her own benefit as much as Gage's.

"I'm all for that," he replied. The intimate look he sent her way spoke of his own desire for some alone time with her.

With a whimper, Humphrey gave up sitting expectantly by his food bowl and slumped down on to his belly.

"Yes, sir, I'm on it right now," Brooke assured him. Once she had the pooch fed, Gage had their drinks on the kitchen table. "Or do you want to go sit on the porch?" he asked.

"Here's good," she told him. "It's cooler, and Humph won't rush in his eagerness to join us."

"Listen to you," Gage teased, as they sat down. "Aren't you turning into a real animal person, concerned that he'll get indigestion?"

"You're such a good teacher, I'd be pitiful if some of your experience and advice didn't rub off on me." She leaned toward him to touch her cut-crystal glass to his. "Thank you yet again."

"My pleasure," he murmured, his blue-gray eyes tender. "You're starting to act like a natural, you know."

"Oh, you are a sweet fibber. The idea of dealing with cat litter on a daily basis, let alone attempting any of the number of things you've told me about doing on calls, is science fiction to me."

"But you'd easily change baby diapers, wouldn't you?"

"This is not a subject I want to deal with sitting at the table."

"The key is to focus on the satisfaction you get in making things better, especially if you're saving a life."

"I'll settle for singing your praises." After taking a grateful sip, she swept her hair over one shoulder and sighed as she rolled her head to ease out the kinks. "I am so grateful the waiting is over." Then she grimaced. "We should have stopped at a drive-through somewhere and gotten you something to eat."

"Me? What about you?"

"I split a sub sandwich with Kiki for lunch, and I swear it's still lying like unbaked dough in my stomach." She started to rise. "Let me check the fridge. I forgot that Naomi sent lasagna over yesterday. Aunt Marsha says she makes the best—"

Before she could pass him, Gage slid his arm around her waist and drew her backward, onto his lap. Slipping his hand under her hair, he directed her nearer, until his mouth could close over hers. Their lips and tongues tasted cool from the ice in their drinks, but they soon grew warm as they yielded to deeper appetites.

"There's hungry, and then there's hungry," he said, when he finally took time to catch his breath. "That couldn't wait. I want to taste the skin along your neck... and other places," he added, his gaze drifting down over her breasts. "But I didn't have time to shave before we headed for the hospital."

"I appreciate the care, considering that I'll be spending some time visiting with Aunt Marsha's minister tomorrow, and who knows who else?" Brooke brushed his jaw with the backs of her fingers, then slid them down the taut tendons of his throat to the V-neck of his white T-shirt. He'd shed his maroon clinic jacket back at his house. "This reminds me... I thought about you today," she added, playing with the soft hair curling there.

Looking as pleased as he was intrigued, Gage smiled. "I'm all ears."

"The UPS man came in with a delivery today, and the top two buttons of his shirt were open—no doubt due to this growing heat. He looked like he had a nice chest, too."

"That's not even remotely amusing," Gage muttered.

"Be patient. It's coming." She touched her index finger to his lips. "I thought, as attractive as he was—

and Kiki was very impressed—he didn't hold a candle to you."

With a soft growl, Gage nipped at her finger, then kissed the tip of her nose and chin. "Better. You didn't imagine kissing him, did you?"

"No!"

"It would be like cheating, wouldn't it?" Gage tightened his arms, bringing her closer until her breasts were crushed against his chest and they were sharing the same breath. "That's how I feel. I don't want to spend a minute with another woman, only you."

Although old habits were hard to break and Brooke's initial instinct was to remind him that he was all but asking for a commitment she couldn't yet give, she realized she could still be honest. "I feel the same way."

Focusing on her lips, he rasped, "One more kiss and then I'm going to finish this drink and get outside and mow after all."

"Gage, it's a steam bath out there, and it'll be dark in an hour."

"That's all I need."

When he took slow possession of her mouth, Brooke felt it all the way down to her womb. Then he took her head in his hands and showed her that she'd experienced nothing about desire and sensuality until now. That made it impossible to keep her own hands still. When hunger coiled more tightly inside her, she shifted on his lap, triggering a groan from him, and suddenly they were both standing upright, and he was pacing, rubbing the back of his neck.

"Sorry," she offered softly. "I got carried away."

"Believe me, it's my fault." After a deep breath, he reached for his drink and downed it in two swallows. Then his gaze slid to her mouth and he winced. "Sweetheart… Crap."

Aware of what he was seeing, since her lips were stinging, she took an ice cube from his glass and started rubbing it over her lips. "It'll be okay in a minute."

"Yeah, right. You'll be lucky if it's better by morning." He looked thoroughly disgusted with himself, only to stop and say quietly, tenderly, "I want you, Brooke. You blind me to everything else. You're staking claim to every corner of my head."

"You must have downed your drink too fast." Bemused, Brooke warned, "I don't think you're ready to get on any monster mower."

Ignoring that, Gage headed for the door. "Take Humph out one more time and then get him inside, and open the back gates for me. You'll save me time in having to get on and off the machine."

His frown of concentration and brusque directives were almost amusing. "Aye, aye, Captain. Anything else?"

"Yeah, cut me a strip of that lasagna and put the package on the back end of your car. I'll grab it as I lock up for you. I can nuke it at my place."

Now she was convinced that he was serious. "You can't come in here and eat it afterward?" she asked, incredulous.

"No, angel, I can't. I'll be sweaty and dirty, and once I shower and get all good-looking and irresistible—" a twinkle of humor lit his eyes "—you won't be able to keep from throwing yourself at me. I'm only human. Besides, a deal is a deal, remember?"

The man was a sweetheart and gentleman—along with being a bigger ham than Humphrey. "I remember." As the corners of her lips twitched from the urge to laugh, and her eyes flooded with tears of mirth and adoration, she admitted, "I can't tell you how you make me feel."

"Your ears aren't old enough to hear how I feel," he muttered.

When Gage let himself into the back gate of Marsha's property at five o'clock the next morning, it was still dark. He came around the tall camellia bushes along the winding sidewalk, only to end up face-to-face with Brooke, who suppressed a scream down to a squeak, as she clapped her hand over her mouth.

"What are you doing here?" she whispered.

"Coming to get Humph. I wanted to get to the clinic for as early a start as possible. I figured you might be thinking the same way, so you can get to the hospital…where I intend to be, hopefully, when Marsha gets wheeled into recovery."

He saw no reason to add that he'd tossed and turned all night, mostly because of her, since he doubted she'd done better herself—probably for different reasons, though, namely worry over her aunt. But he was determined to make the start of her day as positive as possible, which is why he'd used soaps and aftershaves from a reservoir gift drawer of things he never used to hide any hint of antiseptics or animals that might be lingering on his clinic attire. It must have worked because he was suddenly engulfed in a sweetly intense hug.

"You are…incomparable."

She kissed him repeatedly, and he let her, since he'd shaved with a new blade this morning, too. Fighting a surge of renewed hunger, he replied gruffly, "Call me with reports…even if it's about you being frustrated that there are no updates."

Back on her own two feet, Brooke was once again Princess Perfection as she smoothed her hands over her coral sheath topped by a matching blazer. "I'm not going to bother you like that."

"If I'm not there or tied up with a patient, leave a message with Roy. I guarantee you that he and the guys will be hovering over the phone like vultures today. Everyone is thinking about Marsha, and you."

Brooke touched his chest. "That's so dear. Tell them thanks, will you?" She stooped to rub Humphrey, who sat watching their conversation, his tail wagging. "Be a good boy, okay? It's extra important today."

It turned out that Roy beat Gage to the clinic. The older man was busy mopping the front floor and—given his scowl and the fact that the floors weren't part of his job—Gage immediately suspected something had happened.

"What's going on? Isn't Vince Jenson coming this week?"

Roy leaned on his mop and for a moment looked as if he was about to get physically ill. "With all that's going on, I didn't want to trouble you yet, Doc."

No good news ever followed such an opening statement, and Gage ushered Humphrey to the examination area to get him off the wet floors and shut the doors before he returned to Roy. "Consider me troubled. What's up with Vince?"

Looking as if he'd rather be enduring root-canal work without any Novocain, Roy said, "He's been helping himself to inventory."

"Has he now?" Inevitably, Gage scanned the shelves of dog food, cat food, treats, leashes, collars and assorted over-the-counter medications. There were no barren shelves, but Vince would have been a total knucklehead to be blatant in his actions, and had probably taken only a few things per visit. Unless... His insides started to feel like a nuclear meltdown. What if Vince had managed to get into their inventory of prescription drugs? That would require more than calling the sheriff's department, that would mean a call to the DEA. "You can prove that?"

"Via the cameras the fool doesn't know we use."

"But you were on the premises each time and locked up behind him."

That would be an inordinately stupid thing to say to someone at this hour, outside of town, when it would take a sheriff's deputy several minutes to reach here if Roy turned out to be less than the man Gage believed he was. However, he *would* trust Roy with his life. The few times the man had made a mistake with the cash register, he'd insisted on making up the difference out of his pocket. He'd only finished high school before joining the navy, was really sensitive about his lack of education and was quick to take responsibility for his mistakes.

As expected, Roy didn't try to make excuses for himself. Explain, yes, but he was ready to take any and all results on the chin.

"Yeah," he admitted. "But stupid me, I was updating patient files and placing supply orders. I never thought *he* would be the problem, and I believed if someone tried to break in while he was here, that he'd holler."

Gage nodded, his hands on his hips. "How much did he take us for before you noticed?"

"A couple thousand at least."

"Any prescription-restricted drugs that we have to report?"

"Thank goodness, no. I checked that first—and if there had been anything, I would have called you instead of waited for you to get here. Can you believe it, he stole from the storage room? That's why it took me longer to catch on to him. He's probably been carrying the stuff to one of those flea markets popping up everywhere on the weekends. Even selling stuff for a fraction of its worth, he's made several truck payments—all while still paying him for cleaning the floors." Roy hung his head. "I'm sorry, Doc. I let you down."

"As long as you have the disk with proof."

"I definitely do. I just wish I'd checked it sooner. Are you wanting to take a look or call the sheriff?"

Gage nodded. "Call. If it was just a sack or two of food that he needed for his animals, we could talk things out, but this is hardly that. First, tell me how you figured out what's going on. Was he here this morning and you caught him, or what?" If so, Roy could have been in danger.

"He was due and didn't show. I was opening the storeroom door and moving things in preparation for him to clean in here when I noticed some things were different—stock moved to cover what would be obvious holes that would catch my attention faster. Vince is the only other person to go in there besides us, so I called the number I have on file for him—it's his cell, naturally, which he carries with him all of the time.

The mailbox is full. No telling who else he's ripped off and has hit the road."

That was enough information for Gage. He'd known about Vince's past brushes with the law over theft but had been willing to give the guy a chance. "I wish you had called me immediately. You don't know the mind-set of someone who knows he's pushed his luck too far." He left the rest unsaid, seeing that Roy already felt bad enough.

"I fully deserved a knock on my thick skull for thinking he'd changed and pulled his act together the way I did." During his employment interview, Roy had shared that he'd ended up with "police" duty several times while in the service, what old movies described as KP duty, only his disciplinarians had made sure he'd gotten the nastiest jobs available on the ship, which soon had had him getting a new attitude.

"I'm just glad that I don't have to worry about replacing *you,* never mind Vince," Gage replied. "Get that disk loaded. I'm sure the authorities will want to view it, too."

"Yes, sir, Doc." Roy hesitated. "I'm sorry for the timing on this, too. How's Brooke and Miss Marsha?"

"Anxious to have all this behind them." As he began to walk away, Gage stopped and turned around. "I thought we had a steam cleaner of our own?"

Roy bowed his head. "He stole the steamer, too."

Shaking his head, Gage reached for the phone. It was definitely going to be a long day.

Brooke checked her cell phone for what had to be the sixth time since arriving at the shop, and it was still only seven forty-five. It was foolish, of course, since her aunt's surgery wasn't scheduled until later this morning, but after everything else that had gone wrong, she couldn't forget the old adage of not just good things coming in threes.

Striving to focus on what Kiki was saying, she nodded; after all, Kiki had come in early herself so they could talk. "The little purses and the waistband thingies for travelers and joggers, yes, I see your point. If you can figure out a way to display some in the window and then put the rest in the vicinity where we're experimenting with the new charm-bracelet selection, that should work."

"If you don't mind, I'll bring a cute little Tiffany-style lamp from home to light up that area a bit. It seems a little dark to me," Kiki said.

The younger woman continued to impress. But Brooke chimed in. "True. But are you sure you want to sacrifice your lamp? There's one at Aunt Marsha's we could borrow until we find something you like better."

"I bought it on a whim, and it's never quite fit the rest of my room, so I'm more than happy to donate it. Particularly considering all that you're doing for me," Kiki added.

Brooke touched her arm. "You're wonderful. Then that's what we'll do. If you want to run and get it, I'll finish up what I need to here before Naomi arrives so I can head for the hospital."

"Understood. Back shortly."

Only minutes after she left, Naomi arrived as promised. She'd always triggered thoughts in Brooke of Julia Child due to her statuesque frame and robust laugh. No sooner did she set down her things than she had

Brooke enfolded against her bosom, crooning with maternal love.

"How are you holding up, dear? Did you get any rest last night?"

"Enough," Brooke said, fibbing without conscience. "Are you wearing comfortable shoes? Thank goodness Aunt Marsha has a couple comfortable chairs here. I just can't give you a definite time that I'll be back."

Naomi waved away the concern and tied on one of the shop's green-and-white aprons. "There's nowhere else that I'd rather be. I can feel her here." Naomi glanced around only to look a bit bewildered as her gaze settled on the front of the store. "Well, I used to. What is all this? You've changed things quite a bit."

Brooke followed her focus with new concern. Yes, although the painting had to wait, they were making progress to enhance things by creating groupings so that a customer in a hurry would quickly know where to find everything they had in a particular category; but the basic old-world grace of the store remained recognizable, surely?

"There's her angel display she loves so much." She pointed out sections that were still pure Aunt Marsha. "It's just tiered to show off more of her stock."

"I do think I like that better," Naomi allowed. "It rather looks like the choir at church."

That was exactly what Kiki had told Brooke she was aiming for. "What about the front windows?" She knew Naomi had driven by since Kiki had restyled the displays.

"It's eye-catching and…youthful."

Feeling some dismay at the decline in her enthusiasm, Brooke frowned at the two scenes. "The picnic-patio-party theme is supposed to represent family fun through the summer, and a little romance."

"I don't know that I would call two penguins sipping on straws from the same cup romantic. In fact, I can't tell who's the girl penguin and who's the boy."

"What about the decorated wagon with the stuffed animals holding flags as though they were in a Fourth of July parade?" Brooke asked, thinking Kiki had achieved a miracle getting the not-so-small borrowed unit into the window. One of her brothers and two male friends of hers had helped.

"It would have stronger impact if they were wearing military hats or firemen's gear, or even dressed like colonial people? I'm not saying it's not a good start."

Then why was she frowning? Reminding herself that she was talking to someone who had almost as much emotionally invested in the store as her aunt did, Brooke replied, "Those are quite good points. I'll recommend them to Kiki."

Naomi turned to look at the mannequin hands wearing bright rings and bracelets. "She's definitely got an imagination. I couldn't see myself wearing any of that, though."

"We have to draw in a younger crowd, Naomi. The only times the younger generation needs a florist is for homecoming and prom corsages."

"That's true." With a sigh, Naomi returned to the back and checked the computer and fax machine, only to catch herself. "Look at me. I act like I still belong here."

"You do," Brooke assured her. "In fact, I just printed an order that came via email from Pine Country Real Estate. There it is on the workbench. Mrs. Wyman? She seems to be using some code about what she wants. Can you explain that to me?"

Naomi went to the table in the center of the room and held up the order to better read it under the fluorescent lights. "Oh, sure. Mona Wyman wants something sent to the office. It must be time to drive her husband nuts again. She does that now and again."

Brooke shook her head. "Because?"

"Drew, Mr. Wyman, tends to have a short attention span. So along with her efforts in keeping the romance alive in their marriage, she'll periodically turn the tables to trigger his jealousy."

"But if we send the flowers to her office, how does he learn about her fictitious suitor?"

"Oh, they jointly own and run the agency."

"That would explain it." It was one of the newer of Sweet Springs' four real estate firms. "Then you know what she'll want?"

"Something a bit more provocative than a dozen roses. We always include a tantalizing message on the card, too."

"Wicked woman. And how do you know that it works?" Brooke asked.

"Because Drew Wyman always comes in and tries to find out who sent the things. He's tried to bribe me and Marsha both."

Brooke remained perplexed and a little discouraged. "Why would a woman spend so much money to keep a man with such a short attention span interested?"

"Would you abandon a child with attention deficit disorder? If Baskin-Robbins and Ben and Jerry can think up more flavors of ice cream every year, who are we to think there are only so many ways for a relationship to work? It's not my idea of a way to live—or love—but I've seen them at the grill across the street, and they sure looked like they were having a good time making up."

As Naomi giggled to herself, Brooke thought she would stay single the rest of her life if that was the best she could hope for in a relationship. "So what do you suggest?" she asked her aunt's dearest friend.

"The Hawaiian plant with the *long* stamen." Naomi's eyes sparkled with mischief. "I just have to think of the right notation for the card. With luck he'll sweep Mona out of the office and they probably won't resurface in public until sometime tomorrow."

If it wasn't for the visible order, Brooke would have been suspicious. "I think you told me that story just to get my mind off Aunt Marsha," Brooke scolded playfully.

Smiling, Naomi started searching the supply shelves for the perfect base for her creation. "Don't think I'm nosy, although I am, but how did that move go over the weekend? The last time that young man took so much time off, he had to fly back home to Montana when his father burst his appendix."

"Oh, my!" Brooke knew how dangerous that had been due to a fellow classmate enduring the same thing in grade school. "I didn't know that."

"I'm not surprised." Naomi continued to examine vases. "It all worked out okay, although it was touch and go for a while. My point is that I'm glad you've made the decisions you have, and that you have someone that strong and good-hearted to help you."

"He is that." Unable to resist, Brooke had to ask, "Speaking of strange relationships…do you know much about Liz Hooper?"

The older woman snorted with disdain. "Everyone knows about Liz." Choosing an elegant black vase, Naomi cast her a glance over her glasses. "What brings her up?"

"One of the 'everyone' you mentioned is Gage."

Frowning, Naomi scoffed, "The only way someone like Gage would have anything to do with the likes of her is if she kidnapped, drugged and duct taped him to a mattress." She pointed a blossom at Brooke. "Don't you worry your pretty head about her. If Gage took time away from his practice to help you, he's interested in only one woman and that isn't Liz."

Relieved, Brooke immediately backtracked. "Well, it's not like we're dating or anything—neither of us have time—but he's a good man, and a good neighbor. As such, I worried for him."

Naomi drawled, "Liz and flypaper have a lot in common." She glanced at the clock. "Well, girl, why are you still here when you should be at the hospital?"

"I was waiting for Kiki to return," Brooke replied, although she was admittedly eager to leave. "Charles hasn't arrived yet, and Kiki won't return for another few minutes."

"So what? Whether she told you or not, Marsha will be needing the comfort of your sweet, calm self long before they wheel her to surgery. Get going, child!"

## Chapter 6

Brooke made it to the hospital minutes later, only to learn that her aunt had already been wheeled into surgery! She was told that there was a sudden shift in schedules and Marsha had been bumped forward. Worrying that this had to do with a downturn in her aunt's condition, Brooke was brushed off by the senior nurse at the desk, who said, "Let her surgeon do his job, dear."

Her mind spinning, Brooke retreated to the waiting room. Not even knowing if she had a long wait ahead of her, or an abbreviated one due to bad news, she bought herself time by reading texts and listening to cell phone messages. Since the first was from Gage, she returned it first.

"You're not going to believe this, but they took her early," she told him. "A scheduling change they say.

That's all I know so far," Brooke said, fighting new frustration.

"Wow," he replied. "You're worried she had another setback, aren't you?"

"What other reason could there be, unless another patient was either too weak or died?"

"And they're not going to share that bit of information."

Feeling somewhat better, Brooke reasoned aloud, "Common sense tells me they wouldn't try doing this if she was too weak."

"Keep up that mantra." After a slight pause, Gage added, "I'm afraid things aren't great here, either. Something has happened, but I don't want you to worry."

"What's going on?"

"The guy who did our heavy cleaning… He's been ripping us off. Roy confirmed it this morning when I arrived. I've been tied up with the sheriff and police all morning."

Brooke could hardly wrap her mind around the idea. "Are you all right? Have they arrested him?"

"Not yet, but they're hot on his trail."

"You sound incredibly calm for this kind of news."

"That's because I'm talking to you." Gage's voice went low and soft, like a caress. "My one regret is that this will mean that I'll be late getting there."

"I'm fine. It's more important that things get taken care of there. You aren't holding anything back, are you? You're not in danger?"

"I promise I'm not."

"Okay. Then don't do anything to hurt or endanger yourself, either."

He uttered a brief laugh. "Are you kidding? As soon as the old-timers came in this morning and heard the news, they went right back outside and got their shotguns."

Brooke had seen the line of vehicles parked on the side of the building with their gun racks, proof that this was still Texas in more ways than one, and covered her eyes in a mixture of amusement and concern. "You did talk them into putting them back and locking up, right?"

"Everything is fine. I promise. I'll see you as soon as I can."

That wouldn't be quick enough, Brooke thought after they disconnected. She found herself yearning to be in his arms, to feel his heart beating against hers.

Things got a bit busier soon afterward when several people stopped by—Aunt Marsha's pastor, a pair of friends from her Sunday-school class and the elderly couple from across the street. In between Naomi called, as well as dear gentlemanly Charles, asking if she needed him and Chloe to come sit with her after he did the evening deliveries.

Assuring him that what she needed was for him to go home and rest up for the next day's work, she returned to her pacing, until Naomi checked in again. Brooke was surprised to find that it was closing in on noon.

"Well, hasn't anyone come out to explain things to you?" the frank woman demanded.

"No. And I asked at the desk only three minutes ago, but they insisted that when there was something to say, I'd be told. I don't like this, Naomi. I'm worried."

"Me, too. They run a fine operation there, but you

have to believe that if it was terrible news, they would have had to come tell you. Surgeries are busy places. They can't leave bodies blocking traffic."

"Oh, that's reassuring."

"Wait a few years and you'll get more pragmatic, too. Gotta go—the store phone is ringing and Kiki is on a ladder. Tell that girl she needs to wear slacks if she's going to do that kind of thing. We love you."

Brooke was still mulling over Naomi's call when a tall man in surgeon's scrubs approached her. He had salt-and-pepper hair and an intense look, plus a better tan than George Hamilton and George Clooney combined. For all of his suave appearance, however, he was all business, even if he was kind.

"I'm Dr. Zane. She's stable and in recovery," he began. Then he dropped his voice to where Brooke had to lean forward to hear. "But it was touch and go for a while. I won't mince words—we did lose her at one point."

That revelation so startled her that she didn't have time to emit so much as a gasp. Her mind locked on one thought: *"Aunt Marsha?"*

"She should have had this procedure done months ago," Dr. Zane continued. "Last year would have been better yet. She'd just about worn out her equipment. Didn't she show signs of fatigue or complain of dizziness or breathlessness?"

"Work kept me from getting down here as often as I wanted," she admitted, "but she did sound as though she had more business than she needed or wanted, what with one of the other florist shops in town closing."

"Well, I can't dictate to you, but those grueling days are over for your aunt. She'll need to take it easy as she slowly builds up her strength again. No more standing on her feet for hours. In fact, she either needs to hire someone to run the place for her or sell out completely."

Despite being semiprepared for this news, it hit Brooke as though she'd just driven into a wall at breakneck speed. Naturally, her body reverberated with all that meant, and she was glad she was sitting down.

*Don't try to figure it all out this second.*

Drawing a shaky breath, she asked, "When can I see her?"

Aunt Marsha had died. Brooke needed to see for herself that she really was back and was going to be all right.

"Not tonight. We're keeping her sedated and in ICU. By tomorrow morning things should be more stable where you can visit with her a few minutes at a time. Please dissuade anyone else with good intentions, as well. I'd prefer they wait until next week."

"But you're sure she will pull through?" Given his rigid perspective, Brooke couldn't help but press for positive news.

"None of these intricate cases are without some chance of continued complications or even failure, but she should be fine and lead a mostly normal life. A great deal of this is up to her," the doctor added. "Depression will be something to watch for, although it's less prevalent in women than it is in men. But mechanically, things are operating as stably as they should."

"Mechanically. Doctor, she's not a robot."

"No, she isn't. Remind her of that. Remind her that she has grandchildren to—"

"No, she doesn't."

The doctor paused momentarily and edited himself. "Great nieces or nephews?"

"I'm single, and I have no children yet."

"Then Marsha must treasure having you in her life all the more."

Brooke could only hope that was the case. The doctor's news made her doubt things. Had she been doing everything she could? What was best for her aunt now?

As the tired man rose, Brooke thanked him; however, as soon as he'd departed, she slowly lowered herself back on to the chair. Thank goodness, she was the only one in the waiting room. She needed quiet and time to get through what she'd learned.

*Aunt Marsha had died on the operating table.*

Brooke struggled to take in the news. Her aunt had left this world and she'd had no clue; there had been no sign, as in movies. Had Marsha had an out-of-body experience? Would she remember any of it? Would she be in such a condition now that she wished she'd stayed on the other side?

*She should have had this procedure done months ago.*

Brooke couldn't say how long she sat there, but some activity drew her out of her introspection.

"Brooke?"

At the sound of that wonderfully familiar voice, she looked up to see Gage, his long strides quickly covering the distance from the entryway to the reception area. By the time she could get to her feet, he was wrapping her in his arms.

"Oh, Gage," she whispered, hugging him tight.

"Sweetheart, what is it? Has there been bad news? You look—"

"She's all right. Now." Brooke buried her face against his strong shoulder. "She's in recovery, but they lost her at one point."

He hugged her closer. "I should have been here."

"You couldn't have known."

"You're sure they said she's okay now?"

"That's what Dr. Zane just said. They're keeping her in ICU. They won't let me see her until tomorrow."

"Then why are you still here?"

Brooke couldn't answer that, at least not with any intelligence. "I guess I was hoping that a nurse would sneak me in?"

"They know what they're doing, Brooke. There's a sterilized environment to maintain. Also, considering her age and frail state—"

"That's the other thing. The doctor said that she was almost too late doing this. That was part of the problem. Oh, Gage, that's my fault."

"How so?"

"Who else was going to come and take care of things for her? She was delaying having to ask me in the hopes that the prognosis was wrong, or she had more time. All I kept talking about was how busy I was. My not hearing the worry in her voice could have cost her life."

Gage framed her face with his hands. "Don't do that to yourself. You *are* here exactly when she needed you. Focus on the good news. He says she's going to be fine, right?"

"Not exactly. He said she needs to change her lifestyle. That means returning to the shop is out of the question."

Stroking her back, Gage said, "How long have you been sitting here mulling over all of this?"

"I don't know."

"Come on, it's time to get you home."

"I can't. I should go by the store and—" she looked at her watch "—lock up. That will also save me from having to make two of the numerous calls I'll need to make, and to convince Naomi and Kiki not to try to come to the hospital."

After a slight hesitation, Gage nodded. "Okay, but locking up means exactly that. Everything else can wait. I'll be right behind you to make sure you stick with that plan."

He did exactly that, and he followed her into the store as she passed on the news and answered questions from Naomi, Kiki and Charles, who was just back from deliveries. He was the first to ask about the future.

"What do you think you'll do? You sure have a load of decisions to make. Anything you decide, it's fine with me. I like this little job. It gets me out of the house a bit, but mum's the word, either way. Marsha is like family to me. Her business is her business."

"I appreciate that, and you," Brooke assured him, then included the ladies in her look of gratitude. "I honestly don't know what's going to happen. It's Aunt Marsha's decision to make. One thing is for certain, Newman's has been part of this town for too long to close it."

Even though it was a little earlier than usual, once the others left, Brooke locked up, and once again Gage followed her to the house. As usual, he was proving that he was an absolute rock, and words of gratitude were inadequate. She knew she could cope just fine on her

own if she had to—her father had made sure of that—
but it was so nice not to have to. What a pleasure to
have someone who knew what a long day it had been,
or grasp how debilitating some news was. She could
only hope that she'd given him half as much support
or interest in return.

As Gage closed the gate, Brooke studied his handsome profile with new appreciation. "I'm ashamed
that I haven't even asked how things worked out at
the clinic."

"You had a life-and-death situation going on. I think
that takes precedence."

From the sound of things, he could easily have found
himself in a serious altercation. "Tell me, please?"

"They arrested Vince, but we won't recover much
of what was taken because he'd already sold most of
it. Also, even though he's out of circulation, we had
to go through the inconvenience and expense of having the door locks changed, since we're not sure if he
was working with someone and they'd gotten access
to a key."

"How awful. How is Roy taking all of this?"

As they reached the porch, Gage eased her keys out
of her hand and unlocked the door. "Upset that he'd
spoken up for Vince to help him get another chance.
But as I told him, I would probably have done the same
thing. From here on, though, we need to be a bit more
careful if not skeptical, until people prove they're worthy of as much trust as we gave Vince."

As they entered and Gage turned to shut the door,
Brooke slipped her arms around him, pressing her
cheek against his strong back. "Don't change too much.
You're an inspiring role model."

Gage started to turn and reach for her, but Humphrey sped toward them, bouncing around in welcome and demanding his share of attention.

"Well, hey there, Humph. Good to see you, too," Brooke told him. "Aunt Marsha is going to be okay and you're going to see her soon, how's that for something to celebrate?" As she stooped to give him an enthusiastic petting, he licked her wrist in gratitude. With a laugh, she looked up at Gage. "Did you see that? I think he's starting to like me."

"Big surprise."

"There's a sweet boy. Where's your bowl? Is it time? Let's get your bowl."

"I'll take care of feeding him," Gage said. "That dress is too pretty to get messed up."

"Oh, I can manage," she assured him. "Why don't you take a load off? It's about time I repay you for all the TLC you've given us."

"Next time, or else you're going to ruin my little surprise."

Brooke glanced around. "What surprise?" She didn't see anything unusual anywhere, except for the answering machine light blinking on the kitchen bar, and these days that wasn't unusual at all.

"When I dropped off Humph, I snuck a few things into the refrigerator."

"After the day you had?" Brooke was nothing short of incredulous—and touched. Rising on tiptoe to kiss his chin, she hurried for the pantry. "Thank you. I'll give you free reign of the kitchen in a second. I am going to feed Humph, though."

Of course, she slipped off her heels first. By the time she had Humphrey taken care of and washed her hands a second time, Gage had the table set with cute little cut-glass plates, forks and champagne glasses. As she started listening to the messages on the machine, he brought out the heaping bowl of shrimp on ice.

"You call that a *little* surprise?" she asked, eyes wide.

Gage suddenly looked doubtful. "I forgot to ask if you even like shrimp."

"Any way, any day."

"Great. I could eat my weight of them."

"Oh!" Realizing she was hearing messages from two callers she didn't recognize who were checking on Marsha's condition, she quickly grabbed a pen to scribble down their numbers.

"The choir director at the church and the wife of the manager at the grocery store," Gage told her calmly.

Impressed, Brooke shook her head at herself. "You should have been the one related to her."

"Those two are my patients, too," Gage said, with a shrug. "Wayne's constantly coming in for oatmeal shampoo or cortisone spray for his retriever with the skin allergies, and Vicky raises and shows pygmy goats. When Vicky calls in the middle of the night, I know to rush to the clinic to help with a pregnant goat having trouble delivering in the normal way."

Brooke looked at him with new respect. "I'll bet you know their pets' names, too."

"Well, Sadie is the retriever, but Vicky has had enough goats that if they were reindeer, she could have outfitted four or five of Santa's sleighs."

Laughing, Brooke returned her attention to the machine. The other three calls were from people Brooke finally recognized, and she dutifully, but briefly, checked back with everyone to report the blessed news.

By the time she hung up for the last time, Gage had let Humphrey outside, and had even been outside himself to cut one of Martha's roses to put in a bud vase. The tangerine color was as gorgeous as the sunset promised to be.

"I just want to sit here and absorb this," she told him, after he held her chair for her. "I don't want to embarrass you, but I've been to my share of five-star restaurants and hotels, as well as country clubs and estates, and it's all been nice. Seriously well appointed. So believe me when I say that no one has ever tried this hard to make me feel special."

Beaming, Gage poured the champagne. "And I want you to know that's the best compliment I've ever received." Returning from setting the bottle back in the refrigerator, he sat down beside her and touched his glass to hers. "To good endings."

"Definitely," Brooke murmured. "God bless Aunt Marsha…and you, too. I couldn't have managed without you. Now the challenge will be how to tell her that she can't keep the store, that her own surgeon insists it's too much for her."

"Sleep on it," Gage said. "That was good enough for Scarlett O'Hara, wasn't it?"

After a short, surprised laugh, Brooke made a face. "Not one of my favorite so-called heroines in fiction. She was almost harder on Georgians than General Sherman!"

Grinning, as he spooned a serving of shrimp on to her dish, Gage countered, "But she saved Tara."

"Maybe. Remember, the story pretty much has an open ending."

"At least give your aunt some credit for being able to realize the obvious."

"But she's only seventy!"

"A fragile seventy. Not everyone was meant to labor until seventy-five or eighty, or live to be one hundred."

His calm words and soothing tone did help Brooke relax somewhat. "I know you're right, of course, but I thought the surgery was going to be the hard part. I was wrong," Brooke replied. "What's coming next is *really* the hard part. She thought she was going to pick up life where she left off. The truth is that nothing will be the same ever again."

"It could be even better. Don't you think she would like to have more free time to do things she's been putting off until now?"

"Has she said that to you?"

"Not in so many words, but I've seen and heard disappointment when she couldn't do things offered by the senior center or her church because she had business responsibilities here. She would shrug it off, of course, because she does love her store, but those moments happened nonetheless."

"How did you get so wise?" Brooke asked, in open admiration. "Is it that your Big Sky Country upbringing gave you a clearer, broader perspective?" Having grown up at the knee of a man with two degrees and now an ever-growing fortune, Brooke felt her father's advice was increasingly like acid on a wound.

"I don't know," he admitted. "Maybe. One thing I do know," he continued, raising his glass again, "is that we're being way too serious when what we should be doing is relaxing and having some fun."

"And eating!" Brooke declared, after sipping her wine. "It didn't hit me earlier, but I'm just about starving."

"I knew it," Gage said. "You didn't eat, did you?"

"It would have been an exercise in futility to try. My heart felt all but jammed in my throat most of the time." She dipped a shelled shrimp in cocktail sauce and bit it in half. "I'm going to make up for that. Don't worry." Swallowing the other half of her shrimp, she asked, "So what happens with this Vince character? Will you have to testify against him in court?"

"Ms. One Track Mind."

"Please—I want to know what it all means for you."

"Okay, well, maybe," Gage replied, relenting. "But considering how much evidence we have against him— our CD of some of his activity for one thing—he'll probably be convinced by his attorney to take a plea bargain, which will save all of us time and the county the expense of a trial."

"You don't have to worry about retribution from him or anyone else?"

"If I thought for a second that I would be bringing trouble home to you, or to Marsha, believe me, I wouldn't be here."

His calm words were nothing compared to his intent gaze, and Brooke was immediately contrite. "I never thought— My concern was for you."

"I know. But you need to know that works both ways."

Basking in the aura of intimacy, she sighed with pleasure and enjoyed her wine and her remaining shrimp. Before she knew it, both her plate and glass were empty.

As Gage rose to get the champagne to refill their glasses, she refilled his plate and took several more shrimp for herself. Then, too aware of her tired feet to resist, she put them on the chair across from her own. The move didn't go unnoticed by Gage.

"It's good to see that kitten-got-into-the-cream look on your face." Leaning over to peek, he drawled, "I wouldn't have thought you tall enough to reach that far."

"No short jokes."

"Okay, but—" he refilled their glasses "—after I put up this bottle, you can put them on my lap. You'll find me far more comfortable than that hard chair."

Brooke shook her head adamantly. "Ticklish, can't do it. Won't do it. Don't ask." She shivered and giggled at the mere thought.

"Why, Brooke Bellamy," he drawled, looking amused as he sat down again, "are you getting tipsy? It was only one glass of champagne, but it must have gotten into your system before any shrimp did."

"Mmm…it's such a nice little buzz." With a dreamy smile, she removed her jacket, then shook her hair behind her shoulders before sighing and leaning back in her chair again. "There. Now I don't look or sound like Brooke Candace Bellamy, former math head, as I believe you put it?"

"She's rather special to me, but, no, angel, you don't."

His enthralled look had her reaching over to stroke his arm. "You want to kiss me."

"It's a very good idea."

"You kiss better than anyone."

"Anyone?" Setting his right elbow on the table, he rested his chin in his palm. "You have my undivided attention. Have another sip—or maybe not. Just tell me about your research."

"Don't be so literal. I was only being…"

"Adorable."

In the next second, Gage rose and Brooke belatedly realized that Humphrey was scratching at the back door. *Oops,* she thought, setting her feet back on to the cool wood floor. Maybe she did need to leave that second glass of champagne alone. When Gage kissed her, she wanted to be totally present. Realizing how much she meant that, she rose.

As the basset hound waddled to his water bowl, Gage returned to her and gave her a concerned look. "What is it? Do you need to lie down? I can put away this stuff and lock up for you."

Before he could reach for anything, Brooke slipped her arms around his waist. "The last thing I want is for you to leave. Gage. Please stay."

## Chapter 7

Certain that too much fantasizing had him hearing things, Gage hesitated and searched Brooke's lovely face, looking for something beyond the dreamy invitation he saw there, as heart-thumpingly incredible as that was. He couldn't let himself take this next step if she was going to wake in the morning, regretting what she'd invited.

"Sweetheart, are you sure? I'm no poet. I don't even listen to the radio enough to recite country song's lyrics. But I have had enough late and lonely nights to borrow from one of my favorite actors in a favorite movie. 'I won't stay unless I'm here for breakfast.' Is that what you had in mind?"

Delight brightened the sparkle in Brooke's warm brown eyes. "Oh, I *love* that movie! But if I hadn't had even a drop of champagne, Gage, you know that in good conscience I still wouldn't ask you how you wanted your eggs in the morning."

"*I'll* make breakfast." Instead of laughing, as her clever reply deserved, his mouth went dry as he stroked her delicate cheekbones and the soft swell of her lower lip.

"Then stay," she whispered. "There's nothing I want more."

He took another moment to absorb the words that he'd been aching to hear since her return to East Texas. "If I could stop time right now and hold this moment, I would."

"Really?" Brooke teased. "*This* moment?"

"Behave. I'm doing my best not to fling your hummingbird self over my shoulder and carry you upstairs."

"You keep treating me as though I'm fragile. I'm hardly that."

"You are to me. I'm going to show you."

With that, Gage lifted her into his arms and looked over her to nod at Humphrey. "Bedtime, Humph. Good boy."

As he carried her up the stairs, he liked how she slid her arms around his neck and pressed her cheek against his. That and the soft pressure of her breast against his chest had his heart pounding in a way that had nothing to do with exertion. He had in his arms the one, the woman he wanted more than he'd ever wanted anyone, the one he believed he was meant to spend the rest of his life with. That certainty enveloped him in heady joy, as well as an unparalleled peace.

*Try not to screw this up.*

"Are you still awake?" he whispered near her ear, as he reached the top of the stairs.

"I am," she whispered back. "Surprised?"

"I'm about to genuflect for the first time since I was eleven. So which room do you want me to turn into?"

"First on the right," she said nuzzling his ear.

He did exactly that and proceeded to lay her across the queen-size bed covered with a lavender-and-plum bedspread. The miniblinds were almost shut, casting the room in a romantic amber shadow.

Stretching out beside her, he murmured, "I've made it to the inner sanctum. I think I'm suffering from high-altitude syndrome."

With a soft laugh, Brooke drew him closer. "Kiss me. I'll make it better."

She gave him her mouth, her lips parted in invitation, and he wasted no time in seeking the deeper connection she offered, nor did he hesitate in stroking her. He caressed her shoulder to hip and back again, then her breast. "You're unbelievably perfect, as soft as whatever this dress is made of."

"Silk. I love your hands. They're half again larger than mine, but beautiful. Even with the calluses, which tell me you've worked hard."

Gage eased the zipper of her dress down and slid his hands inside, intent on caressing more of her exquisite skin. "Are they too rough?"

"It's too soon to say."

He loved learning that she had a mix of sweet and saucy in her, and continued to ease her dress off her shoulders and lower, until he could respectfully drape it at the foot of the bed. When he learned her lingerie was of equal excellence, he concluded the old adage about quality versus quantity held true. Her peach-colored bra was lacy and sheer, neither denying him the feel of her heartbeat against his lips, nor the arousing sight that her nipples were already taut. "So dainty," he whispered, his touch worshipping, as was his mouth.

After sating the first wave of his hunger, he removed the bit of allurement, then gazed upon what he'd exposed and concluded that it was a damned good thing he hadn't known about any of this before now. As good as his imagination was, reality was far better, and his breath was unsteady as he exhaled. "Lovely."

He continued to explore and pleasure with his hands and mouth until she was naked, and he couldn't continue resisting her attempts to undress him, as well. "Do you know what it means to me to feel you wanting me, too?"

"Then help me."

He let her go only long enough to slide out of his things, and then rolled onto his back and drew her over him.

With her hair flowing around them, Gage felt his heartbeat threaten the walls of his chest. Giving up on words, he sought a kiss to show her what she was doing to him.

Kissing Brooke was an education in sensuality. He found himself striving to earn new utterances, little sounds she made at various levels of pleasure. He reveled in the erotic tango of their lips and tongues. When they paused, sharing the same shallow breath, he opened his eyes to see her watching him and almost climaxed. Foreplay between them was as perfect as though she was a mermaid and he was the current.

When the need to be inside her threatened his control, he groped for his jeans. Swearing under his breath that he might ruin a moment, he dug into his billfold to draw out a cellophane packet.

"I think this isn't so old that it's unsafe."

He hadn't wanted even that much between them; however, safety and common sense were rote when it came to sex, as far as he was concerned—particularly for her. But he could see all was well in her mind. It was in her eyes and in her touch—they weren't just having sex, they were making love.

"Brooke," he rasped and kissed her deeply. He'd never wanted anyone or anything more and was determined to show her, worship her, bring her as much pleasure as she wanted, or could bear, before taking his own.

Resolve bought him some time, and he renewed his exploration of her sleek, increasingly passion-heated body. Regardless of her denials, she was a delicately built woman, while he was anything but. His conscience wouldn't allow him to cause her discomfort, let alone pain. He might not be the current rendition of the Hollywood playboy, but he knew every bit as much about anatomy, and when his soothing kisses came to test the soft petals between her legs, he was reassured by the damp heat he found there...and beyond.

She showed him with her body and increasingly shallower breaths that it was all good, so good she cried out quickly. His name. He went for broke and relished her fingers burying into his hair and clenching, her entire body clenching, and then she collapsed, trembling.

As he slowly rose above her, she opened her eyes and stared at him. "Tell me," he said.

"I've never felt...more. So wanted.... So cared for."

*So loved?* Because he did. His heart, his whole being

soared in the sensation of it. He wanted this moment to never end, but if it had to, when it had to, he wanted to go to sleep holding her. He suspected he would never know another moment's peace if she wasn't in his arms at the end of every day.

"The best is yet to come," he promised, as he resumed kissing and tasting everywhere he could reach. Her nipples kept drawing his attention. The little buds were nearly as sharp as needles. "You're going to be sore, but I can't stop touching and tasting you," he rasped, caressing her with his thumbs and his mouth, as he sought the tempo that would lead them to a joined ecstasy this time.

Soon, with perfect timing and a dancer's graceful glide, Brooke wrapped her legs around his waist. Gage slipped his hands beneath her hips and buried himself as deeply as she could take him.

"Oh, Gage," she moaned. "You're so right. I love this."

"And this?" he asked, slowly starting to thrust inside her.

Her reply was a whimper, as her body rose with a new wave of sensations taking over her body.

"And this?" As she opened her mouth to gasp, he claimed her lips so as to even absorb her climaxing cry, then poured himself into her.

Brooke yearned to stay in the blissful mist of ecstasy surrounding them for as long as she could. *Fly... Fly...* The sensations reminded her of her first time on a friend's trampoline when she had been five or six and she'd thought she had soared high enough to reach the moon still visible in the morning sky. A child's imaginings and a child's measurements…but it was the last time she'd felt such an affinity between her imagination and her body—until tonight.

That experience had ended badly. She'd soared all right, and shot off the contraption, breaking her collarbone. She'd never been allowed to play at her classmate's home again—the start of her slow but steady retreat from making friends. Tonight had to be the start of a turn in her life path, she resolved. It had to.

She'd lost her virginity in her first year in college—pretty much a forgettable experience—and since then she'd experienced a few pleasant relationships, but never something that spoke to her ability to feel more than contentment. She'd concluded that she was just too left-brained—as Gage had teased—like her father, to feel deeply enough to call it "passion," and yet life had taught her that she was capable of feeling deep grief. She had ached for her mother for years, so then why hadn't she been able to feel anything close to that for a man? Now she understood: she hadn't yet met Gage.

Brooke rubbed her cheek against his, absently wondering if he'd suddenly started keeping an electric razor at the clinic or in his truck. How else could he manage to keep such a clean shave at this hour? Lazily stroking his back, she smiled at the thought that he spent so much time thinking about making himself pleasing to her.

"You know you're asking for trouble, don't you?" Gage murmured, pressing a kiss into her hair.

"I hope so."

He shifted to kiss her again in the curve between her neck and shoulder before rising on one elbow to search her face. It was completely dark now, and the exterior lights timed to come on after sunset offered just enough light to see the wonder on his face, but concern, too.

"You're serious?" he murmured, his hand gently caressing her face like a blind man reading Braille. "It was as good as I wanted for you?"

Fairly certain that she now knew what it would do to him, she purred like a feline and arched against his lower body. That won her a strangled groan, and, in the next instant, he stretched her to her full length, lacing his fingers with hers way over her head.

"Minx. Think you're ready for games already?"

"Okay, maybe not," she gasped, under the full weight of his body.

In the next instant, he rolled to her side but slid one powerful leg between hers to keep her in place. "You're too tempting for your own good." But there was a smile in Gage's voice as he added, "I totally approve of the tousled look."

It was Brooke's turn to groan. "If I have raccoon eyes, I'm running for the bathroom."

"I would enjoy the view.... I *really* would if I could find the damned lights."

Brooke swatted his backside lightly. "Leave them off and stop trying to embarrass me."

"I'm not. I'm just..."

He found the small lamp and switched it on. Its shade was eggplant colored and offered only a subtle glow to the room; however, it was enough so that when Gage turned back to Brooke, he took a slow, shaky breath.

"You make me ache, you're so beautiful."

Caressing his chest, she said softly, "Thank you...

for your skill, too. You made me realize that I've been cheated, and was content to be."

"Sweetheart." Gage took hold of her hand and kissed her wrist. "You're breaking my heart—and giving me murderous thoughts." His gaze swept over her, his blue-gray eyes reflecting his internal struggle between renewing desire and lingering concern. "Are you sure you're okay? I wasn't quite in control as I'd hoped to be."

"I'm perfect."

His expression relaxed into a sensual smile. "You are that."

"And getting thirsty." Once again, she splayed her fingers through his chest hair. "Someone didn't let me finish my champagne."

"You know if someone did, this wouldn't have happened."

"So sexy, and still the dashing gentleman."

As she gently scraped her right index finger over his nipple in retribution, he pretended to look suspicious. "You just want me to get out of this bed so you can get a peek at my awesome backside."

"It felt pretty awesome. Now it might be branded by my nails."

Taking hold of her wrist, he pretended to examine each short-clipped finger. "I've seen newborn kittens with more threatening claws." He playfully nipped at one.

"Fine. I'll get my own glass of champagne." She started to sit up, only to be brought flat against the bedding again.

"The idea of you going down there like that isn't something I want playing in my mind. Ever," Gage all but muttered. "Especially since I didn't think to pull the blinds and curtains. Besides, Humph probably needs to go out again." Sitting up, he reached for his jeans. "Rest up. I'll be back."

Brooke grinned as he left the room and listened to him jog down the stairs. Humphrey roused from his bed and uttered a soft "woof" in greeting. Seconds later, as Gage quietly spoke to him, the back door was opened and the dog trotted outside.

Stretching, Brooke relived what they'd just shared and shivered with the residual memory of Gage climaxing in her body. She closed her eyes and let herself imagine what it would be like to be fertile. Would she feel it the moment that special one sperm found her egg? It was such a crazy thought, since only months ago—after sending Parker away—she'd begun to convince herself that she wasn't meant to have children, didn't want any. However, she understood that now: it was easier to reason that way when you knew that you weren't really loved, let alone in love.

Did Gage want children?

*Stop it! It was sex, you fool.*

Even if it was, it had been the best ever. And the night was young, she realized, glancing at the clock. She wasn't going to waste it.

Scrambling off the bed, she hurried to the bathroom.

She didn't think she'd dozed off, but the next thing Brooke knew she felt a delicious dampness around her left nipple. She smiled, sure it was Gage's mouth after he'd taken a drink of something, only to open her eyes and see it was a droplet of wine sliding from his fingertip.

"That's cold!"

"No, it's irresistible."

He leaned over to lick it off. Sure enough, his tongue was warmer and slightly abrasive against her sensitive skin, made all the more tender from his earlier loving.

Stretching and drawing in a deep breath, she paused. "Oh, God, you smell yummy. What did you put on?"

"Sit up and have some of this."

Now fully awake, Brooke did and accepted one of the glasses of champagne he was holding. "Have I been asleep long?" She glanced over at the clock and saw it had only been about twenty minutes. Strange, she thought. Going by the scent of cinnamon around him, she'd believed it was close to morning.

"Long enough for Humph to enjoy a last stroll around the yard, and me to eat a half pound of shrimp while I waited."

Thoroughly confused, Brooke took a sip of her wine then sniffed again. "I'm not smelling shrimp. I'm smelling…breakfast?"

"Because I brought you this." Reaching behind him, Gage picked up a slice of toasted cinnamon bread from a saucer and brought it to her lips. "I thought it would help soak up the alcohol faster than the shrimp."

"Bless you." Brooke took an eager bite and moaned her appreciation as she chewed. Quickly swallowing, she opened her mouth like a little bird. "More."

He laughed softly. "I think I've finally figured out what to make you when I think you need feeding."

After two more bites, Brooke sighed with pleasure. "A picnic in bed…. How fun."

"I can see you missed out on a lot of spoiling," Gage told her. He nodded to her glass. "Sip. You were thirsty, remember?"

She did and was finally awake enough to connect his nakedness with his intent to stay. As her heart did its increasingly familiar flutter, she asked, "So you locked up?"

"I did."

"Thank you," she murmured, glancing at him from beneath her lashes. "Um…with your truck still in the driveway, tongues are bound to be wagging by morning."

Slowly nodding, Gage watched her, his expression surprisingly closed. "I thought we covered this ground already?"

"No, we agreed you should be here for breakfast. I guess… I must have thought you'd put your car in your driveway."

"Would that make you feel better?"

Realizing what he was thinking, she leaned over to kiss him. "It doesn't matter, as long as no one says something ugly to Aunt Marsha. I don't want her upset, particularly while she's recovering."

"Do you think you can keep us a secret for that long?"

She knew what he was really asking, and he had a right to an answer. They both knew her aunt had been doing plenty of matchmaking and should be the last one surprised at her success. However, Aunt Marsha was from another generation. She wouldn't take kindly to hearing about a blatant affair going on in her own house, not from her customers, let alone her church friends.

"No," she admitted. "*If* I'd thought that far. All I knew tonight was that I needed to be with you."

"And now?"

"I want you even more."

Gage stroked the soft swell of her left breast, his expression relaxing into a smile. "Usually it's guys who are so succinct and frank."

"I'm being honest. I thought you would appreciate that."

"Oh, I do." He took another sip of his wine before setting down his glass. Then he set hers beside it. "It helps me gauge how to finish undermining your remaining defenses."

Every inch of Brooke's body tingled with anticipation. Even so, the cinnamon bread continued to play with her senses, and she gave into the urge to peek around him at the plate. "Does your strategy leave me with time to finish that?"

"Nope." Gage brought her against his already aroused body. "You're too irresistible for your own good."

"Okay," she sighed, slipping her arms around his neck. "So I'll have it for dessert."

"Angel, *you* are dessert."

## Chapter 8

"How do you like it?"

Early on Monday, a little more than a week after her latest surgery, Marsha was transferred to continue her recuperation and therapy at the Sweet Springs Assisted Living and Nursing Facility. The relatively new business was a sprawling residence for people in better-than-average health who just couldn't maintain their own homes any longer, as well as those who still needed therapy or other around-the-clock nursing care. Brooke thought the one-story dwelling, shaped like a six-pronged star, was clean and bright. So far, the staff she'd met were friendly and caring, too.

"It's very nice, but can I afford it?" Marsha whispered as though afraid someone might be eavesdropping.

Since she had long been doing her aunt's accounting, Brooke nodded with confidence. "Right now your

Medicare and supplemental insurance are covering things fine. If you think you'd like to move in permanently into the livelier wing, we could sell your house, or your business, or both. There's also the sale of the commercial property to consider, too."

As expected, the older woman looked startled. Brooke knew she would be, but since Marsha had brought up the subject, it was as good a time as any to start some kind of dialogue.

"But all of that is your inheritance!" her aunt insisted. "I can't take that away from you."

Brooke sat down on the pretty floral upholstered couch and patted her hand as she rested in the wheelchair. "Do you think I want to see you scrimping when you deserve to be comfortable? While I appreciate your intent, Aunt Marsha, I'm young and stable financially. There's plenty of time for me to make whatever I'll need for the future."

"But sell the house?" Her aunt seemed to have gotten stuck on that aspect. "I don't suppose I'm surprised that you'd say that about the business, but the house? It's part of your heritage."

So was the other house that she'd grown up in, Brooke thought with some cynicism, and her father had had no problem selling it to move to Houston. Of course, she wasn't about to repeat anything of that to her aunt. The poor dear was rattled enough.

"There's the crib I used and your mother after me, before it was yours," Marsha continued. "I'd hoped someday it would hold your children. Then there are quilts our mother made. I always thought you'd raise your family there and now hoped you'd bring them to visit me here…if I'm still around by then."

"And I'd hoped we would live together while you recovered," Brooke said gently. "But you heard what the doctor said. You'll have a four-to six-month recuperation period with frequent doctor visits, as your heart adjusts. Then there's the therapy for your hip, and the osteoporosis to deal with. Your heart doctor told you that you can't lift anything heavier than your purse anymore, and stairs are out of the question. So returning to the house just isn't an option."

Her aunt's eyes filled with tears. "Well, if we sell, where will you live before returning to Dallas? What about all that's in the house? And *what's* to come of dear Humphrey?"

Brooke knew it had only been a matter of time before they got to the matter of her four-legged companion. "Dallas is way off, if not off the table entirely, and Humphrey is one happy guy. He'll come visit you soon, I promise. And if you behave and do what the therapist and nurses tell you, it might be safe for you to come home for Sunday brunch."

Her aunt gave her a confused look. "What's going on with you? Dallas off the table? You always have to have every *i* dotted and *t* crossed before you make any decision. You don't like things left hanging."

Knowing she needed to be more careful, Brooke said, "That's because this isn't about me. This is about you and what you want and need. In the early days after you broke your hip, you told me that you weren't looking forward to coming home to that big house and having all of the cleaning and caretaking to deal with."

"Who knows what I said, they had me on so many medications. I might have managed…eventually."

"You couldn't. And your golden years shouldn't be

about cleaning. Naomi told me that just yesterday you two talked with some of your friends about taking some trips that the bank offered, not only what your church arranges."

"Well, I'm going to call Naomi and tell her that she has a big mouth," her aunt muttered. "She knows that I have responsibilities with the store even if it was to be put up for sale, which I'm not saying it will be."

Sensing that things were about to get bogged down by one of her aunt's occasional streaks of stubbornness, Brooke decided to throw her a little curve ball to get her focused again. "What if I buy your business?"

Her aunt all but gaped. "Brooke, you're confusing me now. Why should you buy what I wanted to give you?"

"Because first of all, I don't need that kind of generosity, and second, your health dictates that you can't afford to just give it to me," Brooke said gently. "You need the income from the sale. What's more, I could use the purchase to offset some of my gains."

Her aunt grew silent for a few moments as she thought about that. "Are you saying that, in a way, by selling to you, I would be helping you?"

"You would," Brooke replied, hoping her aunt believed that and it would help her make up her mind.

Marsha touched a hand to her temple and pondered the matter. "Naomi did tell me there are a considerable number of changes at the store. You did more than just redo the front windows."

Pursing her lips, Brooke replied, "Naomi is going to find herself fired."

"You can't fire her. She's retired."

"You know what I mean." Shaking her head with

exasperation, even though she'd known all along that Naomi's devotion was to her aunt, she explained, "Yes, I've been having fun with Kiki, and we're starting to see a new wave of customers. Teenage girls. Young professional women."

"I never gave you permission to do all of that."

"Maybe not, but if your health situation got even worse and you had to sell the place to a stranger, these things would draw more commercial attention, too."

"Oh." Her aunt fingered her light-knit pink cardigan and brushed away invisible lint from her dusty pink slacks. "You always did have a good head for business, Brooke. But what about your father? If you stay here much longer, he's going to come and give me an earful for ruining your life."

That was entirely possible, and she couldn't deny it gave her some unease, but she stated firmly, "My decisions are mine to make." Nevertheless, Marsha did know her father only too well. He would bust a vein if he had a clue as to what Brooke was contemplating doing. "Thankfully, he's out of the country again." And hopefully he would stay gone long enough so that, once he returned, there would be nothing he could do about any of it.

Although looking more relieved, Marsha still hadn't run out of questions. "Where's Gage been? I'd feel better if I knew what he had to say about all of this."

Something about the way her aunt kept plucking away at that nonexistent lint told Brooke that Naomi had been talking about more than changes at the store. Since she and Gage had been together each night since her aunt's surgery, Brooke knew it was time to be up front about things—but in her own way.

"Gage is very supportive about whatever I do."

Her aunt slid her a disbelieving look. "So if you told him that you were moving back to Dallas, he would do handsprings at your going-away party?"

"Aunt Marsha…if you don't tell Naomi to quit tattling, I will. Yes, we are seeing each other, but that's all I'm saying. It's our business."

"Naomi didn't tell me that," her aunt replied with a dismissive wave. "Liz Hooper did."

"Excuse me?"

"She was here visiting… I don't know who. Anyway, she heard I was here, so she stopped by, happy to run her mouth. That one never has anything nice to say about anyone." Marsha gave Brooke a bemused look. "Why don't you just say that Gage has been staying at the house with you? I'm so glad. You've been looking far less stressed and lonely these days."

Brooke couldn't believe her ears. "You're not upset with me?"

"You're an adult, dear, and this is the twenty-first century. Besides, Gage is a wonderful man. I couldn't be happier for you both."

Brooke was afraid her aunt was reading too much into things and immediately demurred. "Really, Aunt Marsha, it's too soon to even think what you're thinking. *You* are my priority, as is keeping everything going smoothly to make your life as comfortable as possible."

Looking far less unnerved than she had when they'd first wheeled her into her new quarters, Marsha sighed. "Don't think I'm not grateful. The truth is that I don't deserve you."

"Yes, you do, and it's my pleasure. When Mother died, life would have been far more difficult without you helping me. Reciprocating allows me to show you that."

"You're a dear girl, Brooke." Marsha reached over and patted her hand. "I couldn't be prouder of you than if you were my own daughter. As for the business and everything— Well, you know best. I'll go along with whatever you decided. Just watch out for Liz Hooper. I think she might be the one person in town who isn't happy you're back."

On the drive to the shop minutes later, Brooke felt as though she'd turned another corner—one that was going to renew her sense of empowerment. While she hadn't expected her aunt to take the news about Gage as well as she had, she was delighted about that, as well. Everything seemed to getting on the right track again.

Brooke had another idea gelling, too, but it had been too early to share it with Aunt Martha. She didn't even tell Kiki when she arrived at the shop; however, seeing that they were alone, she did update the young woman, whom she was beginning to see as her protégée, on her plans to purchase the business from her aunt.

"I have a lot of plans for us, so first and foremost, it's time to start thinking about hiring someone to do arrangements full-time," she announced. "By chance do you know anyone who might be interested and qualified?"

"Funny you should mention that," Kiki replied, after enthusiastically applauding Brooke's news. "There was a young girl here a few days ago—goodness, it might have been when Marsha's surgery was going on—and she inquired about a job doing exactly what you're talking about. If memory serves, her husband is a radiologist at the hospital. She seemed sweet, and I took her name and number, but I was so busy, I think I just added it to everything else that I've been piling up on the desk. Let me look." She fretted under her breath as she sifted through junk mail, old catalogs and phone messages from salespeople that weren't emergencies. "I hope I didn't lose it."

"Well, at least you know where her husband works," Brooke replied. "Maybe we can get him to pass on a message to her." Brooke thought the girl sounded exactly like who they were needing. "Did she seem as though she was legit and serious about the business?"

"She was more than that. She had a little photo album. Nice stuff." Kiki gave Brooke a confused look. "I thought Naomi was back to almost full-time?"

"No, Naomi is definitely retired now." Effective immediately, Brooke thought, although she did not blame the older woman for her devotion to Aunt Marsha. But she wanted to be able to know she had her own loyalty among employees. "She and my aunt intend to travel. She was only filling in as a favor to Aunt Marsha."

"Then all the more reason to hope I can find— Here it is!" From nearly the bottom of the stack of papers, Kiki drew out a slip of yellow notepad paper. "Hoshi Burns. I knew her first name was unusual. Do you know anyone with that surname in the area?"

"I don't. They're apparently transplants due to her husband's work. I wonder what Hoshi means?" Brooke said.

"Star," Kiki told her. "I was curious, too, and asked. She's my age. Is that a problem?"

"Not if she's half as talented as you are," Brooke assured her.

Beaming, Kiki handed Brooke the phone. "Then you'd better call. Chances are she's already found herself a position."

It turned out that Hoshi had been turned down at the other shops in town, so she was more than grateful to get Brooke's call. They arranged for her to come down in the next hour, and Brooke put the two orders that had come in while she was at the assisted living facility on the table. Her plan was to ask Hoshi to complete the two arrangements, and if they were satisfactory, she would offer her the job.

In less than fifteen minutes, a petite young woman with an ear-length gleaming black bob and wearing a pressed white blouse and black slacks with ballet-slipper-type flats came in, looking nervous but eager.

"Mrs. Bellamy, I am Hoshi Burns. Thank you kindly to invite me."

Brooke liked her on sight—they were the same size, and there was a quiet dignity underscoring Hoshi's professional demeanor that she hoped spoke to some pride in her skills. "Call me Brooke, please. And I'm not married." She led her to the table and showed her the two orders. "I see you brought your photos of your work. I'm looking forward to looking at them while I give you a chance to show me what you can do. These two orders that came in a little while ago are selections from the florist association's fairly precise styles. Do you think you could duplicate them?"

The girl looked at the catalog photos, then inspected the glass cooler in front. "Oh, yes, thank you. I worked

in Seattle before we came here, and I know this catalog. I can do this."

As she set to work, Brooke watched, enjoying the
young woman's sure but graceful movements. "If you
don't mind my asking, what made you move from the
North Pacific down here?"

"My husband, Sam, was not happy in the city, and
the weather was so gray. We like it very much here and
will save to buy a home and land for a garden, and to
start a family."

"In that order?" Brooke teased gently.

Hoshi lowered her eyes, but her smile was sweet.
"Maybe it is not possible to wait." But on the heels of
that, she looked anxious. "It would not affect my work,
Ms. Brooke."

"I'm not worried," Brooke replied, getting increasingly good vibes from the girl.

Hoshi worked with speed and deftness, and in what
would have taken Brooke an hour and Naomi nearly
that, she had perfected the arrangement so it looked
exactly like the photo in the FTD catalog. To Brooke's
increased pleasure, she was equally successful with the
other arrangement.

"Well, we would be proud if you could join us,"
Brooke said, having already perused her photos. Ex-
plaining what the position offered in salary, she asked,
"So now the question is how is your schedule?"

"Whatever hours you can give me. When you called,
I was about to take a job cleaning motel rooms," Hoshi
said.

Brooke thought of those delicate hands being bru-
talized by harsh cleansers, even if she did wear gloves,
and said, "I think we can spare you that. You can stay

and finish today if you're free, or if not, maybe you can stay long enough for Kiki to start showing you around and explaining all that we offer. She handles the front of the store, but I'm a firm believer in understanding all parts of what makes a business operate. If you already have other plans, maybe you can start at eight tomorrow?" While they had been talking, Kiki had taken another two orders over the phone, and Brooke all but held her breath hoping.

"Oh, I would be very happy to start immediately." The young woman clapped her hands, then bowed her head. "*Arigato*. I am deeply grateful."

"Believe me," Brooke said, with a pleased smile, "you're the gift, as far as I'm concerned."

"I'm telling you," Brooke said to Gage much later that evening, "I was blown away at how skilled those dainty fingers are. And what an eye she has. She's going to bolster our reputation to new heights in no time. Her kind of talent belongs at the finest metropolitan shops. Fortunately, Hoshi and her husband are looking for a different kind of environment."

"Spectacular," Gage said, his gaze radiating pride as much as pleasure. "This is the most excited I've seen you since Kiki sold out on her perfume faster than a banana has shelf life."

"That's because she is the equivalent of Kiki in her own right. Get this—she's been trying to establish a little side business in bonsai plants. She's had a little attention on Craigslist, some nice feedback on Pinterest. I told her to bring in a piece or two and we'd put them in the arbor area of the store by the fountains.

We always have customers looking to give plants instead of flowers."

Gage leaned back against the doorjamb, crossed his arms and legs at the ankles, and grinned. "You're starting to have a good time."

That had Brooke pausing, only to give him a sheepish grin. "I am. This kind of thing—administrating, supervising, directing, overseeing operations, keeping track of the financial results of what I put in motion—this uses my real skills and experience."

"That calls for a celebration," Gage replied. Having more calls to make after closing the clinic, he'd jogged over as soon as he'd had a shower at his place. She was just finishing up doing the store's daily bookkeeping in the front parlor that she was using as an office. "Are you ready for a glass of wine or something?"

"Wine for me." Turning off the desk light, she followed Gage to the kitchen. Humphrey had already said his hellos and was back in his bed by the stairs. "Something else happened today," she said, as she watched him move comfortably around the room. "Aunt Marsha knows about us—about us spending nights together."

Gage gave her a bemused look. "Didn't we agree this wouldn't stay a secret for long?"

"That's not the point. The point is who told her."

"The sweet old dinosaurs across the street?" he said, with a tilt of his head. When Brooke shook her head, he narrowed his eyes. "Naomi."

"Naomi did her share of enlightening my aunt. But no, it was Liz."

That had Gage's handsome face growing annoyed and worried as he eased one of the two glasses of wine toward her. "That's not good. I mean, I know Liz has been angling for my attention, but I thought after my last polite brush-off, she was getting the hint."

"That doesn't mean that she can't try to get at me for interfering with her plans." Sipping the lush cabernet, Brooke added with a wicked glint in her eyes, "You'd better be worth this trouble."

Gage remained serious. "I'll have a word with her."

"Don't you dare," Brooke replied. "Let's just hope that she's gotten this out of her system and moves on."

Although he looked doubtful, Gage asked, "How did Marsha take the news?"

"Extremely open-minded for someone of her generation. On the other hand, despite what Liz said, we have been as discreet as possible."

"No racing naked around the yard and starting to undress each other on the front porch in our eagerness to get at each other."

No, Brooke thought, not on the front porch, but their kisses had caused a few close calls in back. As her body responded to those memories, she changed the subject. "How was this evening? Was it really just herd inoculations?" When he inclined his head, Brooke sighed with relief. She was finding that sometimes he tried to avoid telling her some grim news by using that safe answer. "You are the hardest laboring man that I know."

"Oh, I think there are a few people who beat me— but they don't enjoy it as much as I do. Except when it takes me away from you too much. It's a good thing that you're not one of those people who goes to bed at sunset."

"Just don't ask me to sit on the back porch with you now," she warned him. "At this hour, I'm not offering my body to mosquitoes."

"That's okay. That's not where I want your body anyway." Closing the distance between them, Gage angled his head for a slow, searching kiss. "I like this," he said, skimming his fingers over her black satin thigh-length sleep shirt whose diagonal neckline exposed one shoulder.

"I knew there was a lecher hidden under all that teddy-bear manner," she purred. "It's about time you confess."

"Come sit on my lap and I will. Better yet, come upstairs."

She laughed softly, enjoying this playfulness. "You know, I'm beginning to think you don't even own a bed."

"Of course I do."

"I've never seen it. In fact, you've yet to invite me into your house. For all I know, you could have all kinds of weird stuff over there."

Clicking his teeth, he said in a surprisingly good Eastern European accent, "You only have to worry about me when the moon is full." Growing more serious, he then admitted, "The reason I haven't asked you over is because I sensed how fragile this thing between us was and I wanted to let you set the pace. I thought urging you to come over would only scare you away."

Seeing the irresistible mix of boyish uncertainty and mature yearning in his eyes had Brooke closing her eyes to appreciate the moment.

"I'm still not doing this right," he muttered, clearly misreading her. "I'm taking too much for granted. I should be wining and dining you. Taking you for long rides to show you my favorite places and letting you show me yours. But my work doesn't allow for me to get that far from town because an emergency might come up."

"I know your profession demands a lot from you, Gage. And yours is a noble calling, so I can't resent sharing you for good causes."

Looking relieved, Gage said, "That's good. Very good. So you'll like my news that I'm looking into hiring another vet?"

That was surprising and welcome news—if it meant they could have more time together. "Do you really want to do this? I know you could use the relief, but if you're thinking about this mostly because of me—?"

"To be honest, both." Gage put down his glass and then hers, and slipped his arms around her waist. "We can't really develop this relationship if I can only give you a few hours here and a few there."

"Who's complaining, since most of that time is in bed?"

"I need you, not sleep." Proving it, he closed his mouth over hers and kissed her as though it had been a week, not twelve hours.

Within seconds, Brooke found herself lost in the sensual dance they were developing that was uniquely theirs. He leaned back against the counter and drew her between his legs, his hands cupping her hips and rocking her against him in the same erotic way his tongue was stroking hers.

When he broke the kiss, he leaned his forehead against hers. "The area is growing and so is the town, and only one other of the area clinics offers 24/7 service. They have a big staff, and even they're being run ragged. I've had to limit my around-the-clock service to long-term clients. Yeah, I'd like to build on our staff."

"Fair enough. I would feel guilty otherwise."

"Because you still intend on leaving someday?"

This was the moment they'd been inching toward since she'd first asked him to stay the night. Then, Brooke hadn't been totally ready to face what that meant. She still wasn't, or rather, there was still a great deal to work through; however, she knew it was time to give him some reassurances, too.

"Gage," she began slowly, choosing her words carefully, "if I wanted to get back into 'the game' as I know you see it—my father sure does—I would still need to delay that by months due to my aunt's health and everything. At least through the rest of this year. But… I've been talking to her about options, too. I've even surprised myself by some of the ideas that have popped into my mind."

"You have my undivided attention if you're looking for a sounding board," Gage said.

"Well, this is just a brainstorm, mind you. This is the part that you really are the first to hear about."

"I'm honored."

His caresses made it difficult for her to stay on subject, but Brooke knew that he was trying to seduce every thought out of her head. Out of necessity she eased from his grasp, picked up her glass and began pacing around the kitchen to gather her thoughts.

"Did you know that Aunt Marsha owns pretty much half of that block she's in downtown? That there's an entire second story of space that isn't being used properly in all but two of those buildings?"

"Somewhat, yeah. My schedule keeps me from attending enough chamber and city-council meetings to get it all straight." Gage tilted his head. "So what are you thinking? To fix it up and sell it to where there's double or triple the square footage than what she had before? You'll get her a good price by doing that."

"Actually, I was going to buy the whole thing myself, do the repairs and then lease the space. From what I can tell, the flooring is solid. I'm less certain about the electrical situation and the plumbing. My thinking is that if I could find a few more talented entrepreneurs like Kiki and Hoshi, we could fill the upper floral storage space with enough products to create a whole new retail marketplace. And I'd love to see another restaurant come in on Main Street. Something that won't compete with what's already available."

"I wish you could see your face," Gage said, smiling. "You're literally blossoming into some kind of fairy godmother, minitycoon in front of my eyes."

Encouraged by his enthusiasm, she continued, "Hardly that, but helping the community keep evolving to its full potential appeals. The challenge will be to convince Aunt Marsha to let *me* buy the properties in order to do these massive changes. She thinks everything should be my inheritance, but she can't afford to be that generous. You can just imagine her reaction when I told her that I need to sell this place so she can have that assisted-living suite yet travel, too."

"Hold it. Hold it." Gage paused, taking in her words.

"Your house is on the market and now you're putting this place up for sale?"

"I can't see any way around it. Most of her assets are in real estate."

"And where will you live if both sell tomorrow?"

"I...haven't gotten that far yet," Brooke admitted with a merry laugh.

Gage scowled. "Well, I have. You'll come stay with me."

Brooke had begun to go hug him and stopped in mid-step. Something had gone almost deathly still inside her. *Oh, God,* she thought. He was just being his big kind and generous self, as always. Only...in that instant, she'd heard her father's voice dictating to her, not his.

"That came out wrong," Gage said with a groan. "I all but barked an order at you. Don't deny it, you've gone ghost-white on me."

She sighed and nodded. "Maybe a little. It's not your fault. Listen, it's too soon to worry about any of this. Aunt Marsha may suffer a strong case of sentimentality and resist me, or hate my ideas for her properties. After all, she's still fretting about Humphrey's future, even though I assure her daily that we're getting along so much better."

Gage abruptly reached for her hand. "I need to show you something. C'mon, Humph."

Incredulous, Brooke held back. "Gage, it's nearly ten o'clock, and I'm not dressed."

"It's dark, and we're going next door, not to city hall. Grab that flashlight by the door to see where you're stepping."

As they hurried from her yard to his with Humphrey happily leading the way, Brooke practically had to jog in her flip-flops to keep up with Gage's long-legged strides. "I was only kidding about you not having a bed."

"I know. But it's more than that and you know it."

They reached the sidewalk leading to a patio and porch, every bit as appealing as her aunt's. Also an older building, Gage's house was colonial in design, a boxy main structure with smaller additions branching from it, in a manner that the early Americans had used as family expansion and other needs warranted. Two stories high and painted a country blue, the back had the same white square pillars that supported the front porch, and a picket-fence-style railing. It was a lot of house for a bachelor, unless one was buying it simply as an investment, and Gage wasn't that kind of man.

The hydrangea bushes that Brooke admired from afar ran the length of the porch and surrounded the brick patio where a stainless BBQ and large chiminea kept company with a picnic table and other lawn furniture. "You haven't had a chance to use that much," Brooke said, as they passed the area.

"I'll be throwing a pretty good size cookout for the Fourth, as a thank-you to clients."

"How thoughtful—and generous."

Humphrey scampered up the stairs as though he was heading for his own back door, and they followed. On the back porch was more inviting furniture and two rockers like the set of four on the front porch that Brooke had noticed every time she pulled into her aunt's driveway.

"Does Aunt Marsha know where you hide your extra key?" Brooke asked, trying to tease the small frown of concentration from his handsome face.

"I don't do that, but I'll be happy to give you one if you'll accept it."

He didn't wait for a reply, instead unlocked the door and turned on the inside light. Then he stepped aside for her to enter. Not surprisingly, Humphrey beat her to it.

"Oh, wow," Brooke said, taking in the open-style kitchen with the high ceiling, big stainless-steel hood over the range, granite countertops and stainless-steel appliances. The cabinetry was white, and the back-splash tiles were silver, pewter and gold glass. "I never expected this contemporary style, and yet it's so bright and welcoming."

Gage looked relieved. "I thought the first thing you'd do was make fun of my having the TV in the kitchen."

It was on the kitchen bar facing the stove and sink. "I might if there's also one in the bathroom." It made sense being where he had it, since this is where he probably spent most of his time other than when he was sleeping. He just wasn't a couch potato kind of guy. She eyed him with new curiosity. "I don't even know if you like to watch the business shows in the morning or catch up on sports scores or what?"

"Also the local farm-and-ranch report. If there's time."

"I should have guessed."

The rest of the downstairs consisted of a formal dining room—empty—a living room and family room—almost as bare—his office, a sizable laundry/mudroom and full bathroom. "This makes my little house in Dallas look like an office cubicle." And it was so sadly barren that her voice echoed back at her.

"You haven't seen anything yet." Getting a dog biscuit from the pantry, he gave it to Humphrey, then gestured for Brooke to take the lead up the stairs.

At the top of the hardwood staircase, she saw more doors than were at her aunt's second story. One by one he showed her the bedrooms, and each was empty until they reached one with a simple king-size bed and chest.

"For your family?" she asked.

"On the rare occasion any of them come down here." Gage gestured back down the hall. "See? Plenty of storage room."

Instead of responding to that, she pointed to the door at the end of the hall. "The den of iniquity, I presume?"

"Help yourself," he murmured with a wry smile.

The door was open, and she marveled that the room was easily double the size of the others. Brooke wasn't surprised to see the king-size bed; his long-legged body needed nothing less. Considering the direction the house faced, it got sun most of the day, so she liked the deep ocean-blue walls and the rest of the furniture with its rustic wood and black-iron hinges and handles. "This is so your size," she mused. "But no art? No plants?"

"I'm not here enough to care," he said, glancing around. "That could change, though." Abruptly spinning around, he swept her into his arms, easily lifting her high to gain quick access to her lips. After one urgent kiss, he groaned, "God, Brooke, hear what I'm telling you. I want to make love to you here, and watch the late afternoon sun turn your body golden, and, too, when a full moon makes your skin compete with the most lustrous pearls the sea ever produced."

As touched as she was enchanted, she noted softly, "There's not going to be another full moon for three weeks. Do I have to wait that long?"

"Sweet heaven, no."

As hungry as his first kiss had been, his second was ravenous. Brooke responded with equal need, ready to be transported to whatever passionate destination he wanted to take her to. Once again, they were shortcutting past things that needed discussing, but she was in his arms, and that created an incredible trust factor that made her believe everything was going to be all right.

Gage sat down on the bed, covered with gray sheets, the color of a mourning dove, and equally as soft. With her on his lap he buried his hands in her hair to hold her still for the kind of tender ravaging that had left her breathless and writhing against him numerous times since their first night together.

Stroking his nape and back, Brooke pressed her breasts against his chest, seeking relief from the need building there. Feeling how quickly he became aroused, she immediately started tugging off his T-shirt.

"I can't believe how fast you go to my head," he rasped.

"And other places."

"It's all the same," he drawled. "Where you're concerned, everything I am is all targeted there."

As soon as she pulled his shirt over his head and tossed it aside, Brooke reached for her short gown. "Help me get this off."

"With pleasure."

The moment the shiny scrap of material joined his shirt, Gage rolled her onto the bed and began an avid exploration of her body, which he'd come to know as well as his own. Caught up in the sensations of his magical touch, she barely felt him slide off her satin panties. Then he withdrew momentarily to finish undressing. It took him slightly longer to get out of his jeans because he wasn't wearing briefs, and he was already fully aroused. When he succeeded, though, he stretched out beside her on the cool sheets. "If I could have one wish, it would be to have a whole weekend to do nothing but adore you. Who am I kidding?" he amended immediately. "Anything less than a week would be a wasted wish."

"That is almost too tantalizing to imagine." She reached down to glide her hand over him, loving the look of pleasure that washed over him, just as much as she enjoyed feeling how powerful and hot he already was.

"Right answer. Come here, sweetheart," he said, rolling on to his back and drawing her over him. "I can't wait another minute for you."

Their seductive dialogue temporarily ended then, or rather it became a series of sighs and groans of pleasure as they focused on how to quickly bring each other to the point of ecstasy as this moment demanded. She'd never believed it possible to nearly climax from having her breasts caressed by his hands and mouth, but he proved it to her, while he could be made to shudder with desire from the mere feel of her teeth scoring the muscles of his thighs.

When he desperately drew her up in order to probe her moist center, she eagerly sat up and lured him deeper. Closing her eyes and letting her head fall back, she whispered, "That's perfect."

"Yes, you are," Gage replied, his hold tightening on her hips. "Do it, angel. Take us there."

And she did.

## Chapter 9

"You look too happy for a guy working so much," Roy Quinn said to Gage the following Monday morning.

Gage covered another yawn before accepting the large mug of black coffee from his friend and employee. Smiling sheepishly, he replied, "Well, it's to be expected when you try to cram as much work and living into a weekend that you can."

Roy had accompanied Gage on two of the three ranch calls that weekend and assisted in two more emergencies at the clinic. In between, he and Brooke had visited with her aunt, done some yard work, grilled a few fantastic meals and made love as often as possible. Best of all, they'd fallen asleep in each other's arms every night. Nevertheless, it was increasingly apparent that he needed more for Brooke. Heck, he thought, he needed more for himself.

With a wave to the old-timers in the corner, he jerked his head, indicating that Roy should follow him to the back. There he leaned against a counter and confided in the man who would ultimately be almost as affected by this decision as he himself would.

"Roy, this weekend showed us once again that we're losing ground trying to juggle everyone's needs with just the two of us operating here, so I'm going to accelerate my plans to bring in another vet—even consider a partnership if that's what it takes—and maybe add an intern, or at least a certified technician to help us out. You know I've wanted that position for you, but you're so damned intimidated by the requirements—"

"You know I barely made it through high school, Doc, and that's been over three decades."

"Try selling that excuse to someone who doesn't know about your military service, or hasn't watched you cope with all the paperwork and regulations the state and federal government constantly throw at us. And you're as good with a computer and our software programs than most anyone who comes through that door looking for work."

"Well, I don't have the associate's degree the position requires and I'm too old to go back to school now."

"I can't make you. I accept that." Thinking, Gage sipped at the coffee again, only to rub at the back of his neck. "The fact is, you could use some help yourself."

Roy's dark eyes widened. He didn't often look at a loss for words. A swarthy man with serious whiskers and a shock of black hair that was always slicked back with some product or other to keep it under control,

Roy had intimidated a few women with car trouble the few times he'd stopped to render aid, especially at night; however, he was a quiet, gentle soul, admittedly crusty on the outside, but with a marshmallow interior.

"You know, Doc, funny you should be saying all this, because something came up yesterday, so I guess now is as good a time as any to throw an idea your way. I have someone in mind who could more than carry her share of work around here. Actually, she was primarily looking to relocate her grooming business."

Gage frowned, wondering if Roy had only heard what he'd wanted to hear—and wondered why? Had the fifty-year-old bachelor finally met someone to turn him inside out the way Brooke was doing to him? Sure, the clinic cared for many small breeds of dogs that needed constant attention. But his first priority was to find another vet. "We could probably do that after we find someone to split the main work with me. Do you need a rush answer?"

Roy looked something between worried and apologetic. "I think so."

His cryptic answer triggered more of Gage's curiosity. "Talk to me, Roy."

"The girl I'm thinking about is my niece—you remember Rylie?"

Rylie Quinn, Roy's younger brother's girl. Roy had spoken of her several times through the years and with increasing pride. "Wait a minute—shouldn't she be done or about done with vet school? That's terrific. What's this nonsense about pet grooming?"

"Apparently she washed out and has spent the past year or so establishing a grooming business. It sounds as though she has a nice mobile unit going. As sorry as I am about her schooling, I'm impressed with her work ethic, otherwise I wouldn't say anything to you, Doc, especially when I'm still sick over my mistake with Vince."

Waving away that unpleasant history, Gage focused on how his niece's news must've hit Roy. "You must have been crushed when she told you."

The older man bowed his head. "To have someone in the family do what I wanted to do—my favorite niece, no less? Heck, yeah. But she assured me that circumstances took the matter out of her hands." The rough-edged man held out his hands in a gesture of helplessness. "What does that mean in English?"

"Any number of things."

"That's what I'm afraid of." Roy shrugged. "Then again, if she said that, it's as good as gold. Hopefully, she'll explain more when she arrives." He added quickly, "Not that I'm assuming you're going to want to interview her, Doc, but she's coming regardless."

Gage felt caught between a rock and a hard place. On the one hand, if kids washed out of veterinary school, as far as he was concerned, they weren't committed enough. On the other hand, Roy had been a great employee. He couldn't have managed as well as he had without him. That deserved special consideration regardless of the Vince episode. "I'm glad she wants to see you."

"Yeah. She asked if she could park in back and give you a free trial run of what services she can offer?"

Gage wasn't wild about some cheesy operation going on out in a van in back. On the other hand, maybe Roy's trust was well placed in this young woman, and she could help out Roy when she wasn't tending to her own customers.

"If she passes the interview, I guess she could set up in one of the exam rooms," he told him. "It will look better if she's in the building." It would also be easier to keep an eye on her that way, Gage thought.

Roy looked relieved. "Thanks, Doc. You're the best. I know there are no guarantees, but the kid was heart-broken about the school thing. Maybe this really will be a new start for her."

Nodding, Gage asked, "So when can we expect her?"

"She should be here by the Fourth."

By then it would be jalapeño hot in Texas, but gen-erally not as busy in the clinic as it was out in the field due to people going on vacation. "She can come to our cookout at the house, and we'll introduce her to some folks. Brooke could be helpful in that way, too. It might give us a feel as to what kind of clientele she might pull in."

Looking more than relieved, Roy started to head in two directions at once, caught himself and assured Gage, "I'll get more details for you, Doc."

As he hurried off, Gage returned to the front to see what the rest of the guys had been up to all weekend. He made it through the swinging doors as Jerry Platt entered holding a familiar dog—although Jerry didn't own a dog.

"What the San Juan Hill do you have there, Platt?" Pete Ogilvie demanded.

Looking totally humiliated, Jerry came to Gage. "Can you take a look at this thing, Gage? It's got pine tree sap matted between its toes and Liz is beside herself."

Was Liz setting her sights on Jerry now? Gage wondered. One could only hope. "This is Liz Hooper's Bandy?" he asked, just to make sure.

"Yeah." Jerry glanced over his shoulder at the other men. "Even if you can't do anything, I'd appreciate it if you'd lock it up in a kennel for a few hours. If I don't get a few minutes' peace, I'm liable to do something that will get me sent to prison for the rest of my life." He leaned closer yet. "All I did was open the door for her at the post office, and the next thing I know she's spending the night at my house. And do you know what her solution to her dog getting pine sap on itself is? I should cut down my pine trees. But that's not the worst of it—this little yapping rat keeps relieving himself in my slippers!"

Torn between laughing and sympathizing for the guy, who still cut as handsome a figure as he had as a USAF pilot, Gage took hold of the dog. "Pine sap and dog hair definitely do not get along. I'll see what I can do."

As Jerry headed for the corner table, Gage carried Bandy to the back, where he handed him to Roy. Explaining the situation, he said, "Let's get him cleaned up as much as possible before things get busy."

"Rylie sure would be an asset in this kind of situation," Roy said.

"I wish she was here now," Gage assured him.

"Don't stress," Brooke said to Hoshi, as the phones kept ringing and orders for a funeral service flooded in. The problem was that their coolers were emptying fast, the next delivery truck was running late and even it wouldn't bring all that they needed. "The good news is that the service isn't until Thursday. Granted, the visitation is tomorrow, but by then we'll have enough arrangements done to fill the room to where no one will notice what's late. By then the next truck will have delivered the rest of what we need."

"The gentleman must have been an important person in town," Hoshi offered.

"Brother Jamison had the largest congregation in all of the two-hundred-plus churches in our area," Brooke told her, "and people, being the curious creatures that they are, like to read the florist cards." For various reasons, she thought to herself. She gave their newest employee an apologetic look. "Do you need to call your husband to let him know you'll probably be late?"

"It is not necessary. He is on a longer shift and knows where I am," Hoshi said, seeming to get her bearings. "But thank you for your concern."

Brooke was getting to like the young woman more every day, and liked how her calm demeanor was spreading through the shop, even to Kiki, who had enough energy for three people. Reaching for the phone, she replied, "Then I'll call Charles and let him know that we need to add a few runs for the next few days."

In time, she hoped, Hoshi could handle all this on her own. The young woman was as professional as promised and was learning names and locations fast. But she looked for permission over every minute detail. Hopefully, soon she would believe Brooke when she said she could use her own judgment on certain matters.

As soon as she concluded her call to Charles, the delivery truck pulled into the back. Her pleasure turned to frustration, though, as they realized that little on the truck had anything to do with their order. Fortunately, the driver had enough extra product on board to almost offset that glitch.

Things were busy in the front of the store as well, since this time of year brought graduation celebrations, weddings and a windfall of bridal and baby showers. However, when Liz Hooper walked in, Brooke became immediately concerned for Kiki's ability to manage, as she would for anyone in the path of that female dose of poison. Sure enough, as soon as she spotted her, Liz breezed by sunny Kiki as if she was a store mannequin.

"Brooke, is that you back there?"

Gritting her teeth, since they hadn't officially had a face-to-face since her return to town, making the fake friendliness offensive, Brooke came forward, several orders in hand. She gave the brunette a polite but perplexed look. "Liz Hooper, right? Can we help you?" She emphasized the "we" and slid Kiki a reassuring look.

"I heard about the passing of Brother Jamison, and even though I didn't attend his church, I'd like to send a little something worthy of being the former mayor's wife. Can you do that for me? I've already been to see Rita and Joyce, and they're swamped at their shops."

Brooke suppressed a smile. It would take the Seventh Fleet to block her from catching the insult that the other two florists were busier and more popular than Newman's could hope to be. What's more, considering what Gage had told her about the rest of Liz's conniving behavior, Brooke was determined not to make this yet another "playpen" for the aging former beauty queen.

"Liz, I have to be frank, we were booked solid before either of them were. We do communicate with each other and help out in emergencies. But every blossom coming off the next two trucks is spoken for. Even if you're thinking of something in silk, I can only promise that your order will be delivered to the church in time for the service, not the visitation."

With a sound of scorn, Liz muttered, "Never mind. I'll call Rusk or Tyler." About to leave, she retraced her steps and offered in a saccharine-sweet voice, "I sympathize with how your aunt dumped all this on your shoulders, honey, but you must know you're not helping yourself by acting like the victim in order to latch on to Gage the way you are, just because he was a kind neighbor to Marsha."

So this was the real reason she'd bothered coming in. "I'm not discussing my family or neighbors with you," Brooke replied.

"Oh, please don't put on the ladylike act for me, Brooke Bellamy." Liz sniffed with disdain. "Gage's truck in Marsha's driveway? I thought a niece of a churchgoing woman would have more respect for the dear soul's reputation."

Brooke had run into jealousy and basic female pettiness before, but never to such an in-your-face, nasty degree. Striving to edit down what she really wanted to tell her, she replied coolly, "You've just exposed that you're cruising up and down a street—at night— that you have no business being on. That sounds suspiciously like stalking. If you don't mind your own business, I'll be forced to report that to the police."

* * *

"I can't believe that."

Gage and Brooke were chest deep in the claw-footed tub off Brooke's bedroom, enjoying a soothing soak, and she had just filled him in on Liz's rude visit. Unfortunately, Gage made the mistake of trying to avoid the whole discussion by sounding dismissive.

"What part can't you believe?" Lying against his chest, Brooke struggled with indignation. "That she's as mean as a pit viper, or that after leaving your clinic, where she clearly tried to play you and Jerry against each other, she came to the flower shop looking for even more trouble?" Both Brooke and Gage had already discovered that the other had also been *gifted* with "Liz antics" today.

"What is it about you guys that you don't realize that being so-called 'friendly' to women like that makes them believe that they have a relationship with you?"

"Hold on." Gage paused in stroking the fine line of her collarbone. "You've admitted that you've had problems with male clients."

They had touched upon this subject before, and it further irked that he wasn't quoting her accurately. "I said that I'd protected myself from scenarios that invite trouble. You guys send mixed signals, too worried about losing a client—when you're not getting caught up in some stupid testosterone competition. That's like gasoline and a match to women like Liz."

Gage cupped her chin to gently turn her so that he could look into her eyes. "That is so not fair. I've never led on Liz Hooper. She practically gives me hives if we're the only two people in a room." Ducking his head, he kissed her and reached for the glass of sangria they were sharing. "Net accusations should be illegal," he muttered.

*"What?"*

"Like net fishing, you throw it way out, hoping that you catch something because it's in the wrong place at the wrong time."

Unable to stay annoyed, Brooke replied, a chuckle in her voice, "You'd better not find yourself in the wrong place at the wrong time."

After she accepted a sip of the wine, Gage urged her to turn and straddle his lap. "This is more like it. Three's a crowd in this tub."

"You're also getting most of the soothing water."

"And the best view." He scooped handfuls of the scented, milky water over her glistening breasts. "I'm sorry for what happened. She isn't going to be allowed to threaten our happiness."

Brooke kissed him softly. "Tell me something good about your day."

"I don't know whether it's totally good news or not, but I have my first prospective new employee coming in about a week. It's Roy's niece. She seems to have dropped out of veterinary school." He gave a brief recap of their conversation.

"How strange," Brooke murmured. "And Roy hasn't a clue as to why she gave up? Maybe she failed a class? She might not want to admit as much to him."

"She doesn't sound like a quitter. She's established a mobile pet-grooming business. I'll give her points for not sitting around cashing a free government check. At least some of Roy's genes must have rubbed off on her."

"Is there enough of a market for her to make a go of her kind of work?" Brooke asked, admittedly clueless.

"We'll find out. She's coming in time for the BBQ on the Fourth. That should give her a chance to meet some people and give us a hint if we can find a good fit."

"I thought you were going to hire another doctor?"

"I still plan to. This just came up."

Wrapping her arms around his neck, Brooke rested her forehead against his. "What can I do?"

"Kiss me. Take me inside you."

Slowly doing one, then the other, Brooke said on a sigh, "I meant…about your party."

"What party?"

Brooke laughed softly, then her breath caught as Gage started to rock her against him, sending the water gently lapping against the sides of the tub. "You're right, it is hard to focus on that when you're doing this."

And when he slipped his hand between them to stroke the nub at her core, that ended their conversation for several minutes as they focused only on reaching satisfaction.

"So I'll ask again," Brooke said, when they were in her bed, sharing a last glass of wine. "What can I do to help you with your party?"

"Be there. Help me make Rylie feel welcome."

"How old is she?"

"Mid-twenties?"

"I wonder if Aunt Marsha will be well enough to come. It would give her a chance to spend a little time with Humphrey. Help her feel like things aren't changing too fast."

Her slightly preoccupied tone had Gage craning his

neck to check her expression as she lay on his chest. "What aren't you saying?"

"You know that 'when it rains, it pours' saying? I got a call from Andi this evening before you got here."

Just the look on her face told Gage what was coming. "You have an offer on your house?"

She nodded. "That went fast, didn't it?"

"It's a great house. Andi told you as much." When she rubbed her cheek against his chest, he sensed this was still a jolt to her. "You don't have to take the offer."

"They're not challenging my price, and, barring something surfacing in the inspection, which I know isn't going to happen, and which they're paying for, they're offering to pay all of the closing costs, too." She made a subtle negative sound. "No, I can't turn them down."

"They *really* want the house." Gage caressed her sleek back and kissed the top of her head. "Do you feel as though your freedom is being snatched from you?"

"Maybe a little."

"Can you offset that with satisfaction that your aunt is doing so well and that the business is flourishing?"

"I'm not naturally a glass-half-full person, I'm too left brained and analytical, but I do know how to be grateful."

Gage didn't want her to be wrestling for gratitude. He wanted her to be saying, "None of it matters. I'm here with you." "What will you do?" he asked instead.

Brooke stretched to kiss his chin. "Sleep on you."

For a second, he thought he'd heard her say something else, then he relaxed and allowed himself to breathe. He worried for nothing. She was in his arms, and they were one step closer to forever.

* * *

"How long has it been since you've seen your uncle?" Brooke asked Rylie Quinn.

"Too long. Since my high school graduation."

The Fourth of July party was in full swing. Brooke had liked the perky redhead with the gamine-style haircut from the moment they'd met yesterday. At the time, she'd been picking up Humphrey because Gage had arranged to have a working dinner with Rylie and Roy. The girl looked younger than twenty-five, partly due to her bright smile, sparkling gray-green eyes and sunny personality that matched the exotic-spice highlights in her hair. However, it was clear upon talking to her for a few minutes that she was bright and, considering how quickly she was directing Humphrey, adept with animals.

"Well, from what I hear, Roy has been almost giddy with excitement since he learned that you were coming," Brooke assured the younger woman.

"He's been an advocate for me since I told my parents that I wanted to be a vet on my ninth birthday. My mother wanted me to act and sing, so I could try out for *Annie* on Broadway, and my father bet that the best I could hope for was a day care or kindergarten teacher." Catching herself, she added, "Not that I don't respect what an admirable job that is."

"You don't have to explain," Brooke assured her. "Even parents with the most accomplished children often still wish for a bonus."

"I'm sure your parents think you're perfect," Rylie added.

"My father refuses to give up hope for a Nobel Prize in economics," Brooke replied with proper solemnity.

Rylie laughed and looked back over her shoulder. "I like your aunt. She's a sweetheart."

"She is." Brooke had kept one eye on Aunt Marsha since she'd brought her here to make sure she wasn't get overly tired. "I have to take her back to the assisted living center in a few minutes. She's still recuperating, and she'll weaken fast in this heat."

"Would you like company? I could help you get your aunt situated, and then I'd like to check out the clinic to find out how they feel about canine wellness visits. Do you know if they do anything like that?"

"I honestly don't," Brooke replied. "The center is still establishing itself, and I've only been back in Sweet Springs for a month."

"Wow," Rylie gushed. "I thought you and Dr. Sullivan had been together for ages. You seem so in tune with each other."

Brooke thought that was endearing, but quipped, "Gage could probably get along with a rabid pit bull. But thanks. You're more than welcome to join us." Gently turning the conversation around so that Rylie was answering the questions, she added, "I was startled by the size of your RV. You're only an inch taller than me, and you can actually drive that thing?"

Rylie rolled her eyes. "Well, no more than I have to. For the most part, it was parked at the last place of my employment. The real benefit of something like that thing is having all of the creature comforts of a home, an environment to do my work and being able to keep clients as calm as their pets. But Dr. Sullivan told me that I should use the clinic during regular hours."

"It makes sense to me," Brooke told her. "And I know your uncle has been as swamped with work as

Gage has, so if you're able to offer an extra pair of hands, I'm sure they'll be grateful."

"We talked about that," Rylie said, nodding. "I'll be in heaven."

Hearing raucous laughter around the picnic table, Brooke nodded to the old-timers. "What do you think of the coffee club in the corner of the reception room?"

Rylie followed her gaze and chuckled. "I've started calling them the four musketeers. Mr. Atwood reminds me of a very reserved and intellectual Aramis. Mr. Ogilvie is a tough, lusty, yet sad Athos. Mr. Walsh is Porthos, the life of any party and Jerry Platt has to be D'Artagnan."

Nodding, Brooke said, "So you're a reader, too."

"We didn't have a lot growing up, but we had our adventures, and that book stuck with me."

"Well, if those four rascals hear what you call them, they'll adopt you for sure." Brooke gestured toward her aunt. "If you're ready to go, let's get Aunt Marsha."

Minutes later, after quietly letting Gage know they were heading off for a few minutes and to watch Humphrey, they took off. The moment they pulled into the center's circular driveway, Aunt Marsha was announcing, "Home sweet home."

Brooke smiled as she eyed her aunt in the backseat. "You don't have to sound so cheerful."

"The male residents are probably lined up at the door waiting for your return, Mrs. Newman," Rylie said.

Although she blossomed under the flattery, Marsha demurred. "Not yet, but my girlfriends are. We're playing poker tonight."

"She's a pistol, all right," Rylie said to Brooke.

As they parked and Brooke wheeled her aunt inside, they parted ways. Rylie went to the main desk and Brooke brought her aunt to her suite. "Did you have a good time?" she asked her.

"I did, dear. It was also good to see Humphrey getting good exercise, and you and Gage enjoying each other so much. When do you close on your house?"

"The thirty-first," she reminded her.

"Just checking that was still on schedule."

Brooke locked the wheels, once she stopped the chair beside her aunt's recliner. "You're a little sneak. I'm not about to hold back on you."

"So if there had been talk about an engagement, you'd tell me?"

Heaven help her, Brooke thought. "Aunt Marsha, we've known each other for a whole month. Don't rush things."

Unperturbed, her aunt said wistfully, "I fell in love with your uncle at first sight."

It was probably the twenty-sixth time Brooke had heard that. "Yes, and he said to his friend, who was with him at the time, that you were the girl he was going to marry. I remember."

Brooke couldn't have gotten through these past weeks without Gage's help and support, and she knew she was falling in love with him—*had* fallen in love with him. But she didn't want to jinx the precious feelings between them. Part of her knew Gage was *it* for her. Another part wondered why, for all of his passion, he hadn't said the words yet.

*I love you.*

*Marry me.*

"Do you want to lie down before you meet your

friends?" she asked her aunt, determinedly thrusting away her doubts.

"No, no. The kitchen is preparing a few refreshments, and all I need to do is freshen up. That I can manage. You go on, dear, and get back to the party. Thank you so much for the lovely afternoon."

Brooke kissed her again and promised to check in the following morning. By the time she returned to the front where Rylie was, the young woman was just finishing up talking to Susan Freese, the administrator of the facility. Susan looked pleased with the conversation and waved to Brooke. Brooke found that another good sign. So far, everyone seemed to react positively to Rylie. Maybe Gage had, indeed, found one of the answers to his employment needs.

Once outside, Brooke asked, "So how did it go?"

"Super," Rylie said, as upbeat as ever. "They've had the police department's drug-sniffing canine there for a visit, but you don't encourage those dogs to get touchy-feely. My MG has been with me for three years, and she's definitely the opposite of them."

Brooke had been officially introduced to the long-haired retriever mix at the party. The sleek, shiny-haired black mongrel had the incredibly wise, penetrating brown gaze of an ape. It was so uncanny that Brooke had found herself transfixed by the dog several times.

"She's beautiful and so sweet tempered," she told Rylie. "How did you come to have her?"

"She was someone's throwaway. I happened to spot her alongside the road. There was a jerk driving ahead of me, and he aimed for her, so she threw herself into the ditch. She not only wrenched her shoulder badly, it took me a year to break her fear of being in a vehicle, let alone walking near a road. But if ever there was a dog meant to socialize on virtually any level, it's her."

"MG… I meant to ask you what that stands for."

"Mommy's Girl." Rylie laughed, the sound bubbly and joyful. "This will sound crazy, but she picked up on what I was doing with animals from day one, and when I've been busy with another animal, she would automatically entertain whoever else is around, whether they have two legs or four. She's a doll."

So was Rylie, Brooke thought. "I was impressed when you told her to stay and she lay down by the table you'd been sitting at. She won't get worried and start looking for you? That's a problem that we had with Humphrey."

"She might if something went wrong, or the weather turned bad, but I know I can rely on Uncle Roy and Doc to keep an eye on her, as they are with your aunt's dog." Ryle sent her an impish look. "I suspect when we get back, they'll tell you that the minute Humph tried to mosey around, she ordered him to set his cute self back beside her."

"I would pay to know that really happened," Brooke quipped. "So did Susan arrange for a day for you to try out things with MG?"

With a nod, Rylie said, "Our interview is set for next Wednesday."

"Really? Dogs can be interviewed?"

"Sure. You have to find out how social they are, how they respond to strangers in various environments. They can't panic if something is dropped or there's a siren."

"You've probably been asked this a dozen times already today, but have you always wanted to work with animals?" Brooke wryly admitted, "I'm only just getting where I *almost* think of Humphrey as family."

"Aw," Rylie murmured. "That's a huge accomplishment, good for you! Me? For as long as I can remember. My first pet was a baby rabbit that the mother had ejected from the nest in our backyard. I wasn't in kindergarten yet, so I didn't realize that if she'd done that, there was something wrong with the poor thing. It died later that night. Then came birds falling out of nests—some I actually nursed to adulthood—squirrels, cats, dogs, turtles, raccoons.... My parents did draw the line at baby skunks. That's saying a lot when you realize that I'm the only daughter, and my older brother is adopted."

Amused, Brooke asked, "So you're saying you were spoiled?"

Leaning over, Rylie confided, "To this day, when I hear applause, I have to lock my knees to keep from taking a bow." She grew serious and added, "My folks tried for several years to have kids with no luck, so they adopted my brother, and before his next birthday, they discovered I was on the way."

They talked easily the rest of the way back to the party, and once there, MG, Rylie's dog, came running with Humphrey bringing up the rear. Brooke was delighted when the hound came to her and grinned at her.

"Good to see you, too," Brooke said, stooping to love on him.

Looking proud, Gage came to them. After kissing her gently, he asked, "Everything okay?"

"Aunt Marsha is ready for a big evening with her

gal pals, and Rylie has an in with Susan to bring MG as a prospective therapy dog."

"Hey, that's a good idea." Gage hugged the glossy retriever. "This is the most loving dog I've met in a while. And sharp.... I can even tell she's rubbing off on Humph. While you two were gone, he was content to lay beside her—until a squirrel caught his attention. He glanced at her, as though looking for permission, and she literally laid her paw over his and he rolled on to his side and took a nap."

Getting an I-told-you-so look from Rylie, Brooke replied, "Well, it sounds as though this is the start of a beautiful friendship."

People had been coming and going all afternoon, so when a silver pickup truck pulled into Gage's driveway, that didn't immediately draw attention until Liz Hooper slid out of the passenger side of Jerry Platt's truck.

Brooke barely managed to stifle a groan. "Is that still going on?"

"Actually, he said he was trying to nip that in the bud," Gage assured her. "She must have really manipulated things."

*To get to you,* Brooke thought sourly.

Giving Brooke a look of entreaty, Gage said, "You know he's welcome here, and she could be a great customer for Rylie."

"I take it that she can be a handful?" Rylie asked.

"Enough to make me wish I'd stayed longer with Aunt Marsha," Brooke replied. But she added to Rylie, "I'm wrong to say even that. You need to meet her. She's part of local society—a former Miss Sweet Springs, and Miss Cherokee County."

"I can tell by the hair," Rylie said, slowly nodding.

Seeing Gage's worried look, Brooke said, "And now I'm off to help clean up and refill things, and if the opportunity arises, volunteer for an overseas deployment."

Rylie threw back her head and laughed. "I like you, Brooke."

As they parted ways, Brooke grabbed up empty platters and carried them inside. Once she had them refilled, she brought them back out. There was no missing that Liz had Rylie—and Gage—cornered, and that Jerry had wandered over to his old cohorts sitting by the picnic table. But before she could respond to Gage's look of appeal, a sleek black limousine pulled up in front of her aunt's house.

There was only one person who would make such an appearance—unannounced, no less—and that had Brooke hurrying next door. The doorbell was on its second series of eight chimes when she sprinted through the house and yanked open the door.

"Dad. This is a surprise."

He was carrying a bottle of champagne. In her shock, she hadn't noticed that earlier. Now what? she wondered.

Her father took in her red, white and blue outfit— off-the-shoulder top, swirling gypsy skirt, matching sandals with enough glitter to require their own sunglasses and her hair free and flowing like Gage liked it.

"You look...relaxed," her father replied, as she dutifully kissed his cheek. "I must say the color in your cheeks makes you look healthier than the last time I saw you."

"Thanks." Trying not to be obvious, Brooke pressed her hand to her abdomen to steady her breathing. "I was next door. It's a welcoming party for new staff at the veterinary clinic."

"You've never had a pet in your life," Damon Bellamy replied, clearly not grasping her reasoning. "Oh, wait a minute, you said something about your aunt having a dog."

"He's next door, too." Knowing explanations were useless, Brooke closed the door. "Well, this is nice. Are you celebrating something?"

He held up the bottle. "My latest coup—and a job worthy of my daughter."

Job? Feeling a weight begin to descend upon her, Brooke belatedly gestured to the room at large. "Would you like to sit down?"

"I can't. I'm due in Dallas shortly for an important dinner meeting. But I wanted you to know before word gets out that I've bought The Crystal Group and I want you to run it for me."

She was vaguely familiar with the private investment firm that was about half the size of her father's company. "Me?"

"As CEO, of course."

"I seem to recall that they're not based out of Dallas?"

"That's almost amusing. They're still in New Zealand. One of the up-and-comers in the Pacific Rim."

Dear God, she thought. "Dad…" She tried to maintain her composure. "I'm not interested in relocating halfway around the planet. Besides, I'm needed here."

The handsome but remote man stared at her without blinking. "Needed or used?" he asked, with near disdain. "Didn't you text me that Marsha is settled in a comfortable facility? Your work here is done."

"Not exactly. I'm buying Aunt Marsha's holdings in town. By the time I'm through, I'll have close to a dozen businesses paying rent."

After only a slight pause, her father replied, "Small potatoes." Suddenly, in a totally out-of-character move, he dropped the bottle on to a nearby chair, drew her into his arms and spun her around. "Brooke—think of it! You'll make a dozen deals worth ten times this entire town before you're completely dry behind the ears."

Somewhere in that humiliating and outlandish moment, Brooke saw the back door open and, in the next spin, someone standing in the doorway. By the time her father put her down again, he was gone.

Gage!

"Dad, that was Gage. I have to explain to him."

"Let him go." Damon Bellamy ran a hand over his hair, then adjusted his tie. "I have someone I want you to meet anyway."

Dragging her gaze from the door, Brooke shook her head, willing things not to go from bad to worse. "Excuse me?"

"A merger between our families would be the biggest thing since—"

"Father!"

He fell silent upon hearing her sharp tone.

"You said something about being used a moment ago? I have plans," she said, with quiet dignity. "It would have been considerate of you to ask about them before you started using me as your next bargaining chip."

He looked around and then back at her as though she'd lost her mind. "Do you not understand that I have worked for you, groomed you to be worthy of what you'll inherit someday?"

His words were a blow somewhere even deeper than her heart, but Brooke steeled herself to keep it from showing. "I would say that I'm worthy of being respected for having a mind of my own. What kind of a CEO is it who will be expected to fall lockstep into any directive you make? Thank you for your offer, but I respectfully decline."

Her father took a step back and stared at her as though she was an anomaly. "I won't come to you again. Not with such an offer. When you need help, you'll have to come to me."

"And I'll live in the hope that you will want to see me just to make sure I'm well and to maybe meet your grandchild one of these days."

Without a word, her father walked out.

Brooke watched from the door as he returned to the limo without ever glancing back. She supposed she should be sick that she'd just thrown away a fortune and an even bigger opportunity. However, she realized, in doing so, she'd just freed herself from an emotional and psychological IV that had crippled her for years.

As she closed the door, her gaze fell on the bottle still in the chair. Reaching for it, she whispered, "Whoa," as she recognized the brand and vintage on the label. Then she started grinning.

By the time she returned to Gage's, the party was over, and only Gage and Humphrey remained. They were sitting on his back porch, and it was a toss-up as to who looked more pensive.

Humphrey spotted her first, rose to all four feet and uttered a happy bark. That had Gage sitting forward in his chair as though preparing to rise, then in the last minute, he just clasped his hands between his knees.

"I thought you'd left, too," he told her when she stopped at the base of the stairs. At her confused look, he explained, "When the limo drove away."

How could he think that? She gestured to the empty yard. "So in a state of depression, you ran off everyone?"

"Liz pretty much did that."

"Liz…the gift that keeps giving."

"She arrived two sheets to the wind, so when she downed a margarita faster than a lottery winner can shove a credit card into a slot machine, it didn't take any time at all for her to cross the line."

"And who was the unlucky recipient of that attention?"

Gage slid her a droll look. "Suffice to say that Jerry quickly hustled her back into his truck. Since the concert and fireworks show will be starting at the park in a bit, everyone else decided it was time to head off, too." He nodded at what she'd brought with her. "Celebrating something?"

Brooke glanced down at the bottle of champagne and two glasses. "My engagement."

That had him drawing a slow, deep breath, only to exhale with a loud puff. "Is that so?"

"My father's idea. The pot was sweetened by an offer to make me the CEO of his latest acquisition."

"Well, you knew his intent was to get you away from here."

"Even you would have to allow that New Zealand is a bit excessive."

"Wow. He doesn't fool around." When she didn't expand, Gage rubbed his palms against his jean-clad legs. "So who does your father want to hook you up with? The current owner's son?"

"We never got down to the tacky minutiae, but my hunch is that you're in bull's-eye range. The strongest clue came when the phrase 'merging families' was used. Who wouldn't swoon at the opportunity of being her father's fish bait?"

A look of pain crossed Gage's handsome face, and he momentarily hung his head. But a few seconds later, he rose and strolled to the edge of the porch. He never took his gaze from hers and looked as if the world had righted itself again. "Are you saying you actually said *no* to Big Daddy, Brooke Bellamy? You rejected Damon?"

"Try not to sound so smug."

"Your other option is for you to get up here and let me kiss you senseless."

Ascending the stairs, she showed him the label on the bottle. "Let's try not break a primo vintage."

Gage stared, then whistled softly. "Since Prince William is already taken, and Prince Harry doesn't strike me as your type, who the heck *did* your father have lined up for you?"

Placing the bottle and glasses on the table between the rocking chairs, she returned to stand toe-to-toe with Gage. "I don't care. I'd rather focus on who *I* would prefer."

Gage slipped his arms around her waist. "How many guesses do I get?"

"None. Just show me that I did the right thing."

With an indecipherable whisper, Gage lifted her off her feet and into his arms and kissed her hungrily.

Then again. After the third time, he muttered, "Damn it, Brooke, you scared the hell out of me."

"Be serious."

"I am. I don't have a right to stop you from being all you can be."

"Good, because I will be. With you."

She wished someone had been around at that instant to capture Gage's expression for eternity. Then again, who needed that when she knew she would never forget the blossoming of joy and adoration across his dear face.

"I love you," he said solemnly.

"I love you back."

"Say it again," he whispered.

"I love you. I started to fall the moment you told me so confidently that you were going to ask me out. But it wasn't until this afternoon when I saw you holding those people's new baby—"

"Baby… Oh! The Nelsons' daughter, Victoria. They're fairly new in the area. I'm not surprised that you don't know them yet. What about the baby?"

Brooke replied almost shyly, "I saw that child in your strong arms and thought, 'I want to see him holding our child.'"

He closed his eyes tightly until moisture bled between his lashes. "I ache to see a little angel of our making nursing here," he said, brushing his thumb over her nipple.

Brooke sucked in an unsteady breath as her body awoke with desire. "So we're in agreement?"

"Sweetheart." Gage kissed her with all of his heart. Then he turned her toward the door. "Let's get to work."

# *Epilogue*

*Late August*

On the last Sunday in August, Brooke and Gage were married in the Methodist church that Aunt Marsha belonged to. The couple didn't send out formal invitations. Instead, on the first Sunday of the month, they'd added a card in the program to announce they would take their vows after the late-morning service. Everyone was welcome to attend. Brooke added a stand-alone poster at the doorway to the shop, and Gage had a life-size poster made of Humphrey holding his own announcement at the clinic. A final notice was posted in the weekly newspaper. Gifts were discouraged, and those who insisted on doing something were encouraged to donate to the local animal shelter and the volunteer fire department.

On the big day it was standing room only at the church—testament to most of the community being fond of their local vet and newest business owner. Andi had come in from Dallas to serve as Brooke's maid of honor. Roy stood as Gage's best man. After Brooke's father's secretary sent regrets on his invitation, citing a need to be out of the country, she asked her aunt to give her away.

"I'd be honored," Aunt Marsha had replied, beaming. Although she needed a cane and relied greatly on Brooke's arm, she looked ecstatic and pretty in her lavender suit as they walked down the aisle.

Not even Humphrey was left out of the celebration. He took the place of the flower girl and ring bearer and wore a satin collar holding a pillow on which the wedding rings were tied. His one indiscretion was to offer a throaty howl of excitement upon getting to the end of the aisle. Rylie was in charge of handling him and expertly quieted him down to sit beside a serene MG for the rest of the service.

Afterward there was a brief reception with cake and punch in the church's banquet hall, and then a smaller party with champagne and barbecue at Gage's house—now their house, since Aunt Marsha's house had just been contracted.

Needless to say, the happy couple hadn't had many free moments since the welcome party for Rylie, so as guests began to take their leave, neither bride nor groom protested too forcibly.

"I thought it would be sunset before we got rid of the four musketeers," Gage told his bride, already adopting Rylie's nickname for the bunch.

Rylie had just left, too, with MG and Humphrey. Humphrey had already familiarized himself with Rylie's comfy RV and was looking mighty proud to be going off with his new BFF, MG.

"It was good of Roy to act as the guys' designated driver," Brooke replied, as Gage laced his fingers between hers. Then she added wistfully, "I do wish he had more of a life. He didn't even bring a date."

"Hey." Gage drew her fully into his arms at the top of the porch stairs. "You already have a guy to worry about." He kissed her with a fervor that had been a promise in his eyes since they'd repeated their vows. "Alone at last, Mrs. Sullivan. Happy?"

"Over the moon." Brooke laid her hand on his silver-and-charcoal tie. "I like your parents very much. I'm just sorry the rest of your family couldn't come."

Gage had invited them all, but obligations kept most away, mostly so Gage's parents could come down. They had just left, too, to settle in next door at Aunt Marsha's house. Brooke and Gage had arranged to meet them for breakfast in the morning before taking them back to the airport.

"You'll meet the rest soon enough. My sisters are more curious about you than ever. Apparently my father hasn't stopped raving about you, and Mom gave her stamp of approval the instant you beat Dad at chess. Sullivan women are by nature competitive."

"I don't want to compete," she groaned playfully. "I want a family."

Gage kissed the tip of her nose. "You've got one, angel." But then he looked apologetic. "I'm sorry your father didn't come."

"It's his loss. Maybe he'll realize that down the road." And she meant that. Yes, it would have been lovely to have him here, but not at the cost of making Gage or Aunt Marsha uneasy. As far as she was concerned, everything had been perfect. "But you're sure you don't mind me not wanting a honeymoon?" she asked him. When he'd asked where she wanted to go, she'd answered honestly that she was so excited to start their life together that there wasn't anywhere else she wanted to go but *home*.

"There aren't words," Gage replied, before adding with a grin, "but I plan on trying to find them as I unwrap you out of this enticing concoction."

Brooke glanced down at the gown that her aunt had begged her to buy. She'd been eyeing a pretty ivory suit; however, Aunt Marsha had spotted this and all but threatened a heart episode to get her way.

"You can't go to the wedding as though we're going to the same Easter brunch," Aunt Marsha had argued.

"It's a waste to spend a lot of money on a gown you only wear once," Brooke had countered. But she did have to admit the pencil-slim satin creation with the princess neckline and the sheer free-flowing veil over her hair was lovely.

"You look like a dream," Gage said, as they entered their house and locked up. His expression remained as captivated as when he'd first seen her coming down the aisle.

"You made your mother cry when she actually saw you in this," Brooke replied, admiring his pale gray suit. But knowing how uncomfortable he was wearing it, she sympathetically eased off his tie.

"Well, she'd better grab one of the million photos the photographer took," he muttered, "because I don't plan to get into one of these straitjackets again any sooner than I have to."

With that, he swept Brooke into his arms and carried her up the stairs. Brooke had been merging their things, filling the near-empty house for weeks, but had left the master bedroom mostly as it was because it suited Gage so, and she'd told him it reminded her of their first night here together. Her only addition was a beloved Bombay chest that had been her mother's, which she had already filled with her lingerie. On it was a bouquet of mauve calla lilies—much like the bouquet that she'd thrown earlier to Andi. Interestingly, right afterward, the tall veterinarian friend that subbed for Gage had come over to her and introduced himself.

Setting Brooke on her feet by the foot of the bed, Gage just stood there.

"What?" Brooke asked.

"Earlier today, I wondered if, once we got back here, this moment would feel different. It does."

Brooke helped him out of his jacket and set it aside. "Yes, it does."

"Vows are powerful things," Gage said, unbuttoning his shirt.

"It's not just the vows," Brooke said, stopping him, only to take his hand to bring it against her flat tummy.

"What? *No*." Gage's hand began to tremble against her. "But I saw you drink wine."

"You saw me holding a glass as they toasted us, and pretend to sip," she said, her smile sublime. "Then as discreetly as possible, I put down the glass."

Gage could only look at her and swallow—until he dropped to one knee and pressed his cheek against her.

Brooke stroked his hair. "I don't think I've ever seen you tongue-tied before, Daddy Sullivan."

He pressed his lips and then his entire face against the soft material of her dress. "When?" came his muffled question.

"I'm barely six weeks along."

"How can you know?"

"Well, *Doctor,*" she mused, "when we agreed that night, the night of my father's visit and Rylie's party that this was it and that I should get off the pill? I thought it might take months before I became fertile again, but you can't argue with Mother Nature and a virile man, can you? And remember, after we made love, when I asked if it would be possible to know when it happened? The blinds were open, and the moonlight bathed us in this extraordinary light."

"God, yes. I remember." Rising, Gage picked her up as though she was still a figment of his imagination, only to sit down on the edge of the bed and set her on his lap. "My angel is going to have my baby. I don't know how I'm still breathing. My heart's about to come through my chest."

"Breathe."

"Breathe? I want to shout!" Instead, he laughed, then kissed her with a heart-aching reverence. "You're my life."

"And you're mine," she whispered.

A slow grin broke over his face. "Can we tell my parents at breakfast?"

"I'm surprised you aren't already running next door to give them the news," Brooke teased.

"Tempting." Gage eased them both back onto the bed and tenderly ran his hand from her cheek to her womb. "But that's going to have to wait," he murmured against her lips. "This can't."

\* \* \* \* \*

**Amy Woods** took the scenic route to becoming an author. She's been a bookkeeper, a high school English teacher and a claims specialist, but now that she makes up stories for a living, she's never giving it up. She grew up in Austin, Texas, and lives there with her wonderfully goofy, supportive husband and a spoiled rescue dog.

**Books by Amy Woods**

**Harlequin Special Edition**

*Peach Leaf, Texas*

*An Officer and Her Gentleman*
*His Pregnant Texas Sweetheart*
*Finding His Lone Star Love*
*His Texas Forever Family*

Visit the Author Profile page
at Harlequin.com for more titles.

# PUPPY LOVE
# FOR THE VETERINARIAN

Amy Woods

This one is for the animal rescuers;
thank you for the wonderful lives you save.

And for my Maggie dog, who has my heart.

# Chapter 1

"June, hon, why don't you go on home now? I can finish closing up here myself, and it looks like things may get worse than they originally predicted."

June Leavy looked up from her mop bucket and followed the owner of Peach Leaf Pizza's eyes to the small television behind the counter, tuned in to the evening weather segment. January in west Texas could be unpredictable, but the idea of the twelve to eighteen inches of snow the meteorologist called for actually covering the ground and sticking was just surreal.

She studied her boss's face, not missing the lines around Margaret's mouth and the shadowy thumbprints beneath the older woman's usually lively eyes. It had been a busy day, amid a busy week; they were both exhausted, but the work would be completed much faster with two pairs of hands.

June shook her head, causing a few more strands of hair to escape her ponytail. "Nonsense. I'm almost finished with the floor, and then all that's left is taking out the garbage."

Margaret offered a weary smile as her thanks, but June could see the relief in her boss's face. She would never admit it, but Margaret Daw was getting older. It was time for her to retire and June could feel that the day was coming when her boss would ask her to take over. Margaret had all but asked her about it on more than one occasion—who could blame a new grandma for wanting to spend more time with the adorable twin babies recently born to her pediatrician son and daughter-in-law?—and besides, June was her only full-time employee and comanager. In many ways, it just made sense.

June sighed and sloshed the mop back into the gray water, wondering again how she would respond if and when the day arrived. She could see the pros and cons list she'd pored over so many times in her mind's eye, her options jotted out clear as day on the yellow pad sitting next to the remote control on her coffee table. But no matter how many times she mulled over the bullet points, the decision wouldn't be easy.

Margaret was a wonderful boss—kind and fair—and the job provided steady income. There was something comforting in the daily tasks, in kneading the dough each morning, chopping fresh vegetables and taking orders, in the warm, familiar faces of Peach Leaf Pizza's many regular customers. She would miss the banter, catching up with people she'd known her whole life and the excitement in kids' faces when they piled into the red leather booths after winning baseball games or performing well in dance recitals.

But she had dreams of her own, too.

And until recently, June had been so close to turning them into reality. So close, in fact, that the bruises from losing everything hadn't yet healed.

Now her choice was between picking up the pieces and starting over—letting herself believe that she could somehow regain what was lost—or sticking with the safe option, taking over the pizza parlor and borrowing her neighbors' joy as they lived their lives.

Put that way, it didn't seem like much of a choice at all, but she reminded herself that starting over wouldn't exactly guarantee a happy ending, either.

"Back to square one," she said aloud without meaning to.

"What's that?" Margaret called from the counter.

"Oh… I was just wondering if it's really going to get as bad as they're saying."

She tilted her chin at the television, where the Austin meteorologist gesticulated animatedly, her arms waving in circles and lines to indicate high and low pressure points across a multicolored map of Texas.

"Beats me." Margaret shrugged, her shoulders tapping the pizza-slice painted earrings she wore so that they swirled around beneath her silvery curls. "Wouldn't be the first time, though, you know."

June finished cleaning a blotch of spilled marinara and pushed the wheeled bucket toward the back of the shop, doing a once-over of the black-and-white checked tiles in case she missed a spot.

Margaret wiped the last bit of counter and stood on her tiptoes to turn off the TV before removing her apron. "When I was a girl, we got a couple of feet out at our house, and I'll tell you, it is no easy time getting around town in that much powder." She put a hand on one hip and pointed at June with the other. "Especially when nobody around here knows how to drive in that stuff."

Nodding her agreement, June crossed the kitchen and emptied the mop bucket into the designated sink, then shoved the cleaning supplies into a broom closet. She supposed it was possible that the weather might take a turn for the worse—it had been snowing steadily for a few days, so there was already a little covering the ground—but the thought of that much more coming down in the span of just a few hours in their neck of Texas still somehow didn't seem realistic. Sure, they got a few inches most years, and there was always the danger of ice, especially on the country roads outside of town, but she didn't think there was too much to worry about. She was certain she had plenty of time to get home before anything major hit.

But when she closed the supply closet door and turned around, June found Margaret looking up at her from all of nearly five feet, her boss's clear blue eyes fully of worry beneath a forehead creased with concern.

"Just promise me you'll be extra careful, and if it gets bad, we won't open tomorrow. Just stay home. I don't want you getting hurt trying to make it into work, you hear?"

June gave a reassuring smile, promised that she'd be safe and patted Margaret's shoulder. Over the years, their relationship had deepened into more than just a typical owner/employee situation. Her boss treated her more like a daughter than a paid worker, which only made things harder when thinking about the next chapter of her life. She knew Margaret would hate the idea of June factoring her needs into future plans, but they *were* a factor. A big one. If she ever got back on her feet, if she ever found a way to get back all the money she'd spent years carefully saving to open her own bakery, she would have to leave someone she cared about, someone who'd helped see her through the lowest point of her life. That mattered. Deeply.

She shook her head. There was no use thinking about it now.

The money was gone. In all likelihood, that meant her dreams were gone with it. She'd worked herself to the bone for over a decade earning it and had gone without quite a few comforts to save until it amounted to enough to buy her own bakeshop. Her shoulders sunk as the weight of loss settled once again. It would take years before she could build her former financial stability and credit back up, and even more to get her savings back.

Six months had passed since Clayton left, taking everything with him. Their money. Hers, really, if she were being honest, and she was now—too much had happened for anything less. Her dreams.

And, last but not least, her heart.

Even after all he'd done, taking the cash from their joint account and running off to gamble it away in Vegas, June thought there might be a place inside of her that still missed that stupid man. It wasn't that she loved him still—no, he'd broken her trust and hurt her far too much for that to be the case—but the loss of him and all they'd shared, and the deep chasm of loneliness in his wake, the death of the life they'd built together... June thought maybe those were the things she truly mourned. And it wasn't that she needed him, either, or any man, for that matter. She'd been single for most of her life until Clayton came along and had been happy and fulfilled before his presence.

But that was just it. Until he left, she would have sworn to anyone that he was the one she'd spend the rest of her life with, and when he'd gone, all those promises of a family and a life with him vanished, and she was back where she'd been before—only this time, it wasn't the same. This time, she knew what it was like to share her home with someone she loved, to talk about having kids one day and to dream together, staring off into the future, side by side. This time, she felt the absence.

*Shoulders up, chin up,* she told herself, remembering Margaret's wise words in the aftermath of that mess. Better to make peace with the present, than to dwell on the past, right?

Of course.

Starting with her small, albeit cozy, apartment, June forced herself to make a list of all of the things she had to be grateful for. When she finished, she headed back to the storefront and kitchen to fetch the two large trash bags, hefting them over her shoulders to carry through the restaurant to the Dumpster in the loading area out back.

Things weren't so very bad. She had her job, her friends and a warm place to live, and for that she was thankful. It was a good thing right now to be single and free, to have time and space to decide what to do next, what path to take in putting her life back together. No strings, no one else to care for, no one to put before her own needs. She planned on staying that way for a good while; it would take someone very special to convince her to put her trust in a relationship again, and she was fairly convinced that person might not be anywhere in her future, near or far. It was a…difficult thought to swallow, but one she was doing her best to accept.

June dropped the trash bags near the back door and went to get her coat. Margaret was doing the same. "Bundle up, now."

"Yes, ma'am," she teased, holding her fingers to her forehead in a salute.

Margaret put both hands on her hips, a foreboding figure. "I'm not joking around, Junie. You forget I'm from upstate New York, where it gets dangerously cold in the winter. You Texans don't know from cold, and you're always caught unawares when it hits. Don't let it get the best of you."

"Okay, I promise."

Both women pulled on gloves, hats and purses, and Margaret opened the back door for June when she picked up the garbage bags. A blast of frigid air slapped her across the face and briefly challenged her footing until she steadied herself against its force.

"I'm good here, Marg. I'll drop these off and lock up. See you in the morning," she shouted over her shoulder as she stepped onto the loading dock and into what felt like gale-force winds.

"I'm not so sure about that."

June chuckled to herself. "Okay, then, see you soon."

"All right, hon. Don't forget what I said about not coming in if it's bad," Margaret called, her voice fading as the back door slammed behind her and she headed for her car in the front parking lot, which she always parked next to June's fifteen-year-old jalopy.

June shook her head at the older woman's cosseting, then heaved the bags into the giant metal bin, starting at the loud clanging sound that erupted.

Something else must have heard it, too, and reacted the same way, because June caught motion in her peripheral vision as she turned back to lock up the door. Her heart jumped into her throat, and it fluttered there like so many trapped butterflies as she spun quickly to take in her surroundings.

"Hello?"

She listened carefully and heard...nothing, except maybe her own pulse pounding at her temples.

"Is anyone out here?" she called again, reaching into her purse for her pocketknife and cell phone. There was probably nothing to worry about. This was Peach Leaf, after all, where the running crime rate was pretty much zilch. All the same, she was a woman alone in an alley after dark, so it was only smart to be cautious.

Scanning the view once more to make certain she wasn't about to be attacked, June decided that instead of locking the back door and walking around front to her little car as she usually did, she'd just go through the store.

That was when she heard something again. A quiet rustling, followed by what sounded like a series of soft squeaks. She closed her eyes for just a few seconds, trying to decide whether or not to ignore the sound, knowing the wise thing to do was to walk away. Whatever it was, it was not her problem, and Lord knew she did not need any of those in her life just then.

But then she heard it again, and this time, the soft,

sad little cries were like warm fingers squeezing her heart. As the snow began to fall harder, flakes catching in her eyelashes and forming a thin, shawl-like layer on the red fabric of her coat, June released a great sigh and made the decision to investigate. Whatever was making that noise—*please don't let it be a baby of any kind*, she thought—did not belong out there in a lonely alley on a freezing winter's night.

With the garbage bags out of her hands, June now pulled her coat closer around her and closed all four toggles before carefully descending the loading dock steps. A thin layer of ice had already formed, and she had no intention of tumbling down and breaking a bone or two. She pulled her purse strap up from her shoulder and over her head to secure it tightly, then dug out her cell phone, turning on the flashlight app. Its slim, bright beam shot out into the dark, and June crept slowly behind the pizza shop's garbage bin, the light illuminating nothing but a coating of grimy snow. She stopped and waited a moment, listening for the sound again so she could follow it to its source. Just as she was about to restart her search, she heard it again; this time, it was more distinct.

Placing a palm behind her ear, June tried to zero in on what it was—a kitten, maybe? Something small and helpless and lost? Again, she pleaded that it wouldn't be a baby. The thought of someone leaving a little one behind their restaurant, especially in this weather, was just…unthinkable.

There it was again, and now she was certain it was some sort of cry. Rolling her eyes upward in a silent prayer, she braced herself and started off in the direction of the noise, continuing as it became louder and louder, which meant she must be close. She was half-way down the alley, almost to the street, when she reached it, hidden in a dark corner behind another garbage bin.

Shining her flashlight into the shadows, June gasped, cold air filling her lungs and what felt like the rest of her body. The hand that wasn't holding her phone flew to her mouth as she looked into two pairs of big, brown eyes.

Big, brown...puppy eyes.

The squeaking, she now realized, was the heart-wrenching sound of tiny little canine yips, probably calling for their mother.

There, cuddled together in a heap of trash behind another store's Dumpster, were two itty-bitty bodies coated in black fur, with eight little white, black-spotted boots. But their tiny faces were the clincher. June's eyes filled with moisture, not from the biting air, as she stared at two pairs of fuzzy black ears, each separated down the middle by a thin line of white fur that traced down into identical white muzzles.

For a full minute, June remained frozen in place, her instinct telling her to rush forward and gather the pups in her arms to warm them up, but she wasn't yet positive on what was the right thing to do.

On the one hand, the temperatures had probably dropped to below freezing when the sun had disappeared—at least, it sure felt that way—but on the other, well, what if the puppies' mother returned, looking for them? What if she was around there somewhere and returned to find them gone? But the more pressing question was, of course—what if she didn't? The little ones couldn't have been out there for too long; otherwise they'd be…

No, she didn't want to think about that. Yet…that would certainly be the outcome if she didn't get the little dogs out of the cold, and quick. She could always check the alley the next day and put up flyers to find out if anyone had seen a female dog wandering around the strip mall or a suspicious person dropping off a little bundle. But for now, if she didn't get them out of the increasingly cold night air—and the snow that seemed to be falling faster and thicker each minute—they would surely freeze to death. Not much of a choice there.

Having made up her mind, June hurried forward and opened her coat, then picked up the puppies very gently and with extreme care, and tucked them into the front pouch of her Peach Leaf Pizza sweatshirt. She wrapped her coat across her middle, leaving it unfastened so they could breathe, and, head down, turned the corner out of the alley.

The wind was much fiercer without the protection of the buildings, and the several yards to her car seemed more like miles as June trudged through the now-blinding wind and snow in the direction of the front parking lot. Finally, she reached her car and pulled her keys from her purse to unlock the doors. Opening the trunk, she retrieved her gym bag and slammed down the lid, sliding into the backseat as quickly as possible. She pulled the door shut—no easy feat against the wind—and took a deep breath before unzipping the bag. She took out her jogging clothes and shoes, leaving her towel to make a sort of nest. Opening her coat, she removed the little balls of fluff and placed them carefully inside, close against each other for warmth.

"There," she said. "You guys hang on tight. We're going for help."

Satisfied with the answering squeaks, June pulled a seat belt around the bag and fastened it, hoping it would do, and then crawled into the front seat. Thankfully, her old car started after just a couple of tries, and she was able to pull out of the parking lot.

Snow fell in sheets as she made her way onto the main road with her blinkers on full blast, sifting through her memory for any winter-weather driving advice Margaret might have offered over the years, sorry that she hadn't listened more closely.

Wrapping the fore-and middle fingers of her left hand together for luck as she gripped the wheel with white knuckles, June set off to the only place she could think of that might be able to help her with two very fresh puppies.

# Chapter 2

Ethan Singh cursed before his father's absurdly messy monster of a desk. One of these days, he promised himself for the hundredth time, he would have to suck it up and organize the damn thing. One of these days.

But not today. Or tonight, he supposed, strolling from the office and past the empty receptionist's desk to glance out the front window of his father's veterinary clinic, only mildly surprised to find a dark sky staring back. It was almost a relief to know that, as soon as he arrived at his parents' home and ate a quick dinner, it would be past time to head straight to bed.

Straight to bed meant no time to think about what he was doing in Peach Leaf, Texas, for the winter, and more importantly, what he would do when the season was over and it was time to head back to campus in

Colorado, where he was scheduled to teach several veterinary classes over the spring semester.

Ethan gave his head a little shake and turned back from the window. It wouldn't do to ruminate on that now. The whole point in coming here, agreeing to run Dad's clinic while his parents took a one-month, long-overdue vacation to visit his father's brother in Washington, DC, was to *not* think about what happened in Alaska. Ethan sat down in the receptionist's seat and put his head in his hands. How could he not think about it? How could he not think about *her*—about what she'd done to break his heart into a thousand tiny shreds?

It was impossible.

He had looked forward to that research trip with great enthusiasm, knowing he'd get to spend every day with Jessica Fields, the incredibly intelligent and physically stunning colleague he'd been dating for a couple of weeks, following her recent arrival at his department at the university. And he'd gotten everything he wanted. Their time in northernmost Alaska, a place he'd learned both to love and respect for its extreme beauty and danger, had been absolutely perfect. The team's research on the impact of climate change and infectious disease in polar bears advanced far beyond what they'd initially anticipated, and so had his relationship with Jessica.

It wasn't until their final day that she'd begun to show signs of unease that any scientist worth his salt would have noticed. When he'd leaned in to kiss her on the flight back to Colorado, an action that at that point in their time together had become commonplace, Jessica had pulled away, and he confronted her.

She wasn't single, she said, her eyes full of regret but not, he'd noted sadly, remorse. She was engaged to marry her college sweetheart and had no plans to break it off on account of what she called a "fling." She had led him on, she said.

Well, on that point he certainly would not argue. Sleeping with him, telling him she loved him, making plans with him…yes, he'd say she was damn right that she'd led him on. Ethan had immediately requested an alternative seat on the airplane, enduring the remainder of the flight with a clenched jaw, knotted stomach and the blinding urge to scream at the woman who had, in the space of a few months, turned his life upside down, and then quickly and heartlessly destroyed him.

The department head, though confused at his hasty, fictional explanation, had granted Ethan's request for a short sabbatical, a semester off. Ethan hadn't taken a vacation since accepting the position five years before, and he supposed he was due a break. Though it hurt, not to get started right away on compiling and writing up the Alaskan data for conference presentations. He would never forget the way his breath had caught and his heartbeat raced as he'd knelt next to one of those regal bears to take a blood sample before the tranquilizer wore off. They were the most beautiful creatures he'd ever seen; they deserved saving and he would spend the rest of his life working to do just that.

He pushed out a breath, lifting his head to stare out the window once more as he listened to wind that had begun to swirl and howl. For now, he needed time—even just a few months—to figure out how to go back to the university and face Jessica, who had made it clear she had no plans to leave the team, despite what she'd done to him. He needed to come to terms with the fact that the only woman he'd ever fallen for was getting married to someone else and, worst of all, didn't seem to give a single damn what it would do to him.

In the meantime, he had the clinic, and over the past two weeks, he had to admit, he'd become fond of the locals and their beloved pets, and even of his house calls to care for a few horses and cattle on nearby ranches. He'd always loved the research part of being a veterinary pathologist, but this…this change of pace and reminder of where his career had begun, was nice, too, at least for now.

Ethan's head jerked up at the sound of raucous banging. It took him a minute to realize that it was coming from the front door, which he'd locked an hour ago after closing. Who on earth could be knocking—no, pounding—on the door now? Ethan knew that his father occasionally extended his workday beyond its normal twelve hours when a special circumstance arose, but no one had called to say they'd be coming in late or anything of the like.

He got up from the chair quickly, leaving it swiveling as he paced to the door. Whoever stood on the front stoop wasn't visible from the window he'd been looking out before, and the blinds were pulled down on the other side to cover the spot where the sun hit in late afternoon; he'd have to get much closer and peer through them to identify his visitor.

Ethan rolled his eyes. Yes, it was his duty to help out the local animal population in any way he could, but the day had already been particularly trying—several regular exams on top of two challenging, back-to-back house calls—and he practically ached to warm up a frozen meal, shower away the fur and jump into the cozy bed in his parents' guest room.

When he got to the door, he slid a finger between two blinds and peered out, but the snow was quite thick now, surprisingly so, and the visitor so bundled up that he couldn't make out anything other than the bright crimson of a coat and matching hat. He didn't even see any animals. But the wind was so fierce, and the snow falling in such a thick blanket, that he was compelled to open the door and let the poor person in, reminding himself that this was Peach Leaf, therefore generally void of a large city's potential threats.

Bracing himself, Ethan unlocked and pulled open the door, breath rushing from his lungs as the icy air hit. A tall figure rushed forward, nearly pummeling him to get inside the building, and for a second he regretted his decision to be kind.

"Oh, thank you," came a voice, definitely a woman's, from somewhere in the depths of the coat and beanie. Ethan closed the door behind her.

"Thank you so, so much for letting me in. I thought there might not be anyone here this late and I was about to turn around and go back to my car, but…"

"Whoa, there. Hang on just a minute. Let's start at the beginning. How does that sound?" He clasped his hands in front of his abdomen and gave her some space.

The woman stopped speaking and pulled up her hat, which had fallen down into her face, nearly covering what he now saw were large, green—a very lovely green, in fact—eyes. "I'm sorry," she said, pushing out a puff of air. She reached out a gloved hand in Ethan's direction and he took it, startled to discover how cold it was.

She must be absolutely frozen from head to toe. He'd checked the thermometer that afternoon and, even before the sun had gone down, the temperature was below freezing. If he hadn't let her in, she might have been in real trouble. His semester in Alaska had taught him plenty about the dangers of extreme cold, and even though they were in Texas, which was generally mild, the hazards were the same if one wasn't careful. It didn't matter that the weather was out of the norm; it simply was, and therefore caution would need to be observed.

He hadn't anticipated things getting so bad, and hadn't much of a chance to pay attention to the forecast other than his brief check on the internet as he'd scarfed down a sandwich earlier, but now he could see plainly that the winter storm the meteorologists predicted had escalated quickly.

The woman pumped his hand up and down a few times before letting it go. "I'm June. June Leavy. I came by on the slim chance that Dr. Singh might still be here this late, and, well, I didn't really know what else to do."

"I'm Dr. Singh," Ethan said, doing his best to offer a warm smile despite feeling anything but.

The woman—June—narrowed her eyes and tilted her head to study him, chuckling softly. "Wow, Dr. Singh, I have to say, you look like you've stumbled upon the elusive fountain of youth."

Ethan had to laugh at that. Most folks, unless their pets were ill or aging, only came in for annual check-ups and vaccinations. It made sense that the senior Dr. Singh would not have had a chance to inform all clients of his winter vacation plans.

"No, I mean, I am Dr. Singh, but perhaps not the one you'd hoped to find. I'm his son Ethan."

June's face visibly relaxed as realization hit and she nodded, then proceeded to remove her gloves and hat. As she grasped her lapels and moved to take off her coat, Ethan noticed the bit of roundness at her middle and the thought crossed his mind that she might be pregnant. "Here, let me help you with that," he said, taking her coat.

He couldn't help but catch the subtle, sweet scent of her hair as he pulled the red fabric from her shoulders. Like melon, he thought. Odd that he should even notice. Odder still he should notice that it tumbled down her shoulders in soft, auburn waves, framing a face, he could see after he'd turned back from hanging her coat on an iron rack near the door, that was rosy from the cold and, well, quite lovely.

June smiled, and it occurred to Ethan that she was aptly named. Her skin was as bright as sunshine and the curve of her wide mouth heated his insides, head to toe. Her eyes were lively and warm like summer, although…her smile didn't quite reach them.

Not that he cared, though. Pure observation—like you'd get from any good scientist.

"Thank you," she said. "Now, as I was saying, I drove here on my way home from work and my car broke down about, well, I don't really know how far away, but it sure seemed like a long distance." She took a deep breath and closed her eyes as if willing calm. "Anyway, I'm here now and you're here, thank goodness."

Ethan must have looked confused, and that would make sense because he definitely was. He was glad to help if she was stranded. Perhaps he could call a tow truck for her and let her stay to wait out the storm, but other than that, he wasn't at all sure why she'd been headed this way in the first place.

When she stopped speaking, he took the chance to ask, "Is there something I can do to help you, Miss Leavy?"

"Actually, yes, there is. At least, I hope so."

His heart seemed to speed up as she bit her bottom lip and reached into the pocket of her sweatshirt with both hands. Not that he thought she would pull out a weapon, per se, but because he knew instinctively that nothing she might reveal would be easy to deal with. And what he wanted at that moment, and more than that, for his life in general right then, was just that— simplicity.

But that was simply not in the cards.

So when June Leavy pulled two shivering black-and-white puppies out of her pocket and held them out to show him why she'd driven to his office, walked an unknown distance in a freak snowstorm and nearly pounded down the door, all Ethan Singh could do was sigh.

## *Chapter 3*

As June stared at the junior Dr. Singh awaiting a response, the skin between his brows bunched into a frown over eyes that were cool and impassable, despite what she'd just revealed, making it impossible to determine what he thought of her unannounced arrival on his doorstep. Or rather, *their* arrival.

She knew it was late, that it would be an inconvenience to stop in without even a phone call when the veterinary office had closed over an hour before, but she didn't know what else to do with the two little bundles. She didn't know this man—Ethan, he'd said—but she knew his father, a kind, attentive doctor whose smiles could soothe even the saddest of children when their pets were sick, and for now, that was enough to give her hope that maybe that man's son wouldn't turn her, or her little charges, away on such an awful night.

June hadn't realized she'd been holding her breath until he reached out both hands to take the puppies from her. Letting the air slowly from her lungs, she watched as he tucked them under his arms the same way she had when she'd discovered them in the alley.

"We need to get them warmed up," he said, getting right to business. Ethan turned from where they still stood near the door and lifted a shoulder to motion for her to follow as he headed toward the examination rooms.

June had been in this office many times when her beloved cat reached his twilight years. Being there again caused memories to resurface that she hadn't prepared for when she'd made the impulsive decision to stop in, hoping someone would be there to save two little lives. Trailing behind the doctor, she focused instead on the waves of dark hair that just brushed the collar of his white coat and the broad span of his shoulders. Something about the look of him—the stormy but not unkind dark eyes, the beautiful shade of his skin, like black tea with a bit of milk stirred in, and his height, which had to be considerable to reach well over her own six feet—worked to unravel the tight ball that had formed in her belly.

Driving there in what now seemed to be a full-blast snowstorm was one of the scariest things June had ever done. It was lucky that she knew the roads as well as she did, having lived in Peach Leaf her whole life; otherwise, she wasn't sure there would have been much of a chance of making it this far, not to mention the likelihood that she and the puppies would not have survived if they'd stayed in the car. And until the extreme weather passed, it was impossible to tell what had caused her old lemon to die. Terror had struck when the engine coughed and gave up, the snow coming down so hard as the wind blew fiercely that she could barely see a foot in front of her. She'd followed the road as best she could and somehow, thankfully, had made it to the office.

What was probably only half a mile or so had become a nearly impossible journey until the glass door of the clinic came into view. And now there she was. There hadn't been time to mull over the next step—how she would get home with no working vehicle, especially with the weather throwing such a fit.

At least now she wasn't alone. Even though he didn't seem too happy to see the three of them—and really, who could blame him?—June knew somehow that he would do his best to help. Then they would just have to go from there.

Dr. Singh stopped in front of one of the exam rooms and lifted his chin toward the door, presumably asking June to open it, which she did quickly. When they were all in the room, he held the puppies out to her. "Okay, I need you to hold them for a moment. I'll be right back."

The apprehension she felt must have been poorly hidden because when he saw the look on her face Ethan's stoicism seemed to evaporate briefly; his eyes softened and the thin, serious line of his lips was replaced by a curve at one corner of his mouth that could almost pass for a grin.

"It's okay, Miss Leavy. I'll be right back, I promise. I just need to get some supplies, and it would help if you'd keep the puppies warm for just a moment longer. Can you do that for me?"

June nodded. She'd gotten the babies that far, but

the thought of being responsible for them any longer seemed more daunting now as the stress of the day compounded and the idea hit her suddenly that they might not make it. Even now, in the safety of the clinic, with a trained veterinarian to help, the chance remained that the little ones might not pull through.

"Good," he responded, nodding. "You had a great idea earlier, keeping them close together in your pocket. That way, they had each other's warmth, plus that coming from your body."

A little flutter passed through her chest at the mention of her body coming from Dr. Singh's mouth, but she just shook her head and took back the little bundles of fur, tucking them into her sweatshirt once more.

"All set?" he asked.

"Yes, I think so."

At that, he left the room and June concentrated on snuggling the little pups close, willing her warmth to be enough to keep them alive. She couldn't tell how they were doing, other than that the tiny heartbeats she'd felt for before were still thumping softly, and their sweet brown eyes were open. With any luck, that meant they were okay, but a part of her warned that there could be any number of things wrong on the inside.

She swallowed and closed her eyes, and a moment later Dr. Singh returned with what looked like a pile of fluffy towels. He placed the bundle on the exam table and moved to the bench where June sat, wrapping one around her shoulders and gently settling the warm terry cloth in place, a gesture that was completely logical considering that she still shivered from the cold, but also surprisingly intimate. She couldn't recall the last time a man had done something so simple and caring for her, and before she could think about it, she found herself gazing up at him with a warm smile.

"Thank you," she said. "That feels…wonderful."

"You're quite welcome. We've got a small washer and dryer in the staff room, so I warmed these up for a minute or two."

As he spoke, though he didn't exactly return her smile, soft crinkles formed at the outer corners of those deep brown eyes and it struck her just how exceptionally attractive this man was. She hadn't even known that the older Dr. Singh had a son, but then, they'd only shared a doctor/patient-parent relationship, so it made sense that he wouldn't have gone into detail about his family.

Strangely, now, June very much wished he had.

Ethan went back to the table and returned with another towel, kneeling to spread it on the floor at her feet. He sat cross-legged in front of it. "Here, let's put the pups in this while I take a look at them. Safer than having them up on the table for now."

June nodded and retrieved them from her pocket one at a time, cringing as they squeaked in protest at the brief separation. "Do you think…" She swallowed. "Will they be all right?"

"It's hard to know until I can look them over," he said, wrapping the towel around the puppies. "But I will say this." He looked up at her. "You've done a great job here, keeping them warm and bringing them in. From what I can see so far, I think they have a good chance, all because of you."

June's insides melted a little at his compliments, but she wouldn't feel better until she knew the puppies would be okay.

After a few moments, Dr. Singh pulled the towel to one side and very gently moved one puppy closer to him, stroking it softly behind the ears with one hand as he ran his fingers over each tiny limb, probably feeling for broken bones. He then felt the pup's adorable pink tummy, almost grinning when the little guy—she could see plainly now that the term was accurate—closed his eyes.

June placed her nervous hands into the pouch of her hoodie, crossing her fingers.

"It's a good sign that they don't mind being held," Ethan said, using a thumb to gently pry the animal's mouth open, examining its tiny teeth before listening to its heart with the stethoscope that circled his neck. "Their friendliness toward humans will certainly make it easier to place them in homes when the time comes," he pointed out matter-of-factly. "Where did you say you found them?"

June cleared her throat, surprised at how much she disliked talk of giving the puppies away, even though she had no intention of keeping them for herself. "Behind the pizza shop, where I work."

The doctor winced, then looked up and met her eyes, listening intently as she spoke.

"We were done for the day, and I went out to toss the garbage. That's when I found them behind a Dumpster." Her throat threatened to close up as she thought again of someone leaving two little dogs in the icy alley.

"Any idea how long they were there?"

June shook her head. "No. I wish I had more to tell you, but unfortunately, that's it. I didn't know what else to do."

"Well, you did precisely the right thing, though it would appear you endangered yourself attempting to make it here. These are quite the lucky little guys, having been discovered by someone like you. Their fate might have been much worse, as I'm sure I don't have to tell you." An unmistakable wave of sadness crossed over the veterinarian's face.

"I wasn't thinking about that. I just wanted them to be okay...still do."

Ethan nodded and set down the first pup, picking up the other—a girl—to go through the same exam. "There's a good chance they will, thanks to you." Finished, he tucked the brother and sister back into their towel and folded his hands together in his lap.

"So, how's it look?" she asked, nails digging into her palms.

Ethan stared at her, his eyes warmer now, perhaps resigned to the outcome of his evening. She hadn't even considered that he might have plans...perhaps a wife at home waiting for him. Then again, he wasn't wearing a ring and he hadn't texted or called anyone upon her arrival, or once he'd realized that he would be at work for a bit longer.

"Well, I'll have to do some blood work within the next few days to get a full picture, but from what I can tell at this point, it seems they'll be okay."

Relief flooded through her at the optimistic statement.

"They're about three and a half weeks old, give or take. No broken bones, healthy lungs and hearts, and their teeth are coming in, which is great news."

"So they can eat solid food? We won't have to feed them with a bottle?" June had to admit she was a little disappointed. The idea of holding the tiny puppies and feeding them sounded…nice. She had always wanted children, anyway, but after her experience with Clayton, she wasn't sure she could trust anyone enough ever again to even think about building a life with another person. Another person who had the potential to break her heart. Maybe someday, if she ever had the time and energy to spare, she could have a little puppy just like these to care for. Maybe she could try letting herself love something again…one day…but it would take time, far more than she could spare with her life the way it was, working sixty-hour weeks at the pizza parlor just to pay her rent and keep her car in working shape. She hoped things wouldn't be that way forever; it was a sobering thought.

"Yes, they can eat solid food, but we'll need to mix it with some canine milk replacer that's specially formulated for puppies. Cow's or any other kind of milk would upset their tummies."

For some reason, June grinned at the word, so much more fatherly and sweet than the more technical *stomachs*.

"Do you have that here?"

"Sure do. We've got plenty, and I can have my receptionist, Sadie, order more in the morning if need be." He lifted a corner of the towel and glanced in at the puppies. "For now, we need to get them some water and get a little food in them. We won't give them too much yet, as I don't know what or how much they've been eating and I don't want them to get bloated."

June nodded as he stood and held out a hand to help her do the same, then knelt to pick up the squeaky bundle. He led her to the back area and into a room lined with shelves of food and medicine, handing over the puppies so he could scan the stock for what they needed.

"Ah, here we are," he said, lifting a small bag from a top shelf.

He opened a cabinet and pulled out two shallow bowls, then headed to the back room, stopping at a sink to fill one with water. Into the other, he poured a small amount of pebble-size kibble. He grabbed a bottle from a nearby refrigerator and poured thin, white liquid on top, like milk on cereal. Placing the bowls on the floor in a corner, Ethan motioned for June to set down the towel. At the scent of the food, two little black noses began to wriggle and both humans laughed quietly.

"The little stinkers are cute, aren't they?"

Ethan looked up at her as he spoke and this time his smile reached those gorgeous, mahogany eyes. She felt his gaze all the way down into her middle, as warm and comforting as the towel he'd so recently wrapped around her shoulders.

"Very," she replied, her voice little more than the squeaky sound the puppies made.

Dr. Singh helped her to guide the puppies over to the bowls, and they watched with bated breath, waiting to see if the little ones would eat. Finally, both pups sniffed at the bowl of food and buried their faces in the kibble, and the sound of Ethan's and June's sighs of relief were audible.

As the dogs worked on their dinner, Ethan disappeared into the supply closet and returned holding what looked like a baby gate and paper towels. He set to work in the corner of the room, spreading out what June now saw were puppy pads, which he surrounded with the gate, creating a little pen. "All right. We'll settle them in here for a bit, give them a little time and see if they'll do their business, then we can put them to bed."

He looked up at June. "If I'm correct on their age, they should be able to go to the bathroom on their own."

"What do you mean?"

"Well, if they're too young, they'll need a little help to go, but I'm hoping they're old enough." He winked at her. "Time will tell."

"Ah." June had never been around such young animals before; once again, she was thankful to have an ally who knew far more than she about this unexpected development in her evening.

"In the meantime, is there anything I can get you?"

Her stomach grumbled, reminding her that she hadn't yet eaten and it was almost nine o'clock, but she doubted there was much in the way of people food in a veterinary clinic. "I'd love something hot to drink. That is, if you have anything."

"Come," Dr. Singh said, holding out an arm. June walked through the door in front of him and he left it open, leading her to what had to be the staff break room, where he pulled a chair from a small, round table, motioning for her to sit.

She watched as he took a measuring cup from a cabinet and placed it on a hot plate before pulling milk from the fridge and what appeared to be a few spice bottles from a drawer.

"So tell me, Miss Leavy…"

"Please, call me June."

He set to work, mixing ingredients in the glass cup

as though he were a chef in an upscale kitchen, rather than a very patient veterinarian in a small-town clinic. "June, then. Have you ever had chai?"

It was only one of her favorite drinks. "Oh, I love chai tea."

The doctor let out a chuckle as he stirred the mixture with a spoon.

"What's so funny?"

"Just chai. When you say *chai tea*, what you're really saying is *tea tea*. The word *chai* means *tea* in Hindi."

"Oh, goodness," she said, feeling like a doofus. "I'm sorry."

"Not at all," Ethan said, laughing.

June found she very much liked the deep, warm sound of it tickling her ears. He seemed much more relaxed now than he had when she'd first arrived, almost certainly ruining his night.

"Is your family from India?" she asked, surprising herself. She supposed it wouldn't hurt to find something to talk about to pass the time until the storm let up and she could go on home.

"My father was born in Delhi and came here as a child."

"And your mother?"

"She's American, from New York. They've lived in Texas for most of my life, since my father opened this clinic."

It was quiet for a few moments as Ethan continued to stir the tea and June took a couple of deep breaths, allowing herself to calm down for the first time since she'd found the puppies over two hours ago. Her shoulders ached with tension and her tiredness reached all the way down to her bones; she longed for a hot shower and her bed. For once, she would be happy to go home to her lonely, closet-size apartment, where she hoped to get at least a couple hours of sleep before her alarm clock sent her back to work.

When she opened her eyes, Ethan set two steaming mugs on the table and June lifted hers to take a sip. The hot liquid soaked all the way down into her veins, warming her through and through, the sweet, yet spicy, flavors tingling her throat in an incredibly pleasant way. "Oh, my gosh," she said, rolling her eyes toward the roof, "this is amazing."

Ethan grinned, then took a sip from his own mug. "Better than Starbucks, huh?"

"Um, yeah. Way better. Apples and oranges better."

"I'm glad you like it," he said, taking a few more sips. He got up and went back to the counter, turning on a small television set to the same local weather she'd watched earlier with Margaret. She made a mental note to text her boss soon to make sure she'd made it home.

"We'd better see what's going on out there," he said, returning to the table. "It looked much worse than I thought it was when I opened the door and you brought an arctic blast in with you and those puppies."

"It's pretty bad. I'm hoping it will clear so I can get home soon."

Ethan looked skeptical but didn't say anything as they both turned to watch the screen. It only took a few minutes for them to learn that the weather had gotten worse as they'd been taking care of the dogs. According to the meteorologist, a mass of cold, dry Canadian air had moved south into their area to intersect with a warm, moist air mass moving north from the Gulf of Mexico. Evidently, the cold air had advanced and pushed away the warm air, orchestrating the crazy mess outside. Over a foot of snow had fallen on already-icy roads and the whole of Peach Leaf was now under a winter weather warning.

June put her elbows on the table and lowered her head into her arms. It would be hours before it would be safe to drive home…for a person who had a working ride.

"Well, June," Ethan said, getting up to turn off the steady stream of impending doom on the television. "Looks like you're stuck with me for a while."

"I… I can't stay here. I've got to get home."

Ethan tilted his head. "Not going to happen, at least not tonight. It's really nasty out there—not anywhere close to safe for driving." He finished the last of his tea and picked up both of their cups, carrying them to the sink.

"My car's broken down, anyway. Surely I can at least get a tow truck out here. Maybe they can take me home."

Ethan came back and sat down across from her at the table. "It's not likely we'd be able to get a tow truck out here in this weather. I would drive you if I felt it was safe, but I've spent some time in Alaska and I've seen firsthand what can happen when people don't heed weather warnings." He paused, perhaps not wishing to sound overly concerned. "Of course, I'm not going to stop you from leaving, June, but I have to tell you, I don't think it's safe, and I'd really rather you not put yourself into any more danger than you already have today."

Ignoring the fact that this man shouldn't care about her well-being so much, June ran through all of her options in her head—all zero of them. She sighed. He was right. She was stuck there for the foreseeable future. She'd never in her life experienced such a dangerous storm and she definitely didn't know how to safely travel in one. Besides, she had the puppies to think of now. The minute she'd picked them up, they'd become her responsibility, and she couldn't just abandon them with a doctor who had other patients to care for, especially one who was only temporarily managing his father's clinic.

She looked up at Dr. Singh, who appeared almost as uneasy as she.

"I hate to break it to you, June, but under the circumstances, the smartest thing for you to do is to spend the night here with me."

## Chapter 4

It took June longer than it should have to register what Dr. Singh—Ethan—had said. Mostly because, somehow, she'd gotten momentarily lost in those cinnamon eyes of his. The man was handsome in a way that could almost be described as beautiful, but his looks were also sort of unnerving at the same time, as though they had the potential power to unravel her completely.

It occurred to her that looks like his didn't really fit in with the men she was used to seeing in Peach Leaf, almost as though she'd woken up still inside a dream involving a movie set. Men who looked like Ethan Singh were generally employed as actors or male models… not small-town veterinarians. And they usually associated with other exceptionally attractive or powerful people, or in his case, highly educated people…people nothing like her.

Staring at him made her think of all the ways she couldn't quite measure up. Though she wasn't sure where that notion had even originated from. After all, why would she need to measure up at all?

It wasn't like he was interested in her, at least aside from his medical duty to assist her in getting the puppies healthy. He certainly wasn't interested in her as a woman, as well he shouldn't be, because she was not interested in him as a man.

Really, she was not.

She shouldn't be, at any rate, not after what she'd been through the past several months. No woman in her right mind would seek to get back out there after the burn she'd suffered. And even though she might not be thinking clearly, what with her only real possession stuck out in the snow enduring God only knew what horrors, which might prevent it from ever working again—and with this man staring at her with unmistakable amusement as she waited for appropriate words to arrive—she could at least be certain that she was, in fact, in her right mind.

With that, she cleared the cobwebs from her throat and finally spoke, hoping her voice wouldn't come out too rusty from lack of use.

"Um, okay. I guess that makes sense." She swiped a hand across her forehead, suddenly warm despite the weather outside and the room's cool temperature.

"Of course it does," Ethan answered, his tone final as if the issue had been decided and there was nothing more to be discussed. But June thought there was plenty in need of discussion. Like, for example, the fact that she was suddenly starving.

And not, it would seem as she found herself in danger of falling deep into those eyes again, just for food.

The thought rushed in unbidden and was stuck there in her mind before she could stop it, meaning that the mature thing now would be to address where it had come from and what it meant. At some point. For now, feeling more ragged than she did after a double shift at work and hungrier than she could ever recall having been before, maturity was the last thing on her mind.

"Is something wrong?" the devastatingly handsome doctor asked, his voice even sexier thanks to its thick note of concern.

June shook her head. "No, it's fine. Or in any case, I suppose it has to be." She looked away from him and, not surprisingly, her mind was instantly clearer.

She would have to be careful around those eyes from now on, especially if she was meant to endure an entire night—possibly more, if the weather didn't clear up—with a man who looked like he'd just walked out of the latest glossy issue of *GQ*.

He made her want things she shouldn't want, things she couldn't have.

"What is it, then?"

When she didn't answer, he tilted his head like a curious puppy—like a ridiculously adorable, curious puppy.

"Come on now, I can tell you were thinking about something."

Like a tickle of wind against her cheek, she sensed him staring at her, willing her to speak.

"It's just that, well—" a hand flew to her stomach involuntarily "—I'm starving."

Ethan threw his head back and laughed, the sound

low and sultry and full of mischief, leaving June almost frustrated with his level of physical perfection. Couldn't he at least have an absurd-sounding, high-pitched laugh or something? Was there nothing about this guy that wouldn't make her want to kiss him?

It was just her luck—she should be used to this by now—to be stuck overnight with the most distractingly attractive guy she'd ever met, right after the absolute worst breakup she'd ever endured.

*Come on, Junie*, she chastised herself. *That's about enough negativity for two lifetimes, don't you think?*

Best to push on. Besides, with the cards she'd been dealt, what choice did she have?

"All right. What's so darn funny?" she asked.

"Nothing, really. It's just that here you are looking so incredibly serious and come to find out you're just hungry."

"Hilarious," she responded, this time allowing a hint of playfulness to escape. "But seriously, I haven't had anything to eat since lunch, which now seems like years ago. I know it might be useless to ask, but is there anything to eat around here? That is, anything we can get to without risking our lives."

Ethan grinned, his full lips setting in motion a series of thoughts that she wasn't entirely certain were legal.

"Actually, this might be one problem we can solve."

"Don't tease me now. I'm this close to sneaking some of that puppy kibble from the storage room."

He laughed. "I wouldn't dare. There's a bakery a few doors down. It might be a rough trip, but I think if we stay right next to the building and, well, right next to each other, we can probably make it with only minimal danger."

"Stay—" June swallowed "—next to each other?"

"Of course. For warmth."

June felt her cheeks heat, hoping they weren't turning as ghastly pink as they were in the habit of doing—the eternal curse of redheads like herself. "Yes, right. Warmth. Of course."

It made perfect sense under the circumstances; it really did. But the mere thought of being near Ethan for the duration it might take them to reach sustenance raised her temperature enough that she was fairly certain she could comfortably walk all the way to her apartment in the wind that had begun to howl outside the clinic like a wild animal.

Without a coat.

"Let's check on the puppies, get you bundled back up and see if we can't get some food," Ethan said, tossing his new companion a sweet smile. "I could go for some dinner myself."

While that was definitely true—his stomach had been protesting against its emptiness since he'd seen his last patient, and that had been hours ago—there was another reason, equal in weight to the first, that he'd suggested leaving the office and grabbing something to eat.

That reason was June Leavy.

A few hours before, his life in Peach Leaf had been simple and clear, intentionally so.

This morning, he'd woken with a relatively muddled head for the first time since leaving Colorado.

Since he'd left *her*.

Sure, he still thought about his ex a few times a day still; that was perfectly normal following the demise of a serious relationship. But aside from those few painful moments, things had actually started to look up, and he'd gotten into a comfortable groove. Wake up and go for an early run, shower and eat breakfast, arrive at the clinic before sunrise to relieve the night technician and check on the overnight patients, work through his father's back-to-back appointments, breaking only for a quick lunch, and then go home after he'd completed evening rounds and closed up. He'd say goodbye to the staff and head home, too tired to think. Working from dark sky to dark sky suited him at this odd juncture in his life. The routine kept him busy and, most importantly, left little time for ruminating over all he'd left behind.

At least it had, until that evening, when June Leavy had burst through the door, literally bringing with her a blast of fresh air.

The image made him smile. As cold as it had been when she'd walked in, June was about as different from his frosty ex as she could be—a truth he didn't really want to examine closely.

But as beautiful as June was, as sweet and warm as he could clearly see she was even in the limited time they'd spent together, the truth remained that her presence was simply not welcome.

She filled the room in a way that, while extremely pleasant—intoxicating, even—made him uncomfortable. Tall, bright in color and in mood and lively, June was impossible to ignore. Sharing a cup of tea with her had been difficult enough, but offering to let her stay the night—something he'd had no choice but to do on account of the growing danger outside—was going to take an iron will.

He didn't want her in his clinic, didn't want her on his mind. Being in the same room with her for the past while, as warm as she made him feel, he'd almost forgotten about the blizzard wailing away outside.

All of which was dangerous. What he needed was space, and a clear head.

Taking June for a bite to eat was the perfect solution. They were both hungry, and it would give him a chance to get a grip on whatever spark she'd ignited within him. Plus, he'd like to check on his father's business neighbors—the couple who owned the German bakery next door had been there for years and were close with his dad. They were elderly, and it would be good to make sure they were holding up through the freak snowstorm.

A blast of frigid air would do him good, and then he could figure out how to handle himself around June for the rest of the evening.

Things came to mind. So many things.

None of them realistic, or even appropriate for that matter.

A guy like him was in no position to be picturing those endless legs curled up next to his on the office sofa, for example, or better yet, wrapped around his middle as he kissed the daylights out of those undoubtedly soft lips and…

No. He couldn't let himself go there. Not again. It was stupid enough that he'd allowed his thoughts to wander this far. It seemed any time he ventured away from work for five minutes, he landed in trouble. He didn't want to be the sort of man who was so easily distracted by a pretty face and a pair of killer legs.

He looked up to find the object of his musings worrying her bottom lip as she studied him.

It wasn't sexy, the way she did that. Not at all.

The resultant swelling of those soft pink clouds did not affect him. Not in the least.

Also, he needed to check the thermostat—had it gotten warmer inside the clinic?

"So, what kind of place is it?" June asked, her cheeks slightly more flushed than they'd been when she first came in from the wind. Surely she wasn't... she couldn't possibly be having similar thoughts to the ones he'd been entertaining. The idea was absurd. He'd been radiating a cool demeanor and a general *leave me alone, I'm busy* attitude for weeks now that would put off any woman. More likely, she was just in a hurry to get out of there as much as he was.

"I mean what kind of food do they have?"

"Oh, well, there's the rub," he answered, trying not to get distracted again by those wicked lips, which had reddened to a pretty ruby shade—from the cold or from her nibbling, he no longer cared.

And what difference did it make, anyway?

It certainly didn't matter that they looked good enough to feast on himself, like fresh cherries ripe for the picking.

*Dammit!*

What the hell had they been talking about again?

"The rub?"

*Ah, yes.*

"It's just a little German bakery, you see. So we won't be able to get any real dinner. We'll have to skip straight to dessert. Hopefully it'll do until the weather lets up and you have a chance to head on your way."

A thought that disturbed him far more than he cared to acknowledge.

Something crossed her features very briefly—a shadowy hint of darkness, perhaps—and then disappeared.

Was it something he'd said that had so quickly stolen the light from her eyes?

He didn't have time to figure it out before she spoke again.

"Oh, that's right. How silly of me to forget. I've been working such weird hours the past few years that I haven't been to Bauer's in ages—I'd forgotten about the place until now." Her features softened into wistfulness. "My mom used to take me there as a kid, on special occasions. They have the best pastry and…"

She blushed again and he wished to touch the crimson apples on her cheeks. He enjoyed her rambling—quite a lot actually. But what good would it do to say so? After that night, she would be gone and he would go back to his temporary, if somewhat lonely, life.

Still, it was nice to see her talk about something so obviously important to her; it was nice to see inside her just a little.

"Anyway, I'm rambling, but that will be just fine. I'm so hungry I really don't care what we eat, as long as it passes for food."

"And is preferably intended for human consumption," he teased, recalling her earlier comment about kibble, and wanting to restore her brightness.

"That would be great," she said, beaming.

Pleased, he gestured for her to follow him to the back room and she did so. When they stepped through the door, the puppies were curled so tightly together that he and June had to check to make sure the little ones were both accounted for. After changing out the potty pad, they watched the critters sleep for a few moments, Ethan checking their breathing before he gently touched June's elbow, whispered that the pups would be okay with only each other as company for a short while longer and led her out to the front of the clinic.

"I feel like I'm leaving my kids alone at home," June said, shrugging into her coat, which he held open for her.

"I completely understand, and sadly, I don't think this is their first time on their own," Ethan said, wanting to reassure her, "but we won't be long and I promise they'll be fine until we return."

What was he thinking, making a promise like that? Yes, the animals appeared relatively healthy and strong, considering their situation, and yes, he was confident in his ability to usher them back to full health, but he had no history of clairvoyance and therefore no business making guarantees regarding things he couldn't fully control.

What had gotten into him? Would he say anything to make this woman smile?

Catching the worried crease between her brows as she glanced once more over her shoulder in the direction of the pups, Ethan tucked his hand beneath her elbow. "Trust me, June. They'll be all right. Their bellies are full, they've had fresh water and have done their business, they're safe inside the pen and they're not alone."

The answer was yes, apparently, he would say anything.

At his words, her expression softened, and though

he didn't want to examine why it mattered to him at all, he found himself relieved at the idea of having provided some comfort. "Also, I would not leave them if I believed them to be unsafe, okay?"

She nodded.

"So then, do you trust me?"

She wasn't quick to answer, a fact that made him like her even more. After all—though he wasn't entirely sure any longer whether he believed time to be a reliable factor in the decision to invest trust in someone—they'd only known each other for little over an hour.

"Yes," she finally said. "I do trust you."

He smiled, more pleased than wisdom should allow.

"Good." He squeezed her elbow, then let go. "I figure the best thing to do now is grab something to go and come back here. That way, we won't risk getting stuck at the bakery. Even though it's only a few yards away, we could end up unable to get back, and I don't want to leave the puppies alone for a full night."

"Sounds like a plan," June agreed.

Ethan pulled on his coat and wrapped a scarf around his neck and face before donning his hat. By the time he'd finished, June had done the same and looked adorable, a description that, despite being worlds apart from characterizing the women he was typically attracted to, seemed somehow more enticing.

June looked like someone he could curl up and have hot chocolate with after a long day at work, someone who would be joyful when a guy walked in the door, happy to spend an evening at home with him just relaxing, doing nothing in particular.

That was just it—the sight of her evoked *home* to

him, something he could never ascribe to the women he'd dated before, women who preferred nights out on the town on the arm of a successful professor. It didn't escape him that, over the past few years, being a "nerd" had become an asset, one he'd not hesitated to take full advantage of, and there had been plenty of young women, even a few former students, who had been eager to date an up-and-coming scientist who'd begun, much to his dismay, to attract media attention.

But June was part of a different world than the one he'd become accustomed to. For reasons he couldn't explain, she brought to mind everything he missed about living in a small town, being close to family and so much more. He'd spent a good portion of the last decade thinking only of his career, dedicating all of his time to furthering his research and, if he was honest, to impressing his department at the university.

June made him think of other things. Things he used to want but truly thought he didn't need any longer— things like home, and family, and someone to share it with. Someone to love.

None of which he would entertain, because that word—*love*—was no longer part of his vocabulary when it came to women.

Of course he loved his parents, his siblings and his nieces and nephews, but that was the safe kind of love. Loving a woman, which would inevitably lead to a broken heart again—well, that was an experience he'd rather not repeat. Especially not when his heart hadn't quite healed from the last.

What kind of scientist would he be if he didn't learn from failed experiments?

"Remind me again why we're doing this?" June

asked as he opened the door and snow crashed through with the force of a speeding train.

He reached for her hand and, when she grabbed it with her own, pulled her close to his body, tucking an arm over her shoulders. He chose to ignore the way she stiffened as their figures came together, not caring to assess whether it was aversion or pleasure at the contact that made her react in such a way.

"Because we're starving, remember?"

"Oh, right," she said. "Somehow the idea of having my face frozen off made me forget how hungry I am."

He started to laugh but stopped when icy air hit his lungs, and set his focus on moving ahead instead. As they made their way in the direction of the bakery, Ethan was careful to keep his free hand against the wall of the building as the wind's forceful blasts threatened to send them flying into the white abyss that used to be a parking lot. June's head was down, her chin tucked into the top of her coat as he led the way. Despite the circumstances, Ethan couldn't help but enjoy the way her tall, slim figure nestled against his own, her body's warmth seeping through the layers of his clothing, strong enough to set off a flame in his lower abdomen.

Astounding, the lack of discipline he'd allowed in letting himself get carried away over June. Having her huddle against his skin for warmth was one thing; that just made practical, biological sense.

Letting her under it, though, was another matter entirely.

"Looks like there's a note on the door," Ethan shouted to June, who was still tucked under his arm. It was virtually impossible to hear himself think, let alone to communicate with each other with the high-speed wind whipping around them. They were only a couple of yards from Bauer's Bakery and, Ethan hoped, his stomach growling like an angry dog, something hot to eat.

He felt June nod beneath his shoulder as it occurred to him for the first time, stupidly, that the Bauers might have closed up early and hit the road once the weather started to get worse. He certainly couldn't blame them; it's exactly what he would have done if he didn't have so many little furry creatures depending on him. Even if he'd been able to earlier before June showed up, after he'd told the overnight tech not to risk the trip in, he would never have left the babies alone on a night like this.

As soon as they made it to the door of the bakeshop, June emerged from his side and reached for it, only to find it locked. He wasn't surprised, but he sure as hell was disappointed. The note on the door had been taped at all four corners, three of which were now torn. Peeling off the last, he read it only to confirm his earlier assumption that the Bauers had gone home, and he was glad for their safety.

"Well, crap," June said, turning to face him. "Guess we'll have to head back to the clinic. Maybe we can find a granola bar to split or something. Or… doggy biscuits are basically flour and water, right? So, maybe if we use our imaginations, it would be like eating cookies."

He'd have to be a little more desperate to try a canine treat, but if they did find a granola bar, Ethan would let June have the whole thing. However, it was too early in the game to consider giving up just yet.

"Hang on a minute."

June's face was bright pink from the well-below-freezing temperature and the wind's icy fingers slapping at her cheeks. He needed to get her inside that building, needed to get her warm.

"I've got a key." He took off one mitten and, reaching under his coat, pulled his wallet out of his back pocket and dug through the compartments until he found what he was looking for. "My dad gave it to me in case the Bauers had an emergency."

June didn't look too relieved; probably she was holding out to make sure it worked. That made two of them. He hadn't paid much attention when Dad went through all the important numbers and files and such that Ethan might need while caring for the clinic, and it hadn't occurred to him to check and see if the key worked. Who would have guessed that the worst storm in Texas history would hit during his stay?

"Well, what are you waiting for?" she yelled so he could hear, her eyes squinting against the brutal air.

With fingers on the brink of frostbite, he gripped the key and shoved it into the lock, releasing an audible sigh when it fit and the knob turned.

"Oh, thank God," June said, her eyes shooting toward the sky.

Ethan opened the door and ushered her inside, pulling it closed against a turbulent gust.

Once inside, Ethan leaned his back against the door, then they looked at each other and both started laughing as relief and the possibility of getting their hands on some food settled in. The moment of relaxation didn't last long, though, and suddenly Ethan heard a sharp, incessant beeping.

"Oh, crap!" he shouted, echoing June's words from when she'd thought they were locked out in the cold. This could be worse.

When she met his eyes, hers were wide as salad plates. "Is that what I think it is?"

"Uh, yeah. 'Fraid so."

"Oh, no. No, no, no." Her hands flew to her cheeks and she stared at him with obvious fear. "We are going to be in so much trouble when the police…"

He held up a hand in an attempt to prevent her panic from gaining momentum.

"Hang on. It would take them ages to get here if they were coming at all, but I've got a strong feeling that's not going to happen. Luckily, I also have a plan." He reached into his pocket once more, praying his phone was still in there; he hadn't checked before they left the clinic, a distraction he could justifiably blame on June. He pressed his thumb against a button, unlocking the cell, and dialed as quickly as his icicle fingers would allow.

"What are you doing?"

"Just trust me, okay?"

She nodded at the same time his father picked up.

"Dad, hey, I'm glad you answered. I need you to listen carefully. I don't have much time."

"Ethan, is that you?" his father asked.

He rolled his eyes.

"Yes, Dad, of course it's me. Look, do you have the alarm code to the Bauers' place?"

He waved at June to get her attention and motioned for her to open the keypad near the door where the alarm continued to blare its warning.

"Just a minute, son, I think I have it here somewhere." Ethan could picture the older man digging through the kitchen junk drawer of his uncle's apartment in DC.

Ethan groaned—getting his father to hurry up was about as futile as trying to force a cat to walk on a leash—but thankfully, he'd set to work without an argument.

"Time is of the essence here, Dad."

"All right, all right. I've got it right in front of me now. Just let me put on my reading glasses." More shuffling ensued. "Are you ready?"

"Of course I am. Go ahead."

He listened as his dad recited the code, repeating it to June, who promptly punched the numbers into the keypad. When the inane beeping stopped, Ethan dropped the phone to his side and they both let out the breaths they'd been holding since the noise began.

"Is everything okay now?" his father's voice chimed from the cell.

"Yes, Dad, it's fine. Thanks a bunch. It's a long story and I can't talk now, but I needed to get into the Bauers' and I've got the key you gave me. I just hadn't considered the alarm system."

"Tell Dr. Singh thank you for me," June called out.

He nodded that he would.

"Is that a girl?" his dad asked.

Ethan rolled his eyes. "Yes, Dad. And she said to tell you she's thankful for the help, as well. But like I said, I'll have to explain later. I have to go…"

"What girl?" came his mother's voice in the background.

Grumbling rose up from his throat when he heard her snatch the phone from his father's hand.

*Here we go.*

"Ethan Singh, do you have a girlfriend you haven't told us about? Are you on a date? You should not be on the phone while on a date. I raised you better than that and…"

"Mom, Mom! I'm not on a date." He shook his head at the curious, teasing smile that sprung up on June's face. She crossed her arms, clearly enjoying his misery just a little too much.

"Look, like I told Dad, I've got to go. I'll talk to you guys later."

"You'd better not be out with a woman and keeping it a secret from us, Ethan. I'm your mother and I deserve to know if your heart isn't broken anymore and you're back out there. Are you back out there, Ethan? I certainly hope so. I never liked that last girl and I know you can do so much better."

"Jessica, Mom. Her name was Jessica. All right, thanks for the lecture. I really do have to go, though."

"Bring her by the house so we can meet her, son," his dad interjected from the background. "I don't know if your mother has told you yet but we're coming back down for Neena's birthday party in a few days. We will see your new friend then."

"Yes, do so," Melanie Singh agreed. "And sooner rather than later. I don't like to see you so down all the time."

He could practically see the maternal finger shaking in his face.

"You're not getting any younger, Ethan," she continued, "and I want to see you settled before you're old and gray."

He gazed heavenward, hoping maybe the guy upstairs would throw him a bone. As if getting stuck in a blizzard without dinner wasn't bad enough, now he had to endure an inquisition from his overinvolved parents while a woman he'd been attracted to the moment he laid eyes on her looked on with thinly veiled amusement.

June could at least have the courtesy not to look so thoroughly entertained.

"Yes, Mom. Tell Dad I said bye. I will talk to you later."

"Not so fast. First, promise you'll bring this young lady by for Neena's birthday party. The more, the merrier, I always say."

He'd never heard her use that expression before in his life, but this was a time for picking battles.

"I can't do that."

"And why ever not?"

His jaw clenched and he withheld choice words. "Because as I said, we are not dating. If you'd been listening you would know that we've only just met, June and I. Now I really do have to go."

"Oh, June is such a pretty name, but, Ethan, if you're not dating this young woman, then what are you doing with her in the middle of this weather? After the clinic is closed?"

"She's not...we're not..." He closed his eyes, drawing in a slow breath and hopefully a hefty dose of patience, too. "I will explain later."

"I know you, Ethan," his mother said, her voice stern now. "The party. Next weekend. You'll call me later for the details."

"I..." Oh, what was the point in fighting her? When

Melanie Singh got an idea in her head, there was simply no talking her out of it. "All right, Mom. I promise."

"Good boy," she said, the sound of victory clear as a bell in her falsely innocent voice.

He knew when to admit defeat. "Okay, Mom. Goodbye."

He pushed the end call button with a bit more ferocity than was necessary. June was standing there staring at him, arms still crossed, a pleased grin curling her lips up at the corners.

"You don't have to look so smug, you know."

June's eyebrows shot up. "Smug?" she asked, pointing at her chest. "Who, me?"

She batted her eyelashes, a gesture that was meant to be silly but instead ticked up his pulse a notch.

"Yes, smug. I can see you got a kick out of watching me get dominated by my overbearing family, and you're enjoying it far too much." He shoved his cell back into his pocket and took a few steps nearer to the woman who'd turned his evening upside down—whether in a good way or bad still remained to be seen.

Something in her eyes darkened, but she quickly brushed aside whatever had bothered her for half a second. "Not at all. I mean, I did enjoy listening in on your conversation, I admit, but probably not in the way you think."

"I'm intrigued. Go on." It was his turn to cross his arms, and he did so with a smile on his face, enjoying the easy banter with her. It had been a long time since he'd felt so tranquil in a woman's presence, and even though he wasn't willing to invest his heart in one again, what harm could there be in having a bit of fun? They were stuck in each other's company for the night, after all. Maybe it wouldn't hurt to enjoy the short time they had.

He expected June's next words to be playful, flirty even, but instead they were serious.

"It's just that…well, it sounds like your parents are very sweet. You're a lucky guy."

"Oh, June, you have no idea," he said softly, trying to set the tone to light again. "My parents are many things, but sweet is not one of them."

Her eyes crinkled at the corners and registered disbelief. "You're bluffing. They sound incredibly sweet."

"They are kind people, I'll allow that. But—" he made a clicking sound with his tongue "—meddlesome to an unholy degree."

He stood only inches away from her now, and the heat radiating in that small space was enough to warm the entire cold bakery.

"At any rate, I'm in debt to them for that alarm code, so I'm in no position to complain."

"Goodness, me, too," June added. "I think my butt was literally about to freeze off."

"Wouldn't that be a shame?" he quipped, the words popping out before he could reconsider.

June would have been justified in socking him a good one, but the thing was, he didn't for a second regret the comment. It was true—the woman had a great ass—and he wasn't afraid to admit it.

For a second, her pretty mouth hung open in surprise, and then it did something rather unexpected.

She smiled—a gorgeous, sexy smile—even a little naughty, he would say, and he couldn't help but grin back.

They stood there like two teenage idiots on a first

date until finally June gave a little cough. "Right. Food," he said, more than a little sorry to see the moment pass.

## Chapter 5

"Obviously no one's here, so what are we going to do?"

Ethan pulled off his outerwear and made a motion for June to let him help with her coat. He plucked the garment from her shoulders and she was instantly grateful for the air that slid over her skin like cool water.

He'd gone and done it again—made her uncomfortably warm with that silky voice and those delicious brown eyes. Not to mention she was certain her heart would melt as she'd listened to his humorous but charming conversation with his folks.

June swallowed, willing the lump in her throat to dissolve.

She loved her own mom fiercely, but that had never stopped her from wanting more as a kid, from wanting a real family. A whole family. It was easy to admit that she wasn't a kid anymore, that she should grow up and accept reality, but some wishes did not go away.

When her ex had deceived her, stolen every cent of the money she'd saved to start her own bakery, then topped that off by leaving her in the dust with a shattered heart, she'd thought more than once how comforting it would have been to have a sister. And yeah, she had good friends—not many that she kept in touch with, considering the long hours her job required, but a few close ones nonetheless. Her best friend, Katie, was always there for her, when she and her husband, Ryan, weren't too busy with their kids' many activities. It was just that sometimes she couldn't help thinking how wonderful it would be to have someone she'd grown up with, someone who knew her history— who loved her deeply and unconditionally—to have her back when things got really tough. Really, really tough. Like you're-on-your-back-and-someone-kicks-you-in-the-face kind of tough. That's certainly how she'd felt when Clayton had taken everything she'd ever invested into the bakery.

And, it sometimes seemed, much more.

On the loneliest nights in her tiny apartment, without even a cat to keep her company anymore, June sometimes felt like he'd taken her very future from her. To her name, she had a rented apartment, a car she didn't yet own and a job that paid only slightly over minimum wage. Nothing that really, truly, belonged to her.

Sometimes her whole life felt borrowed, as if someone could come collect at any time and she would have nothing left but the clothes on her back.

Of course, she would never admit that to anyone—not ever. She was June Leavy, the positive girl who'd grown up poor with a single mom who broke her back at multiple jobs to put food on the table but could never scrape together enough for a much-deserved vacation—all with a smile on her face.

Because if she didn't smile, there was only one alternative. And even on her lowest days, feeling sorry for herself was not an option.

And then there was Ethan Singh, saving puppies and rocking her world during the biggest storm of her life.

If she didn't watch herself, he might convince her that she was not a woman who no longer trusted men. Or, at least, he might make her want to try.

She gave herself a mental shake.

No way. She wasn't going there again. She knew to stay away from a face like that when she saw one. Her ex had been a good-looking guy and she'd been the envy of all her friends, until he'd broken her heart into a thousand little pieces.

She was a much stronger woman now, and would not fall victim to a handsome face, liquid-gold voice and a knock-your-pants-off body.

"We're going to do what we came to do—get something to eat."

His comment brought her back to the present situation. She was starving, yes, but she wasn't about to steal food from a sweet old couple who'd pinched her cheeks as a child. Perhaps they could leave a note and pay later.

"We can't just take food when no one's here."

"Of course we can. These are dire circumstances, June, on the off chance you haven't noticed."

Something about the way he said her name turned her insides into custard.

"I've known the Bauers since my dad opened the clinic, and they won't mind one bit."

She was skeptical and it must have shown in her expression.

"Look, there's nothing to worry about. I'll leave a note and some cash and drop by to explain when the storm is over. No worries. Besides, I'm pretty sure Mrs. Bauer would hate to see us leave here empty-handed. She's always bringing the clinic staff cookies and trying to fatten us up. If anything, she'll be happy we helped ourselves."

He had a point there. The Bauers were childless and seemed to take immense joy in spoiling other peoples' kids with their stellar baked goods. The bakery was their passion and the older couple loved nothing more than watching people savor their homemade desserts.

She wasn't exactly keen on the idea, but desperate times and all…

"If you're sure."

Ethan pulled a large bill out of his wallet and left it on the counter, promising to find a pen and paper before they left.

"I'm sure."

She raised her hands in surrender. "I suppose we don't really have a choice, now do we?"

"That's my girl."

The words hit her harder than the wind outside. Why did she like them so much? And why, when she'd only been around him for a few hours, did this guy have the power to unravel her with a couple of words?

Yep, she definitely needed to watch out.

As if to remind her that biology had a say in things, June's stomach let out a lion-worthy roar, making Ethan laugh and lightening the mood.

She covered her mouth to stifle a grin. "Sorry about that."

"Nonsense. Let's just get something in there already."

"Deal."

With that, they made their way behind the glass cases, which had been emptied for the night, and into the kitchen. June didn't see any pastries, but the scent of fresh dough tickled her nose and made her even hungrier, if such a thing was possible at that point. And yet there was absolutely no food in sight. Which made perfect sense—under normal circumstances, the Bauers would be there early in the morning to make everything from scratch for the day. Unfortunately, there were two ravenous people in need of immediate sustenance, and baked goods weren't exactly known for being made quickly.

Ethan appeared as disappointed as she felt.

"Okay, so I don't see anything to eat, and now's probably as good a time as any to admit that I know less than nothing about baking."

June chuckled, scanning the shelves stocked with flour, sugar and other products. She had an idea that just might work if she could drum up the right stuff. "You're in luck. I do happen to know a thing or two."

"Oh, really?" Ethan asked, his dark brows lifting in hope.

"Really." She rubbed her hands together. "I just need the proper ingredients, so let's see what we can find."

"By all means, then. Put me to work."

"I'd really rather not use the Bauers' electricity by turning on the industrial-size ovens, and I'm anxious to get back to the clinic and see how the puppies are doing, but I think I know just the thing to make back at the clinic." Now it was her turn to ask. "Do you trust me?"

He grinned, giving her a full view of his perfect white teeth between chestnut-colored lips that looked good enough to bite.

"I do."

"Okay, then. If you can grab a sack of sugar and one of flour from those shelves—" she pointed behind him "—I'll see if I can't manage to scare up some cocoa powder."

He clapped his hands together and headed toward the rows of neatly organized baking supplies. "I don't know what you're up to, Miss Leavy, but if it includes cocoa, I'm in."

There were lots of things she'd like to do with him that included various forms of chocolate, but she supposed she'd have to settle with baking. Especially since, she reminded herself, no matter how sexy he was and no matter how many unwanted but delicious images he brought to mind every time he graced her with that smile, she wasn't looking for a relationship. Her stay in Singlesville was meant to be permanent.

Having given him an assignment, she made her way to the walk-in refrigerator and, shivering at the climate that matched the one she'd just escaped from, grabbed a carton of eggs.

She opened the door and ran smack into Ethan.

The eggs were safe as she had instinctively pulled their carton against her chest to shield the contents from impact, but when he grasped her shoulders and stared into her eyes, she was very, very far from safe.

"I'm so sorry, June. Are you all right?"

His lips were too close to hers, but yes, technically she was okay. She looked away, fighting to slow the sudden surge in her heart rate.

"Yes, I'm fine," she lied, averting her eyes. "What were you doing here, anyway?"

Perhaps he wasn't immune to her, after all. She caught a tiny jump in the muscle of his jaw, and he was definitely breathing more heavily than the situation warranted. And his pulse was tap-tap-tapping against the velvety skin of his throat, almost in time with her own.

"I was just… I came to check on you. I got the flour and sugar like you said, and, well, you were in there for longer than I liked."

*Oh, God*, she needed to get away from him. Now.

She pulled back and he let his hands drop.

"Great. I just need to get some vegetable oil and we'll be set."

If she just kept busy, the awkward moment would pass and they could both forget about it.

Ethan cleared his throat but didn't have the decency to stop looking at her. If she hadn't been mistaken, for a second there, it seemed like he might have been on the verge of kissing her.

Far worse, she could not guarantee that she wouldn't have stopped him.

She watched as he moistened his lips, reassuring herself that this was reality and he could not, in fact, read her mind. He could see that, in spite of herself, she would have allowed him to press those lips against hers, just to see what it would be like to have that sensual-beyond-words mouth covering her own.

But the moment was gone forever, and that was a good thing.

It was.

She pushed her shoulders back, remembering where she was and what she was doing there.

"Right," he said. "We'd better get back and check on the puppies."

Her head bobbed rapidly up and down.

"I couldn't agree more."


"You're making what in a what now?" Ethan asked when they were back at the clinic.

June rolled her eyes in exasperation.

"Brownies. In a cup. Like I said."

"I'm not following. I have had brownies a time or two and I really do not see how you could successfully make such things in a coffee mug."

"Well, you'll just have to wait and see, then, ye of little faith."

Having traipsed back through the weather carrying zippered bags of flour, sugar and cocoa, the little bit of oil she'd poured into a mason jar, along with the couple of eggs she'd stuffed in her pockets, they were both dying to eat.

While she'd set out the ingredients on the limited counter space of the tiny break room, Ethan had checked on the pups, returning to say that he'd freshened their water, changed out their potty pad and given them a little more food to eat, and they were snuggled back up for additional, much-needed rest.

The poor little ones were doubtless exhausted from

the sheer effort of staying warm in below-freezing temperatures, not to mention having fended for themselves for who knew how long. She knew they would need homes soon, but she didn't want to think yet about giving them away. There was no way she could keep a puppy—not with hours like hers at the pizza place—but their little faces made her heart ache.

So much had been lost to her over the past several months that, even though she knew the tiny creatures did not belong to her, the idea of losing them might threaten to push her over some invisible edge of grief.

"All right," she said, winking at her companion and focusing on the task at hand, trying to block those little brown puppy eyes from her mind, "prepare to be awed and amazed."

Ethan smiled at her, looking ridiculously adorable with his elbows on the counter, chin in hands, watching her like an eager little boy.

She pulled their tea mugs from earlier out of the dish drying rack and mixed ingredients into each one. As Ethan stared, intrigued, she then put the mugs into the microwave. Only a minute and a half later, out popped deliciousness.

She presented him with a mug and stood back, ready to watch him take a bite. When he did, he closed his eyes and remained still long enough to worry her.

"Oh. My. God," he said, barely in time to take another mouthful. "This is amazing."

She shrugged and picked up her own serving. "It's not that exciting, but it's the best I can do with limited time and materials."

"You're being too modest, June. I'm not kidding—this is possibly the best brownie I've ever tasted."

She covered her mouth and a laugh escaped as she swallowed a large bite of moist chocolate. "That's just the starvation talking."

It was true. Microwave brownies were no secret—they had been trending all over the internet for a while—and she was absolutely not the first one to make them. But in a pinch, they'd have to do.

Out of nowhere, something hit her in the gut, and this time, it wasn't hunger.

It was longing, deep and pure.

She couldn't recall the last time she'd baked anything. Not microwave brownies, not her favorite apple caramel pie or any of her secret cookie recipes that were famous among her friends.

It had been…months.

And she missed it. So, so much.

She had a sudden, desperate urge to bake something for Ethan. Something far better than the stupid brownie he was digging into so hard and clearly enjoying, if the periodic moans he emitted between bites were anything to go on.

While it was absolute bliss to see him loving something she'd made for him, it would be a thousand times more satisfying to see him dive into something really special, something that was truly an original creation of her own.

Baking had been her passion, the one constant in her life. Despite working a full-time job, June's mom had always made time for her when she'd had the chance, time they usually spent in the kitchen mixing up delightful things to eat.

June disagreed with the common conception that baking was a science, not an art. On the contrary, she and her mom had thrown caution to the wind when it came to treats; they played with ingredients and measurements to their hearts' content, never afraid to risk disaster for the possibility of unearthing new greatness.

June released a soft sigh. Those were some of her very favorite memories.

She made a mental note to give her mother a call as soon as she got home, and not another of the short Sunday night check-ins they usually shared, but a real, long, catch-up call. And as soon as she had a break from work, she would visit, and they would bake something fun, something new that neither had tried before.

She could use a little adventure in her life, at least of the safe variety.

Closing her eyes, she poked her spoon around in the last bits of gooey chocolate at the bottom of her mug, the best part in her opinion, and took her final bite of the impromptu dessert. When she slid the clean spoon out of her mouth, June found Ethan studying her, his expression a strangely pleasant blend of curiosity and…joy, as though he'd happened across an interesting painting.

"Something on your mind?" he asked, resting his spoon in his own mug and setting it on the counter.

The way he did that—put down the dish to focus all of his attention on her—was simultaneously intoxicating and unsettling. He gazed at her as though what she might say next was the most fascinating thing in the world, before he'd even heard it. She wasn't entirely sure she liked being examined so intently; there was great potential to make a fool of herself in front of someone she was slowly coming to respect and even like.

She decided to be honest, to be brave.

"The truth?"

He nodded affirmation.

"I was just thinking about my mother."

Ethan's features softened. "Ah, mothers. A complicated bunch, aren't they?"

It was alarming, how much she enjoyed the sound of his voice, that singular mix of accents she'd never heard all in one place before and couldn't quite identify. His words were more carefully formed than the looser, more drawn-out cadence of the locals she'd grown up around; they were tighter but also smoother—not better, of course, just different. And his vocabulary, his way of putting sentences together, was more formal than any man she'd ever spoken to before.

Ethan Singh was a rare, increasingly fascinating gem. He was cool and direct, almost hard, at first meeting, but like a fine baklava, she had the sense he would be infinitely more complex inside, lovelier. Hearing the way he'd talked with his parents on the phone—his tone warm and indulgent, the opposite of his annoyed words that didn't fool anyone—she knew already that he cared deeply for his parents and he placed great value on family.

As did she.

It seemed as the evening progressed, she and the doctor had more and more in common.

"It's true," she conceded. "They are complicated, but I can tell you adore yours."

His cheeks shaded to a slightly darker almond. "Guilty as charged," he answered, raising up his palms.

June giggled. "An admirable quality in a guy."

"I try." He winked at her and took another bite, not at all shy about how much he relished the experience.

*You're doing very well*, she wanted to say, but didn't.

"Is she the one who taught you to bake?" he asked. "Your mother, I mean."

June moved to wash out her cup so as to have something to do with her hands. She was used to being in perpetual motion, on her feet all day at work, then crashing into her bed at night. It had been a while since she had been in one-on-one company with someone else for this length of time. To tell the truth, she was nervous she'd run out of things to say—not that she'd said much, as it were—and Dr. Singh, highly educated, was way out of her league.

She rinsed the last bubbles of soap from her cup and set it to dry. "Yes. Or…at least at first."

"Ah. Did you then go to culinary or pastry school before you started at the pizza shop?"

She knew the question wasn't judgmental, but the subject of school was a sore spot for her; her features must have registered as much because Ethan looked suddenly worried.

"Did I say something wrong?" he asked.

"No, not at all." She stopped fidgeting and did her best to show him the same courtesy as he had her, by slowing down to really listen. She knew that must not be easy for a man as busy as he must be—the sole doctor in a clinic that served an entire small town full of furry clientele—so she could at least try to do the same.

She raised and then lowered her eyebrows. "I wish I could have gone to pastry school." She heard the dreaminess in her own words. "In Paris or someplace far off and amazing like that."

She didn't know what else to say, so she simply

stopped there. She'd wanted so many things, but the money had not been available, and though she'd worked her butt off to ace her high school classes while keeping up with part-time jobs, her grades just hadn't cut it; they were good, but not exceptional. Not enough for scholarships. And her mom's income had been on that fine line that partially determined the future of so many hopeful kids. According to the government, her mom's finances were healthy enough to put a roof over their heads, to feed and clothe the both of them, and they were too high for her to qualify for aid. But, alas, not enough to help her pay for school. She'd tried combining community college with a full-time job for a few months, but the long days and nights of fighting desperately to keep juggling all those plates had gotten to her, and she'd felt like a failure.

Her mom had wanted June's life to be better than her own, and June wanted to make her proud. She'd let them both down.

"So, why didn't you? Go to school like you wanted, I mean?"

"Lots of reasons." The last thing she wanted was to talk openly about education and money with a man like Ethan Singh, who had likely excelled in school and who, she knew from small-town gossip, was blessed with wealthy parents.

"June," he prodded, his eyes as soft and warm as melted caramel. "I'm sorry to have to tell you this, but that is a pathetic excuse for an answer."

"No, it isn't."

"Yes." He laughed softly. "Indeed it is."

She almost asked what difference it made, but she

didn't want to know the answer to that question. The only logical solution was to change the subject.

"Why do I have to talk about my education?" Or lack thereof. "I'd be willing to bet that yours was much more interesting."

His eyes bore into hers for several long seconds and she wondered what he was thinking, what picture he was forming of her in his mind.

*It's better this way*, she thought.

If he didn't know the truth—that despite her heavy and eclectic reading habit, her attempt to give herself the knowledge she hadn't been able to formally obtain, she'd never be as smart as he was.

She would never fit into his world, even if she had reason to.

At one point, she'd had a chance to be as successful, but that had been stolen from her.

She would get it back—oh, yes, she would—but each time her car broke down or she made another rent payment, she gained fresh understanding that it might well take the rest of her life to do so.

Ethan Singh did not want to hear about that. Heck, she didn't, either. She'd much rather go back to the beginning of the evening when their only subject of discussion was a pair of precious fur babies.

"Really?" he asked, skepticism written all over his face. "You seriously want to hear about my time at a boys' boarding school and then my grueling years as an intern in the biology department of a university that spent the bulk of students' tuition hiring new football coaches?" He moved his face closer to hers. "I think not."

"Oh, come on. You've lived all over the world, while

I've been digging my heels in good ol' Peach Leaf, Texas." She injected an exaggeratedly thick drawl into her words. "So, tell this country girl what it's like in them big, fancy cities."

She was teasing, but when he gave a short laugh in response, it wasn't the full, loose sound it had been before. Was it possible that, in making fun of herself, she'd unintentionally offended him?

How could that be? Wouldn't he have to care for her to be affronted by something she'd meant to be self-deprecating?

"So you really want to know about my past, huh?" Ethan asked.

She nodded, a tad too vigorously.

"All right, then, but this is a two-way street, you know."

"Fair enough," June said, biting her lip. There was something mischievous in his tone.

"So let's make a deal, then, shall we?"

## Chapter 6

June forgot everything around her except being there with him, listening to that accent that melted over his words like butter and, of course, sinking deep into those decadent eyes.

It shouldn't have surprised her by then that his charm came with a generous side of cunning. The rules he'd proposed were simple on the surface; she was allowed to ask one question at a time, which he would answer truthfully, but then it was his turn. The problem was, every time he started to speak, follow-up questions popped up in her mind like whack-a-moles, and she was forced to wait until it was her chance to ask another.

It was just that his life had been so starkly different from hers. His father had come to the US to live with family while attending veterinary college and met his mother, who'd been working as an intern at the Library of Congress. Despite their cultural differences—he was from India and she was American—it was classic love at first sight. The couple married quickly, and a son, Harry, and daughter, Sani, had followed before they finally had Ethan.

Because the senior Dr. Singh had become renowned in the field of veterinary science, specializing in the prevention of infectious disease, he was frequently asked to speak at conferences and even to work on long-term research projects abroad, always opting to bring along his family.

"Sounds like a dream childhood," June said, her voice sounding wistful even to her own ears.

"It was certainly interesting, I'll give you that." There was a hint of sadness in his tone.

Her eyes narrowed as she studied him. "You didn't like it?" Such a thing was hard for her to imagine. It wasn't until adulthood that June had even set foot outside of Peach Leaf. She'd never had reason to complain, and she knew she was fortunate for the blessings in her life. But one thing had always bothered her: her world had always been very small, and she wasn't sure why, but for some reason that fact made her self-conscious and overly careful, as though she feared saying something that would reveal a deficit in her intelligence.

He pondered the question for a bit before answering. "I suppose I did like it sometimes, but like anything else, it wasn't always perfect."

"What do you mean?" To June, endless opportunity for travel sounded like a dream come true.

"Well, it was lonely, for one thing, moving around so much. Seeing the world was a lovely gift my father gave me and my siblings, but it's not exactly easy to make and keep friends if your address changes frequently."

"That makes sense," she said, not about to remind him that he seemed to have forgotten his own rules and she'd sneakily asked more than one question in a row.

"I suppose there are two sides to every coin." She paused. "I guess I am lucky in that I've always lived in the same place, so I'd have to really make an effort to get away from my friends," she said, chuckling. "Small-town life has its ups and downs. You can't exactly run away from your mistakes, and if you try to forget them, someone else will inevitably be there to fill in the gaps, whether you want them to or not. It's almost like the whole town has a collective memory. Everybody knows everything about everybody else, including all the bad stuff."

He watched her carefully. "You don't seem like someone who would have any bad stuff you'd like to forget, June."

How wrong he was there.

"In fact, you're one of the most thoughtful people I've ever had the pleasure of meeting."

His words came out slow and with intention, as though he'd been planning them for some time, a thought that made her knees a little weak.

She swallowed, careful not to meet his eyes. "You can't possibly know that about me. We've only just met."

"You have a point," he said, "but I don't know many people who would have driven to this office in such a terrible storm to try to save a couple of puppies. Not to mention your reluctance to take food from the Bauers, even though it was compensated fairly."

He was grinning, only teasing her; nevertheless, her cheeks went suddenly warm.

"In fact, I don't need to see much more to believe that the world would be a much better place if there were more like you in it, Miss Leavy."

The next few seconds seemed like an eternity, as the absolute last thing she'd ever expected to happen, happened.

Ethan leaned forward and kissed her—the softest brush of his lips against hers. It was so sudden and so surreal, and over so quickly, she couldn't swear it had even actually occurred. That is, until she opened her eyes and found his face still very near her own, the pleasing scents of sandalwood and lemon blended with something male and uniquely Ethan, tickling her nose. She couldn't keep her eyes from those lips as the corners kicked up in a sultry smile.

Finally, he pulled them away. This was a good thing because June was pretty sure that if he'd left them lingering much longer, achingly close to hers, she would have wrapped her hands around his neck and devoured that mouth, and possibly anything else she could get her hands on.

It had been such an innocent kiss in its softness, yet somehow it had sparked a flame that had rapidly caused her to burn for more.

"You've cheated me, June."

"Hmm?" Apparently he'd rendered her unable to form words, much less full sentences.

"I said you cheated."

"What do you mean?"

"And there you've done it again. Asking questions of me without letting me have a go."

Ah, so he *had* noticed. Evidently she wasn't as sneaky as she'd assumed.

"All right, then. Go ahead." Great, now her voice was embarrassingly creaky.

*Way to keep it cool around the hot guy, June.*

If she kept this up, he'd regret having kissed her at all, a thought she couldn't bear because now she wanted more, more, more of him.

She glanced up into dark, soulful eyes.

"Here's my question, then. What is it that you'd like to forget?"

"Way to keep it light, Dr. Singh," she joked, but he wasn't having it.

"You know the rules," he said.

She licked her lips, the chocolaty taste of his kiss still lingering there; it took a concentrated effort to refrain from touching them, just to see if the buzz she felt would spark against her fingers.

She focused on the question, organizing her response carefully. Since Clayton had left with everything she had, June had not talked to anyone about how painful that experience was, how badly it had broken her. Her friends pressed from time to time, but she knew her role among them. She was the positive one, the upbeat girl. Letting herself be vulnerable might change how they saw her, and she worried it might scare them away.

She wasn't the one who let her tears show, who wore her heart on her sleeve. She was the one who'd always been the romantic—who'd truly believed that love was out there in some form for everyone, and they just had to find it. She couldn't let anyone see how wrong she'd been, how naive.

"Come on, June. What is it?"

She hesitated. Why did he want to know? And what about that kiss?

Part of her wanted to force the subject, to make him talk about why he'd done it, but the other part was content to just let it be. It would go down in her history as one of the best kisses of her life, possibly *the* best, as it had been completely unexpected, sweet and without any strings attached.

Couldn't she just leave it at that?

No, she could not, and she knew the reason as well as she knew, from an evening of charting them like stars, the pattern of gold flecks in Ethan's brown eyes.

"All right, then. Fair enough." She glanced up at him again, as much to make sure he wasn't something she'd dreamed up as to see if he really did want to know.

"It's a really short story," she started. "There was a guy. I loved him. I gave him everything I had and planned to spend the rest of my life with him. He broke my heart. The end." She waved a hand, emphasizing the relationship's finality.

Ethan's eyes narrowed and appeared to be full of pain, which was impossible. They were not friends; they certainly weren't lovers. So why did he look so sad? Further, why did he appear as if he knew exactly how she felt?

"I'm very sorry to hear that, June. I truly am. And trust me when I say I've been there myself."

Somehow, she didn't find that the least bit comforting.

"You have?"

"I have. Same song, as they say, different tune."

"Why would anyone…?" She stopped, placing a hand over her mouth. She'd been so caught up in the moment, so enraptured by the feel of these eyes on her, that she'd almost said too much. Her bruised heart needed protection, not more exposure to potential harm, so it was good she hadn't blurted out her confusion over how any woman in her right mind could possibly ruin a chance to be with a guy who, she was quickly learning, was kindhearted, gentle, attentive and thoughtful.

And whose kisses came straight from a fantasy.

"Why would anyone what?" There was a tinge of hopefulness in his expression that she could not have explained for the life of her. So when she heard a low, buzzing sound that startled them both and interrupted their conversation, she almost shouted with relief.

"That's me," she said. "I'd better get it."

Pushing away from the counter where they'd been standing so long her legs were a little wobbly with use, she began following the sound. Finally, she reached her purse, discarded earlier in the reception area, and grabbed it on the last ring.

"Hello?"

"Oh, June, thank goodness." Margaret sounded relieved to hear her voice. "I was worried when you didn't pick up. It's getting late and I hated to call, but I've got some news."

"It's okay. I'm glad to hear from you. It's a long story, but I found some puppies behind the restaurant and ended up bringing them to the veterinary clinic. I've been stuck here with Dr. Singh's son—" she gave

Ethan a little wave as he joined her "—for the past few hours. Looks like I might have to spend the night."

"Do you mean Ethan? I haven't seen that boy in years, but last time he was home from college I ran into him at the market. Lord, he's a handsome one."

"That's the one," June blurted. "I mean, not handsome, just that, you know, you've got the right person."

Margaret gave a low whistle. "Sweetie, you are one lucky girl. I'm telling you if I was still young, stuck overnight with a good-looking man like that, I'd make the most of it."

"Margaret!"

"Oh, hush, Junie," she said, but when she spoke again, her words had softened. "You've been hung up far too long on that damn jerk that broke your heart. It's time you moved on, so if this guy is single…is he single?"

"Yes," she reluctantly admitted, knowing the mess she'd walked into.

"Good, then take my advice—get back on the horse, kid."

June refrained from pointing out the fact that, being in her late twenties, she was hardly a kid, but she knew all the same that her well-meaning boss had her best interest at heart.

"What was it you wanted to tell me?"

"Oh, yes. Hank called a few minutes ago," she said, referring to an elderly restaurant regular that lived in the neighborhood, across the street from Peach Leaf Pizza. "He told me that the power lines are out. Several people nearby have called the electric company and it looks like it could take several days to a week to get things up and running again."

"A week?" June's hand went to her forehead as a series of figures flashed across her mind's eye. A week of no work meant…it meant she likely would not be able to pay her rent the next month without cutting into the miniscule amount of savings she'd managed to scrape together after Clayton had wiped her out.

"That's right." The older woman's voice sagged. "I'm so sorry, honey, but listen, we'll work something out. I did some math before I called you and I'd like to pay you three-quarters of what you'd make if you worked the week. I know it's not the same, and you know I'd give you all of it if I could manage, but without the business coming in…"

"Margaret, stop. It's okay. That's more than generous, but I'll manage."

"Nonsense, June. I…"

"I mean it. I can't take money from you without earning it. I'll be fine."

"I don't like this at all, dear."

"Well, neither do I, but I'm not changing my mind."

Her boss made a dissatisfied noise. "You're allowed to change your mind, hon. Anytime. You know I consider you like my own daughter and it won't do you any good to be proud among family, you hear?"

"I know," June said, emotion welling up in her throat at her boss's kindness. She desperately needed the money, so much so that with an ounce more prodding, any pride she had left would fly out the window. But she wasn't about to take payment without working for it. "But this is final."

"Well, I know stubborn when I see it, and you're a gal after my own heart, but don't you forget that I'm here if you need me. And I want to hear more about those puppies when we're back at the shop. And more about you-know-who, of course."

"All right, that's it. I'm hanging up."

"Details. I mean it."

"Talk to you later, boss," June said, forcing back laughter. "Call me when I can come back to work."

"Hint taken."

"And, Margaret?"

"Yeah, sweetie?"

"Are you going to be okay? With all of this going on, I mean."

"I'll manage. I've got Vince's little Social Security check every month for when the pizza business is slow. Besides, I'm as hardheaded as you are and I've been around a hell of a lot longer, so don't you worry about me."

When she hung up and tucked the phone back into her purse, Ethan's hypnotic gaze was on her again. Her cheeks warmed, remembering that kiss.

"Everything okay?" he asked.

"It has to be." She sighed as the long hours caught up with her, knotting something awful in her shoulders. She'd been going full-force all evening and into the night—first with the puppy emergency, then braving the crazy weather to get something to eat, and finally enduring the shock of that world-rocking kiss. Intense longing for a hot shower and her lonely, albeit warm, bed was almost enough to send her into tears.

"It doesn't sound okay," he said, coming to her side. "And you look tense enough to crack in two." He stood behind her and placed his hands on her shoulders, the touch of them shooting electric warmth all the way down her arms. "Mind if I help?"

Did she mind? Did the man even have to ask?

"No, um, that sounds nice actually."

When he began to rub her muscles, she had to bite her tongue to avoid moaning. Evidently, his skill wasn't limited to healing members of the animal kingdom; he had expert hands when it came to humans, too. She closed her eyes as the knots loosened and her bones turned to jelly.

Maybe Margaret had a point. Maybe she should take advantage of her limited time with this sexy, tender, animal-loving wonder-god she'd accidentally stumbled upon. With his hands on her like that, did it really matter that he looked like he'd walked off the set of a magazine shoot, whereas her hair had probably frizzed into a puffball and she hadn't set foot in a gym since college?

She didn't like the answer. *Yes*, it did matter.

In case she'd forgotten, the last guy who had wooed her with a fit physique and slick words had broken her heart. She didn't want to be that girl—no, she refused to be that girl—who slipped right into one bad relationship after another.

Ethan Singh might be handsome, and he might even be kind and all the other things she'd seen that night. None of that mattered. She simply wasn't ready to start over, to risk putting all of herself into someone new, only to have it blow up in her face.

Even if he proved to be a good guy, even if he was interested in her, she needed things only she could give herself: time, self-respect and space in which to put her life back together.

Grabbing his hands, she removed them from her shoulders and let them drop as she pulled away and turned to face him.

"Thank you. That was…wonderful, but I—" she hated that hurt expression on his face she'd caused "—I just need a minute. Excuse me."

With that, she left him standing there as she walked quickly away from emotions that threatened to undo her.

Ethan followed, still confused about what had happened.

He hadn't meant to be so forward. Hell, in the space of half an hour he'd not only kissed the woman, but had pulled the most cliché move ever known to man by offering to rub her shoulders.

*Dammit*, could he be any more of an ass?

What had come over him?

All he knew for sure was that when he saw June hang up from what had obviously been a difficult conversation with exhaustion practically crumpling her body, he'd have done anything he could to make her feel better.

He stopped abruptly in the hallway.

His instinct had been to go after her, to fix the awkwardness that hung in the room after she'd gone, but she had asked for a moment alone. And as his head began to clear, sifting through that spontaneous, intoxicating kiss from earlier, and the way his hands felt digging into her muscles, he realized he needed to give her what she'd asked for.

He needed to back off.

*But that kiss.*

It made him want to do anything but.

That kiss had wrecked everything he'd been so certain about. Up until it happened, his lips moving toward hers, propelled by a will of their own, he'd been so sure he didn't want a woman in his life. Not when he'd come to Peach Leaf for the sole purpose of getting over the last one.

But with June...it was like he wasn't even in control. Every minute he spent with her made him want another to follow.

Which was ridiculous, considering she'd told him her own heart had been broken recently. What kind of guy forced himself on a woman who clearly didn't want that kind of attention?

What he needed was some air, and for the storm to be over so that he could get her out of his space and off his mind.

When he stepped out the front door, the wind was still blowing with greater than normal force, but it had calmed down significantly since he and June had returned from the bakery. It was a pleasant break from the heat that had developed back in the office between the two of them.

He hadn't expected to feel that way again for a very long time, if not ever. It disturbed him, how much this sensation, this primal drive to be with a woman, resembled those first few days with Jessica.

The two women didn't abide comparison. Jessica had been cool, cosmopolitan, gorgeous in a cold, almost untouchable way, like a model from the cover of a magazine, and fiercely competitive—things he'd admired at first, until he'd discovered the heartlessness she was capable of.

June, on the other hand, was girl-next-door-beautiful, soft and curvy in all the right places and sweet.

Sweetness was an underrated quality in a woman, he now believed.

A gust of wind swiped at his face and he had to go back inside. The storm had subsided, but it clearly was not over yet.

Being in the cold made him briefly miss Colorado, and he wondered what June would think of the place he called home, the place he'd lived the longest now and where he'd begun to put down roots. She'd said she had always wanted to travel, and before he stopped the train of thought, it crossed his mind that he might like to take her there one day. Her eyes had sparkled when she talked about wanting to see the world, and that would be a good place to start.

He imagined her face lighting up when she saw the Rocky Mountains for the first time—how drastically more majestic they were in real life than in photos. He would take her to Estes Park to visit the haunted Stanley Hotel, and to Aspen to ski, and the list went on and on, nearly bursting out of him.

Unlike Jessica, who had been near-impossible to impress no matter how hard he tried, somehow he knew June would relish every minute of it, and he longed to feel that way again about a place he loved so much.

As it were, returning would be painful. Those ugly memories would be waiting for him at the university, and even in his home, and he didn't want to face them alone.

"Ethan?"

June had stuck her head out the door to call after him. He turned to follow her inside.

She looked at him like he'd lost his mind.

"What the hell, Ethan?" She gasped, hugging herself against the cold. "You're not wearing a coat." She slammed the door behind them. "What were you thinking?"

He didn't answer the question, ignoring the concern etched in the crease of her forehead. "I'm fine. Just got a little too warm."

The response in her features told him she knew how he felt, but it passed quickly and she forged ahead.

"Ethan, something's wrong with one of the puppies."

His heart lurched into his throat. He'd promised her he wouldn't let harm come to them.

Without speaking further, she grabbed his hand and led him to the back room. When he saw both puppies still inside their little pen, each of them wiggly and energetic, his breathing slowed a little.

"I think one of them threw up," June said, her voice catching in a way that made him ache. "But I can't tell which one."

He crouched down onto his knees and lifted one puppy at a time, palpating their stomachs and checking the rest of their warm, squirmy bodies. When he realized that the pups were completely okay, he almost laughed, but caught himself.

June would be hurt if she thought he was making fun of her for worrying. It wasn't overreacting for her, he reminded himself, because she wasn't used to looking for symptoms like he was. She just followed her heart, an admirable quality.

He put the puppy he'd been holding back into the pen and spent the next several minutes cleaning up and replacing their soiled towels with fresh, warm ones. Then he set his hands on June's shoulders, urging her to meet his eyes. When she did, he noticed glistening at the corners.

"Hey," he said, giving her shoulders a little squeeze. "Hey, it's okay. They're fine." As soon as he'd said the words, a tear slipped down her cheek and, without thinking at all, he reached up to wipe it away before pulling her shaking body against his chest.

He let her cry for a few moments, hating it but wanting to give her a chance to release some of her pent-up emotions. When she pulled back, she wiped her eyes and leaned back on her heels, looking embarrassed.

"I'm so sorry, Ethan. I have no idea what's gotten into me."

He shook his head. "Please do not apologize to me when you didn't do anything wrong."

She grinned, her eyes shimmering with dampness, greener than any emerald he'd ever seen.

"You must think I'm a complete idiot," she said with an unsteady voice.

"Absolutely not. Look, it's been a crazy, long day, and I think we both might be on the verge of simultaneous nervous breakdowns, but don't you ever say you're sorry for being concerned about something you care for."

As she finished wiping her face once more, her eyebrows rose in surprise. "Thank you for that. That's incredibly sweet of you." She was quiet for a moment, and he wondered what was running through her mind.

"I just saw the…" She pointed at the place where one of the little ones had regurgitated its supper, clearly a tad bit grossed out. "And I just lost it. I don't really know why." She tossed up her hands.

"It's okay, June. I'll run some tests again in the

morning, but from what I can tell now, they are still holding up really well. It would probably be safest to put them in a crate for the night, but I'd rather not, and this pen is fine."

She nodded and he tucked a strand of auburn hair behind her ear, taking his time in letting his finger slide along her soft cheek before pulling it back. "My educated guess is that they just ate a little too much. Sadly, if they've been without food for a while, it might take some time for their stomachs to get back to normal so they can eat the portions they'll need to gain weight."

June looked as relieved as he felt.

"In the meantime, they'll just need for us to be patient."

He met her eyes as a surge of emotion threatened to overwhelm him.

"After all, this will take some time. What they've suffered simply cannot be healed in one night."

## Chapter 7

The rich scent of coffee brewing pulled June from the short nap she'd finally managed to sink into. Her eyes slowly opening, she glanced around at the unfamiliar room, realizing, as the fuzzy edges of sleep slipped away, that she was in Dr. Singh's office.

The black leather couch squeaked as she pushed up to lean against its back. Chilly, she decided not to give up the blanket that Ethan must have draped over her as she'd snoozed. As the smell of delicious caffeine beckoned her further into wakefulness, her mind drifted back to the night before—and that kiss—the oh-so-delicious kiss that had seared her lips and sent sparks zipping through her veins.

That kiss—spontaneous, incredible, though highly unexpected—made her feel like a woman again.

It was the first time she'd been that close to anyone

since Clayton and, she thought with more sadness than she wanted to admit, probably the last.

After she'd had that slightly humiliating breakdown over one of the puppies' mild tummy ache, which she'd replayed over and over until deciding to chalk up her emotions to lack of sleep or an adequate meal, Ethan had dried her tears and sent her to bed, promising to take care of the dogs while she got some rest.

There hadn't been the slightest hint of judgment in his tone or expression, but what had been there instead scared her a little.

She'd looked up into those intense, mahogany eyes of his and found only concern.

He'd been sweet, nurturing even, and had shown her a softness she wasn't used to in men, but she got the feeling that wasn't really Ethan's usual style.

Perhaps the strange magic of a Texas night covered in snow had affected them both. She'd resisted him at first, had not wanted to like him so easily, so much; she hadn't wanted to enjoy his company, but her attempts to not care had been futile, and now her heart had jumped into the game, forcing her to admit that she didn't want their time together to be over.

That sentiment had even kept her from sleep for a while, as she'd tried desperately not to let her eyelids slam shut. But they'd been so heavy from exhaustion, Ethan's voice so soothing as he'd sat in his father's desk chair telling her stories of his Alaskan research trips.

Like a desperate Cinderella, she hadn't wanted it to end.

But in real life, pumpkins weren't carriages and tattered shoes weren't glass slippers...and Prince Charming did not exist.

She needed the reminder; Ethan could have fooled her last night.

But finally she'd succumbed to rest, and it was over. For better or worse, her normal life would resume.

She stretched her arms behind her head before taking a moment to rub a charley horse out of her neck. Wrapping the blanket around her shoulders, she made a quick trip to the bathroom, careful to avoid the mirror, adamantly not wanting to know what she'd be met with following a full shift and a night without a shower. She splashed water on her face and headed to the front of the clinic to check the weather.

"Morning, June," Ethan said, turning as she entered the room. Dark stubble covered his jaw and chin and, instead of looking like hell, which would be perfectly appropriate after being awake for over twenty-four hours, he was even sexier than he'd been the day and night before. And when he graced her with a sleepy smile, she almost threw herself across the room and kissed him. It took effort to remind herself that she'd only stumbled into this situation through a weird turn of events—it didn't truly belong to her. He had not chosen to spend the night with her; it was forced, and he'd been kind to let her stay, as she knew he would have anyone else.

"How'd you sleep?" he asked. "Considering, I mean. I know my father's office couch isn't exactly like a king-size bed in a five-star hotel."

Beds, hotels, unkempt but perfect Ethan with a shadowy beard following a night of…

June shook her head. That wasn't real. The reality was that she'd stumbled upon him due to a freak snowstorm. Reality was, that if the snow had melted enough and the roads were moderately safe, she'd be back at her car and home to her empty apartment in a matter of a couple of hours at best.

The fantasy would be over.

As it should be.

Clayton, with his smooth talking, his well-toned body and those promises he'd made with a straight face while looking right into her eyes—it had all been a fantasy, too. And June needed no reminders of how that turned out.

She may not be highly educated like Ethan, but she was smart enough not to make the same mistake twice. A woman who couldn't trust herself, who couldn't protect her own heart from destruction, was better off alone.

Ethan was staring at her, waiting for her to respond.

"The couch was fine." She smiled. "I can't thank you enough for letting me get a little rest."

He waved a hand, brushing her gratitude aside. "It's nothing. Not my first twenty-four-hour shift, and probably not my last. You get used to it after a few times."

"All the same."

"Don't mention it." He beckoned her to join him at the window. "Looks like we're in luck. I watched the weather on the news a little bit ago and it seems the snow is starting to melt. Also, half the town lost power last night and some won't get it back for a few days. We were pretty fortunate here, with the heater running and all. Would have been a cold night otherwise."

Not if they'd snuggled together, she mused.

He took a sip from the mug in his hand. "The pups were doing great when I checked in and fed them a few minutes ago, and in an hour or so, we'll be able to head out and check on your car."

The news should have been welcome, but for some reason her heart sank. She plastered a smile on her face and crossed her fingers it was convincing. She didn't think she could bear any more of Ethan's insightful kindness or another second of those dark eyes boring into hers, seemingly capable of unearthing her most private thoughts.

"That's excellent news. I can't wait to get back to my place and take a shower."

"I'm with you there. I probably smell like my furry clients," he said, laughing as he turned back to the window.

Outside was a veritable winter wonderland. Snow had blanketed the parking lot, glittering like sugar in the sunlight.

"It's beautiful, isn't it?" he asked.

"Very."

"Have you ever seen snow like this before, June?"

She nibbled her lower lip, stopping, suddenly self-conscious when his eyes followed. "I've seen snow, yes, but never like this. It usually melts so quickly that it doesn't cover anything."

"So you've never really gotten to enjoy it, then? Never built a snowman? Gone sledding?"

She shook her head. His eyes lit up when he'd spoken, and he made all those activities sound so fun.

He tsked. "Well, that is a shame. We get plenty of snow in Colorado, and of course we did during my time in Alaska, too. Most people don't like the weather in the more remote areas, but for some reason, I took to it during my research there."

"Do you miss it?" she asked, instantly regretting the question when a muscle in his jaw jumped, betraying some reaction he probably hadn't meant to reveal.

"I miss the place, not the memories." He was far away somewhere for a moment, but then quickly returned to ask if she'd like a cup of coffee.

"How selfish of me, standing here drinking mine without checking if you want one of your own." He turned, surprising her by tucking a finger under her chin, lifting it to look into her face. "It's been a long time since there's been anyone to ask. Too long."

She licked her lips and his eyes snapped to her tongue. In a matter of seconds, he moved as if to kiss her again and alarms went off inside her, louder even than the one at Bauer's had been.

June pulled her face away from his with effort, disappointment spreading through her body like a virus. If she thought she could let him kiss her again without strings, without involuntarily building an attachment that she knew would be one-sided, she would have allowed it. But that was the thing about mistakes; if you were smart, you learned from them. She supposed she could thank Clayton for that—she knew herself better now, knew she couldn't go in halfway.

It was all or nothing from then on, and nothing was by far the safer route.

*Safer, maybe, but a hell of a lot less fun,* a little voice chided in her mind.

Unmistakable hurt clouded his features the second she made that decision, but he quickly, expertly erased it.

"I'd love a cup," she said, the air thick with static between them. "It smells amazing."

He nodded, giving her a soft grin. "Stay here. I'll be right back with it."

* * *

Ethan was halfway to the break room before he realized he hadn't even asked how June took her coffee. The oversight was just another testament to the trouble he'd gotten into.

She was intoxicating, mesmerizing like a siren, and like a fool, he couldn't stay away from her song.

And if he didn't watch out, he'd be back in the same place, drowning once again as he had with Jessica. Even though everything in him wanted to do the exact opposite, he would have to be more careful.

He pressed his fingers into his tired eyes, then pulled a clean mug from the dish dryer, a reminder of the night before. Those delicious brownies and those even more delicious lips. The taste of her was almost gone, and he'd stupidly attempted to get it back, only to have June turn away from him.

He should be grateful—at least one of them was thinking clearly.

Grabbing the carafe, he poured her a cup of the expensive, delicious brew his father indulged in and shared with everyone at the office, adding a splash of half-and-half from the fridge and just a little sugar, feeling like an idiot for wanting to get it right. He stopped himself from adding a sprinkle of cinnamon. It would just have to do.

And with any luck, he'd have her back in her car and out of his life soon enough.

He gave the coffee a quick stir and headed back down the hallway, taking a deep breath to steady his nerves.

It had just been a long night; that was all. June was

a beautiful, sweet girl, and he enjoyed her company, but that didn't mean it had to turn into anything more.

If only someone could tell his stupid-ass heart the same.

June was still standing at the window when he entered the reception area, the blanket he'd draped over her the night before wrapped around her shoulders. Her red hair draped across the soft white material, and she looked like an angel.

Which gave him an idea. Snow angels, snowmen— June had never experienced a real chance to enjoy this kind of weather.

"Here you are." She turned and reached for the coffee, closing her eyes as she drew in her first long sip.

"Oh, my God, this is *sooo* good. How'd you know how to fix it just the way I like it?"

"Wild guess. Speaking of wild, finish that coffee and put your coat on."

She raised an eyebrow.

"I'm going to give the pups their breakfast and I'll meet you out front in ten minutes." She opened her mouth to ask questions or to argue, but he held up a finger, stopping her.

"Out front. Ten minutes. See you there."

Ethan's pulse raced and his heart felt lighter than it had in months. He didn't want to believe that it was June making his body behave that way, so he gave credit to the snow. The problem with that theory was that he'd seen a hundred snowfalls, most of them even more magical than this one. Paris, London, New York—the small-town Texas weather couldn't even begin to compare. He loved the idea of sharing this one with someone he barely knew but who'd reminded him that life could go on after heartbreak. He knew there was no future with June for lots of reasons, the most basic being that the two lived in different cities and probably had different goals, but right then, none of that mattered. The only thing he wanted that morning was to show her a great time in his favorite weather.

After checking and feeding the puppies, he threw on his coat and dashed outdoors, regretting that his father didn't keep a sled in his office. The temperature was perfect when he opened the back door and stepped into several feet of powder that reminded him of fresh whipped cream. There was not a hint of the previous day's harsh wind, just cold, crisp air on an occasional whispery breeze. The snow stung his hands as it seeped through his mittens, but Ethan didn't care.

He worked as if in a trance, determined to make June share one of those beautiful smiles with him again, the kind she'd tried to hide after he'd kissed her berry lips. What harm could there be in making a woman smile? It didn't have to mean forever, and it wouldn't. But didn't he deserve a moment's happiness after the way the past year had gone? Didn't June?

Just as he'd thought her name, the woman stepped outside, glancing around before she caught his eye.

"Ethan, what are you up to out here?"

He watched her as she paced nearer, enjoying the way the sun's bright rays danced over her hair, causing it to glisten like a crown adorned with rubies. Her eyes were impossibly green in the dreamlike morning light.

"What's that behind you?" she asked, veering right so she could get a glimpse of what he'd hidden.

He couldn't stop himself smiling like a little boy as

he stepped out of her way, waving his arms like a magician's assistant.

June's hands flew to cover her mouth, and those emerald eyes lit up, glistening in the sunshine that reflected off the snow.

Then he heard the best music ever as she threw her head back and laughed, before her feet did a little dance. She squealed. "Is that a snowman?"

"Just for you," he answered, taking far too much delight in her reaction to his simple gift, the only thing he could think to give her for making him feel like the frost inside him had begun to melt a little.

"He's perfect." She held out her arms and spun in a little circle before running toward him. Ethan opened his arms just in time to catch her, but lost his footing as she threw her body into his, plunging them both into the snow.

His laughter mingled with hers, and he didn't at all mind the wetness starting to soak into his back. All he knew was her weight on top of him as she raised up on her elbows and stared down into his face, and the curtain of auburn that came down to tickle his cheeks as she bent to kiss him, her mouth warm and eager, pressing hard into his. When their lips parted, he pulled her close into his chest and held her there for a long moment, unwilling to let her go just yet.

Finally, only when he began to freeze and thus worried that June would be vulnerable to the same, he twisted his body to the side and rose, holding out his hands to help her up.

Her smile disappeared as they stood face-to-face, and all he heard was their matched heavy breathing.

"Ethan, I…"

He covered her lips with a finger. "Shh, don't say anything. Just...just enjoy this with me, will you?"

She was right, of course.

"I get where you're coming from," he said, the words pouring out of him before he could measure them to make sure they conveyed what he wanted them to, not necessarily exactly what he was thinking. "But that's just it, June. I don't want to talk about it, at all. I don't want to try to figure out what's going on between us."

Her eyes had narrowed and there was a crease between her brows.

"Wouldn't you rather just let this be what it is?"

She looked down at her hands.

"That's my point, though, Ethan. We just met. I don't know what this is, and I don't think you do, either."

He rubbed a soggy mitten over his forehead. "I know, I know. But why do we need to understand it at all? Why can't we just enjoy it while it lasts?"

Her expression changed, and as she took time to think of what to say next, he thought he saw something new register.

"I'm not sure where this is going, but I think I see what you're saying."

He waited.

"And, well, the more I think about it, and even though it sounds crazy, you might be on to something."

He took her hand.

"All I mean is that, we both know this thing won't last—it can't, anyway—because I'm leaving in a few weeks and you've got a life here."

She cringed at that last part, but he didn't want to stop and examine that. He needed to convince her to let him spend more time with her, before it was all over. He wanted to soak up her sweetness, to let it seep under his skin so he could take it with him. It didn't need to mean anything more. Maybe not everything happened for a reason. Weren't some things in life just pleasant coincidences?

"We seem to get along, you and I, and if I'm not mistaken, we both had some fun last night, despite the evening not going the way either of us had planned. So while I'm here, and while you've got those puppies for the next few days and they'll need some medical care, let's just enjoy each other."

She bit her lip again, that sexy little gesture that let him know she was considering it.

"But, Ethan, is that wise? You've had your heart broken recently, as have I, and we both need time to mend. Does it really make sense to start something up right now?"

"That's just it, though. We wouldn't be starting anything. Look at it like this. We'll just be having a little fun before we both go our separate ways and get back out there. You're right that we're both unprepared to get into relationships again any time soon, so let's… use each other as practice…for lack of a better term."

He grabbed her hand and pulled her into his chest, pushing past her resistance. "Let's enjoy each other's company, make each other better and have a few laughs, before we go back to real life. What do you say?"

A look of sadness whispered across her features, but was gone instantly. She smiled up at him, making his heart flutter a little.

"All right, Dr. Singh," she said. "You have yourself a deal."

He placed his hands on each side of her face and brushed her chilly nose with his lips.

He didn't care what kind of fire he might have been walking into, as long as he got to see her again after that morning.

"Deal?" she asked.

"Deal."

With that, he picked her up and swirled her around and around until they were both dizzy, from the spinning, yes, but also probably from something else. When he set her down, June headed over to examine the snowman, giggling with joy over the jerky treat nose, kibble mouth and doggy biscuit eyes he'd scrambled together. As she studied his creation, Ethan knelt to form a snowball, gasping in surprise when one of June's own smacked him right in the middle of his back.

"I don't know why, but it surprises me a little that you like country music so much."

Ethan grinned, the corner of his eye crinkling behind aviator glasses. Of course they made him look even more stunning.

"Is it because I'm half-Indian?"

She considered his question; she hadn't really thought much about his ethnicity, other than the fact that his father's heritage had obviously given him the most gorgeous, terra-cotta skin she'd ever seen in her life.

"Nope, not that," she said, drawing out her answer to make him sweat a little. He tried to pretend he didn't care, but the longer she spent with him, the more she could see how much he wanted her to like him.

Even though they'd discussed their intention earlier that morning, that whatever their odd little relationship was would not turn into anything serious, it was still a refreshing quality in a man, to be able to see that he wanted to please her.

"I've got it," she said. "I think it's just that country music doesn't mesh with your worldliness or something." She poked his side, making him laugh. "Seems like you'd be more of a classical music type." She eyed him up and down. "I can totally see you fake-conducting an orchestra as you drive to work or something."

"Ah, but that's why I like it so much." He turned and flashed a smile full of perfect white teeth against incredible copper skin. "Reminds me of the simple things in life."

They were in Ethan's large black SUV, headed in the direction where June had left her car. The weather couldn't have been more different than it was the day before; not a cloud in the blue sky, thick mounds of snow gradually beginning to melt as the sun reclaimed her throne. It would take time for the powder to turn back into liquid, and then Peach Leaf would face the possible threat of flooding.

They weren't out of the dark just yet, but things were beginning to look up. She said a silent little prayer that they would find her car in decent shape, but it wouldn't do much good to hold her breath. The old thing wasn't in great health to begin with; it would be a small miracle of it survived the beating it had taken the night before.

Loosening her seat belt a little, June turned toward

the backseat to check on the pups. Ethan had nestled blankets into one of the crates from the clinic, then wrapped the little guys inside so they'd be safe on the way to her apartment, where June was thrilled she'd get to watch them until Margaret called her back into work. Ethan had said they'd figure things out from there, but she'd made him promise he wouldn't let anyone adopt them until they were one hundred percent healthy. She wouldn't say it out loud, but the idea of never seeing them again made her stomach churn.

Gently, she poked a finger between the bars, squealing when the male pup bounced over and began to nibble on it. She took that as a sign that he was having a good morning.

That made two of them, she thought, reminiscing about the impromptu snowball fight with Ethan and the adorable snowman he'd built for her, completely out of the blue. She tried not to overanalyze how good it made her feel to be with him, to play, and to have the freedom to kiss him with such abandon without expecting anything serious in return.

She knew it wouldn't last, but maybe he had a point. It was a hell of a lot of fun to be spoiled, to be enjoyed, and even though she hadn't agreed with him at first, she was beginning to come around to his way of thinking. Perhaps their plan would work out fine, after all. No strings, no attachments and, most important, no promises.

Just pure, unbridled fun between two people on the mend. Surely, everything would be fine.

"Okay, that's starting to hurt, mister," she said, taking back her nibbled finger.

"I wouldn't let him do that too much, June. He might start to think it's okay."

"I won't," she promised. "I just like seeing him up and full of energy."

"Well, you'll get plenty of it over the next few days." He tossed a glance her way before refocusing his attention on the road. "Are you sure you want to do this?"

"What? Take care of a few puppies? How hard can it be?"

He coughed out a laugh. "I'd love to hear you say that again in a few days."

She started to retort, but paused as Ethan slowed the SUV.

"Is that it?" he asked. "Your car."

She turned back to the front and caught sight of the old hunk of metal out the front window, barely recognizable underneath a mountain of snow. "Yep, has to be."

He turned off the road, getting as close to her vehicle as he could manage without pummeling into a bank of powder. When the SUV stopped, June reached into her purse and pulled out her keys. Without lifting her head, she grabbed at the door handle only to find Ethan had gotten out, come around and opened the door for her. Such a gentleman. She accepted his offered hand and stepped out of the warm vehicle, which he'd left running to keep the puppies from getting too cold.

By the time they reached her car, moisture had soaked the bottoms of her jeans, but that problem took a backseat to a bigger one pretty darn fast.

She shouldn't have been surprised, but that didn't make it any less annoying when she stuck the key in the ignition, only to find the engine wouldn't turn over after a dozen tries.

Someone in control, someone who had her life together, would have bought a new battery before the weather turned so cold and sapped the last dredges of energy from the nearly four-year-old one. But June had not been so responsible. Between her full work schedule and not wanting to part with the hundred or so bucks a new one would cost, this was what she deserved.

She looked up to find Ethan staring at her, his long body blocking out the sun as he leaned over her driver's side door.

"Thought you were getting rid of me that fast, did you?"

She tossed her shoulders back and tilted her head, debating whether to punch him in those toned abs or straight on the nose.

"What the hell do you look so happy about?" Her question was genuine; shouldn't he be getting tired of her just about now? Shouldn't he be dying to get back to his parents' house so he could get cleaned up and take a much-needed nap?

"Nothing," he said, but the grin didn't fade. He offered her his hand. "Come on, then. No use beating a dead horse."

"I've never liked that expression," she said.

"Neither have I actually, but it suits the situation. There's no point in trying that key again."

She did just that as he rolled his eyes, then shook his outstretched hand.

They tried jumping her car a few times, but it wouldn't take the juice. The old thing had simply given up.

"Come on. Let's get you home. Once you've had something to eat and we get the puppies settled in, we'll call a tow truck."

She hated to admit it, but she liked the sound of that *we*. Exhausted, hungry and craving a near-boiling bath, it was nice to have someone with her, someone who still managed to drum up energy after the long night, someone who put her needs first. It was a good quality in a man…a good quality in a boyfriend…or even a husband.

She almost gasped when the word entered her mind, but the more she tried to shoo it away, the stickier it got.

Once they got back at her apartment, Ethan was relentlessly sweet, making oatmeal for them both while June took the puppies out of their crate and onto her small back patio. She cheered them on and gave them treats when they went to the bathroom on the least snowy patch of grass she could find, which seemed to come naturally to them since they'd likely been living outside. Her heart ached at the thought of their mother, and she promised then and there that she would take good care of them until she found them good homes. She knew it might not be possible, but she hoped she could find a way to keep them together.

When she went back inside, Ethan had made himself at home in her kitchen, and she couldn't help but think he looked good there. They ate together and he sent her off to take a hot shower while he fed the puppies some of the kibble he'd packed up for her from the clinic's supply closet and texted his vet techs to find out if either of them would be able to drive in and take over that morning while he went home to take a nap.

By the time she finished relishing the steamy water

as it thawed her cold skin and wrapped herself in comfy sweats and socks, Ethan had fallen asleep on the couch. The puppies had done the same, snuggled together, safe inside their shared crate with full bellies.

She stood in the doorway for a long time, just enjoying the view. The stunning, kindhearted doctor passed out on her couch after a night spent caring for the two most adorable little fur balls she'd ever seen, all nestled into her small living room.

If she'd been certain it wouldn't wake them all, she would have dug out her phone and taken a photo.

It was an image she didn't want to forget as long as she lived. Instead, she went with her very next impulse. For once, she allowed herself to do exactly what she wanted, without thinking.

Ethan sighed as she lay down next to him on the couch, eyes remaining closed as he drew her against his chest and tucked an arm around her. She looked up just in time to see him smile before drifting back to sleep.

# Chapter 8

"Over here!" June called when she caught sight of her mother's strawberry-blond head passing through the front door a few days later. The coffeehouse, which had the unique luxury of being the only such place in their small town, did not belong to any competitive chains and was especially crowded.

"My goodness," Abigail Leavy said, joining June at the long counter by the window. She set her purse on the bar stool June had saved for her. "Looks like folks got a little case of cabin fever in the storm."

"I think you're absolutely right," June said, standing to give her mother a big hug. "Hi, Mom. I'm glad to see you're okay."

"Hi, sweetheart," the older woman answered, squeezing June in response.

Her mom was tiny and resembled a pixie with

her short, stylish haircut, sparkling blue eyes and cheeks that always looked as though they'd been recently pinched. At sixty-five, Abigail looked a decade younger. Despite having worked since she was fourteen, June's mother had not slowed down after retiring from the grocery store, where, over the years, she'd climbed from bagger to manager; the woman made a point of spending time regularly with her numerous friends, walked several miles per day and took pride in her commitment to a healthy diet. June always teased her that she put her daughter to shame.

"Let me go get a cup of joe and I'll be right back." She pulled out her wallet and pointed a finger at June. "Don't you run off now, girl. I haven't seen you in ages and it's getting harder and harder to track you down."

June waved her away and took a sip of her peppermint hot chocolate, a foray from her usual Americano. For some reason, since that first cup of coffee Ethan Singh had made for her a few days ago, nothing she prepared for herself or purchased tasted anywhere near as good.

She smiled, whipped cream tickling her nose as she let her mind circle around and around that man.

Though, at the time, she'd thought that night with him would go down as the longest of her life, it had been nothing compared to the past few days.

He'd gone back to his regular shifts at the clinic, of course, and she'd been happily soaking up her lazy days at home as the power company worked to restore electricity at the pizza place. Only the challenge of training the puppies occupied her time, and she was loving every minute of it.

Despite being busy with the clinic, Ethan called

every day on his lunch break to check on her and see how the little ones were doing, and they'd met for coffee once.

But *dammit*, she missed him.

And nothing she tried could make that fact go away. He'd gotten under her skin.

"All right, sweetheart," her mother said, setting a ginormous cup of black coffee on the counter. "Let me just get some of this stuff into my veins and I'm all yours."

"It's certainly no mystery where I got my coffee addiction," June said, giggling.

Abigail took a long sip before putting down her extra large cup. "Come on, girl. You ain't foolin' nobody." She gave June's frothy beverage the stink eye. "That is not coffee."

June looked down into her delicious but admittedly oversweet drink. "You've got me there."

"What's up with that, anyway? Why aren't you having your normal Americano with cream and sugar? What's on your mind?"

"Nothing's on my mind, Mom. I just wanted to try something different."

Her mother glared at her, without a word, and that's all it took for June to break.

"Okay," she said. "Maybe there is a little something on my mind."

Abigail looked a little too satisfied.

"But that's not why I'm here. I really just wanted to spend a little time with you while I've got a few precious days off work."

"That's more like it. I knew something was up.

You're usually so chipper, and today you look like you've got a bug in your biscuit."

June snorted at her mom's goofy expression, one of many in the woman's vast collection of odd colloquialisms. Even after hearing it all her life, that particular one still made her laugh.

"It's just the puppies, Mom. Nothing more."

Her mom smiled. "How are those little squirts? Have you given them names yet?"

"No, not yet. I want to, but Ethan—Dr. Singh— keeps discouraging it for some reason."

Abigail was silent for far too long before speaking again. "Ah, so that's what this is about."

June kept her features as neutral as possible, determined not to give in. If her mom caught a glimpse inside her head and managed to figure out how stupidly smitten June was with the doctor, she would never let it go.

She cleared her throat and glanced out the window with as much nonchalance as she could muster.

"That's what *what* is about?" she asked awkwardly. "I have no idea what you mean."

The statement rang false even to her own ears.

Her mom set aside the massive coffee and June knew she was in for it.

"It's this Dr. Singh, isn't it? You've got a thing for him?"

"Mother, I do not…"

"Don't give me that." She held up a palm. "I know my daughter, and I know when she's been bitten by the love monster."

June chuckled in spite of her good intentions. "Mom, you're so silly sometimes."

"Don't you try to change the subject on me. You've got a thing for this guy and I want details."

"Mom," she said, injecting seriousness into her tone as she tried to conjure up sad images to keep from grinning like an idiot at the mere mention of the man's name. "It's nothing. Really, it's not."

"Like you'd tell me if it was." Her words were teasing on the surface, but underneath June detected the hint of hurt feelings.

"Mom." June rested a hand over her mother's and squeezed. "Why would you say that?"

Abigail shrugged. "I didn't mean it, sweetheart. Really, I didn't." Her eyes settled on something out the window, but June could see they weren't focused and her mother's mind was far away.

"I guess what I mean is that, well, I don't see you much anymore."

"I'm sorry, Mom." June cringed. "I had no idea you were feeling neglected lately."

"It's okay. I know you can't help it and I did not mean to guilt-trip you."

"No, really, I'll make more of an effort to see you." June's shoulders sagged. "It's just that I work so much, and when I'm not at the pizza parlor, I'm resting up to *be* at the pizza parlor."

Her mother nodded. "I understand what you mean, June Bug. It was like that for me after your father left."

Her mom didn't talk about her father much, and June had never met the man; all she knew were bits and pieces she'd picked up over the years. He and her mother had never had a real relationship and June had essentially been, as her mom put it, "a happy accident," but she'd always felt loved. Not once had her mom ever made her feel unwanted.

"I've probably never said this before, Mom, but I know how hard you worked to give me the things I needed growing up, and I've always been thankful for it."

Abigail's eyes filled with moisture. "Oh, honey, I did it because I loved you, and I wanted you to have the best I could give you, but all the same, that means a great deal to me."

June's mom wrapped her in a big hug, then pulled her torso back to study her daughter, a hand on each of June's arms. "I just don't want you to make the same mistakes I did."

"What do you mean?" She sipped her lukewarm hot chocolate.

Abigail released her and then did the same with her own drink. "Well, you work so hard, and you've always been so independent, like I was. I certainly can't blame you for that, because you got it from me." She winked a pretty blue eye. "At the same time, I don't want to see you miss out on the same things I did, honey."

"What mistakes, Mom?" she asked. "When I look at you, all I see is a strong woman who worked hard her whole life, who has a daughter and lots of friends who love her."

"Oh, sweetheart, thank you."

"I mean it—I don't see any mistakes."

Abigail's forehead creased as she studied her fresh manicure.

"Surely there were times when you were a kid that you wished your father was around or that I didn't work so much."

June nodded. "That's true. I did wish those things sometimes, but if my father didn't make you happy, and if you wouldn't have been happy with him in our lives, then I trust that you made the right decision."

"He wasn't a bad guy, but he didn't want to be a dad, and no kid needs that kind of burden. Plus—" she gently touched June's cheek with her palm "—I was so excited to have you, and you were such a sweet little thing, always smiling and happy to see everybody."

Though there had been times when she'd wished for a brother or sister, it was true that she'd enjoyed a happy childhood, and she knew that some kids didn't have any parents; she was always just glad to have one that loved her so dearly.

"I'd love to see you back to your old sunny self, Junie. I know you're working hard and you probably won't let me, stubborn girl, but is there anything I can do to help?"

June shook her head. "I'll be fine, Mom. Just need to keep working and save up again so I can change things." She swallowed, wishing she could believe it would be that simple to start over. "I'll find a way."

"I know you will, sweetheart." Abigail paused. "I swear, if I could find that Clayton Miller, I'd kick his ass into next year."

June laughed so hard she almost snorted hot chocolate out of her nose. "I know you would, Mom. I know you would."

"Seriously, though, don't work yourself too hard and forget to live your life. You're too young for that." Abigail's voice quieted, her tone softening. "I dated a guy once, back when you were little—a good one—and I should have let him in more. He wanted to build a life with us, and he was so wonderful with you, which mattered to me more than anything else, but for some reason—I guess because I was too afraid to let any man near us again because he might disappoint you like your father did—I let a very good person go. Now I can't tell if that was the right or wrong choice, and life's too damn short to dwell on such things. But I'm telling you this because, if it happens to you, I don't want you to miss out on love by being afraid that what happened with Clayton might happen again."

June's eyes were tearing up, and she dabbed at them discreetly with a napkin, not wanting to attract attention.

"The point is, I don't want you to stop living life to the fullest. No one can promise that your heart won't get broken again, but if something good comes along, don't be afraid to take it, June Bug."

"Mom, I can't…"

"Just promise me you won't be too scared to try flying again."

She pulled in a breath, then released it slowly. "I promise."

"June?" Her ears picked up the low, smooth voice in the distance and she turned.

"Ethan. Hi," she said, standing up from the stool, righting her cup after nearly tipping it over. *Very smooth indeed.*

He waved over the crowd, so tall she had no trouble seeing him. His hair was still damp from a shower and he'd shaved all that sexy stubble off, which would be a pity if he didn't still paint a gorgeous picture. He wore a deep silver button-down shirt the color of storm clouds, the sleeves rolled up, revealing toned forearms with a coating of dark, silky hair.

The thundering in her heart increased as he neared, women looking up from their tables to catch a glimpse of him as he passed. The thing that really set off her pulse, though, was that he didn't notice a single one of them; he had eyes only for her. She wondered if it was possible that he'd gotten more handsome since she'd last seen him a few days ago.

When he stood only a foot or so away, the intoxicating scent of his skin caused all rational thought to fly out the window.

"June, it's so great to see you here," he said, seemingly unsure of what to do with his arms. For a man who had previously exuded confidence, seeing him a little flustered was just plain cute.

Her little heart completely ignored her and went to town—the traitor.

"It's good to see you, too," she said, helplessly grinning from ear to ear. "The puppies are doing really well. My neighbor—who is supertrustworthy, by the way, and has a rescue dog of her own—practically jumped at the chance to spend a couple of hours with them."

"That's wonderful to hear," he said, reaching out to touch her forearm, a gesture that was both unexpected and incredibly intimate. His touch tingled all the way up her arm, making the fine hairs stand at attention.

*Good Lord*, the things he could do to her with such simple, innocent contact.

She wondered if he had any idea what kind of effect his presence had on her. On her body, her mind, deep inside her most intimate places.

"But how are you doing?" he asked, lowering his head to make up for their difference in height so he could stare straight into her eyes. Heat blossomed in her belly and spread all over.

"Me? Oh, I'm… I'm good," she stammered. "Thanks for asking."

"Ahem." The sound of June's mom clearing her throat startled her and Ethan.

"Ethan," she said, turning to include her mom, "this is my mother, Abigail Leavy. Mom, this is Ethan Singh, the veterinarian I told you about."

His eyebrows rose in response to that last part. "Ms. Leavy," he said, and June reminded herself to thank him later for not assuming she was a *Mrs*. "It's so very nice to meet you."

"Likewise," Abigail said, flashing those baby blues at him. "I hear you were quite the hero the other night, saving those puppies."

June was tickled to see his cheeks darken. Suave, classy, worldly Ethan Singh, blushing over a simple compliment? She hadn't thought she'd live to see the day and, of course, she made a quick mental note to tease him relentlessly about it later.

"I was just doing my job. It was nothing out of the ordinary."

June's mother practically burst out, "Oh, I'm sure June would disagree."

"Mom," she said through clenched teeth. "I'm sure Dr. Singh has to get back to work."

"It's true," he said, those illegally sexy lips curving upward. "But I was hoping I could borrow you for a moment first, June. There's something I'd like to talk to you about, if you can spare the time."

"Oh, she absolutely can. Can't you, sweetheart?"

"Yes, Mother." She turned and shot daggers at her mom. "I think I can take it from here."

"I certainly hope so. Remember earlier when I advised you ought to say yes to a good thing, should one come along? Well, this is exactly what I was talking about, so do yourself a favor," she whispered quickly to June, then turned and offered Ethan a million-dollar smile. "I'll leave you two alone," she said. "Call me later, June Bug."

Abigail picked up her purse and remaining coffee and hurried off, blowing her daughter a kiss over her red acrylic fingernails.

June rolled her eyes, but was unable to help grinning at her mother's tenacity.

Ethan watched the older woman go, then turned to June. "She's a firecracker, that one, isn't she?"

June chuckled. "That's one way of putting it."

"She seems like a lot of fun."

"Never a dull moment with Mom around." They both stopped talking, and uncomfortable silence filled the space between them until he motioned for her to sit down. He took her mother's chair.

"There's something I wanted to ask you, June."

She nodded, then took a sip of her now-cold drink and immediately regretted it.

"A friend of mine, Isaac Meyer, owns a companion animal training facility in town."

"Oh, yeah," June chimed in. "Friends with Fur."

"Oh, so you know it. Good."

"Well, not really. I mean, I've met Isaac and his wife, Avery, but I haven't ever been to their facility, though I have heard only good things about it."

"Yes, it's excellent. Isaac and Avery are really great with animals and they do a lot of important work in the community to encourage people to rescue shelter pets. Anyway, what I wanted to ask you is, they're having an event next Sunday that I thought you might like to take the puppies to."

"The puppies?"

"Yes, well, it's an adoption event, where people can come and see rescue animals and get to know them a little—see if they want to apply to take one home."

Her heart lurched into her throat at the thought of giving away either of the dogs she'd grown so fond of after the past few days. She swallowed, reminding herself that the animals did not belong to her; soon, they would need permanent homes, and it would be her duty and responsibility to help them find forever families.

Besides, there wasn't room in her life for a pet right now, much less a brother and sister pair.

So why, then, did it hurt so much to even think about letting them go? Especially when that's what was best for them.

Ethan continued speaking, and she didn't think he'd noticed her hesitation. Thank goodness for that at least; she had no desire to explain something she couldn't even understand herself.

"I think it would be a great way for them to have a chance to find homes, don't you?"

"Yes," she agreed, her voice a little squeaky. "Of course I do."

"Good, so you'll come with me, then?"

"Sounds like a plan."

"Oh, and that's not all," he said. "What time should I pick you up tomorrow?"

"Tomorrow? What's tomorrow?"

"Don't tell me you've forgotten."

All she could do was stand there, mouth gaping open.

He crossed his arms, grinning. "You really don't remember, do you?"

She absolutely *had* forgotten.

"My niece, Neena's, birthday party. Remember, when we were at Bauer's Bakery and my parents insisted I bring you by and you seemed okay with it."

"Oh, my gosh! I can't believe I forgot. Ethan, I'm so sorry."

Mixed emotions surged through her at the thought of spending time with him around his family, at how intimate that would be considering they'd agreed that this…thing…would not get serious.

Not serious, sure. And here she was about to get introduced to the people who cared the most about him.

"My family can't wait to meet you, and after all, you did promise you'd go."

She must have looked as nervous as she felt because he gently squeezed her forearm, chuckling. "Hey, they don't bite. We don't have to stay long, but you'd be doing me a major favor. If I don't bring you, I'll never hear the end of it."

She swallowed down the nervous lump that was taking up far too much space in her throat. "I did promise, didn't I?"

He nodded, clearly enjoying the sight of her squirming far too much.

"All right, then. It's just meeting your parents." The words nearly choked her. "It'll be fine. What's the worst that can happen?"

# *Chapter 9*

The following Sunday, June found herself victim to the oldest curse known to woman. There she stood in front of a closet full of clothes, yet she had absolutely nothing to wear.

"I really need to give some of this stuff away, huh?" she muttered to a furry audience of two. The puppies were curled up on a towel in the cushy dog bed Ethan had given her to take home from the clinic, and when she spoke, their little heads tilted adorably.

She didn't know too much about dogs, having only ever had a cat, but she could tell that the puppies were starting to learn a few words after only a couple of days. After observing that, she'd started intentionally naming things when they were exposed to them, like their water, food and toys.

At first, trying to keep track of them had been challenging—she'd started a little notebook to record their eating and potty schedules so she could take them outside at regular intervals and to avoid accidents. Ethan taught her that it was better to try to keep those from happening altogether and instead to give the puppies treats when she took them outside and they were successful.

If someone had told her a month ago that she'd be that interested in the bathroom habits of a couple of baby border collies, she would have questioned that person's sanity.

She laughed.

Yet here she was recording everything the little ones did. Beyond enjoying their company and going through their daily routines, she hadn't thought much about the mechanics of caring for them, but it occurred to her suddenly that she'd basically become a dog mom.

And, oh, she loved it so much.

Being an only child and then working so hard all of her adult life, June had never really given much thought to having kids, but every time she cleaned up a little mess or woke up in the middle of the night to take the puppies outside, she felt a little less afraid of the idea of having a child of her own someday.

The thought of children reminded her of Ethan, whose family was large and full of kids.

*Oh, gosh. Ethan!*

June's eyes flew to the clock on her nightstand and then absorbed the chaotic hurricane of clothing scattered all over her bedroom. Skirts hung from the closet doorknob; tops littered an armchair in the corner; there were bras and underwear hanging from the lampshade and the unused elliptical trainer. Still, she hadn't settled on anything yet, and he was due to pick her up in less than five minutes.

The doorbell rang, sending shock waves up her spine.

*Oh, God.*

Her hair was still wet and she stood there wearing nothing but a towel.

That was another lesson the dogs had taught her— they always needed more time for bathroom breaks than she planned for. If they weren't so cute, she'd be tempted each time she took them out to shout at them to pick a patch of grass already—they were all the same, for goodness' sake.

But they took their time, and now she had none left.

So she did the only thing she could think of, digging through the fashion debris until she found her pale blue bathrobe with the fluffy white clouds on it. She could only hope that when Ethan saw her wearing it, he wouldn't instantly change his mind about taking her to spend time with his family.

"Coming," she called out as he pressed the doorbell one more time.

She moved as quickly as she could, wanting to curl up and die when she opened it and saw Ethan standing there, the perfect specimen of modern masculinity. Beneath his unbuttoned overcoat he wore a navy-blue, long-sleeved henley and dark jeans. His hair waved a little above his collar—she loved that it was just a little too long—and his face was clean-shaven.

There wasn't even a trace of the annoyance she'd thought she might meet when he saw that she wasn't anywhere near ready to go. Instead, his toasted-almond eyes twinkled as he looked her up and down, making no attempt to hide his approval.

Wait. Was that really what she'd seen in his expression? The perfectly put-together, insanely gorgeous Dr. Singh had just seen her at her most unkempt—wild, soggy hair that hadn't had a proper trim in months, old, ratty bathrobe that she'd thought whimsical when she'd purchased it and which now just seemed childish and not a stitch of makeup.

After looking down at herself only to confirm that, yep, it was as bad as she thought, she finally worked up the courage to meet his eyes.

"Ethan, I'm so sorry I'm running late." She wrung her hands and flicked a thumb in the direction of her bedroom by way of explanation. "The puppies…"

He crossed his arms over his wide chest—firm, too, she knew, after the closeness they'd shared the other night.

"Not what I'd expected, but I see nothing to complain about." He winked at her. "My parents and siblings, on the other hand, well, they might not be so keen on…"

"Ha, ha," she teased, opening the door wider so he could come in.

As soon as he did, two little black-and-white fuzz balls galloped over, their ears bouncing up and down.

"Well, look who it is," he said, crouching down to scoop them up.

She was tickled to see that he didn't care at all about his clothes getting hairy. That quality made her like him all the more.

"Have they been behaving for you?" he asked, moving farther inside the living room and sitting cross-legged on the floor.

June closed the door and sat on the couch, extra careful to wrap the robe tightly around her body. The way Ethan had eyed her in the doorway made her think about things she probably shouldn't. Being pretty much bare underneath the robe increased those feelings until they hovered at a dangerous level and she had to force herself to think of anything but…that. Anything but being naked and alone with a man who made her insides burn with need.

She focused on the question he'd asked.

"They've been great," she said. "I've gotten their feeding schedule down pat, and potty training them has been a cinch, thanks to your helpful tips."

"Are they eager to get treats for following through with what you ask?"

*Good*, she thought. If he kept the conversation along that line, she'd have no trouble forgetting her growing fantasies about what it would be like to…

"Yes, they seem to want to do what I ask as long as they know they're getting doggy snacks. Is that a good thing?"

"Definitely. It means they're food-motivated, so as long as you're handing out the goods, they'll aim to do what you need them to."

"I've had my neighbor, Ainsley, and her dog, Max, over to work with them, as well. She's the one I was telling you about who sometimes fosters dogs, and she'll be watching the puppies tonight as soon as I text her to come on over."

"That's great, too."

"What is?"

"That they're spending time around an unfamiliar human and dog. That will help get them socialized so that when they're ready they can go to good homes even if there's already a dog living there."

Her heart lurched and she started to ask him when he thought that day might come—she wasn't even close to being ready for it—but she closed her mouth, quietly watching for a few moments as he rubbed their tiny bellies. "I'll leave you here with them and go finish getting ready."

She headed to the bathroom and closed the door, resting her back against it as she tried to slow her breathing.

Every time they were apart for a few days, and then she saw him again, things got so much worse, meaning, she wanted him so much more. The sparks between them had become more frequent and much stronger and she could feel the chance of an explosion increasing at a terrifying rate.

Since running into each other at the coffee shop, he'd called each day, often more than once, and he'd even stopped by a time or two for a few minutes to ensure that the puppies were thriving.

Each time they spoke on the phone, and when he'd come over, she could sense that he was going through the same thing—wanting to take some elusive next step with her, but afraid of what that might set in motion.

The other morning when they'd had that snowball fight, and after briefly discussing what to do with their casual, not-friendship, not-relationship thing, it had all seemed so risk-free.

Surely, if they had agreed not to let things get too emotionally serious, then they were both on the same page and that very thing would not be allowed to happen.

But then, what about all the physical longing? What about the way her body seemed drawn to his by some unseen force? What in the world were they supposed to do about that?

If they let things get too far, she couldn't be certain that she would be able to inhibit herself from wanting some kind of commitment, something more permanent. She could not promise herself that she would be able to indulge in getting physically closer to him without her heart following along.

Neither could her growing affection for him be ignored.

But she didn't think she could stand to be in the same room with him for much longer without giving in to temptation.

And that's exactly what she faced that day—hours and hours by his side without being able to touch him the way she wanted to, tell him what she was going through every time he was around.

It would be absolute torture, she thought as she pulled on a pair of dark purple skinny trousers and a soft, silky black sweater with sparkly gems along the collar. They were the first pieces she'd put on earlier and then discarded in the bathroom, and now, with a tornado of garments covering her bedroom floor, it was of course what she ended up wearing. It was an outward testament to how little she trusted herself these days.

Her favorite outfit, the only one guaranteed to act as a confidence-builder, and along with a pair of black high-heeled boots, it would have to do.

Because Lord knew, she needed confidence that day more than ever before.

A soft knock rapped on the other side of the door and she opened it.

"I'm sorry to bother you and I don't want you to feel like you have to rush, but I just got the puppies to sit on command, and I wondered where you keep your treats."

"Oh. Of course." She passed by him into the hallway, catching that light but heady scent that hung on his clothes and skin, and started to head down the hall toward the kitchen; but Ethan caught her hand and spun her to face him.

He pulled her to his chest until her forehead touched his chin, then put a palm on either side of her face and covered her mouth with his own.

Shots of electricity buzzed up her spine as the moist heat of his tongue touched hers, deepening the kiss. Without thinking, she wrapped her hands around his hips, tucking her fingers just under the hem of his shirt, moaning when her skin made contact with the warmth of his.

Encouraged, he moved his hands to her shoulders and backed her up until she was against the wall, both of them gasping for air as they gave in to the heat between them.

Finally, she pulled away from his mouth, forcing breath into her lungs.

"What was that for?" she asked, a smile playing at the corners of her lips.

As she fought for composure, Ethan just stood back and flashed that sexy grin of his. Though his motions were smoother than hers, she could see the way his chest rose and fell rapidly, and her own swelled with pride that she'd agitated him to such a degree.

"I just wanted you to know," he breathed, "how beautiful you look today, June."

She coughed out a very unsexy laugh. "Thank you. Very much. But my hair's still wet and I haven't even gotten around to putting on makeup yet."

He stepped closer, threatening to start it up all over again. She wanted to cross her arms over her chest, to keep him at a distance, but her body wouldn't let her. It seemed to crave his in a way she couldn't control.

His eyes plunged into hers. "I meant what I said," he whispered, leaning in again.

She worried he might kiss her once more. Somehow she knew that if he did, there would be no chance of them making it to the party.

Instead, he brushed his lips against hers in the softest of touches, then let her go, padding back down the hall, leaving her breathless and shaken to her very core.

Half an hour later, standing outside an entirely different door, Ethan possessed even less control than he had when he'd arrived to pick up June.

He'd anticipated that evening all day.

Yes, he wanted to see his family, especially his niece Neena, whose tenth birthday they would be celebrating, but the bulk of his eagerness he'd have to attribute to seeing June. He'd been looking forward to a casual, fun evening and maybe an equally casual kiss at the end of it, but when she'd answered her door wearing that tattered old robe, her red hair wet and in complete disarray, she had absolutely thrown him for a loop, caught him totally off guard.

It wasn't hard to imagine her naked under that robe, and after pressing his body up against her in the hallway of her apartment, he could trace her curves in his mind's eye with no effort at all.

She was even more beautiful that way than she'd been when they first met the other night. Without any adornment, her green eyes shone clear and bright, and her hair was like satin as he'd weaved his fingers through it. She had a body that was made to be adored—ample curves for a man to hold on to, soft, creamy skin…it was such a shame he would never have the chance to be that man.

The way she'd responded to him back there, the way she'd reached under his shirt to dig her cool fingers into his burning skin and kissed him back with abandon, he knew he could have her. He knew it wouldn't take much to get her into his bed.

So why wasn't he doing just that?

He watched her face out of the corner of his eye as they stood outside his parents' front door, his heart going soft at her nervous expression.

"No worries, June. My family is a mess but they are nothing if not kindhearted. They will love you, trust me." He squeezed her hand and didn't let go.

Something knotted in his throat as he said the L-word. The last time he'd used it had been for Jessica, and he'd expected using it now to leave a bad taste in his mouth.

But it didn't. And what he'd said was perfectly true. His family would love June, which distressed him to no end.

The only time he'd brought Jessica to meet them had been awkward and uncomfortable for everyone.

She simply didn't fit in, did not understand his family's warm teasing, the way they'd tried to get her to open up to them and to make her laugh. She'd been like oil to their water, everything they said hitting her the wrong way and prickling under her skin.

It was a day he'd like to forget.

It didn't escape his understanding that he was bringing Jessica's polar opposite with him this time, fully aware that she would be met with a completely different reaction.

They would love June's sweetness, her easy smile, her softhearted nature and her sense of humor.

All the things *he* loved about her.

That thought crashed into him like a sucker punch, and he thanked his lucky stars when the door opened and his mother wrapped him in a bear hug.

"Ethan, sweetheart, I'm so glad to see you," she said far too loudly into his ear.

"No need to shout, Mother. I'm right here," he said, grinning.

Melanie Singh whacked him in the side and turned her attention to the woman next to him.

"And you must be June," his mom said, folding her hands together in front of her. He knew that meant she was trying not to be too huggy and it made him cringe. Jessica had complained about his family being overly physically affectionate, a trait he'd never noticed until it had been pointed out to him. A trait he happened to treasure.

He'd grown up feeling loved and surrounded by affection. Of course, he'd apologized on their behalf when Jessica had complained, hating himself for doing so when, even at the time, he'd known it was she who'd been too cold.

A smile spread over his lips as he watched June hold out her arm, as if to invite his mother in. The two women embraced like they'd known each other their whole lives, and seeing their instant connection set off butterflies in his stomach.

"I'm so happy to meet you, Mrs. Singh," June said, holding his mother at arm's length, her eyes sparkling as she chattered easily. "Ethan's told me so much about you. I've heard lots of stories about all the places you've visited as a family, and I'd love to hear more from you if you have the time."

"Absolutely. Oh, I'm so glad. I think sometimes we embarrass our boy, and I hope you'll forgive us if we roped you into something you weren't wanting to do, but we're just so proud of him and we're so excited he's met someone new."

His mother gave him a pointed glance that said a thousand things all at once—the topmost being that she instantly liked this girl he'd brought into her home.

And though he did not like what such a thing implied, not in the least, knowing that his mom approved of June pleased him an inordinate amount.

He would have to keep that to himself. If his mother knew, she'd have the two of them married before Neena's party concluded.

"Come inside, you two, and let me get your coats. How silly of me, letting you freeze out here while I yammer away."

June laughed and followed his mom inside, tossing a smile over her shoulder as he closed the door behind them.

Inside his parents' home, after their coats were taken, they were met with a flurry of friendly chaos as siblings and their children, aunts, uncles and anyone else collected along the way descended upon them. June's eyes glowed at the rainbow of saris worn by some of the Indian women in his family. Several others wore jeans and T-shirts, but June's eyes were drawn to the rich jewel-toned fabrics of his father's place of birth.

"They're all so beautiful," she whispered when they had a second without anyone's attention on them. "I feel so plain in my outfit."

"Nonsense. You look amazing." He pulled her close so that his lips touched her ear. "I thought I made that quite clear earlier."

He loved the rosy apples that instantly blossomed in her cheeks at what he'd said. Images flooded his mind of all the other areas her skin might turn pink for him in exchange for whispered words.

She looked at him, her eyes huge under bright fairy lights that were strung all over the house. "I mean it, though. Are you sure I'm dressed okay?"

"Absolutely." He touched her elbow to soothe her. "You would look beautiful in traditional Indian clothing. Don't get me wrong. But no one expects you to wear it. I would have told you if that was the case. See," he said, holding a hand out to encompass the room. "Plenty are dressed similarly to you, so you fit in just fine."

"Good," she said. "I was a little worried I'd underdressed."

"Not at all. Just breathe, June. They already think

you're wonderful—my mother in particular, and that's not a common occurrence."

*Me, in particular*, he'd really wanted to say.

She looked down at her feet. "I'm so glad."

"Ethan!" He turned from June to see his brother, Harry, hurrying across the room with open arms. Harry grabbed him, then greeted June with his usual, friendly bear hug, making her laugh.

"Is my brother bothering you?" Harry asked, sending June into giggles. If the man wasn't already happily married with two excellent children, Ethan's hackles might have risen. Harry was stupid-handsome and taller by several inches than any of the other Singh men. But he was also too sweet and goofy to invite jealousy. He teased June for several minutes until she was almost doubled over in laughter. Finally, Harry's wife, Amani, caught Ethan's eye, rolled her own and came over to join her husband.

"Take my advice," Amani fake-whispered to June, "and stay far away from this family, unless you want to become crazy like the rest of us."

As she spoke, Amani tossed adoring eyes at Harry and he gave her a big smooch on the cheek. The four of them bantered for half an hour about the couple's recent vacation, how Ethan was managing the clinic, Amani's work in civil rights law and their children, Neena and Suresh.

"Neena's having a blast," Harry said. "But I'm afraid she'll be disappointed when she finds out she's not getting the present she asked for."

Amani's soft eyes met Harry's. "She'll be all right. I think between the cake, her grandparents and aunts and uncles spoiling her and her friends, she'll forget all about it."

Harry glanced at Ethan and then June. "Neena's been asking for a puppy since she first started to talk. I would love to look in to getting one for her, but Amani insists that she and I are too busy to take care of a pet for Neena. Between you and me, though, I think she's at just the right age to start learning the responsibility of caring for a pet."

Amani gave Harry a worried look, but he brushed off his wife's concerns.

"You worry too much, my love. The best way to teach her responsibility is to give her some. What do you think, Ethan?" Harry asked.

Ethan glanced between the two.

"Ordinarily I'd say not to drag me into it, especially when I know Amani will always win—" he winked at his sister-in-law "—but in this case, I'm inclined to agree with you, Harry."

"Well, that would be a first," his brother teased, gently punching Ethan in the shoulder.

"No, I mean it. I think you might be on to something. There are plenty of studies supporting the idea that children who are given pets to care for at a young age—with their parents' supervision backing them, of course—become more caring, conscientious and reliable adults."

Amani tilted her head. "Truly?"

Ethan nodded.

She put a finger on her chin. "Wow, I had no idea. I mean, it makes sense, but I didn't know there was evidence to back it up. You might have to send me some of those articles, Ethan." She leaned closer to him and

June. "And don't you dare tell my husband this, but if you're right, I might have to consider changing my mind," she said, plenty loud enough for Harry to hear. "Besides, you know I love dogs."

Ethan looked at June to see if she was tracking his line of thought, but her eyes were aimed down at the glass of champagne someone had placed in her hand earlier.

"And it so happens that I may have just the puppy for her."

At that, June's eyes snapped up to his.

Something wasn't right, but he couldn't read her expression. He would ask her as soon as they had a moment alone. It was possible she was just feeling a little overwhelmed; his family could have that effect on new people.

Harry and Amani seemed interested in hearing more, and he had two puppies to find homes for, so he went on. "As a matter of fact, that's part of how June and I got to know each other. It's a long story, but the short of it is that she came into the clinic during the storm the other night and was carrying two puppies with her."

Amani put a hand over her heart and her face softened as he told them about June's rescue, unable to hide his pride in her.

"Anyway, if you'd like, June and I can bring the pups by later this week and Neena can meet them."

As he spoke, Ethan's brother and sister-in-law nodding in agreement, he noticed June's skin had turned a little pale. As Harry and Amani discussed the idea of their daughter getting to see the dogs, he took the opportunity to ask if June was all right.

"Me? Oh, yeah," she said, her voice faltering a little. "I'm fine."

"Are you sure, June?" He placed his hands on her shoulders. "Look, if this is too much, being here with all these people you haven't met before... I mean, it might be too much, just let me know and we'll get out of here."

"No, Ethan, it's not that, it's just..."

"All right," Harry burst in. "We've talked it over and we think it's a great idea. As long as you don't tell Neena what the plan is. I just want you to make sure you don't say anything about her possibly getting to keep one, since my wife isn't completely sold on the idea yet."

Ethan pulled his eyes away from June for just a second.

"Hang on one sec, Harry." He turned back to her, and her features had released some of the tension that had been in her face. "Are you okay, sweetheart?"

"Yeah, um, yes." She closed her eyes and took a deep breath before speaking again. "Yes, I think I will be."

He touched his fingertips to her elbow, willing her to feel his tenderness toward her, to know that her will was his command. "Are you certain you wouldn't like to step outside and get some fresh air?"

June shook her head and he forced himself to let go of the issue, hoping that by now, she would surely tell him if he'd done something to bother her.

It shouldn't matter, he knew.

They were merely friends, destined to end that friendship when they parted ways in a short time.

But something was changing between them, something that made him believe it did indeed matter.

The puppies, what she thought of his family, and of course—most of all—how she felt about him.

Warm awareness prickled up his neck.

All of it mattered.

# Chapter 10

The ride home from Neena's party was the epitome of awkwardness, and June kicked herself for being the cause of the uncomfortable silence. Ethan had asked her what was wrong more than once, but had given up the third or fourth time she told him it was nothing.

But how could she tell him what was really bothering her? He would think her silly, or worse, she might scare him off if she opened up her heart that much. What had been bugging her for the week since they'd met, since she'd been the main caretaker of two new little lives, had only become crystal clear to her as of that night when Harry had brought up giving one of the puppies to his daughter and Ethan hadn't objected.

She knew it was nothing personal, knew he wasn't deliberately trying to hurt her by rushing to find homes for the puppies—he was only doing his job and trying to make sure they were cared for—but it made her heart ache nonetheless. She'd finally figured it out, and she wanted to share her thoughts with him, but she wasn't brave enough. If he knew what she'd realized, it would be too much for him, too serious, and he'd run.

Ethan pulled his SUV to a stop outside her apartment and walked her to Ainsley's unit to pick up the puppies. Once they were back inside June's home and had put the dogs to bed, there were no buffers left; she would have to face him.

He took her hand and led her to the couch, his eyes tender as he brushed a piece of hair back from her cheek, rubbing the auburn strand between his fingers before tucking it behind an ear. The way his gaze held hers the whole time made butterflies gather in her stomach, their wings tickling her insides.

"June, look, I know something's been on your mind."

She pulled her eyes away from him and down into her lap, focusing on the sad state of her nails.

"Look at me, June, please," he said, tilting her chin up toward him. "I know that this—" he waved a hand between them and she understood that he referred to their odd pseudo-relationship "—is weird. But the fact is, well, I've begun to care for you." He swallowed, his nervousness out of character. "Quite a lot actually."

Her eyebrows lifted and one corner of his mouth kicked up in response.

"I know. I didn't mean for it to happen, either. It just did." He closed his eyes and sucked in a deep breath, and as he let it out, the impact of what he was trying to tell her pummeled into her.

"We don't have to discuss the way I feel, or if…if

you're feeling something similar—" she opened her mouth to speak, but he held up a palm to give her pause "—and, in fact, I'd rather not do it tonight. There's always time for that later."

She closed her lips. They both knew there wasn't going to be time later, not if he left Peach Leaf and they both went their separate ways.

"But as I said, I care for you, June." He reached out and took her hand, flipping it over to rub a finger against her palm.

The touch resonated all the way up her arm and sped up her breathing.

"So I *do* want to know what's been on your mind that you've not been telling me."

June swallowed and took some time to gather her thoughts. She wasn't ready for this, especially after hearing his confession that he'd developed stronger feelings for her than he was supposed to have let happen. If he hadn't stopped her, the chances were high that she would have blurted out the fact that she was going through the very same thing, if not something even more.

She wasn't ready to put a label on it, was most certainly not ready to call it…*love*. But that flutter under her ribs each time she saw him, that gravitational power he seemed to have over her that made her want to get as close to him as possible—none of it could be denied anymore.

Add to that the new knowledge of how sweet he was around his family, how much she'd enjoyed watching him play with his nieces and nephews and the way he supported his brother and sister and welcomed any stranger as a new friend, and the evidence was clear.

Maybe it wasn't quite love, not yet at least, but one thing was for sure; she absolutely adored Ethan Singh.

Still, she couldn't tell him the truth just yet—that she'd begun to think of the puppies as a symbol of the new life she was trying to build. That, somehow, even though it didn't entirely make sense, she'd begun to believe that if she failed the animals, she would fail herself. She knew she didn't have the resources or the time to nurture them and be there for them the way she should, but neither was she willing to let them go.

If she gave up on them, she felt, it would be as if she'd given up on herself.

Worse, selfishly, she knew that once the puppies were no longer her responsibility, Ethan would have no real reason to see her anymore.

A week ago, she hadn't known the dogs or Ethan Singh, and now the loss of all three was a real threat, a specter of darkness hanging around her future.

Imagine if she told him all of that; she wouldn't blame him for wanting to disappear from her life. And she wasn't ready to face it herself.

Still, he stared at her, waiting for a response, the question of what was on her mind hanging thick in the air between them.

Maybe it would be safe to tell him just a fraction of the truth, especially since, for whatever reason, it seemed to be almost impossible for her to lie to the man. He acted as her own personal truth serum.

"You said you don't want to talk about this tonight, and, well, I guess I'm feeling some of the same things you are. I think that this thing between us just overwhelmed me a little tonight, meeting your family and all."

"I'm sorry, June." He smoothed a hand across his forehead. "I shouldn't have pushed you into going."

She shook her head. "No, don't apologize. I agreed to go and you didn't push me. It's just that I hadn't imagined how much I would enjoy being around them and I guess the thought of never seeing them again—after you're gone, I mean—is a little sad to me."

His lips formed a thin line and his eyes narrowed as he considered her words.

"Maybe it doesn't have to be like that," he said. "But let's not talk about the future." He leaned in until his lips were mere inches from hers. "Right now, I want to know only one thing."

"Mmm," she mumbled, apparently unable to form whole words when he was that close to her.

He smiled and ran his tongue along his lower lip, moistening it. "What can I do to make you feel better tonight, in this moment?"

"Anything?" she asked.

"Anything."

Instead of spelling it out, she wrapped a hand behind his neck and slowly, tentatively, pulled him in, pressing her lips against his, relishing his signature taste—cinnamon, as always, from the chai he drank so often, layered with a hint of champagne from the party. Emboldened by his hungry response as he wrapped his arms around her waist, she parted his lips with her tongue, deepening the kiss, smiling against his mouth when he gave a soft little groan.

She moved her hands from his neck, over his shoulders and down his muscular arms, grasping his hands in hers. She moved them to her breasts and he responded by softly massaging the mounds over her sweater, her nipples rising to meet his touch.

She groaned in protest when he moved away.

"June," he said on a heavy breath. "Are you sure you want this? I mean, don't get me wrong, I absolutely, definitely do, but I don't want to pressure you. I know we're both just out of bad relationships and I don't want to…"

She held up a finger to quiet him. "Shh. Don't think so much, Ethan. Just go with it."

He smiled, lips parting to reveal perfect teeth, and she grinned in response. "I can do that," he said.

"Good. That's what I hoped you'd say."

He kissed her again and ran his hands down her sides, pausing at the hem of her sweater. When she nodded briefly, he lifted it slightly, tucking his hands under the fabric. His hot fingers against her skin, still cool from being outdoors only moments before, caused a slight intake of breath, and then she relaxed into his touch as his hands slid up her back. They slowly, expertly glided along her spine, then back down, circling around to the front where he smoothed them over her abdomen. When they trailed upward to her chest, his fingers toying with her nipples until they perked up to meet him, she closed her eyes and relished the sensation.

When she opened them again, she met Ethan's dark irises, his pupils dilated with arousal, letting her know he'd like some attention, as well.

So she moved until her back rested against the arm of her couch, pulling him until his torso rested against her. She was glad that a certain part of him was far away from her hands, though she could feel him growing when his groin came in contact with her thigh, the knowledge that she'd turned him on so thoroughly setting off her own response.

She ran her hands up his back, stopping here and there to admire the muscles before running them back down to his abs, and then to the waistband of his jeans. His mouth covered her own as he grabbed her hand and guided it to the front.

June didn't hesitate in removing his belt and unzipping his fly.

But that was as far as she got before her nerves settled in. Ethan seemed to understand that she needed to slow down a bit, and he lifted his upper body away from her, pulling her over until she rested against his chest, his arms wrapped around her. She looked up and saw that dark stubble she loved so much beginning to show along his jawline. He smiled down at her, his eyes full of desire but warm and patient. She rested her face against his chest and attempted to slow her breathing.

Was she really ready for this? Had she truly healed enough from the last person she'd been with, the person who'd so completely shattered her heart, to be able to give herself to someone new?

Even if they'd agreed that this wouldn't turn into a relationship, she still owed Ethan that much, that he would be the only man on her mind without her dwelling on the past if they went through with this; she forced herself to use the actual words—if they made love. She wanted to give him her whole self, not a broken collection of parts. He deserved that, just as she did from him.

When she looked into his eyes again, she found confirmation that she was the only woman on his mind; he wasn't far off somewhere, recalling the last time he'd held someone like that. The way he gazed at her, making her feel like she was the most beautiful, most amazing woman in the world, told her she had all of him.

And, for that night, that's all she wanted. It was enough. It had to be enough.

With renewed confidence, she placed a hand on his shoulder and pulled her body up, straddling his waist with her legs.

"God, you're gorgeous," he said, as breathless as she felt. His arousal was there between them, causing June to long for more from him. She kissed him again and again, until hunger mounted on both sides and they couldn't stand it there any longer.

In one quick motion, Ethan rose from the couch, lifting her as if she weighed nothing.

For once, she was more than satisfied with the size of her apartment, as it was so small and uncomplicated she didn't have to point out where the bedroom was.

Ethan smiled at her as he carried her there, laying her down gently on her lavender bedspread, shoving aside the clothing she'd discarded earlier.

He lifted her legs one at a time to pull off the socks she'd worn inside her boots, stopping to kiss the ticklish parts of the soles of her feet, making her giggle.

She was thankful for his lightening the mood, as intensity had begun to build and she knew they were both close to breaking. He seemed to know instinctively when she needed a softer moment before he started in again, sending desire spiraling through her.

He pulled off her pants and tossed them aside, then she leaned up until her head was at the level of his torso. His jeans were still undone, so she made quick work of removing them completely, her pulse rocketing up as she ran her hands along his firm behind, covered only by black boxer briefs.

She looked up at him and he nodded, his eyes black as night in the dark bedroom. With her eyes locked on to his, she pulled off the underwear, running her hand along his hard length until he shut his eyes and his legs slackened.

"June, I can't survive this much longer," he said, grabbing hold of her hand. "I want you."

She smiled and pulled him down onto the bed, where he relieved her of her own underwear, leaving only her bra and top. His hands worked fast but gently, pulling her sweater over her head and unhooking her very last piece of clothing.

When all of the garments were gone, they stared at each other for several seconds. June loved the contrasting colors of their skin, her lighter tone against his darker one, and she couldn't wait to blend them together into one.

Ethan softly pressed her shoulders back until her head lay on a pillow. His hands slid up her thighs until they reached her center, and he spread her legs, then bent forward to kiss her, plunging his tongue into her mouth as he caressed her heat, slipping a finger inside. When she was very wet, she grabbed a condom from a drawer of her bedside table, allowing him to slip it on before he dove deep inside her.

Everything faded away until all that was left was his pulsing, faster and faster until her core buzzed with desperate need. At his final plunge, they burst open to each other until there was nothing left to give. And when Ethan slid from her body, he lay down behind her, pulling her against his warm form.

Both of them wordless from exhausted pleasure, he ran his fingers through her hair and along her arm, until she drifted off into the deepest sleep she'd enjoyed in as long as she could remember.

A terrible noise ripped Ethan from sleep, and it took almost a full minute for him to realize where he was, and that the god-awful sound was an alarm tone coming from June's phone on her bedside table.

He almost laughed when he looked down to find her still in his arms, her eyes slammed shut, completely oblivious to the ripping sound.

"June," he said, chuckling. "June, wake up before I throw that damn thing across the room."

One eyelid rose revealing a pretty green iris, but fell again almost immediately and it took several more tries before Ethan was able to fully wake her.

"Good Lord, woman," he said. "You sleep like the dead."

She stretched out her arms and tossed a sleepy smile in his direction. He crossed his arms over his chest and watched her, just enjoying the view. The sun wasn't up yet, but when she flicked on her bedside lamp, soft light flooded over her ivory skin and all that luscious red hair fell over her shoulders, rendering June so ethereal and beautiful that she resembled a wood nymph.

Her beauty was unique and warm, and he wanted to wrap himself in it like a blanket. As fresh thirst began to build, he reached for her, ready to quench it with her body.

But as June picked up her phone, her eyes widened

and she launched out of the bed before he could catch her.

"Oh, my God, I am going to be so late for work." She ran to her dresser and grabbed clean underwear, mumbling to herself. "So late, so late, so late!"

Ethan had to get to the clinic himself to relieve the night vet tech, but he wanted to enjoy the show for a few more minutes—June's naked curves moving quickly around the room as she gathered clothing. He didn't know when he would next get the chance to see her like this, and he wasn't about to miss relishing that moment; it would be worth arriving a half hour late to work. It would also be the first time, so he was confident his father's vet tech would forgive him.

He leaned back and rested his torso against the headboard. "June," he said, but she didn't register him calling her. "June!"

This time, she looked up as if from a trance, and her eyes softened as they landed on him.

"Yeah?"

He curved a finger. "Come here for a second."

If he was honest, he enjoyed the battle raging in her eyes, clearly weighing the cost of missing work with another hour of lovemaking with him. It had been the best of his life with June, without contest. For the time being, coming off a night of it, he'd be willing to give up everything to spend another day wrapped up with her in those lavender sheets.

As it were, he would never get her out of his mind, and he could already tell that the day at work would be the longest of his life. Finally, the battle was over, and he was disappointed to realize that she'd made the mature, adult decision.

*Dammit.*

"I can't, Ethan. I've got to get to work."

But at least she walked over, her berry lips curved upward, and his eyes latched on to her creamy breasts as they hovered above his chest when she leaned in for a kiss.

"I really do have to go," she said, the very same moment he took her forearm and pulled her down on top of him. His heart buzzed at the giggle she gave in response.

"Ethan," she said, trying her best to be serious. "I'm going to be late for work, and it'll be pretty hard to come up with a legit-sounding excuse when Margaret's already given me a full week off."

"But I'm not finished with you yet," he argued, attempting to strengthen his case by nibbling at her neck and dotting tiny kisses along her shoulders. "There are so many spots I haven't yet kissed."

She indulged him a little, but finally pulled away. June put her hands on either side of his face.

"Last night was…amazing. It was beyond amazing," she said, echoing his thoughts, "but it can't last forever." She ran her thumb along his lip, sending vibrations all throughout his body.

"Do you know what you do to me, June?" He grabbed her hands and held them to his chest. "Do you have any idea?"

She closed her eyes as he felt his heart beat against her fingers. "I have some idea," she answered, eyes wide and full of desire, "if it's half of what you do to me."

He grinned at that and leaned in to kiss her. She kissed him back with the same hunger that tore at his insides. Everything in his body burned to take her again, to be inside her, where he felt better than he ever had before in his life.

It was even possible that he...

"But I really do need to get out of here." She took her hands back from him and touched his face once more before rising from the bed. As she stood before him, hands at her sides, doing nothing to hide her form, he let his eyes wander from her lovely, fiery mane, past her spectacular breasts, all the way down to her purple-painted toes.

"You're the most beautiful woman I've ever laid eyes on, June." He'd thought the words might come out cheesy, and that June might rightfully laugh at him, but his voice was strong and as he spoke them he realized that no truer words had ever escaped his lips.

And then it hit him.

What the hell had he done? What had he allowed himself to get into here?

He hadn't meant for things to go this far. Obviously, he'd wanted her physically more than he ever had anyone else, but he'd sort of convinced himself that, once they'd slept together and the novelty wore off, the mystery was gone, that things would calm down between them.

He'd mistakenly believed that he could get the woman out of his system.

On the contrary, she was more present in him, had more of a grip on him, than he'd thought possible.

Instead of getting her out of his system, he'd invited her in, all the way.

And he knew now that nothing he could do or say would get her out.

He swallowed, bringing a hand to his forehead to brush off the beads of perspiration that had sprung up there.

She was right to get away from him now, and he would let her go.

He dropped his hands to his sides.

"Right," he said. "Right, you should get ready for work and I'll do the same or we'll both be seriously late."

Something in her features let him know she'd registered the sudden change in his demeanor, but she didn't have time to question it.

He offered a small smile, hoping she wouldn't ask about his abrupt decision to come around to her way of thinking.

Thankfully, she turned and left the room.

If she'd stayed, she would have seen the way he buried his face in her pillow for what he somehow knew would be the last time, inhaling her sweet jasmine scent. If she'd stayed, she might have heard him groan as he realized what a mess he'd turned their casual nonrelationship into. And worst of all, if she'd stayed, she might have seen the first bud begin to grow as love— yes, *love*—blossomed in a heart he'd thought dead.

## Chapter 11

On Saturday morning just a week after she and Ethan first made love, June's hands shook as she pulled into the drive at his parents' home. She turned off the ignition and forced herself to take ten deep breaths.

She couldn't put her finger on why she felt so nervous all of a sudden. She and Ethan had been seeing each other off and on the whole week, Ethan taking the puppies to work each day with him and bringing them to June's to spend the night. Just the puppies, though, not Ethan himself.

Maybe that was the problem.

Something had changed after they'd slept together, but it wasn't the type of thing she expected. Sure, now and then a guy spent the night with one of her friends and never called again, and it had happened to June once a long time ago, but this was something entirely different.

Ethan still called, he still visited, and if anything the two had gotten closer...but they just hadn't been to bed together again.

And it was making her insane.

This was exactly why they had agreed to keep things casual, and yet he'd gone and taken it to the next level.

She stopped herself, recalling that perfect night a week before.

Her assessment wasn't fair; she had been the one to take that first step, and she'd been more than happy when he went along with her. Without a doubt, it had been the best night of her life. Ethan had been wonderful—attentive, but not demanding, letting her take the reins, but giving as good as he got—and, oh, he was an amazing lover.

The problem was that he was also more than that. She'd seen a change in him that next morning when she'd been running late for work. He'd been so tender, so...well...*loving.* He'd been in no hurry to leave and had even packed her a lunch while she'd showered, and then had driven her to work and kissed her when he dropped her off, promising to call that afternoon—a promise he then kept.

She knew what the problem was; it was all too good to be true.

At least now she had her own car back, complete with a big-ass bill for a new battery and the cost of a tow.

She rested her head on the steering wheel for a moment before opening the door and lifting the puppies out of the backseat in their crate, along with a tote full of baking supplies.

She slammed her car door shut with a foot, careful not to jostle the puppies too much, and then she looked up just in time to see Ethan jogging in their direction. Her heart swelled the second she met his gaze, further proof that something wasn't right.

Over the past few days, she'd had plenty of time to realize that she had been kidding herself when she'd agreed to keep this thing with Ethan casual. It would be easy to blame it on the way their physical relationship had changed, but in her heart of hearts, June knew it was so much more.

As she watched him approach, she was reminded once again just how much she genuinely liked this man, how incredibly, purely happy she was in his company. No one had ever made her come alive the way he did, and she had him to thank for bringing her natural optimism back. She'd even gotten the urge to bake again and to risk hoping that she might still someday see her dreams come true.

He was special, no doubt, and he'd gotten a hold of her in a way that no man ever had. Not her horrible ex—not anybody.

She recognized the feeling for what it was, but still she resisted naming it. Doing so would solidify it, somehow, and she wasn't ready to do that just yet. Because she knew that, the second she did, it would all be lost. If Ethan found out what was going on in her heart and in her mind, he'd back off and possibly out of her life. And she didn't want to, but she needed him now. Though he was still as wonderful as ever with the puppies, it also had nothing to do with them anymore.

"Hey there," he said, drawing up in front of her, reaching for the tote bag and dog carrier. "Let me take those from you."

He leaned forward and kissed her cheek before leading her to the door.

Though they had seen each other since that night they spent together—doing the puppy exchange and going out to dinner a few times—this was the first time they'd be in a house together. She prayed she could keep her hands off him, keep from making a fool of herself by wanting him to sleep with her again when he'd made no motion to take her to bed over the past week.

She got the sense he was being careful with her, as though he didn't want to hurt her. But not being with him again, after they'd shared each other that way, hurt even more.

He led her through the door he'd left propped open and she followed as he brought the crate and bag into the dining room that attached to the Singhs' kitchen. He pulled a few child gates out of a linen closet and set them up. "So we can watch them while we go in the kitchen," he said.

June nodded.

Ethan glanced at a clock on the wall. "We've got about three hours until we have to be at Friends with Fur. Anything you'd like to do until it's time to go?"

June's cheeks went warm at the same time Ethan's turned a slightly darker shade and she knew he'd heard it, too. Of course there were things she'd like to do in that time, all involving clothes on the floor and lots and lots of bare skin.

He cleared his throat and looked away, disappointment clouding his features.

Her heart sank and she changed the subject before the sharp pain could do any more damage.

"I brought baking stuff, and I was thinking we could make some canine treats for the adoption fair if that sounds good to you."

He managed a soft, sad smile, but it was a smile nonetheless, and she would have to take it. "That sounds like a great idea."

He took her hand and led her into the kitchen. He asked what he could do to help and she gave him the task of measuring out the dry ingredients while she whisked together eggs and water in a small bowl.

"This isn't my recipe," she said, leaning against the granite countertop to admire the Singhs' chef-worthy kitchen. "I found it online. But I did make a few modifications that I think will make these biscuits even better."

Ethan glanced over his shoulder. "I'm sure they'll be excellent," he said, his voice sounding distracted. He stirred flour and baking powder together in silence for a bit. Finally, he turned to face her, dropping the wooden spoon to his side.

"Listen, June. I…"

She put the bowl down and held up both palms. "You really don't need to say anything."

"I would like to, though. I feel like we need to talk and we're both dancing around an elephant in the room, hoping it will go away. But, June, it won't. We have to discuss some things."

"Actually, you're completely wrong. That's the beauty of our little arrangement. You said friends only, nothing serious. So we absolutely don't have to talk about it, now do we?"

She noticed, too late, that her voice had gone up an octave, making it all too clear that she was agitated, that she cared far too much. Of course, the way they'd set things up, caring *at all* was too much.

He closed his eyes and then put down the spoon, crossing his arms over that toned chest she'd loved resting her head against. "I know that's what we said, but I don't think either of us can deny that our boundaries really don't apply anymore."

She tilted her head. "Of course they still do, Ethan." Without them, there was too much freedom. Anything could happen between them if there weren't any limits, and she just wasn't ready for that. Was she?

His brows lowered over stormy eyes. "How can you act like nothing happened between us, June? How can you stand here baking dog cookies like nothing's changed at all?"

"I don't know, Ethan. You tell me. It's probably the same way you can take me out to dinner and then leave for the night without even kissing me goodbye."

He brushed a hand over his face. "You're right. I know I've been doing it, too." He looked up and met her gaze, his eyes burning with the same things she felt but was too afraid to speak out loud. "But don't you think it's time to cut the crap?"

She was quiet for a moment, knowing that anything that came out of her mouth had the potential to define their relationship in permanent ways.

She stood at a precipice, looking down into a pit, the bottom of which she couldn't see and held both danger and possibility. Here was her chance. Here was a guy who was willing, pushing even, to define what was going on between them, and maybe even to acknowledge that they both wanted more.

An amazing, kindhearted, hardworking, absolutely gorgeous human being obviously cared for her. Wasn't that what she'd always wanted? Wasn't that her dream? Hell, wasn't that every woman's dream?

So why would she even consider cutting their conversation short and throwing it all away, which was exactly what she knew would happen if she refused to engage in that discussion with him?

There was too much at stake. Their hearts were both still too tender from being broken by careless people. Not to mention the fact that, even if she wanted him to stay with her, or better, to go with him, she knew she couldn't have that. Could she?

"I think the crap, as you called it, is the only thing saving both of us from making a huge mistake."

The look he gave her then—that look that said all the things she couldn't articulate—nearly undid all of her resolve. It would have, except that she'd succeeded in her goal of getting stronger, of resisting the temptation to give her whole heart to someone again. As much as it hurt, she wasn't going to open her heart and tell him how she really felt. She sure as hell wasn't going to admit to him, or even to herself, that she was falling for him so fast she couldn't keep the walls from caving in on her.

"June," he said softly, unwinding the strings around her heart as he stepped toward her, "I'm not so sure anymore that it would be a mistake."

She closed her eyes so she wouldn't melt into his.

"So, how can *you* be so sure?" he asked.

She gasped when his cell phone began to buzz in his pocket.

"Aren't you going to get that?"

"No, it can wait. We're having a conversation here."

She turned away. "I think you should take the call."

Even though she was no longer facing him, June could feel the heat from his eyes blazing into her back. She felt sick. She'd been rude and awful, and she wanted to kick herself for it.

He didn't deserve this. Ethan was a great guy, willing to rehash their initial boundaries so that they could talk about their growing feelings and possibly go forward. And what was she doing?

Acting like a complete and total immature idiot.

She groaned and turned around, ready to apologize, but was met with Ethan's broad back. He was stirring the ingredients again and the only indication that anything had changed was the forceful, angry way he beat at them with the spoon. And, of course, the thick, tense ball of terrible energy that had taken up all of the air in the room.

Her nerve endings were frayed so that June felt everything at double the normal intensity. Standing there, watching the moment slip by, with her heart hanging off a cliff, June wasn't sure if she was relieved or furious when his phone started up again.

His head tilted backward against his upper spine and then he looked back down, hands clenched into fists at his sides as if he fought to gather his composure.

He picked up his phone, voice tight as he greeted the caller.

She didn't know who was on the other end, but she was grateful for the chance the call gave her to pull herself together. Now that she'd elected to forego a conversation that could have changed her path, her entire life, all she could feel was a tight disappointment in the pit of her stomach, the absence of anything good.

She knew instantly that she'd made a severe mistake, and it would cost her if she didn't fix it. The problem was, she didn't know how.

Before Clayton, she'd been an open book, a romantic, a heart-on-her sleeve kind of girl, but he had crushed that out of her when he'd stolen her life savings and skipped town without so much as a text or a note. She'd spent the following months trying to figure out what had happened, how her dreams had seemed so clear, right at the tips of her fingers, only to disappear overnight.

It wasn't the only time her life had changed in such a short amount of time. The other night when she'd made love with Ethan, it had changed again, but this time she didn't feel like curling up in a ball and quitting; this time, it had made her want to grow wings and soar.

But she couldn't tell him, because if she did and he didn't return her feelings, didn't want the same new life with her, where would that leave her? She had nothing left anymore; if she let Ethan have her heart and he broke it, all that would remain would be a shell of a person, and June would rather not become someone she would grow to resent.

She stood, unable to get her limbs to move until Ethan finished his call.

When he turned around, all of her raw emotion was reflected in his eyes.

He fidgeted with the phone and then finally slipped it into his pocket. "I have some good news," he said, and she could see that he was trying to offer her a smile.

She put her hands in her pockets, afraid that if she didn't give them something to do, they might reach out for the man she'd begun to fall hard for. So. Hard.

"Yeah?" she asked, but the word came out more like a choking sound.

"Yeah, um…" He raked a hand through his hair "That was Harry, my brother."

"I remember," she said, folding her hands in front of her torso, hoping he would understand that she meant she remembered far more about that night than the names of his family members.

"Right." His eyes were dark and narrow as he studied her. "Anyway, he says that Amani is on board and they want to take one of the puppies for Neena, after all."

"Oh," she said, not making any attempt to inject joy into her voice. She certainly didn't feel any, and this new revelation only made that worse. But if it would make him happy, she would lie. Just this once, because she needed to see light return to his face. "That's—" she swallowed over the pain rising in her throat "—that's wonderful. I know they'll be the perfect family for one of the puppies."

*But what about the perfect family I want?*

"I thought so, too. They love and respect animals and they'll take good care of a puppy." His eyes were tired now and his shoulders sunk as if he felt defeated. "We should go," he said, glancing at his watch. "Isaac will be expecting us soon."

Had that much time passed? She checked the wall clock and got her answer. No, it had not. Ethan probably just wanted to get away from the suffocating room, away from her. She didn't blame him—she wanted away from her, too.

Friends with Fur was bustling with activity when Ethan and June arrived less than an hour later. It was early—dog food and supply vendors and animal rescue organizations were still getting their booths and pens set up—but he couldn't have stayed in that kitchen with June for a single minute longer.

Seeing her struggle to talk to him about whatever it was she was feeling, and not being able to communicate himself, had been the worst form of torture. The sadness in her eyes had made him want to run, to get away from her, because what could possibly be causing it, if not his presence in her life?

When she'd come into his clinic a couple of weeks ago, she'd been like a breath of fresh air, her passion for saving those puppies only a fraction of the kindness that defined June Leavy. From that instant on, he'd wanted nothing more than to get to know her better, to get lost in her sweetness so he could forget about Jessica and his broken heart.

He'd told June that the boundaries he'd set, the "rule" that things wouldn't get too serious, were for both their benefits. But in reality, his doing so had been purely selfish. He saw that clearly now—now, when it was probably too late.

He'd tried to protect his own heart from getting broken again, but he truly had not realized that doing so might be the very thing that would cause her pain. It caused him pain, too. Keeping her at a distance had been a mistake. He realized that now. But if she wouldn't talk to him, wouldn't tell him what was wrong, how could he help her?

He hadn't thought it possible that they would end up wanting more from each other, and now that he knew that to be the case, he had no idea what to do about it.

This had not been in his plan. Their short-term relationship was supposed to be casual, a stop on their respective routes to healing from past heartbreak; instead, falling for her and not being able to do anything about it for fear of hurting her was causing more harm than good.

And still, she was sweet to him, letting him hold her hand as they walked around the open training arena inside Isaac's facility, June having insisted on carrying the crate with the puppies inside. They were getting bigger and would need their own separate crates soon.

For some unknown reason, even though he'd been campaigning to find them homes, the thought of giving them away so soon, especially to separate families, caused his throat to catch.

"Ethan!"

He turned to see Isaac Meyer, his wife, Avery, and Avery's dog, Foggy, headed toward the two of them. Isaac shook his hand and he introduced his friends to June. He couldn't help but smile as he watched June ask to pet Foggy, and Avery, who was always just a bit shy, seemed to take to her instantly.

That was his girl—warm, kind, drawing people to her like bees to honey.

"Are these the puppies you've been telling us about?" Avery asked, crouching down to peer into the crate.

June's eyes brightened and her whole demeanor

changed as she regaled her new friend with stories from the past couple of weeks. She'd gotten so attached to the little guys.

And suddenly it hit him—he'd been awful about the puppies. Nonstop, he had talked only about finding them homes, giving them away, thinking it was the right thing to do. And all the while, June had been falling in love with them.

That must have been why she had become so distant the past few days, and why her thoughts had gotten so far away each time he mentioned Neena wanting a pet or bringing them to the adoption expo.

By dragging her there that day, he had, against her will, set in motion events that would break her heart yet again. He hadn't been careful with her feelings the way he so badly wanted to be, and he'd overlooked the fact that the puppies really did in fact belong to June. He didn't have the right to make decisions about them without consulting her, and now he wanted to kick himself for neglecting to put her needs first.

"You know," Isaac said, playing with one of the pups June had released from the crate, "this one could have all the makings of an outstanding service dog."

"Really?" June asked, her voice faltering so subtly that he knew he was the only one who'd caught it. He knew her so well now, and it had become more and more difficult to imagine returning to Colorado to resume his former life without her.

He hadn't realized until that moment how much he loved having her by his side.

How much he loved…her.

And yet, as he wanted to be closer and closer to her, the thing he'd been encouraging her to do—find homes for their little furry charges—was the very thing pushing her away.

"Yes, really," Isaac continued. "He's got a calm temperament, he's alert and curious but not impulsive and he responds well to treats." Isaac beamed at June, his face full of excitement.

Ethan knew his friend was passionate about training service dogs, especially for victims of combat PTSD, and his father often donated veterinary care to keep costs down for people who needed service animals. Ethan had done the same for the time he'd been running his dad's clinic. He admired Isaac's work, but right now, all he wanted to do was to get June out of there before her kind heart let someone take a puppy, even though she didn't want to give them away.

It was so clear now. All she'd been trying to tell him was that she wanted to keep them herself. It didn't matter that she wasn't in a position to do so at the time; that could be dealt with and he would help her any way he could. All that mattered then was letting her know that he understood what was going on behind her facade of pretending to be okay.

"Isaac and Avery, would you guys mind watching the pups for a minute?"

They shared a glance and then nodded. "Of course, no problem," the two said in unison.

June set down the puppy she'd been holding and watched him carefully.

"June, would you join me for just a minute? There's something I need to talk to you about."

Her eyes narrowed but she did as he asked, taking his hand and following him to the only spot in the arena that wasn't covered in furry bodies or free dog toys and treats. He pulled her to a stop and grabbed both of her hands.

Confusion was etched into her features. "Ethan, what's wrong? Isaac was in the middle of telling me about training the male puppy to be a service dog and I..."

"How do you feel about that, June?" he interrupted. "Tell me the truth."

Her face fell and moisture sprung into her eyes. She quickly wiped away the first tear before it had a chance to fall. "It's just about the last thing I want, Ethan."

He pulled her against his chest, his heart breaking as she cried softly.

"God, June. Why didn't you just tell me that you didn't want to give them away?"

"I don't know," she said, her voice cracking in a way that made him think she wasn't telling the whole truth. "I guess it's just that you were pushing me so hard to do it, and you're the expert when it comes to dogs." She sniffed and pried her chest away from his. "I guess I felt that if you didn't think I'd be a good dog owner, then you were probably right."

"You've got it all wrong, June. If you'd have told me that what's been bothering you this whole time was that you didn't want to give the puppies up, I would have helped you find a way to keep them. I can't believe that's all it was and you kept it from me."

He thought they were having a heart-to-heart, a moment that would fix everything and get them back to normal, whatever that meant. But June was shaking her head.

He'd missed something crucial, but he had no idea what.

"No, Ethan. That's not all it is."

He was genuinely confused, and the way she was looking at him gave the impression that she was still sad and angry with him. But if that wasn't it... "Then what is it?" he asked.

More tears ran down her cheeks, making him feel like a total jerk and an idiot at the same time.

"If you can't see what's been bothering me, Ethan, then me spelling it out for you isn't going to change anything."

With those final words, she stormed off. And he knew she was very, very upset because she didn't take the puppies with her.

He wanted desperately to follow, but something in him caused him to pause. She'd made a comment in passing that morning of the snowball fight, one he hadn't paid much attention to at the time but that now stood out, marring an otherwise glowing, perfect memory.

*That was it.*

She'd said she needed space, time to heal from what that previous jerk did to her. And more than anything, he did not want to give her reason to lump him in with a guy like that, a guy stupid enough to let her go.

So he vowed to give her a little space, a little time, just like she asked. Maybe she would realize, as he'd begun to, that she wasn't at peace with the idea of their relationship coming to a close.

And after that passed, after her heart healed, nothing would stop him from going after her.

Nothing in the world.

## Chapter 12

From the parking lot of her apartment building, even with tears still blurring her vision after driving aimlessly for hours, June could see her patio light blazing. The hairs on the back of her neck stood up; she did not recall flipping the switch by her back door before leaving earlier in the day.

She shut her car door and paused to grab pepper spray from her bag before making her way up the stairs to her unit. Not for the first time, but for a new reason, she wished the puppies were with her. They were still small, but their barks were deceptively loud, and lately, the little squirts had begun to put up a fuss if anyone they didn't know got too close to their mom.

Another tear slipped down June's cheek; that was how she thought of the situation. She'd basically adopted them, after all, and she still felt guilty for leaving them behind at the pet fair. Ethan would take care of them, but from the bottom of her toes all the way up to the top of her head, with every cell in her body, she hoped he wouldn't give them away that day.

But she didn't have a chance to think about regrets at the moment, because as she approached her building, June was fairly certain she caught movement on her back porch out of the corner of her eye.

She jammed her key into the lock and got in as quickly as possible, slamming the door behind her. Her back against it, she peered into her living room and down the hallway, the only light coming from a lamp on her bedside table.

"Hello?" she called, but there was no answer.

She looked out from the sliding glass door to try to see if there was someone on the patio, but the light didn't reach too far and there were shadows everywhere, so she settled for checking the lock and the dead bolt. Setting her purse on the couch, June flipped on a single lamp, checking the closets and in every potential hiding area she could think of.

But as soon as she returned to the living room and plopped down on the couch, she heard a soft knock, and it wasn't coming from the front door.

As icicles formed along her spine, she picked up the pepper spray and the golf club she kept under the couch and, one in each hand, headed over to the sliding door.

When she pressed her nose against the glass to better see out, a face stared back at her and a blood-curdling scream erupted from her throat before she recognized who it was.

"Clayton!" she shouted, anger coursing through her veins to replace fear. Her first instinct was to call the police, but as her pulse calmed and her breathing slowed, June reminded herself that, for all his faults, he'd never been a violent man.

Clayton Miller held up his hands and turned around, showing her that he posed no threat. Convinced he didn't intend to hurt her, she dropped the golf club and unlocked the door, sliding the pepper spray into her pocket, just in case.

*Hell*, she thought, *I might use it just because.*

When she slid the door open, he walked slowly past her into the living room. He still stood nearly eye level with her, of course, but he'd lost weight and his thinner form didn't suit him. There were dark circles under his eyes when he looked at her, as though he hadn't slept well in weeks.

She crossed her arms over her chest, suddenly feeling a chill that had nothing to do with the January temperature. "Clayton, what in the hell were you doing on my porch?"

He cringed. "I needed to see you and my key didn't work in the lock, so I figured I'd just wait out there until you came home. Where were you, June? I've been here for hours."

She choked out a laugh, feeling sick to her stomach. "Of course your key didn't work. I had the locks changed. And after all you've done to me, your audacity continues to amaze me, Clayton. I shouldn't have to tell you this, but you don't get to ask questions like that anymore."

He looked down at his sneakers. "You're right. I... I'm sorry."

Her eyebrows rose in genuine surprise. "Well, that's

the first I've heard those words since you walked out on me and took every dime I'd saved up."

"I know, June, and there's a lot I need to apologize for. I'd like to do that if you'll give me a chance."

Up until she'd found him standing on her porch, looking like something a cat had dragged up, there were a lot of things June would have wanted to say if Clayton Miller ever graced her with his presence again, and even more she'd have wanted to throw in his face. But seeing him there, she realized she no longer cared what reasons—excuses, really—he would give for leaving her and everything else he'd done.

She could finally say, with absolute certainty, that she gave less than a damn.

"I don't have anything to say to you, Clayton, and to be frank, there's nothing you can say to me that will change anything. So, if it's all the same to you, I'd like for you to get the hell out of my life for the last time."

This time, it was her choice, and she wanted him gone.

He held up a hand and she saw that his eyes were closed. "That's fine, June. I will get out of here like you asked, but there's something I wanted to give you first, if you'll let me stay just a second longer."

As he pulled an envelope from his back pocket, she tilted her chin up so she could stare down at him as though she were ten feet tall. "What's that?" she asked, not allowing her hopes to climb, not wanting to let herself wish it was what she thought it might be.

"It's…it's the money I took from you."

Her jaw dropped and she quickly pulled it closed.

"All of it," he said, holding out the paper. She

stopped herself from snatching it away, opting to take it slowly instead.

"It doesn't feel like much."

"It's a check," he said. "It's not everything I took. Some of it I… I gambled away. I still owe you the rest and I plan to make good on it as soon as I can."

June rolled her eyes.

At least he'd had the courtesy to look guilty. Perhaps there was room for growth in a person as twisted as Clayton.

"Come on now, June, don't do that. It'll clear, I swear. Would I come all the way down here and give you this, knowing it wouldn't?"

"I honestly don't know, Clayton. I thought I knew you once, but then you stole everything I had and left me alone to pick up the pieces, so I really can't answer that question."

She shoved the check—if that was really what it was; she still didn't trust a word the man said—into her pocket and pointed at the door.

He gave a sad nod and turned to go.

She'd given him everything once, and he'd smashed it all, and she'd believed that if she ever saw him again, all of the rage she had felt for him would return. But standing there in the tiny living room of the only place she could afford—a place she paid for every month with hard-earned, honest money she made herself—June felt nothing but pride. Pride in herself, for putting her life back together, even if it wasn't much yet, for picking herself up off the floor and drying her tears to go to work the day after Clayton abandoned her, for telling him to hit the road when she had the chance.

She hugged herself as another chill spread through her body.

Clayton stopped, his hand on the door, and turned back. She only saw the side of his face.

"What I did was wrong, June, and you're right that it doesn't matter why. Hell, there are times when I don't even know why I did it, because some days I miss you like crazy. I know I got my own garbage to sort out, but I do want you to know that I'm sorry. I'm sorry I hurt you. If I had it to do over, I'd do things different."

With that, he opened the door. She'd thought that would be the last of him, but a second later, he was backing into her apartment as though held at gunpoint.

As he passed through the door, she saw Ethan on the other side of Clayton, shoving the man back into her living room.

"Ethan," she cried. "What are you doing?" She rushed over to where the two men stood.

Ethan's fists were curled and there was murder in his eyes. "June, who the hell is this man and why is he bothering you?"

Clayton flinched but didn't respond.

She walked over to Ethan's side and put a hand on his forearm. "It's okay. I've got this handled and you can relax."

He met her eyes. "You sure, June?" He turned to face her, jaw trembling. "I shouldn't have let you go earlier today. I should have fought for you." He tipped his chin in Clayton's direction. "I'm prepared to do that now. Just say the word."

An unexpected little flip happened in her stomach and she had to fold her lips together to keep from grinning. "I mean it, Ethan," she said, her heart going soft with tenderness toward him. "I'm fine and everything's okay. I was just telling Clayton to go on and get out."

Clayton nodded, looking relieved that he'd avoided getting punched in the face, pepper sprayed or whacked in the noggin with a golf club. Finally, the man walked out her front door, taking their dark past with him.

When June turned back around to face Ethan, even though they still had a lot to discuss, a part of her knew there would be mostly light from then on.

She walked to the door and closed it, hard, not taking her eyes off the man she loved.

"June, I have so much I want to tell you. So much I understand now that I didn't before."

"I do, too, Ethan. Oh, I shouldn't have left you earlier. Even though I was hurting, it wasn't the right thing to do, and I'm sorry."

"No, I'm the one who needs to apologize." He took both of her hands in his and led her to the couch. Recalling what had happened the last time they'd ended up there together, June's cheeks warmed and she took a deep breath. There would be time to think of that later; right then, she needed to focus on the conversation she should have had with him ages ago—the one they'd both feared, until that moment when all their walls had finally come crashing down.

For her, at least, all that remained was an exposed but ready heart, and she hoped he would offer her the same.

When they were seated, she took her time before speaking.

Ethan looked handsome, as always, but there was a little vulnerability in him just then, wearing the same hooded sweatshirt he'd put on for the pet adoption event earlier that day, his hair a little mussed, that five-o'-clock shadow she loved so much making an appearance. She longed to touch him, to reach out and run her fingers along his jaw, but there would be time for that later, she hoped.

His eyes were dark in the dim light coming from her bedroom—she still hadn't switched on any additional light, and doing so then could potentially break the spell they were under. It was one of those moments in life when she knew everything was about to change, for better or worse, and it felt as if even the quietest breath had the potential to destroy it all.

"Listen, June, I know we have a lot to say to each other, and I'd love to start if you're ready."

She offered him a tender smile, holding back from reaching out to wrap her hands in his. "No," she said, her voice firm. "Let me."

He started to open his mouth but thought better of it when he saw the determination in her expression.

"That guy that just left?" she asked, pointing a thumb in the direction of her front door.

Ethan nodded.

"That was Clayton Miller." She drew in a long breath and slowly released it. "I was in love with him for six months, so much so that I thought he would be in my life forever. We never actually talked about it, which I see now was probably a red flag, but I just assumed we would get married someday. Every moment that we weren't working, we spent together, and we both shared a dream of owning a business together."

She shook her head. "I was stupid to believe him—I see that now—but he convinced me that he'd found the perfect building for the bakery I wanted so badly, and I trusted him. I went there with him, once, to an empty store in a cute little strip mall in Dallas, and fell in love with the place."

Ethan nodded, his eyes narrowing as he followed along.

"Because I worked so much and Clay—Clayton—had a more flexible schedule, he convinced me to transfer all of my money into his bank account so that he could make an offer one afternoon. That morning, he kissed me goodbye like always."

Ethan cringed.

"And I didn't see him again until today." Even after all that time, admitting such a thing was still embarrassing.

"Did you go to the police?" Ethan asked.

"I did, but because I'd willingly given Clayton the money and I wasn't under duress or threatened or anything at the time, there wasn't much they could do. They tried to track him down for a little while, mostly as a favor to me, I think, since this is a small town and everybody knows most of the force, but after a bit, they let it go."

She wrung her hands. "I tried to do the same, but honestly, until you came along, I was having a hard time believing that I'd ever get over that pain of being abandoned."

Ethan reached out and took her hands. "I'm so sorry he did that to you, June."

She shook her head. "And the worst part is, he made me stop trusting myself. It's a miracle I didn't extend that to everyone around me, but thankfully I didn't. I've got a lot of good people in my life that I would have pushed away if I'd have done that. But no, it was just me."

"What do you mean?" he asked, his voice gentle.

"Well, I figured that if I was that stupid once, if I trusted someone like that—someone who took every-thing I had without breaking a sweat—then I should never let myself get close to a man again."

"It wasn't your fault, June." The words were true, she knew, but still so hard to digest.

"So when you came along, even though I started to fall for you from pretty much the moment we met, I didn't want to let myself get too close. You seemed wonderful, but if I made such a mistake before, who was I to judge?"

"Do you still feel that way about me?"

"Of course not, Ethan," she said, willing her words to convey the extent of what was in her heart. "You have to see that."

"I do. I do see that, June, and I'm so sorry that I didn't go after you today. I'm so very sorry if I made you think I didn't care that you ran off."

"Ethan, I know you care. I can see that, even though I know you didn't really want to from the beginning."

"June, please let me explain…"

She held up a hand, then placed it back over his. "Of course, but let me finish, okay?"

He nodded, his brown eyes so warm.

"I want you to understand what happened today, when I left the pet event, I mean."

"Absolutely," he said. "I mean, I think I have some idea now, but I want to hear your story."

"Those puppies, Ethan—they mean more to me than I think you realize."

He looked like he wanted to say something but he kindly let her go on without interrupting.

"I think I've come to see them as a sort of…symbol…for lack of a more accurate word. They've come to represent some things for me that I hope make sense. If it doesn't, and you think I'm crazy, you're welcome to walk right back out that door."

"June." His voice was rigid, final. "If you'll allow it, I will never walk out that door without you knowing I'll be back. So, I'd love to hear what you're going to say, but know this—I am not that man that left here a few minutes ago. I am not him. I will never treat you like he did. I will never do what he did to you."

Ethan swallowed, his jaw ticking in that nervous way.

What he'd confessed certainly made it hard for her to continue, but it also made her heart swell with joy.

"I definitely want to hear more of that," she said, giggling, which made him laugh, too. "But what I was saying is that, the puppies are sort of like this representation of…well…us. Look, I know it's weird, but they brought you into my life, and even though we got to know each other apart from them, I always had this sort of fear that if they went away from me, well… you would, too. What I mean to say, or ask, really, is… would you still be here if it wasn't for them?"

She wanted to think she knew the answer—Lord knew she did—but at the back of her mind there was still an inkling of fear that, contrary to what Ethan said, he might just walk out that door and not come back. She hated that fear, and recognized it for what it was—Clayton's last hold on her—the last little piece of her trust he'd stolen. No apology could return it to its rightful place, she knew, but giving her heart to Ethan, letting him teach her to trust again, would be a pretty good place to begin.

Ethan leaned forward and took her face in his hands. "Absolutely, I would still be here, June. Absolutely. I *am* still here, and I'm not going anywhere if you don't want me to."

"Oh, Ethan, I'm so glad to hear that."

"Jessica broke my heart, too, not in the same way as yours but close enough. She abandoned me in a different way."

"Do you mind if I ask how?" June whispered.

"No, not at all. I want to tell you everything. After we'd been together for a while, I found out that she was engaged and had been cheating on her fiancé with me. I know it's not the same, but it hurt so much, and I really thought I'd never be able to trust a woman ever again. When I found out she'd been lying to me the whole time, that I'd been played like a damn fool, well, I decided then and there that I was done giving my heart away."

June nodded, her heart aching for him, but glad he'd felt close enough to her to share what had happened to him. Everything made more sense in light of that knowledge.

"So when I met you—" he smiled "—when you came crashing into my father's clinic with those two puppies under your coat, I was instantly attracted to you, and it only grew from there. I thought that if I put boundaries around our relationship, I could keep that attraction from becoming something more, but I was powerless from the beginning. I see that now, and my only regret is ever trying to keep you out."

He squeezed her hands, kissing her cheek before continuing. "I should never have compared you to Jessica in my heart, June." He shook his head. "You're nothing like her, in all the best ways possible. You are kind, sweet, openhearted and brave—so very brave— to have put your life back together after that asshole took everything from you. I can't even begin to tell you how much I admire your courage. I also should never have tried to keep from letting you in, because ever since I did, I've been happier and a better man than ever before."

His eyes bore into hers as her own moistened with tears of joy. He was saying everything she'd wanted to hear since she'd met him, and it was all she needed it to be.

"I love you, June. I love you with everything that I am."

"Oh, Ethan," she said through tears, "I love you, too. More than anything. And, just as importantly, I trust you one hundred percent, with my whole heart."

He grabbed her hands then and pulled her up from the couch and straight into his arms, swirling her around like a movie heroine. But it was better than a movie because Ethan was real. By being trustworthy, honest and willing to open his heart to her after having it broken so badly, Ethan Singh was all the hero she could ask for.

Finally, he set her back down and kissed her long and hard, his lips conveying all the passion that had built up between them, stronger and fiercer than the first time they made love.

"One more thing, June."

"Yes?"

He looked down at her with twinkling eyes. "I'd like for you to give the puppies names. You can call them whatever you like, and they'll be ours to keep."

Her heart nearly burst. "I was so afraid you'd given them away at the adoption event… Wait, what about Neena?" June's hands flew to her mouth. "I love those puppies, and I feel like they're my babies, but I'm not going to be the kind of woman who takes a puppy from a child who's been promised one."

Ethan looked at her with enough warmth to heat her entire apartment building, plus the whole block. "That's something I was going to tell you. I got a call from Harry earlier today and he gave me some news."

June clenched her hands until her nails dug into her palms.

"It turns out Neena is severely allergic to dogs and we just had no idea." Ethan let out a deep laugh.

"Oh, my gosh," June gasped. "How awful!"

"No, no, sweetheart. It'll be fine. Harry and Amani are going to get her a rabbit instead."

Now it was June's turn to laugh. "So I really get to keep the puppies, then?"

He nodded, brushing a finger along her cheek. "You really do. And I'm sorry I was such a jerk. I was so focused on trying to figure out how to keep myself from loving you that I completely missed the fact that you'd fallen in love with those little fur balls. And I have to admit—I have, too."

She wrapped her arms around his neck and held him close for as long as she could stand. When she let go, he pressed his lips against hers, igniting a spark in her belly that she knew could only be quelled by spending the rest of her life with him.

"Well," he said, pulling his breathless mouth from hers. "You know what you have to do now."

"What?" she asked between the kisses she was busy dotting along his deliciously-scented neck. "Take you back to my bedroom and have my way with you?"

"Obviously that, yes," he growled, the low, throaty sound sending sparks to her groin. "But first, something else."

"What?"

"You have to name the puppies."

June threw her head back and laughed, all the tension and pain from the past flowing out of her. "What should I name them?" she asked.

"I can't tell you that," he said. "I was the idiot trying for so long to get you to give them away. They're ours now, but you're the one who gets to decide what we'll call them."

She bit her lip, looking up at the ceiling as she considered all of the possibilities.

"It's so hard," she said, grinning. "Naming one puppy would be difficult enough, but two?" She tossed up her hands. "That's going to take a while."

He looked down into her eyes, his own reflecting all of the joy that threatened to burst out of her. "That's absolutely fine, June. Take as long as you need."

He kissed her.

"We have all the time in the world."

# *Epilogue*

*One year later...*

The weather for their wedding could not have been more different than the season in which Ethan and June had met.

There wasn't a snowflake in sight as June walked down the aisle toward Ethan, her smile shining brighter than the July sun. He didn't even try to contain the grin that spread over his mouth as he watched her draw nearer, going a little too fast—adorable—as though she could not wait to start their life together.

He could not have agreed more. Their hearts were absolutely on the same page.

She joined him underneath the archway her brides-maids had covered in her favorite lilies, and he took her hands in his, joining them together forever as they exchanged vows.

The next hours whizzed by in a blur as they were congratulated by one family member after another. Even though the official ceremony was that day, the wedding had lasted far longer in his father's Indian tradition.

Ethan had enjoyed every moment, his heart alive and full to bursting, surrounded by family, friends, their two growing puppies, Salt and Pepper, and the most wonderful woman in the world, whose beauty in a sari was beyond all imagination.

But a part of him had to admit that he'd be relieved when it was all over and he could take his bride home.

They'd been discussing their next move for months, Ethan having accepted a new position as department head at a university in Montana. Although he hadn't pressured her, June had jumped at the chance to join him, sad to say goodbye to her hometown and the people that loved her there, but excited about the new chapter they planned to start together.

She still carried a dream of opening a bakery of her own, but she'd been willing to put that on the back burner so that she could be with him in his new state, which made the surprise he had for her that day all the more special. June wasn't expecting it at all, and he couldn't wait to tell her the news.

Finally, after they'd eaten dinner and had a moment of quiet to themselves amid the storm of attention, he managed to pull his new wife aside. The light in her eyes was incredible as she looked up at him, glowing even beyond their normal brightness.

"You look beautiful, Mrs. Singh," he said, taking her

hand and leading her out to the gazebo in his parents' backyard. Fairy lights—numbering in the thousands, he was certain—had been strung up for the occasion and twinkled like June's eyes.

He pulled her close against his chest and held her there as they swayed back and forth in a slow dance. They had done the classic first dance as husband and wife, but that had been in front of everyone. This special moment, he wanted to share only with her.

"June, I will never be able to properly thank you for agreeing to be my wife."

She gazed up at him for a second and then tucked her face back into his chest. She felt so right, there against his heart, and he vowed, as he had hundreds of times before, to always keep her safe and, to the very best of his ability, as happy as she made him—though he wasn't sure such a thing was possible.

"You've made me the happiest man alive, my June, and thanks to you, I always will be." He felt her lips curve into a smile. "And you've already shown me more support than I've ever had the right to ask for."

She raised her head as they continued dancing. "What do you mean?"

"Everything," he said. "But right now I'm talking about your agreeing to come with me to Montana."

"Of course," she said. "But why wouldn't I, Ethan?" Her pretty ruby lips parted in a grin. "If that's where you're going, and that job will make you happy, then there's nowhere else in the world I would rather be."

"And I'm so thankful for that, June."

They moved slowly to the music as he enjoyed the warm night air, the stars sparkling above and the feel of a beautiful, happy woman against his body.

*His* woman, *forever.*

The joy he felt at that knowledge was almost too much to keep inside, so he twirled her around and around until she laughed for him, the sound of her voice as refreshing as a cool spring on a hot day.

"There's something else I want to share with you, though, Mrs. Singh."

Her nose crinkled adorably as she grinned at the sound of her new name.

"You like that, do you?"

"I do," she said, wrapping her arms around his waist. "Very much."

"Good, because I can't wait to say it to you when we're really alone."

She swatted him, then, moving her arms to his neck, pulled herself up so she could kiss him.

It was nearly impossible not to be aroused by the feel of her warm body against his. She was so beautiful in the ivory dress she'd chosen, the heart-shaped neckline showing off her gorgeous curves.

"I can't wait to get this incredible dress off you," he said. "But there's something else I wanted to tell you."

She stopped dancing and opened her eyes; they were like emerald gems when she glanced up at him. "What is it, my love?"

"June, I know we've been talking about you opening up a bakery someday, somewhere near my work and the home we're building."

"Yes?" Her expression was a mixture of apprehension and excitement.

"Well, I hope you won't be upset with me, but I've sort of taken the liberty of…buying you a bakery."

She jumped back, her arms flailing to her sides. "Ethan! Are you serious?"

"Completely. And, June, it's truly amazing. Ready for operation, stainless-steel, top-of-the-line appliances, the works."

Her hands flew to her mouth. "Oh, Ethan."

She threw her body into his torso and squeezed his waist. "Thank you so, so much. I've wanted this for so long."

Unable to contain his joy at her pleasure, Ethan pulled his cell phone from the back pocket of his tuxedo pants. "Here," he said, sliding a thumb over the screen to unlock the phone. "I've got pictures for you, and specs, and everything else."

She thumbed through the photos, making approving noises at each one. He'd spent ages looking for places online, calling folks in the area to see if they thought it was a good place for the kind of business his wife wanted to run. Everyone he'd spoken to had been ecstatic about the idea of a new bakery coming to their area.

And now he had confirmation that June was happy with his choice.

It wasn't possible for the day to get any better; he would have bet money on that.

"So, you like it?" he asked, needing her to put into words what he could already see on her face.

"Like it? Ethan, it's the best gift anyone's ever given me, with the one exception of this." She held up her wedding ring, tilting it so that its angles caught the light.

He'd chosen an ample round emerald circled by seed diamonds because it reminded him of her lovely eyes.

"I'm so thankful, and so happy, Ethan, but I do have one question."

"Go for it."

Her eyebrows knit. "Why did you do this, when you know I got the money back from Clayton and it's more than enough to buy a bakery?"

He'd thought long and hard about the answer to that question well before she'd asked it. He knew her money was earmarked for a bakery, and he'd taken a risk in buying the place himself, aware that she might be disappointed she hadn't done it completely on her own.

But that was just it. She wasn't on her own anymore, and he wanted her to know that without a doubt.

"I know you could have bought the bakery yourself, June, and I hope you're not angry with me for doing it as a surprise. But the thing is—I wanted you to know that I'm all in, one thousand percent. Buying that place for you, in the town we're going to call home together, was the best way I knew to show you how committed I am to this marriage."

"Oh, Ethan, how could I be angry? It's the most wonderful thing anyone's ever done for me and I am over the moon about it."

"I thought it would be a symbol of how much I love you. Your dream was stolen before, and I wanted to give it back. I wanted you to know that you can trust me to love you well." He grabbed her hands. "Do you trust in me, June?"

"With all my heart, Ethan. With all of my heart."

With that, he swirled her around the dance floor once more.

When he set her back down, though, June looked up

at him, a mischievous grin on her lips. "I have a little surprise for you, too, Ethan."

He held her out at arm's length and caught the split second her eyes flickered to her midsection.

"You're not…"

June nodded, biting her lip. "I am."

"I'm going to be a father?"

"You are," she said, bursting into tears and laughter all at once.

As he lifted her into his arms to carry her off into their future, Ethan realized he'd been wrong about one thing that night—it definitely could get better.

In fact, now that they had the promise of everything they'd wanted in a life together—it was the very best.

\* \* \* \* \*

SPECIAL EXCERPT FROM

**HARLEQUIN®**

# SPECIAL EDITION

™

*Runaway bride Mayor Maggie Spencer doesn't*
*anticipate the fallout from fleeing her wedding.*
*Or her ex-fiancé's brother riding to her rescue!*
*Griffin Stone used to run from challenges, but now he'll*
*have to fight—for Maggie and their forbidden love.*

*Read on for a sneak preview of*
Falling for the Wrong Brother, *the first book in*
**Michelle Major**'s *new Maggie & Griffin trilogy.*

"What's going on here, Griffin?"

"I'm on an amazing date with an amazing woman and—"

"This isn't a date," she interrupted, tugging her hand from his.

He shifted, looking down into her gray eyes. Strands of lights lined the pier, so he could see that her gaze was guarded...serious. Not at all the easygoing, playful woman who'd sat across from him at dinner.

"You're sure?"

"I'm not sure of anything at the moment. You might remember my life turned completely upside down last week. But even if that wasn't a factor, I can't imagine you wanting to date me."

"I'm not the same guy I used to be."

She laughed softly. "I get that you were an angry kid and the whole 'rebel without a cause' bit."

"I hated myself," he admitted softly. "And I was jealous of you. You were perfect. Everyone in town loved you. It was clear even back then that you were the golden girl of Stonecreek, which meant you represented everything I could never hope to be."

"But now I'm okay because my crown has been knocked off?"

"That's not it," he said, needing her to understand. He paced to the edge of the pier then back to her. "I can't explain it but there's a connection between us, Maggie. I know you feel it."

She glanced out to the ocean in front of them. "I do."

"I think maybe I realized it back then. Except you were younger and friends with Trevor and so far out of my league." He chuckled. "That part hasn't changed. But I'm not the same person, and I want a chance with you."

"It's complicated," she said softly. "A week ago I was supposed to marry your brother. If people in town caught wind that I'd now turned my sights to you, imagine what that would do to my reputation."

The words were a punch to the gut. He might not care what anyone in Stonecreek thought about him, but it was stupid to think Maggie would feel the same way. She was the mayor after all and up for reelection in the fall. He stared at her profile for several long moments. Her hair had fallen forward so that all he could see was the tip of her nose. She didn't turn to him or offer any more of an explanation.

"I understand," he told her finally.

"I had a good time tonight," she whispered, "but us being together in Stonecreek is different."

"I get it." He made a show of checking his watch. "It's almost eleven. We should head back."

Her shoulders rose and fell with another deep breath. She turned to him and cupped his jaw in her cool fingers. "Thank you, Griffin. For tonight. I really like the man you've become." Before he could respond, she reached up and kissed his cheek.

*Don't miss*
Falling for the Wrong Brother *by Michelle Major,*
*available September 2018 wherever*
*Harlequin® Special Edition books and ebooks are sold.*

www.Harlequin.com

# HARLEQUIN®

# SPECIAL EDITION

### Life, Love and Family

Save **$1.00**

on the purchase of ANY
Harlequin® Special Edition book.

Available wherever books are sold,
including most bookstores, supermarkets,
drugstores and discount stores.

---

# Save $1.00

## on the purchase of ANY Harlequin® Special Edition book.

Coupon valid until October 31, 2018.
Redeemable at participating outlets in the U.S. and Canada only.
Limit one coupon per customer.

52615913

5  65373 00076  2    (8100)0 12381